WINTER'S FALL

BOOK ONE

THE WINTER SAGA

WINTER'S FALL

BOOK ONE

CHRISTIAN RIVERS

Winter's Fall
The Winter Saga
Book One

Christian Rivers

BookWise Publishing

Cover Illustration: Steve Argyle
Olympus Illustration: Yvan Feusi

Library of Congress Control Number:2019916733

ISBN 978-1-60645-242-4 Trade Paperback
ISBN 978-1-60645-244-8 ebook
ISBN 978-1-60645-245-5 Audiobook

10 9 8 7 6 5 4 3

Order online at Amazon.com
www.WinterSaga.com

3/21/2022 version

DEDICATION

To the Truths that open our eyes.

TABLE OF CONTENTS

OLYMPUS

For full color illustration, please visit www.WinterSaga.com.

CHAPTER ONE

Stillness.

Utter silence.

The pre-morning light glowed on the lip of the horizon as she dipped her sweat-covered fingers into the bag of chalk at her waist. Her calloused skin sank deep into the dry colorless dust, and the excess fell away in a wispy puff that dissipated in the air.

No wind, no sound. Nothing in the world existed but the peace, and the calm, and the climb. Far beneath her feet, as they wedged against the vents and divots, clouds of deep purple floated like a thick blanket. They showed nothing of the distant surface world far below.

Breaching the third leg of her climb, arms shaking, mind so focused and clear, her sharp, icy blue eyes lifted to the horizon. Suddenly, their crystalline surface reflected an explosion of color as the breathtaking dawn burst over the radiant cloud blanket in the east.

Her mouth fell open, breathing in the sweet, fresh air at the glorious onslaught of dawn. Like a silent yet thunderous conqueror, it chased all the shadows from view, horizon to horizon. The warm radiance lit up her fair features and glinted off the long waves of her braided ebony tresses.

The dawn empowered her resolve. It shed light on the darkness, symbolically creating symmetry in her mind between nature and her own life—the light that she and those like her, by their efforts, gave to their people. The thought took root in her heart as she watched the molten light spill slowly over the sea of clouds.

Invigorated by its presence, she greeted the sun's emergence with renewed effort and dug her fingertips into the next ledge. The metallic structure gave her few options, but she had never been one to be limited by those she was given.

Ascending the convex terrain, she relished the peace and tranquility of her utterly empty and silent surroundings but at the same time fed off the rush and burning within her. Her limbs radiated with the heat of exertion as they worked methodically together. Enamored by the clarity that these mornings of isolation in the quiet, empty vastness gave her, she wished every second of the day could be as serene and meditative as this moment.

The only sound was her own breath—timed and controlled to perfection as she worked up the structure's face with years of honed skill and concentration.

"January!" a female voice rang out suddenly from overhead.

Both the silence and her concentration were demolished. Her foot slipped, sending her heart rate sky-high. In a single breathless moment, she looked down into the gaping expanse beneath her. The ground was not even visible through the clouds. Teeth clenched, fingers straining, and heart throbbing in her throat, she struggled to find her foothold once more. A bead of sweat rolled down her forehead as she channeled all the newfound adrenaline into reaching the top while ignoring the continuing calls.

"January Winterton!" the voice shouted again.

She sighed in frustration and attempted to finish out the most difficult part of her climb without slipping and falling to her death. Finally able to throw one leg up over the railing, she laid eyes on the young woman who had interrupted her morning quiet.

"Janey?" the newcomer greeted as she approached with a surprised smile. Her big brown eyes blinked in disbelief.

"I go . . . by . . . Winter now. Just Winter," the exhausted climber corrected as she pulled herself up over the ledge and came to stand on solid ground inside the East Quarter Gardens. "Nalara, I thought we were meeting in the conference room later." She leaned down on her knees for support while she steadied her breath.

"Yes, of course, but after my commencement, I just couldn't wait to see you!" She bounced. "I was told I could find you out here . . . climbing—although I didn't really believe it."

Winter breathed deeply and righted herself. "Believe it."

Limbs still vibrating, Winter glanced over Nalara's pristine uniform—heather green and accented with gold buttons, with no patches of note or honors from all her years spent in preparation for this day. There was simply a digital display over her right breast that read:

ARCHANGELS
NALARA GRESSEN
RANK 100

Winter blinked, taking a moment to turn off her hyperawareness. Her icy, meticulous gaze melted into a smile. "You're right," she said, taking her friend into a tight hug. "I haven't seen you for so long."

"So many years," Nalara agreed. "Winter, huh? Wow! You've really changed. The Formulation Quarter just wasn't the same after you graduated. You were always my hero." She glanced over the lip of the city where the scenery plummeted down into the clouds forever. "You still are," she added with a smile.

Winter shook her head, not voicing her random thought: that she never realized until this moment how very young a Purifier is at their commencement. Could she possibly have looked that soft and immaculate four years ago when she graduated? Nalara's flawless ivory skin and shiny brown hair pulled into a neat bun above her untouched formal uniform made her look more like a doll than a soldier.

"Don't worry," Winter spoke at length. "Today, you'll become a hero in your own right."

"After orientation?" The newly graduated cadet beamed.

"Exactly," Winter said. "You nervous?"

"Ahh, no . . ." Nalara replied without confidence.

"Don't worry. I was nervous, too." Winter started moving toward the walkway, through the manicured flora that bordered the ledge. "Come on, walk and talk." She clapped her hands together and swept the last traces of chalk from her calloused palms.

"Well, yeah. I guess everyone is a little nervous their first time out, right?" Nalara shrugged and followed her friend. "I mean, look at it out here!" She turned in a circle, rife with wonder. "It's so big and open, and it's so beautiful."

Watching Nalara take in the world after being raised in the lower decks was humbling. It was difficult to stay objective with such a history as they shared, but Winter focused her mind on being in trainer mode.

"Just remember, these gardens are for the Elite," Winter warned. "If you're ever caught loitering, and they're not in the mood to mingle with us, you could get in serious trouble."

"Sovereign's blessings, I didn't think—"

"It's alright. I pass through here all the time. You just don't want to stick around for too long and push your luck."

"But it's just that you're so amazing, and having you as my initiator . . . I really don't want to mess up."

"Oh, come on, I had my first day, too," Winter said as they stepped up onto the footbridge that arced across the fields and farmland below and reconnected with the street of the Second Tier, where the Purifiers and other middle-class citizens resided. Below them, Winter and Nalara could look down and see Third Tier workers laboring in the Food Production Sector alongside harvesting drones and watering apparatuses.

Across the bridge, the Second Tier swarmed with citizens fulfilling their vocation or on their way to it. The shining buildings glinted in the morning light as citizens walked through the perfectly maintained streets.

"There's so much life up here in the city." Nalara's jaw hung loose as they climbed the arching bridge, her brown eyes wide as they drank in the bustling cityscape.

Winter nodded in agreement. "Yeah. Sometimes I forget what it was like living down inside for fifteen years." She thought of the first time she had seen green grass and colorful flowers . . . the warmth of the sun. "For a while, it's overwhelming." She spoke almost to herself.

Nalara scoffed. "But that was after you passed the trials with a *record-breaking score,* and accomplishing a feat that had only been achieved once before in the history of Olympus."

The sudden, forced reminder of her trial made Winter flinch. Goosebumps crawled over her skin as she struggled to banish the memory. The tightness in her chest subsided as she forced a long, slow breath. Rattled somewhat, she felt she could refocus the conversation by saying something to boost Nalara's confidence. Purifier life wasn't exactly easy, and Sovereign knows there had been no one there to pat Winter on the back when life felt intimidating.

With a soft sigh, she spoke. "Listen . . . it's okay to feel nervous."

Her statement seemed to take Nalara by surprise.

Winter bit her lip as they walked, her mind racing to get a handle on some elaboration. "I know I always had your back at the FMQ, but you're not a kid anymore, and I'm not your hero now; I'm your comrade. You're a ranked Purifier just like me, and people are counting on you. You're going to do your best—I know you will. You've trained your whole life for this." Winter smirked playfully. "And if you screw up during these first few weeks, I'll be there for you. After that, you're on your own."

Nalara jostled her friend's shoulder in good humor, a sign that Winter's pep talk had touched her heart.

They paused simultaneously as they reached the apex of the bridge where the view of the entire city lay before them.

The Second Tier, which comprised the surface deck of Olympus, was a bustling metropolis of industry. For the churning population that it held, there was always a surprising peace and quiet in the air as the residents traversed the streets from their modest living chambers to their designated vocations. Every day was like witnessing a masterpiece of efficiency and congruence. The clean streets and practical buildings were sectioned into 'Quarters' based on specific vocations, and the citizens rejoiced to live under the gaze of their dear Sovereign.

The very center of the Second Tier boasted the magnificent, towering, cylindrical arena, covered in intricate carvings and crowned with a pantheon of statued heroes. The arena served as the base for the First Tier, where the blessed Elite lived in lavish glittering towers and mansions. Hanging gardens of lush green speckled with flowers of every hue graced the lip of the First Tier, and crystalline waterfalls poured from its ledges and splashed into massive pools at the arena's base.

From their perch on the apex of the footbridge, Winter and Nalara could just sneak a glimpse of the living paradise. As a rule, Second Tier citizens could only dream of witnessing the First Tier's glory with their own eyes. The marble walkways and crystal fountains glimmered in the morning light. However, the perpetual gardens and pleasure pools, with their gilded filigrees and silken house banners of vibrant hues, all stood as nothing when compared to the breathtaking majesty of the golden Sovereign Tower, which reached so far into the sky that any citizen could look up from any point and see its monolithic glory.

"If you ever feel frightened because of what we're called to do," Winter spoke reverently, "just think of this moment and remember: this is why we fight." She held up her right fist, indicating her Purifier's mark: the blade wreathed in flame on the back of her hand. "Olympus is our home, and even if it means my life is sacrificed today in the defense of our home, I'd never want *any* other vocation."

Nalara looked into Winter's determined blue eyes and accepted the surge of resolve her resilient friend exuded.

Chime, Chime

The city-wide intercom signaled.

Winter and Nalara reacted instinctively and turned to face the Sovereign Tower, smoothly falling to their knees with their right hand clenched over their hearts. Throughout each tier, they were joined with every living soul on Olympus in the posture of worship. As the sound of chimes concluded, four giant hologram projectors generated the beaming face of their cherished leader on each side of the Sovereign Tower.

Light and happiness filled their hearts as his portrait materialized before their eyes. His snow-white beard and softly cascading hair framed a handsome face exuding elderly wisdom and quiet strength.

Tears rimmed Winter's eyes as she steadfastly gazed at his image. She couldn't help it; the blessing of seeing his face each and every day was almost more than she could contain. His power had given her life, his wisdom had given her purpose, and his mercy had given her strength to fulfill a divinely appointed mission.

Winter joined her voice with those of a hundred thousand Olympians, from the highest Elite to the lowliest core worker down in the depths of the floating city ship, and they recited the sacred pledge in flawless unity.

Not an ounce of power or meaning was lost from speaking the same words, the same way she had every single day, twice a day, since she was first able to speak. They filled her with resolve and courage now as they always had throughout her life.

Hail to his supreme holiness.
Hail to our Sovereign ruler.
Hail to our living god.
Your name is a light to our path.
Your wisdom guides us through darkness and death.
Your power governs the whole earth.
It is to you and you alone, o gracious lord, that I swear my life, my loyalty,
and my unconditional obedience.
I swear to live for you.
I swear to die for you.
Live forever, o glorious king—for in you, we are granted life.

The intercom chimed again, the visage disappeared, and the residents, rising to their feet, returned to their morning.

Winter and Nalara stood as the brightening morning sunlight gleamed off the golden tower. A shimmering wave of color washed over the sky. The iridescent bubble surrounding the entire city ship of Olympus rippled with shifting hues in the morning warmth.

"Wow." Nalara gaped upward. "Is that the barrier?"

"Sure is." Winter glanced up. She had seen it so many times that it had somehow lost its wonder, but witnessing Nalara's gaping amazement rekindled the passion in her heart. "The barrier is another testament of our Sovereign's power. With it, he protects us every single day from the toxins outside, also from freezing temperatures, the lack of oxygen at this altitude, lightning—anything at all that might harm us. That's why what we do is so important. As Purifiers, our vocation is the path to safety and prosperity for all of Olympus. Through our efforts, someday, he won't need to protect us with the barrier up here in the clouds. We are the strength of his arm in reclaiming our homeland. That's more important than our insecurities." She smiled. "Even more important than our own lives."

Nalara couldn't help but return the smile. Her friend Janey was always speaking strength and courage into existence. She hadn't changed in four years, it seemed. Well, perhaps she had changed in the way that she was more direct. Her manner was very abrupt and to-the-point now. When they were children, they both had delighted in talking for hours and hours in lighthearted, meaningless conversation. But now, it seemed like she said nothing unless it had a specific purpose—no time or words wasted.

One thing was for sure: Winter was fully invested in her vocation. She always said she wanted to be the greatest Purifier in history. Just when Nalara thought that she had seen the last of her old friend Janey, Winter spun around with a playful smile.

"Okay, we're definitely going to be late now." Winter shrugged. "We should probably run!"

Stunned in surprise, Nalara protested loudly and scrambled to catch up.

Olympus sped past as the two Purifiers sprinted steadily through the immaculate city streets. Large digital billboards displayed the current Purifier rankings, spotlighting the highest achieving Purifier of the previous month and announcing the upcoming bout event where qualifying Purifiers would be given a chance to boost their team's numbers.

Second Tier citizens turned their heads at the sight of the sprinting Purifiers but continued undeterred in their commute to their respective labs or offices.

"There are so many people!" Nalara called to her friend as they ran.

Both genetically superior and honed by years of training, Winter spoke easily as she sprinted. "The middle tier is always a busy place. Educated and skilled contributors to society are allowed to live and work here in the sun and beneath the blessed gaze of our Sovereign."

"Not like the Elite, though," Nalara mused.

"No, definitely not like the Elite." Winter glanced up at the First Tier that towered over the rest of Olympus like a golden, gardened balcony.

The steady stream of commuting middle-class citizens was freckled with the presence of immense Guardians, the policing force of the city, as they stood in silent observation at every security point. Their imposing stature and build were designed by the Sovereign to make a statement of strength.

Nalara was pleasantly surprised when random citizens smiled at her and Winter when they passed by. A few even addressed Winter by her callsign and wished her the best of luck. Nalara noticed that her initiator neither thanked nor even acknowledged these people and didn't break stride until they reached a security checkpoint where a towering Guardian lifted his hand in a silent command to halt.

Winter and Nalara slowed to a stop.

The muscular Guardian spoke in the low, gruff tone characteristic of their class. "Census study."

"Identify," spoke the slight, bald census worker at the Guardian's side. His clean, hairless head was adorned only with an earpiece and view screen over one eye.

"January Winterton," Winter said and held out her right hand.

Wave analysis flicked across the Unifier's view screen, and a green light emitted from the worker's headgear, playing over Winter's hand mark. The census worker was silent for a moment as he read the display.

Nalara looked unsure. "There are Unifiers up here, too?" she asked.

"Of course." Winter nodded. "They're the lifeblood of Olympus."

"Heart rate, excellent," the Unifier stated. "Physical condition, excellent. How are you feeling today?"

"I'm well," Winter affirmed. "I thank the Sovereign every moment for the service I can render."

A green light blinked on the Unifier's display, and he turned to Nalara. "Identify," he requested.

"Uh . . . Nalara Gressen," she replied timidly and held out her hand.

The green light scanned her hand, and the Unifier studied the readings. "Heart rate, slightly elevated," he said. "Physical condition, excellent. Records show that you have just come from formulation graduation."

"Yes."

A yellow light blinked. "You are due to receive *Intervene* treatment before you begin active service. Please turn your head."

Nalara obeyed dutifully while the Unifier produced an injector and loaded a capsule of yellow liquid. Nalara flinched as the device came in contact with her skin, and a little puff of air projected the needle and fluids into her neck muscle.

"Treatment complete." The Unifier put away the device. "Your next treatment will be due in two years. I am putting a note on your permanent record. And how are you feeling today?"

"Um, good," Nalara responded, rubbing her neck.

A green light blinked on the display. "Both of you may proceed in your service to our Sovereign."

Winter and Nalara moved on as directed and joined the flow of symbiotic citizens on the other side of the checkpoint.

CHAPTER TWO

The lift slowed, and the display centered on *Purifier Command: Level Four*. The hydraulics hissed, and the doors pulled to the sides. Winter and Nalara were greeted by a flood of voices and musky, stale air.

The teams were separating already—quickly and efficiently dispersing to their respective hubs, which made their tardy entrance even more conspicuous and awkward.

The Grim Reapers, already in their full battle gear, passed by on their way to the shuttle bay. Their team's insignia, a skull crossed with a black scythe, was emblazoned on their chests, and their faces were obscured behind dark green and black paint.

"Can't be the best if you don't show up," their captain teased. He was a man of average height, with intense eyes and a stocky build.

Winter smirked despite her annoyance and clenched jaw.

The Grim Reapers all chuckled as they disappeared down the corridor.

"Who was that?" Nalara asked sheepishly.

"Eagle Eyes," Winter replied. "Derrick Zinda."

"No kidding?" Nalara's mouth fell open. "The Master Purifier? You know him?"

"Sure, he's the best." Winter casually backhanded her friend's shoulder. "Come on, this way. Derrick's great to everybody." She led her initiate to their team hub. "He volunteers for extra training after the jumps, and he's an excellent team captain."

"The Grim Reapers have been the top team for years," Nalara gushed. "I've always dreamed of meeting him."

"Mm, you won't have a lot of opportunities to," Winter commented with resolve. Her eyes lingered on the Archangels' insignia as they passed through their team hub's threshold. Their symbol, an imposing six-winged figure whose base formed together like the blade of a sword, adorned the bulkhead above the door. "But I hope you do get a chance to meet him before his Ascension."

"He's lucky," a sharp, grating voice cut in.

Nalara's large brown eyes opened wide.

Their hurried walk was abruptly halted by the appearance of a truly formidable man in full Purifier gear, holding his helmet under one elbow. He stood at an intimidating six feet four inches, built like a tank, with close-cropped sandy hair and a perpetual scowl lining a chiseled, wide jaw. The saying around the hub was that he'd been formulated as a Guardian but branded as a Purifier by accident.

His scowl grew deeper as he continued. "Lucky to have a team that *at least* honors the code of conduct, let alone scores higher than all the others."

"Captain Priest." Winter saluted, followed in kind by Nalara.

"You know, I think to myself sometimes," he mused, shrugging sarcastically, "what it might be like to have a team that followed orders . . . or protocol . . . or even just the base set of rules. But I'm sure I'll never know." He grew louder with each syllable. "Because I have this problem, where some of my Purifiers can't even show up for orientation on time!"

Winter breathed a steadying calmness into her reply, "Sorry, Wraith. It won't happen again."

"Well, I wouldn't want to inconvenience you!" he snapped, his voice again increasing in volume. "Eight extra hours of PT for each of you. Now, if you shiftless amateurs are done wasting all our time, perhaps you should *gear up now!*"

"Yes, sir!" Winter responded without losing a beat. "Captain Priest, this is the initiate, Nalara Gressen." She took the opportunity to change the subject and make the introduction.

It worked. Wraith's indomitable professionalism won out and he turned to the recently graduated cadet. His eyes narrowed.

"Welcome to the Archangels." He nodded.

"H-honored to be here, sir." Nalara swallowed.

Wraith pursed his lips in approval. He took great pride in his team. "I expect nothing but the very best from you—not only today, but at all times. The Sovereign is watching us all."

"Yes, sir!" Nalara saluted again.

With one last glare at Winter, Captain Priest moved away to the team armory.

"This way," Winter said, indicating down a corridor.

"Wow . . . he is so *intense!*" Nalara whispered.

"His leadership is first-tier," Winter replied. "He's very focused on making us the best we can be. With Eagle Eyes ascending, we have a good chance of overtaking the top position soon."

"Wow," Nalara breathed. She looked down at the rank on her uniform. "I hope I'll be able to make up for taking the place of . . . of . . ." she trailed off.

"His name was Logan Hanson." Winter completed her initiate's thought as they entered the gear chamber. "And don't think of it as taking his place."

The gear chamber was a circular room with ten shielded alcoves; inside each was hung a set of gauntlets, a helmet, and utility gear.

"Hammer Hanson, right?" A tall, grinning, redheaded man jostled Winter's shoulder as they entered. "What a way to go out!" He cringed.

"Everyone," Winter spoke from the center of the room. "This is Nalara, our initiate. Sorry we missed orientation; it was my fault."

Several of the team mumbled greetings in reply as they continued to don their tactical suits.

Winter led Nalara around the room, introducing as they went.

"This is Bulletproof." The stoic man nodded as they passed. "Whether that's true or not is yet to be seen," she added, eliciting a playful snort in reply.

"Viper." The short, compact woman smiled as she extended her hand to Nalara.

Winter moved on. "This is Sapphire." The stunning woman with high cheekbones glanced at them briefly.

"Havoc." The strong young man shook Nalara's hand.

"Here's Savage." Nalara recognized her from the FMQ, but she didn't look up.

"This is Trigger." The handsome gentleman smiled openly at Nalara and winked.

"And the one with the big mouth is Scorch," Winter concluded with a jeer. "Though I'm usually the one *burning* him."

Scorch turned on his heel with a smirk. "Yeah, right, Winter. You know only I can melt that icy heart of yours."

Winter sucked air through her teeth and shook her head as they shared a laugh.

Nalara was sure it would take her forever to remember all her teammates' names. She felt overwhelmed by the experience and more self-conscious than ever.

Winter stopped in front of an unoccupied stall; she pressed *New Entry* on the access panel and typed in her security code. She then typed Nalara's name and stood aside.

"Enter your code there," Winter prompted. "Once you do, no one but the team's captain, the team's lieutenant, and yourself can access your gear."

Nalara moved to comply but briefly experienced an internal panic attack as she forgot her security code for a moment. She was glad that Winter had moved on to her station. Having successfully entered the correct code, Nalara breathed a sigh of relief when the shielding around the alcove disappeared.

"You excited, cadet?" The redheaded man approached Nalara's side and grinned widely.

Her blank expression spoke volumes.

He laughed and held out his hand. "Scorch," he spoke simply. "The name's Seth Sahara, but call me Scorch. You got a callsign, cadet?"

Nalara shook her head. "No, I guess not."

"Ah, you'll probably have one by the end of your training, so no worries!" He let out a low guffaw. "And don't worry about replacing Hammer—the guy was a wreck. And not just on the day he died, I mean. I'm talking like his first day—he couldn't even put on his gauntlets without Winter's help." He shook his head. "Sure glad he wasn't my initiate while I was lieutenant."

"Y-you were the lieutenant?" Nalara asked, hoping she didn't sound impertinent.

"Aw, yeah, no doubt." He nodded eagerly with a grin. "You see, Winter wasn't always the stone-cold machine she is now. I sure as dyin' trained your girl over there." He jerked his thumb at Winter.

Winter laughed. "Oh, yes, and I'm *still* trying to forget everything you ever taught me." She finished zipping up her jumpsuit and then pulled on her boots before standing up and twisting her long black hair into a tight, functional bun.

"Yeah," Scorch sighed. "She was a keeper, alright." He wrinkled his nose at Winter and turned back to Nalara. "Sure wasn't surprised when she passed me up and became lieutenant. Not like Hammer—boy, what a sad case! He got so lost down there on the surface, it took us a whole week to track down his communicator." He made a sullen grimace. "Just to find it inside a wild dog. Mm . . . when we found what was left of him, we couldn't tell if it was the blighters that killed him or the pack of dogs that ate him."

Nalara's color drained.

"Some sights you just don't forget, you know?" Scorch continued without noticing. "Like, what was left in his boots and gauntlets were the *only* parts intact. You feel me?"

Winter shoved Scorch away. "Don't pay attention to him. He's got a connection issue between his brain and mouth."

Scorch relented with one final laugh and withdrew to the station with his name displayed above it.

Nalara gulped hard and gazed at her trainer with desperate, wide eyes that cried for help.

"Just get changed and put your boots on," Winter instructed. "That's the easy part."

Nalara quickly sat on the simple, cushioned stool at the base of the alcove and pulled off her shiny dress boots. She hung up her formal uniform with care and pulled on the tactical jumpsuit that served as the base for her gear.

The jumpsuit was softer than she imagined it would be. She loved how the Archangels' insignia looked on her chest. The thick fabric felt durable but slipped on easily. The digital feedback relays began monitoring her vitals the second she zipped it up. She tried not to show her fascination with the remarkable technology and quickly slipped on the boots that were beneath the stool. She noticed with surprise the long, jagged gash running from the ankle to the toes of the left boot.

"These are *my* boots from the trials," she voiced her inner thought.

"Sure, same ones you wore to victory," Winter confirmed. "These are mine, too." She clicked the heel of one to the floor.

Nalara sighed. "Yours don't look like you nearly died . . . I barely survived by sneaking and hiding through the whole thing." Her countenance fell hard.

Winter stifled an impatient sigh. "What matters is you passed. You're an initiated Purifier now," she affirmed resolutely. "Stand up. Let's go over the gear belt."

They both clasped utility belts around their waists.

"These are your flares." Winter pointed to each item in turn. "Here are the extra fuel cells for your rifle. This is your sidearm and its fuel cells. On the other side is your knife." Winter demonstrated. "You want to clip the sidearm holster around your thigh like this. There. Now, grab your gauntlets."

"How do they work?" Nalara held them with uncertainty.

"You just put them on." Winter slipped hers onto her hands. Their simple design contoured the curves of her forearms almost up to her elbows. The palms were a heavy mesh material, with carbon steel plating on the outer surfaces and a touchscreen template across the arms. Winter entered her access code on the keypad, and a subtle blue light emanated from the outer edges of the gauntlet.

"This activates and monitors the stability of your armor," Winter explained. "You can also access your location relative to your teammates and view simple topography. This is important because it's the only way to find our loading zone once coordinates have been sent out." Winter demonstrated the functions. "Look, you switch like this—very simple."

Nalara followed suit and experimented with her gauntlets' operation.

"Alright, now activate the armor." Winter smiled and switched on *Full Armor Mode* for surface engagement.

The gauntlets hummed ever so subtly and issued a thin layer of translucent film that slowly crept up her arms and met together at the center of her chest before making its way down her torso. It connected at her belt before descending down her legs and sealing at the tops of her boots.

"It's called six-point nano-armor shielding." Winter moved around to show Nalara. "The helmet completes the circuit. Once all six points are engaged, the armor filters out the toxins of the surface and repels high levels of kinetic energy. It's a similar technology as the city's barrier."

"Whoa, it's so first-tier . . ." the starry-eyed cadet breathed out as she watched in awe while Winter retrieved and donned her helmet. Her face was obscured by the digital targeting system as it came online. The liquid nano-armor melted upward over and around Winter's neck and sealed against the helmet's base. Once the circuit was complete, the gauntlets ceased humming.

Nalara switched the armor on and watched almost uncomfortably as the sheer liquid slowly covered her entire body. She locked her helmet in place and took a deep breath as the circuit completed.

The digital display was confusing at first, but she soon figured out what it was doing. She understood the green outlines of her teammates, the energy levels in her rifle's fuel cells, the status of her armor, and some other readings that she couldn't quite make out—but didn't dare ask about, because it had most likely been a part of her training that she simply couldn't remember at the moment.

"Alright, Archangels!" Captain Priest commanded everyone's attention as he entered the room.

His sudden arrival made Nalara jump, while all the others simply stood to attention.

"Today, we're sweeping a hot zone," he continued. "Teams of two for everyone. I don't want anyone caught alone down there. This area is thick with blighters—don't take any unnecessary chances. I want to see some big numbers up there by the end of the day." He looked directly at Nalara. "No excuses, and no pussy-footing around. Any third-tier behavior will be met with harsh and extensive extra training assignments. Some of you think we're a shoo-in for first team now that Eagle Eyes is getting out of the picture." A tiny smile in the corner of his mouth betrayed his true feelings. "You're wrong. The Grim Reapers still hold first by a long margin—so let's close it!"

The team cheered with enthusiasm.

"Not by default, but by raw effort!" Wraith clenched his fists and looked at Winter. "No one here gets by on talent alone."

Winter shifted her stance and took a steadying breath.

The Archangels all pounded their fists into their palms in camaraderie.

Wraith latched on his helmet. "For the Sovereign and for our home! Let's move out!"

CHAPTER THREE

Winter glanced over her shoulder at Nalara as they stood in line with the rest of their team. She looked apprehensive. Through her helmet's visor, beads of sweat could be seen gathering on her brow in the hot shuttle bay as they all waited in the boarding corridor.

"What are we waiting for?" Nalara whispered.

"Protocol is that each team awaits the departure of the one before them before boarding their own," Winter explained. "It helps keep negligent crowding down."

"What does that mean?" Nalara asked innocently.

"The barrier is a one-way shield," Winter expounded. "Anything can pass through from inside to outside. To help keep the pilot's job simple, only one shuttle at a time is given clearance to depart."

Nalara looked around at her team. The helmets mostly obscured their faces, but what she could see was tinted red with the overhead light. All of them were so focused and confident. She recognized Savage and Sapphire from their time together in the Formulation Quarter, even though they had gone by their names Kressara Sutlin and Neera Solis back then. They were only one and two years older than she was, but they were full-fledged, seasoned Purifiers now—their eyes stone cold and fixed forward.

Nalara couldn't help but envy their calm. She glanced at their ranks and mentally took note: *seventy-eight, eighty-two.*

Winter noticed her initiate's worried expression. "You okay?"

Nalara noted Winter's rank display with a quick glance: *thirteen*, and sighed. She nodded in silence. Except for Captain Priest at rank *two*, no one on the team even came close to Winter's rank.

It was a big shadow to live in . . .

The overhead light turned green, and Flight Control's voice flooded the bay through the intercom: "Grim Reapers are clear of the barrier. Archangels are go to board."

The bay doors near Wraith hissed open to the sides.

An orchestra of organized bustle, the shuttle bays appeared to resemble intricate timepieces of motion. Technicians in orange jumpsuits ran with supplies and checklists in arm this way and that through the rows of aircraft. Pilots in their blue uniforms marched dutifully to their assigned team's station. Sharply scrutinizing mechanics fine-tuned and adjusted the engines. Beneath the vaulted bay ceiling, giant mechanical arms lifted the prepared shuttles from their docking station and positioned them on the launching chute.

"Iron Raiders on deck, prepare to board," Flight Control prompted.

Winter turned and nodded to signal Nalara to follow before moving forward with the team through the busy bay and entering their shuttle.

Their craft, like all the others, consisted of two chambers. The entrance was a circular room wide enough for only one passenger to pass through at a time. The floor of the entrance was covered in curious vents. Beyond the entrance was the main cabin, where five seats with overhead locking restraints lined each wall, facing inward. A small alcove in the rear housed a rack of Purifier rifles, locked behind a glass panel. The cockpit was adorned with an intricate set of desk controls and a steering apparatus; a single pilot sat in the command chair and nonchalantly followed pre-flight procedure.

Winter saw the trepidation in Nalara's eyes and guided her by one shoulder to her seat. "Pull this down, and lock it between your legs," she instructed, tapping the overhead restraint. "The second we get the signal on the surface, you unlock and get your rifle from the captain."

Nalara nodded, wide-eyed.

"*The area's hot* means we might come under fire the second we disembark, so stay sharp!" Winter smacked Nalara's shoulder briskly.

Nalara nodded again. She was so overwhelmed taking in all the new things, she couldn't have mustered words if she had wanted to. So worried that she would say the wrong thing and embarrass her trainer, Nalara held her tongue and observed while everyone around her found their seats and locked their harnesses. She noticed with interest that neither Captain Priest nor any of the team addressed or even acknowledged the pilot. Sitting in his command chair, not even separated from the main cabin, he sat and worked carefully over the controls, vastly unaware of all of them as well. Fulfilling his vocation diligently, the pilot worked as all the Purifiers settled.

"Flight Control," the pilot spoke into his console. "Purifiers on board. Requesting launch permission."

"Shuttlecraft 3FGD-4FRWE," Flight Control's voice returned from the console. "Permission granted. You are go for launch."

"Copy that, Control. Initiating flight sequence," the pilot replied and adjusted his cap before playing his hands in expert motion over the buttons on the panel before him. The craft's door slid closed and sealed. A slight shutter in the structure and a humming whine in the air signaled the engines' ignition.

Nalara seized the handles on her restraints and clenched her jaw as the craft shifted suddenly.

The pilot gripped the steering device, and Nalara's stomach lurched. The walls of the shuttle bay zipped past the windows and transitioned into blue sky as the craft emerged from Olympus and flew out into the open air.

Winter smiled, watching Nalara's reaction. Seeing her experience her first team jump made her think of the great good they were doing. Someday, because of their sacrifice, the surface would be clear of the blighted. Then, young girls like Nalara could remain sweet and innocent; they could enjoy their lives without fear—as it was meant to be.

Winter watched her friend's eyes grow wide and knew at this moment she was seeing their home come into view as the shuttle pulled away. A technological marvel, the city ship of Olympus held her initiate in awe and admiration. The gleaming metropolis reached upward in beautiful spires and stately towers. Two miles across in diameter, the outermost circumference was lined with breathtaking gardens and organic farmlands. Fusion thrusters covered the cone-like base. Suspended thirty-thousand feet above the surface world, Olympus was like a glittering crown for the clouds.

Winter searched the lower portion of Olympus and spotted the access door she had used that morning to begin her climb up the outer hull. The shuttle shifted, and Winter lost sight of her home as their craft descended through the clouds. Nothing solidified her resolve more than seeing what she was fighting for with her own eyes.

"Jump time, cadet!" Scorch laughed. "You never know what's going to be waiting for you down there. It's been over two centuries since the surface was touched by civilization. Nothing but savage beasts and frenzied mutants live there now."

"And that's exactly why we exist," Winter explained. "To reclaim our ancestral home from the blighters."

"Didn't we have a colony on the surface once?" Nalara asked.

"That's what they teach the cadets," Wraith growled in his low voice. "What they don't teach is that it was wiped out—totally demolished by blighters."

Nalara looked to Winter in alarm.

Winter nodded solemnly.

"The story goes, they called for help, and the Purifiers were dispatched," Bulletproof elaborated. "But by the time they got there, they say the barrier was down, the structures burned to the ground. Livestock was slaughtered, and the colonists who were killed before they turned into frothing mutants were strung up like a human chain. Tree to tree in a bloodbath, they hung— their infected, blighted relatives left there to slowly chew off their feet."

Nalara swallowed, gripping her restraints so hard that her knuckles turned white.

"No more colonies until we wipe them off the face of the planet—every last one of them," Winter summed up. "Nothing like that will ever happen again." She shot a silencing glance at Bulletproof, but Nalara didn't seem to take any hope at the thought. "You'll see for yourself. The blighted aren't boogeymen; they're just animals. Mindless creatures. We have the power of the Sovereign and the just cause of Olympus on our side."

The team all nodded and mumbled in agreement.

"Oh, speaking of animals!" Scorch interjected with enthusiasm. "That's something you'll get to see just about every time you're on the surface."

"Really?" Nalara asked in trepidation and excitement. "Are they mutated horrors like in the trials? O-or . . ."

"Some of them, yeah," Scorch replied. "Get this—"

"Zeus spare us, here it comes." Viper rolled her eyes.

"—there's this thing called a *'camel'*," Scorch continued without hesitating. "Large, hairy, humped creature. Long nightmarish face, big teeth, eyes as black as death. It spits acid that melts you down to your core in seconds. It then slurps you up and takes you down in one gulp!"

"Whoa . . ." Nalara breathed. "Have you ever seen one?"

"Yeah, Scorch," Viper jabbed. "Have you ever *seen* one?"

"Well, no, not me personally, thank Sovereign!" Scorch confessed as he cleared his throat. "But, I read all about them in the FMQ. Scary, nasty beasties!"

"Sure sounds scary." Nalara looked again to Winter for reassurance.

"Look, I was scared of everything, too, my first day," Winter admitted, "of the animals and the blighted. But then I saw a blighter for myself. I took aim, shot, and just like that, it was dead. From that moment on, I never feared them or anything else. As far as I'm concerned, they're nothing but in the way."

The teammates all pounded their fists into their palms in applause and affirmation.

"Don't get too cocky," Wraith warned. "Every time we enter those doors," he pointed to the shuttle entrance, "we risk breathing our last. You have to make the decision to give your life for Olympus and our Sovereign before every single jump—or you're a naive fool." He locked eyes with Winter. "You think Zinda's taking it casual during today's jump?"

Winter didn't answer.

"You think he's about to let his guard down?" Wraith prodded. "You don't get to be the best on talent alone, and you don't achieve Ascension by underestimating our enemy."

"Ascension . . ." Nalara whispered in reverential awe.

The shuttle rattled as it hovered down below the canopy.

"Drop zone 20242," the pilot said. "Grid twelve, sector one."

A glass partition lowered at the entrance, sealing off the door area.

"All of you, get your head in the game, and score me some killshots today!" Wraith shouted.

"Sir! Yes, sir!" the Archangels resounded.

He and Winter both unlatched their restraints and stood. Wraith entered his code into the security panel on the rifle rack, while Winter took up position by the hatch and entered her code.

"Bulletproof, Viper," Wraith barked as he dismounted two rifles and held them out.

The two specified Purifiers unlocked and stood forward, accepting their weapons. Winter entered the command to open the departure chamber, and they stepped in.

"Airtight," Winter explained to Nalara as she sealed them in. "A failsafe to ensure no tainted air makes it to Olympus." She waited for a nod from the two in the chamber, then opened the shuttle door.

Bulletproof and Viper jumped down onto the surface and hit the ground running. Winter closed the door and the sealed chamber filled with disinfecting gas while the pilot moved the shuttle to the next sector. They repeated the process for Sapphire and Havoc, then Scorch and Trigger.

"Drop zone 20242," the pilot said again. "Grid twelve, sector nine."

"Winter, Gressen," Wraith signaled.

Nalara almost jumped at the sound of her name. She unlocked her restraint and left a trailing glance at Savage as she stood and received her rifle from Wraith.

Winter was given her rifle before she placed a hand on Nalara's shoulder and guided her into the departure chamber. Wraith operated the airlock once they were both inside.

"You're doing great," Winter assured her initiate as the shuttle door opened.

Nalara caught her breath as the terrain became visible. Dirt and grass below, trees and sky above; she had never felt so small in her life. Everything around her was big and unfamiliar and imposing. The deafening hover thrusters blew torrents of dead leaves and dust into the air.

The liquid nano-shielding protected her from feeling the forceful gusts, and it repelled every tiny particulate of sand, but the chaos on her view screen was maddening.

Winter patted her shoulder. "Jump! Jump!"

Nalara acted on instinct and launched herself out the door, followed closely by her trainer. Nalara stumbled as her feet hit the ground, crunching in the sparse patches of early spring snow. Everything felt so heavy all of a sudden. Winter immediately began sweeping the area. Nalara dutifully did the same while trying her best not to look lost and panicked.

The shuttlecraft hummed upward and screeched away above the trees for one last drop zone for Wraith and Savage before returning to Olympus.

A female computer voice droned over the intercom inside their helmets: "Loading Zone: Grid twelve, sector ten." The terrain display on their left arms reflected this announcement: "Rendezvous at 17:00 hours."

Winter took a moment after securing their immediate surroundings to check the progress of her teammates, represented by little dots in the grid on her gauntlet.

"Looks like everyone's making good time," Winter commented. "Let's get to it!" She checked the fuel cell on her rifle and took lead. "We need to clear this sector and meet up at the LZ before the sun goes down."

Nalara settled into her training and took flank.

"Eyes open," Winter cautioned. "This is a hot zone. There's been activity tracked here within the last week. We don't know what we're going to find. Could be a migrating herd of animals, could be a pack of blighters taking up habitation in the area."

"Those guys on the shuttle . . ." Nalara ventured, "they were just giving me a hard time . . . trying to scare me, right?"

Winter's icy eyes flitted across Nalara's view.

"They say a lot of cadets don't even make it through their first day." Nalara glanced around at the trees and the ancient, decrepit structures—completely unrecognizable and overgrown.

Winter's focus was on the landscape, analyzing every inch of their surroundings. She was completely methodical, almost like a machine. Every single movement was deliberate and graceful as she moved silently through the terrain. After a moment, she responded without pausing her gait. "Most cadets don't make it past the trial of Tartarus. Do you know how strong and proficient you have to be to even make it to your first day?"

"All I can think of is how this may be someone's last day."

"Don't worry about what Wraith said," Winter was quick to respond. "He's wrong. If you concentrate on the possibility of dying, you're doing it wrong. We're not here to die—we're here to make a better future."

"What about Eagle Eyes?" Nalara asked. "It's one of his last jumps, right?"

"And he's earned it." A kind of longing glow entered Winter's eyes. "Not only on the verge of Ascension, but retiring at the first rank position of 'Master Purifier'."

"Amazing," Nalara whispered in awe.

Winter nodded. "Only the second in the history of all Purifiers to achieve both."

"Oh, I remember; your hero, right?" Nalara grinned. "Nereza 'Nightmare' Vossen."

"Exactly." Winter smiled in genuine admiration. The very name filled her with ambition.

Some movement caught her attention, and she snapped the rifle sights up to her eyes. Nalara brought her rifle up, too, not sure what they were looking at. Winter stepped forward stealthily, firearm trained on the foliage.

A rodent of some kind darted up a tree before them; its beady blank eyes scanned for danger.

Nalara breathed.

"No threat," Winter spoke over her shoulder, not lowering her rifle.

"Why isn't it mutated?" Nalara asked.

"They say the Blight was created to target human DNA," Winter said dolefully. Warily skirting the creature, they continued their sweep. "But you can never be too careful down here."

At length, they reached a summit overlooking a small dell. Winter scanned the topography and froze. "Three blighters," she spoke quietly—with great urgency—while stepping closer to cover.

Nalara's heart pounded in her ears as she struggled to find the targets that Winter saw.

Winter raised her sights and took careful aim. "There," she said softly. "Hundred-fifty meters. By the second structure to the right of the metal fence."

Nalara squinted and searched the clearing to see them. She let out a tiny gasp as her view screen outlined three figures. She put her eye to the scope of her rifle and peered at the blighted near the tree. Even from this distance, their gruesome forms were enough to make her grimace, seeing the effects that generations of the Blight had caused. Their bodies twisted, their limbs having lost all definition of what they once were. It was difficult to think that this grotesque creature, hunched and cowering in the distance, had descended from the same ancestors as she, hundreds of years ago. The Blight had removed anything that had been human, leaving nothing more than a monster behind. They looked so small from this distance, yet they still filled her heart with trepidation. These were the stuff of nightmares—the reason civilization fled the surface in the first place to find refuge on Olympus.

"They're . . ." Nalara breathed. "They're . . . so . . ."

"Disgusting, I know," Winter said, finishing her thought. "Point in," she ordered quietly.

"Oh, right," Nalara complied as she snapped out of her trance-like fascination. She tried to focus on the front sight, tried to remember this was the whole reason for her existence, but the overwhelming excitement and terror of seeing a blighted mutant for the first time clouded her mind. All her life was spent training for this moment, and she simply could not focus.

"I'll take out the two on the left, you take the one near the tree," Winter instructed. "On my mark."

Nalara swallowed. The moment that followed seemed like an eternity.

Winter exhaled. "Now." She fired twice in rapid succession. Both kills were confirmed by her view screen. The instant replay appeared, tracking the last millisecond of the bullets before they made impact.

Nalara paused to reset her focus, then fired.

Miss.

When two blighters dropped like stones one after the other, the third fled.

Nalara's mind flew to recall all of her marksman training. She breathed out and fired again.

Miss.

The target was almost out of range; she clenched her teeth and fired again with another miss.

Winter saw Nalara's hands start to shake and holstered her rifle to her back. Swiftly and directly, she seized Nalara's firearm and took aim. She fired a resounding shot and dropped the last target mid-stride, like it was as easy as breathing.

Nalara's eyes met Winter's as she returned her weapon. Winter's steady, even breath set the pace for her initiate and settled her nerves somewhat. Nalara tried to find reassurance within those cold blue eyes but found only death and detachment within.

"Why did you do that?" Nalara asked at length.

Winter took out her own rifle again. "Trust me," she said. "You'll see. Ready to get down there?"

"We have to go purify those blighters now?"

"Yes. Stay close, stay alert. There might be more in the area."

Nalara bit her lip. She put her best effort into emulating her trainer. She tried to mimic her silent footsteps and steely gaze as they picked their way down into the clearing.

Winter noticed Nalara fall back slightly as they approached the felled blighters. One look at her initiate's pale, terrified expression and Winter knew she wasn't prepared mentally to approach.

"Secure the area," Winter ordered and switched her rifle from *single shot* to *purify*.

Nalara watched from a healthy distance as Winter fired a blasting stream of white-hot flame that washed over the horrible remains.

Winter concentrated the stream and watched as Nalara's curiosity got the better of her. She circled around the perimeter and took a few steps closer to the third fallen blighter.

"Careful," Winter cautioned. "The Blight releases into the air after death."

"Isn't the air already contaminated down here?"

"Yeah, but you don't want a concentrated dose seeping through your nano-armor."

"It can do that?" Nalara asked in horror.

"Sometimes." Winter ceased the flames, revealing a charred, ash-covered section of ground where the corpse had been. "You just don't want to risk it." She began purifying the second corpse.

Nalara gripped her rifle and stared at the monstrous thing.

Winter watched in silent pride as Nalara switched her rifle to *purify* and, after only a moment of pause, did what she was created to.

Winter smiled. She knew Nalara would hit her stride. She just needed the right nudge.

"Winter, Scorch here," Scorch's voice crackled over the intercom. "Winter, you there?"

Winter cut off the flames and switched back to *single shot*. "Read you, Scorch, what's up?"

"Hurry up and finish your sweep, then come to sector three." He laughed.

"You need support?"

"Nah. You've just got to get your cadet over here to see this. Something I'm sure she won't want to miss."

Winter looked up at the sky, then glanced at her gauntlet. "Copy that. We've got a lot of ground to cover, but expect us in a couple hours."

"See you then. Scorch out."

Winter turned to Nalara. She looked aghast and unsteady, her rifle boring a fiery crater into the ground long after the carcass had disintegrated into ash.

"You're good to stop now," Winter said, stifling a laugh.

Nalara cut off the stream, staring at the charred ground. Her breathing was rapid with exhilaration. It took her a moment to regain her composure before she turned and smiled sheepishly at her friend.

"It's best to make sure, right?"

Winter scanned the blasted area and saw absolutely no remains of the blighter. "I think it's safe to say it's dead." She tried to show a hint of levity to her uptight initiate. "Let's get our sector finished out, then Scorch wants to see us."

Winter led the way from the clearing, rifle ready.

Nalara was a mixture of awestruck and fearful while following this woman, who used to be her childhood friend. In her trainer, there was neither hesitation nor aversion at approaching and destroying these monsters of the surface. Transformed into a methodic purifying machine, there was no sign of the warm little Janey that Nalara once knew.

A cold efficiency had taken her place, and all that was left was this . . . *Winter.*

CHAPTER FOUR

Like a monument to a past age without history, a once-white stone building stood. Dead for so long that nature had crept over it and made it a part of the landscape, the giant structure was surrounded by a sturdy iron fence corroded by time. The forested terrain was flecked with patches of snow still clinging to the fading season.

Winter scanned the area surrounding the ancient structure watchfully and checked her gauntlet display. They were getting close to Scorch and Trigger's position, but she didn't want to slip up and get caught by surprise in transit, especially with so many large buildings nearby that could hide any number of blighters.

Nalara seemed to be more comfortable in her vocation by the end of the day. Her face still cried for help, but her body language spoke confidence.

Winter knew her FMQ training would kick in.

Together, they traveled up what looked like it had once been a road. The mossy growth was lower and flatter, and the crumbling remains of vehicles lay on all sides.

Nalara stumbled suddenly and looked down at the ground.

"What is it?" Winter asked.

Having kicked over a clump of dirt, Nalara apologized and regained her composure.

Winter smiled at the overturned soil. Her initiate's movement had revealed a cluster of small circular objects. She couldn't stay her curiosity. These trinkets of the former world had always fascinated her. Switching her rifle to *purify*, she gave the objects one short burst of flame.

Nalara looked puzzled.

"You need to be very careful handling anything on the surface," Winter offered. "It's possible that even things like these could have traces of the Blight on them. The nano-armor protects, but, like you said, it's best to make sure, right?"

"Definitely," Nalara agreed with an affirmative nod.

Winter stooped down and picked up one of the purified objects. Flat and thin, perfectly circular and covered in soil, the metallic item sat in her armored palm so unassumingly. Winter didn't communicate her thoughts to Nalara but felt a swell of excitement as she swept the imprinted surface clean. Her fingers revealed what appeared to be a man's face and lettering so old and faded that time had erased its message.

What had their civilization been like? Winter wondered.

"Hey, can I see it?" Nalara chirped.

Winter snapped out of her inner wanderings and stood up to show the object to Nalara.

"What do you think it is?" Nalara asked.

"I honestly don't know. I've seen many like them in the four years I've been in active service, but I have no idea what they are."

"Do you think they could be like allotments?"

Winter shrugged. "Your guess is as good as mine."

Nalara leaned closer and squinted. "Is that . . . a face on it?"

Winter nodded. "And there are words on it, too." Winter dropped the object in Nalara's receiving hand. "Make anything of it?"

"They're really faded, but I think I see . . . *'Un'* . . . and then *'mer'* . . . *'In'* . . . There's the letter *'G'* . . . *'ust'* . . . and *'Lib.'*" Nalara shook her head. "Weird. I wonder what language this was. I mean, I recognize the letters, but . . . it doesn't make any sense."

"Anytime you two feel like joining us would be nice." Scorch's voice crackled in their helmet's intercoms.

Nalara dropped the object at the suddenness of the voice, her eyes darting up to scan for its source.

Winter had already found it. She gave Nalara a nudge and pointed.

Nalara followed the line of her finger and spotted Scorch and Trigger a hundred meters off through the trees.

Winter switched on her communicator. "Be right there."

The two men turned and waved.

Winter initiated movement, treading the ancient item beneath her boot as she moved on. She and Nalara came up to stand by them at the edge of a large clearing.

"See what we found?" Trigger jerked his helmet toward the field near which they stood. His swept sable hair fell over his hazel eyes as he did.

Winter and Nalara stepped up closer and looked out over a wide clearing lined with young fruit trees only weeks away from blossoming.

"You found a nest." Winter nodded in approval.

"We cleared half a dozen out of a structure over on the east bank. They scrambled when they spotted us," Scorch said. "Only got one killshot." He shrugged.

"Sounds like your average," Winter teased. "One out of six."

"Hey!" Scorch laughed.

"We thought your initiate would want to see the Eye of Zeus in person," Trigger said with a smile.

"Not bad, right?" Scorch jostled Nalara with the butt of his rifle. "Getting to see the Sovereign's full, unconstrained power on your first day? Can't ask for anything more than that!"

"Did you call it in yet?" Winter asked.

"Nah, we were waiting for you."

"You should have called it in," Winter almost chided. "Do it."

"Yes, ma'am." Trigger hit the communicator on his helmet. "Flight Control, Archangels: Ashton 'Trigger' Cross."

After only a moment, a woman's voice came over the com in response. "Trigger, Flight Control. We read."

"Requesting Eye of Zeus support for purge and suppression," Trigger continued. "Authorization code P.A. dash sixty-one."

"Recognized." Flight Control paused. "Your request has been approved. Relay coordinates."

Trigger replied with a string of numbers.

"Copy that, Trigger. We're on our way," Flight Control responded. "ETA four point five minutes. Get your team clear of the area."

"Copy. Trigger out." He switched off the channel.

Winter looked over the field once more. "There has to be close to five acres here." She shook her head.

"Olympus hasn't circled back to this area for at least four years." Trigger shrugged. "Maybe they've gotten bold in our absence."

Winter smirked. "After today, they won't be."

"It's gonna be a good show!" Scorch laughed. "Come on, let's get to high ground."

Winter took point and led them away from the clearing. Her legs pumped mechanically, unwavering as her teammates struggled to keep pace. The crunch of dead leaves beneath the patchy sheet of fading snow, the soft impacts of her boots, her view screen constantly analyzing her surroundings, and her hyperawareness that came with being on the surface—it all made sense to her.

This was a good day.

She hoped Nalara took everything to heart. Perhaps it was the fact that her last initiate broke protocol and was killed in such a gruesome manner, or perhaps it was that she was training her childhood friend from the FMQ. Whatever it was, Winter *needed* Nalara to excel.

Reaching a summit nearly a quarter-mile from the field, Winter shielded her eyes and looked up at the sky. Olympus was nearly overhead, a large dark disk filling a portion of the sky. No longer were the shining towers visible, just the imposing, metallic underbelly. Winter smiled and sighed with satisfaction at the thought of their great Sovereign and creator being able to protect them even from that distance.

"Archangels, Flight Control," the voice came over all of their intercoms. "Confirm that all personnel are clear of grid twelve, sector three, subsection j alpha."

"Clear," Wraith's voice growled over the wave.

"We're clear," Havoc cued in.

"Clear," Viper chimed.

"Flight Control, we're clear," Scorch said.

"Clear," Winter acknowledged.

Above them, within the monolith of technology, multiple Flight Control technicians sat around a hub of projected touchscreen displays.

"Confirmed, Archangels," one of the women replied to their affirmations.

All of their eyes trained on the projected grid display, they dutifully fulfilled their vocation in monitoring the teams' progress and positions on the surface.

"Stand by for the Eye of Zeus," the technician beamed. "And be sure to enjoy the fireworks, honored Purifiers."

"Nothing quite like 'em!" Trigger's voice came through the com.

"Thank you for your service," the technician gratefully expressed before switching channels. "Engineering, you are go for energy discharge."

Inside the depths of Olympus, dwarfed by the massive, glowing fusion core, lay the vast and complex Engineering sector, where a core worker stood on a catwalk near a communication panel.

"Copy that, Flight Control," the engineer responded. He cleared his throat and took a calming breath before removing his hard hat and switching the channel. "Supreme Sovereign," he spoke reverently, his right fist placed dutifully over his heart, "my lord, Olympus is prepared to harness your power. Hail, mighty Zeus!"

The technician bowed his head in reverence as he flipped the toggle that communicated the massive weapon's readiness directly to the Sovereign Tower. No reply was made, but the technician's eyes grew wide as the core began to pulse and glow brighter.

Perched on the hill overlooking the field, Winter looked up at the city and pointed. "Look, it's starting!"

Nalara turned her eyes upward and gasped as a blinding ruby-red light gathered at the base of the floating city.

"The Eye of Zeus . . ." she breathed.

The tops of the trees began to shudder, and all sounds of wildlife ceased instantly. There was a sudden pressure in the air, and a faint ringing so high it was almost imperceptible.

The hairs on Winter's neck stood on end, and she shifted her stance slightly in preparation.

Without warning, a deafening thunderclap suddenly shook the forest, and a blinding beam of energy shot from the Eye of Zeus and struck the ground, causing vehement tremors. The explosion was ear-shattering. Fire and smoke belched up in billows from the point of impact.

Nalara fell backward, shaken from her feet, her eyes and mouth all agape.

The gigantic beam lasted only seconds, but it covered the entire target area and left a sizzling crater in its wake.

The group on the hill paused in reverential silence.

Nalara's eyes were rife with shock—even terror. "Oh . . . my . . . god."

Winter turned to her and nodded. "My thoughts exactly."

Looking back at the crater, Winter smiled slightly, admiring the simplicity of it all. She wished to herself that she could be as calculating and efficient as the Eye of Zeus. It simply pointed in the right direction and channeled the power of their Sovereign to eradicate evil.

Beautiful metaphor—how she longed to be like it.

Trigger took Nalara by the hand and helped her to her feet. "Well, now that the show's over, you girls just about ready to get back?"

"Mm. We should be getting to the LZ." Winter glanced at her gauntlet, then to Nalara. "You alright?"

"Y-yeah," she replied breathlessly, placing her hands on her knees to steady herself. "Yeah. At least . . . I think I am."

"Crazy, right?" Scorch exuded enthusiasm.

"'Crazy' is not the word I'd choose," Winter corrected, glancing once more at the smoldering crater. "More like . . . 'awe-inspiring.'"

Trigger jostled Nalara's shoulder, causing her to stumble. "So, the fireworks didn't disappoint?"

Nalara felt limp, as if her mind were disconnected from her body. All she could do was laugh weakly in response.

"Consider yourself lucky, cadet," Trigger continued. "It's not every jump you get to see the full wrath of the Sovereign unleashed against the Blight. Must be a good omen." He flashed his handsome smile again.

"Agreed." Winter turned to her young initiate. "Do you remember what you were taught in the FMQ about Zeus? About the legends of the ancient world?"

"I . . . I think so," Nalara said, still trying to regain her balance on legs that refused to stop shaking. She paused to take in a deep breath. "Didn't they say that Zeus had the power of lightning? To hurl lightning bolts to the earth . . . or something?"

Winter smiled and gestured to the hot glassy crater, the light of the late afternoon sun reflecting out of its massive basin. "They weren't far off," she stated. "Not lightning, though. Fire. Fire that purifies all." Her cold blue eyes locked with Nalara's. "I want you to always remember what you saw here today, Nalara. What you've now witnessed for yourself is the awesome purifying power of the Sovereign's Eye. But also remember that you are his Purifier. If you work diligently to fulfill your calling, you act as his Hand." She lifted her armored right hand up in a fist. "That's what the mark of the Purifier means. The ancient world may have created the Blight, but you were created to crush it. *You* are the Sovereign's Hand. Remember that."

Nalara's brown eyes widened in awe. Winter's words were pure conviction, an infusion of strength. Nalara's legs stopped shaking. She nodded resolutely. "I will. I promise."

The hard cold in Winter's eyes softened as her face warmed in a smile. "Good." She consulted her gauntlet display once more. "LZ to the southwest, three klicks. Move out!"

Winter took point, perfectly comfortable in her leadership. Her promotion to lieutenant earlier that year had taken a while to get used to. It was awkward at first to be in charge of the people who'd trained her, but she had worked hard since then to ensure that her team had the very best leadership possible. Winter imagined that if it had been up to Wraith, he would never have chosen her for his second in command, but she strived to meet his standards nonetheless.

Sometimes, she longed to be a simple team member once more—to be able to joke and relax. But she had worked too hard to get this far. Going back was not an option.

Her eyes trained on the route, she picked the way deliberately and carefully. Winter avoided any hollows in the terrain; she kept them to high ground and watched the openings of buildings for any signs of movement. She mentally latched on to her mission like a steel vice and could not be distracted.

Winter breathed out a release of tension once the sound of shuttle engines finally reached her ears. Her small group broke through the trees to find some of their teammates already loading onto the transport.

Each team member stepped individually into the entry chamber and was scanned thoroughly by sweeping emerald beams. When the scan was done, they were doused by a thick, opaque fog of disinfectant that vented out the floor before the glass opened, allowing the Purifier access to the shuttle. Once sanitized, each Archangel handed their rifle to Wraith before strapping into their seat.

Winter held back and secured the loading zone, ensuring her team's safety as they all boarded before her.

Nalara hesitated outside the entry chamber.

"You just step in," Winter instructed, her rifle still low and ready.

"It's easy." Scorch stepped in to show her.

The glass partition slid closed, and the green lights swept over his whole body. The disinfecting gas filled the chamber and voided out the vents, then the inner partition raised, and Scorch gave his rifle to the captain.

Her confidence bolstered, Nalara followed suit and held her breath through the whole process. Once on the other side, she allowed herself to breathe again as Trigger entered the chamber in turn. Nalara handed her rifle to Wraith.

"Well!" His eyebrows rose in surprise. He shot Winter a sideways glance through the glass partition but then looked back to her initiate. "A confirmed killshot on your first jump?"

"I . . ." Nalara quickly glanced at Winter's cold visage through the glass. "Yes, sir."

Wraith smirked and clapped her on the shoulder. "That's what I expect. Excellent work, Purifier."

Nalara almost smiled in response; she felt a sudden swell of accomplishment, but her mirth was cut short by a loud alert in the entry chamber.

Everyone snapped their heads to serious attention seeing the scanners turn red.

Outside the shuttle, a pit sunk deep into Winter's stomach as she winced and cursed inwardly. She knew what this meant, having seen it before.

Trigger's handsome face contorted in terror.

"Beginning purge sequence," the pilot stated unemotionally.

"No, please! Sir, I swear I wasn't touched; it has to be a mistake!" Trigger shouted in fervid desperation. His sweat poured down his face like raindrops as he pressed his hand against the glass in fear. A breathless second transpired as all eyes turned to their comrade.

"Pathogen detected," Wraith stated flatly. "You . . . are Blighted."

Winter's heart fell hard.

Wraith's stony eyes held his doomed comrade's in silent respect. "I'm sorry, Trigger," he spoke through clenched teeth.

Trigger's hand dropped from the glass. His eyes swelled and grew red as he fought back tears. His voice was steady. "No. I'm the one who's sorry, sir.

I've failed you, and I've failed . . . our Sovereign. I'm sorry." He apologized at length, then quickly turned away from his team. His eyes met with Winter's as she stood outside the shuttlecraft.

Winter couldn't bring herself to break eye contact with him. She wanted to, but her teammate needed her strength. He had turned so the others wouldn't see his tears, so there she stood as they fell—his sole, silent witness.

The floor vents glowed red and Trigger dropped his rifle. He leaned his helmet gently against the glass and exhaled.

The void where once vibrant life had sparkled was now an empty gaze of despair.

Winter swallowed and raised her chin, keeping their eyes locked together. She sent every ounce of strength and honor she could muster to her comrade.

The floor vents snapped open, instantly filling the chamber with a blinding inferno.

Winter's lips parted in shock at the sudden burst, and her jaw quivered as a tear escaped her crystalline eyes. It rolled down her cheek unnoticed as the chamber vented and blew a cloud of flaky gray ashes into the wind.

The chamber filled once more with disinfecting gas and vented before opening and inviting her inside as if nothing had transpired.

Winter could still feel the residual heat inside the chamber and shuddered to think of the unforgiving, purging flames. But with no other choice, she stepped inside.

CHAPTER FIVE

Approaching Olympus in a graceful, steady sweep, Winter gazed blankly out the shuttle windows and swallowed down her emotions at the loss of their teammate. She sighed out her sadness and breathed in the mission.

Someday . . . *someday,* there would be no losses. Someday, the Blight would be eradicated. Someday, good men and women wouldn't be in peril of death just by stepping outside. The planet was going to be theirs again; it was just a matter of time.

The sun's brilliant orange rays split the clouds like blades through silk as the vibrant orb cast long shadows across the billowing terrain in the sky. The golden spires of the city burned in the evening splendor, and the dazzling Sovereign Tower stood tall above the rest, looking down in loving warmth to assure them that everything was going to be alright. Winter hugged herself and held on to the thought of a better tomorrow for her people.

The city rose over them higher and higher as the shuttle made its final approach. The entire team sat in somber silence, many of their helmeted heads hanging, eyes closed.

"Flight Control, this is Shuttlecraft 3FGD-4FRWE," the pilot spoke at the console. "Requesting shield clearance."

"We see you, Archangels," the voice replied. "Reversing Hex 42. Enter and proceed to Bay 7."

"Hex 42, Bay 7, copy that."

Nalara sat up with sudden interest and swiveled her head to see what they were talking about.

"What's Hex 42?" Nalara almost whispered.

Winter leaned forward against her restraint and directed Nalara's vision out the front, past the pilot. Swiftly approaching the city's barrier, the shuttle maneuvered expertly toward the reversed hexagonal pattern.

"Like I told you earlier, the barrier is a one-way shield," Winter explained. "Anything can pass through it from the inside going out, but it's completely impenetrable from the outside coming in. Any one of the many thousands of hexagons that make up the shield's grid can be 'reversed,' so that something from the outside can penetrate through."

"So . . . does it make a hole in the barrier?" Nalara looked shocked. "What about the toxic air?"

"No," Winter said flatly, seeing the fear in her initiate's eyes. After what just happened to Trigger, that fear was to be expected.

She cursed inwardly, hating that it happened at all, but even more that it happened on Nalara's first day of active service. She thought back to what Trigger had said after they witnessed the glory of the Eye of Zeus, that it was a 'good omen.'

Not for him and not for Nalara, she thought bitterly.

Winter felt her hatred for the Blight intensify as she clenched her right hand into a fist. How many more lives would it claim before they eventually purified it from the surface? How many more would have to needlessly die for the sins of the past? Winter cursed inwardly again, knowing that Trigger's death would remain with Nalara for a long time.

"You're right," she finally responded. "If there *were* a break in the shield, we would be in danger of the Blight. But," she said, trying to dredge up something resembling confidence for her initiate from her own well that had gone dry, "we praise the Sovereign that he doesn't allow that. When a shuttle is ready to enter Olympus, Flight Control simply reverses the directionality of one single pattern, called a Hex. The shield remains completely intact against all particulates. Something with the force of a shuttle is able to pass through, but something as weak as a free-floating pathogen can't, especially at these altitudes."

"But . . ." Nalara protested, "you said our armor was a similar technology to the city's barrier. Isn't it possible—?"

"Nalara," Winter quickly interjected, "they're similar, but not the same. Trust in the Sovereign. He's never failed us before, and he won't fail us now."

Nalara nodded slowly, the fear reluctantly loosening its grip. She turned to the window and watched with big eyes as the shuttle passed through the barrier.

Winter eased back into her restraints, glad for the silence again.

The bay doors scooped them in, and the shuttle disappeared into the belly of Olympus.

Winter and her team silently exited the shuttle and entered their gear chamber to begin the melancholy transformation. They hung up the gear in their respective alcoves and wearily removed their boots and slipped them under the bench.

"I remember him from the FMQ," Viper spoke softly of Trigger, breaking the heavy silence. "He seemed kind of shy at first. But then . . . he changed. More confident, maybe."

The other Purifiers continued in their routines.

"Yeah," Scorch eventually said. "The guy was a whole lot of fun once we got him going."

"And cute too," Sapphire added. "That smile. I don't think I'll ever forget that smile."

"Anyone remember how he got his name?" Havoc asked, smirking.

Scorch laughed. "Oh yeah! First year in the field, he was so nervous down there that his hands would shake whenever he put his finger to his rifle's trigger. 'Shaky-Trigger,' we called him. But," he continued, his eyes staring off into space, taking in all the memories, "he kept at it, and kept at it, until he had earned the name 'Trigger.' You should have seen his hands today." He extended his own hands in demonstration. "Rock solid."

Seeing Trigger's tear-streaked face appear in her mind, Winter took in a steadying breath as she again stood as the sole witness to that face disappearing in purifying flames. In the field, Winter had known Trigger to be an average-level Purifier. Not incredible, but also not terrible. Average. But home on Olympus, far above the blighted horrors of the surface world, Winter knew him to be kind and genuine, always ready to flash that winning smile that seemed to chase away all despair. Her heart sank at the thought that Olympus had forever lost that smile.

Winter slowly opened her mouth to add to her teammates' reminiscing—

"Enough of this," Wraith grumbled from the armory, cutting her off and silencing the topic. "Focus on your service, and get to the conference room."

Silence reigned once again and the Archangels moved on. The team members changed into their rec clothes and, one by one, took their leave.

Nalara took Winter from her inner musing by speaking softly. "I'm so sorry," she said simply.

Winter glanced at her initiate and smiled slightly. "He was a good Purifier," she stated. "Our team will miss him." She paused, knowing in her heart that somehow, Nalara needed to finish the day out strong. "His sacrifice is one more added to the glory of our Sovereign. One more against the Blight and toward reclaiming our ancestral home." She breathed and swallowed and smiled. "This was a *good* day."

"Thank you," Nalara replied. "I know you took that shot from my rifle so I could feel good about my first day."

"You did your best."

"Wraith thinks I did . . ." Nalara grimaced. "But it was—"

"Next jump will be all you." Winter moved on. "Right now, we have the evening tally; then the rest of the night is yours to rest up and recover." She walked with her friend to the briefing room. "Tomorrow is training in the Hive for our team, and you want to make sure to get plenty of sleep beforehand. Also, there's a bout coming up." She smiled.

"Yeah, but I'm not going to compete," Nalara said. "Only you and the other top achievers get to."

"Every day is a chance to overtake the person ahead of you. There are no limits on your performance except the ones you give yourself." Winter paused for a breath when she realized she was nearly snapping. "You and the others," she started again, "need to stay in top shape, whether you're competing as part of a team or in the individual bouts."

Nalara nodded as they entered the active briefing room. It was filled with tired faces and sluggish movement. Each team sat together in their section; within a matter of moments, the room was settled and quiet.

Eagle Eyes took the podium and cleared his throat. "There's not one of you who didn't leave his or her heart down on that surface." He spoke in a strong and encouraging voice. His intense eyes locked on each of them in turn as he spoke. "I saw some great numbers, and I saw true effort. It makes me a very proud and satisfied man to be retiring soon on such a good note." He nodded in approval. "Now, call off."

As Eagle Eyes spoke the names of each team and read the tallies from the view screen on the podium, the teams responded with a simple cheer.

"Grim Reapers, seven killshots today. Broadswords, two. Archangels, six killshots . . . and one casualty. Name: Ashton 'Trigger' Cross. Iron Raiders, one killshot." He shifted his posture. "On the roster tomorrow we have Shadow Lords, Knight Hawks, Black Ghosts, and War Wolves." Eagle Eyes closed the view screen on the podium and looked up at his teams. "Hive training tomorrow for all teams not jumping. Good work, Purifiers." Clenching his right hand, he saluted by hitting his fist over his heart, showing the Purifier mark to his fellow soldiers. "Hail, Zeus!"

Everyone quickly rose to their feet. "Hail, Zeus!" they returned in unison, likewise saluting with their fists over their hearts.

Eagle Eyes nodded. "Dismissed." He touched the *update* button on the podium, transferring the updated statistics to the digital boards throughout the city.

Citizens on every level of the city congregated impatiently under the scoreboards to see the results. The anticipation built as individuals jostled each other for a better view. The boards blipped and displayed the new scores; wild cheers and scornful dismay erupted from the onlookers as their favored teams rose or fell in rank. The exchange of allotment tokens followed as it did every day. As one of the primary forms of entertainment on Olympus, the Purifiers and their feats of battle were heavily wagered upon.

Winter set her jaw as the Grim Reapers and the Archangels both held steady at first and second place. Exhaling through her nose in silent frustration, Winter looked away from the scoreboard and noticed Nalara standing near. She looked beat and desperate, standing there in silence, awaiting instructions.

"You're good to go," Winter said. "Go take a shower; relax."

"Okay," Nalara replied. "See you tomorrow?"

"Yes. Show up for training at the Hive when your alarm sounds, and get some good rest until then." Winter encouraged her initiate.

Nalara nodded and exited the conference room with the crowd of Purifiers.

As everyone filtered out slowly, Winter made her way forward to the front where Derrick Zinda still stood by the podium.

His focused face appeared to bear the cares of a man much older than thirty.

"You again?" He muttered without looking up.

"Yeah, are you free?" Winter asked.

"You have all of tomorrow, you know," he replied, studying the screen.

"Yeah . . . I know."

It could have been the cold calmness in her voice, but somehow, Eagle Eyes' attention was pricked. He looked up and studied her features. "It's always hard to lose a teammate. Are you sure you don't just need some rest?"

Winter paused. "I'm sure," she asserted. It was distasteful to her—the thought of needing rest like some initiate.

He looked incredulous.

"Please, Derrick. I need this."

"Alright, listen," he sniffed and continued. "You go home and shower, and *after* you do . . . if you feel up to it, meet me at the Hive. I've got to finish up here logging in the teams' movement patterns anyway."

"Thanks, Derrick." Winter smiled.

"Spoiled brat," he muttered.

Winter winked at him and retreated from the room.

Olympus was filled with joy as the citizens celebrated the safe return of the Purifier teams. Everyone on the Second Tier wanted to shake her hand. Everyone wanted to fawn and glorify her for the allotments they'd won or for the service she gave.

Their congratulations were lost upon Winter's ears as she ignored them in swift passing. Even though the vocation was paramount in her life, the praise was never important to her. She found it distracting, and she did not like distractions.

Holding her chalk belt from her climb at the break of dawn, Winter recalled her day of physical exertion, and suddenly, her limbs felt used and exhausted. Emotionally, she was drained and uncomfortable. She felt the need to ignore her physical discomfort and stay on task; if she took the time to let her muscles rest, she might have the time to feel grief at the passing of her teammate. That was a risk she wasn't willing to take.

Winter had already been interviewed by a Unifier today and thankful she would not be held up in their security line on her way to the living chambers.

The order and uniformity of Olympus was such an established

reassurance in her mind. No matter what happened on the Blight-stricken surface, her society would always tick on like a masterwork clock—reliably. It filled her with confidence to see and feel the steadfast consistency all around her.

The Purifiers' housing building was a simple structure made up of three levels. The ground floor level was composed of a huge cafeteria, which serviced all but the top twenty achievers, and dormitories for the bottom fifty achievers. The second level was a bit more spacious and boasted fifteen small apartments and full communal bathrooms, complete with showers. The middle thirty achievers lived there.

Winter exited the lift at the top floor. This level was reserved exclusively for the top twenty Purifiers. She made her way down the empty hall to her room.

She remembered the day she graduated from the FMQ, where all the cadets slept in a giant barracks together. Moving to the ground floor of the Purifier housing seemed like a dream at the time. Sharing a room with only three others, having a bathroom across the hall that was shared with only eight other people, was absolute freedom.

Only three years later, having spent only a brief stay on the second floor, Winter earned her place as a top twenty achiever and received favored lodging. She had been given an apartment here on the top floor all to herself, with furniture and her own private bathroom. The exclusive comforts came with the opportunity to mingle with the highest achievers of Olympus on a daily basis. At the end of the day, this level was filled with the people Winter emulated.

Winter entered her security code on the door pad, and the panels hissed open to the sides.

"Winter," her captain's brusque voice hailed her from behind.

Winter breathed deeply, internally setting her will.

Here we go.

"Yes, sir." She turned around and waited while Wraith approached, his demeanor as stern as ever.

The sheer size of the man was truly daunting. He would fit right in had he been formulated as a Guardian, but here among the Purifiers, Captain Priest stood out like a bough among twigs.

Wraith came to stand over Winter and stared her down.

Winter averted her eyes and waited patiently for him to finish posturing.

"I know what you did today," he accused.

"Did, sir?"

"No games with me, Winter. That no-name, third-tier initiate has a file so small, I've never been so underwhelmed in my life. I'm astounded she made it through Tartarus alive!" He paused, waiting to see her reaction. "I watched the blast-cam footage."

Winter looked up at him.

"She couldn't have made a shot at that range, even if the Sovereign had blessed the bullet himself!" His enormous, muscular body shifted forward, and his voice lowered. "I don't like you skirting the rules. And I do *not* like your uncanny knack for always justifying it. If we have a problem like this in the future, you're going to answer to me. Understood?"

"Completely, sir."

Wraith paused, eyeing his lieutenant suspiciously. "Just tell me why."

"Why, sir?"

"Yes, why." He leaned closer. "Why did you make that shot for her?"

Winter sighed and placed a hand on her hip. "An attempt to bolster her confidence on her first day," she said after a moment's thought.

"To coddle her, you mean."

"No, sir. Not to coddle. To lead."

"By holding her hand?" the towering figure accused vehemently, his voice carrying down the corridor. "This is what I do not need, Winter! Not now, not ever! I need soldiers for my team! I need soldiers like . . ." his voice trailed off into silence.

Winter finished his thought. "You need soldiers like Trigger."

"*Better* than Trigger, as is plainly evident," he shot back. He lowered his voice again. "I've now lost two middle-grade Purifiers in just the last month. I don't need a third! Even the caliber of Hammer and Trigger would be a *very* welcome addition instead of some pathetic, weakling pod-child!"

Winter stiffened and set her jaw. "With all due respect, sir, Nalara is not a child. She's fifteen and has earned the right to be an active Purifier—no different than you or I, or anyone else. Like you said, she made it through Tartarus alive."

"Only by Sovereign's blessings, I'm sure," Wraith scoffed, rolling his eyes.

"He carries us all, doesn't he?" Winter quickly returned, her voice resounding with confidence. Her rhetorical question took him by surprise. With his guard now lowered, she moved in to quickly bring an end to the hostilities. "However she did it, sir, she still made it through the trials, and what she needs now is some guidance—guidance, a little encouragement, a little help. I know she'll prove to be a valuable member of the Archangels."

Wraith's scowl persisted, but his eyes flitted into her living chamber momentarily.

Winter shifted uncomfortably in the moment that transpired.

He huffed. "We'll see." He eyed her for just a moment longer, but even he could see the battle was over. His posture relaxed. "Dismissed, Lieutenant."

"Very good, sir," Winter replied, turned on her heels, and retreated into her room as Captain Priest moved back across the hall to his chambers. Winter sighed in relief as she closed the door on that encounter.

Very good indeed, she thought.

In the four years since she'd been an active Purifier, she and Wraith had not seen eye-to-eye on many things. But ever since she had been promoted as the Archangels' lieutenant, their working relationship had only become more strained. Punctuated only by brief glimpses of approval, these encounters had become more frequent.

The bigger room and nicer furnishings were still somewhat unfamiliar. In the moment, it occurred to her that she didn't know if she had sat on the couch even once yet. Winter slipped off her climbing shoes and tossed her chalk belt onto the kitchen counter before moving to stand near the large living room window.

The sunset was beautiful. Meditatively removing the pin from her bun, Winter let her hair fall in its messy braid as she watched the sun's last light dissolve through the clouds. The milky-hued barrier shimmered in its arcing dome around the city ship.

She removed the band from her braid and began separating the sweaty, tangled strands from each other. She watched the citizens down below on the Second Tier as they steadily walked from their vocations to their respective sleeping sectors. The streets were cleared quickly and efficiently before dusk even began to set in.

Winter sighed and stretched her sore muscles on the way to her bathroom, where she took out her brush and worked it carefully through her obsidian locks.

A wave of calm washed over her as she watched her hair in the mirror. Most Purifier women liked to keep their hair short and manageable; but she had always made time for it and loved the way it looked. It was the one luxury she allowed in her life, and it afforded her immense satisfaction.

Chime, Chime

The citywide intercom beckoned.

Winter dropped her brush and rushed to the main room where the outer wall that faced the city center dissolved from opaque to transparent.

The sides of the Tower up on the First Tier lit up with the face of their Sovereign, and Winter fell to her knees automatically. She spoke the words of the prayer in sync with every living soul throughout every deck and within every station.

> *Hail to his supreme holiness.*
> *Hail to our Sovereign ruler.*
> *Hail to our living god.*
> *Your name is a light to our path.*
> *Your wisdom guides us through darkness and death.*
> *Your power governs the whole earth.*
> *It is to you and you alone, o gracious lord, that I swear my life, my loyalty,*
> *and my unconditional obedience.*
> *I swear to live for you.*
> *I swear to die for you.*
> *Live forever, o glorious king—for in you, we are granted life.*

Winter remained on her knees as long as his divine face was visible—and a little longer. Even after the wall of her apartment had returned to its solid appearance, Winter sat on her feet and pondered the coming of the morning. Her eyes lingered steadily upon the Sovereign Tower, still visible through the large window. Her heart swelled within her as she knew—*knew* that her Sovereign saw that she was doing her best.

CHAPTER SIX

The stars above Olympus were clouded by the milky barrier. The night was as warm as day inside the perfectly maintained, temperate sphere of life.

Soft footfalls, timed breathing—Winter glided like a silent shadow across the urban terrain. Long strides and careful foot placement carried her forward like the swift, steady rush of time itself. The empty streets were her playground; stairs and ledges transformed from obstacles to pathways. Nothing hindered her course, because nothing could be a blockade to her honed physique and conditioned lifestyle.

The dark onset of night grew deeper as she became poetry in motion—completely unfettered as she sailed through the darkened city streets and across balconies and rooftops.

Winter ran the same course often, having memorized how to avoid the movements of the nighttime Unifiers long ago. Their primary duty was to enforce the standard curfew. Since Purifiers needed less sleep than the average citizen, Winter saw no harm in honing her skills even more with the time she had. It was in the best interest of Olympus for her to be in top condition.

Although she knew it to be true, Winter firmly denied all evidence that she used her training to run from her emotions. The simple fact was that if she used all her time and energy to train, there would be nothing left for the intense gnawing within her heart.

Winter made it across the city to the center of the Second Tier, where the immense coliseum stood in monolithic majesty.

This structure served as the pillar that elevated the First Tier above the rest of Olympus. The coliseum, or 'Hive' as it was called, was perfectly circular and surrounded by fragrant garden beds and waterways that spilled from their source far above on the Elite's tier. Its walls were covered in ornate carvings depicting the Elite in gold filigreed gardens, worshiping at the foot of the Sovereign Tower. The immense structure was crowned by arcing columns in which could be seen the statues of the Ascended, standing in eternal decorum.

The only entrance from the Second Tier was always locked at night, but Winter was undeterred.

Veering off to one side, she came to a staggered halt and took a moment to catch her breath. Blood coursing, legs throbbing, eyes and heart opened by the life-affirming free running, Winter approached the gigantic wall and glanced up the daunting, sheer surface.

With years of practice on her side, she approached the structure confidently and began her ascent. Winter dug her strong fingers into the tiny crevices and methodically worked her way upward.

Somehow, it was more nerve-wracking to climb this structure within her own tier than it was to climb the outer hull of Olympus from the Engineering sector all the way up to the outer gardens. The thought of being found the next morning in a splattered mess on the street was terrifying when compared to the romantic dignity of softly falling forever and ever through the clouds and being joined permanently with the unknown home she had been fighting for as long as she had lived.

Her calloused hands reached over the lip of the stadium, and Winter pulled herself up onto the highest row where the honored Ascended stood, forever transfigured in towering marble.

Winter was very familiar with their faces. The twelve-foot statues of Purifiers that had gone before formed a long row, partially encircling the arena. A reverence washed over her as she passed by them one at a time. Gazing at their peaceful, heroic countenances, Winter honored their memories and efforts in her heart. Happiness and hope sprung up inside her as she approached the Purifier that had most inspired her life.

A gorgeous, muscular, gracefully proportioned woman stood immortalized in flawless marble for all generations to see. Assuming the same position of all Ascended, her left hand was outstretched, palm up, and her right hand, balled in a fist, saluted over her heart in perpetual reverence. Her stone eyes were fixed on the eastern horizon, and her hip-length hair was frozen in lustrous waves.

Winter smiled openly to see her hero in person again.

The plaque beneath her feet read:

THE IMMORTAL NEREZA 'NIGHTMARE' VOSSEN

Nereza Vossen is recognized as the greatest Purifier of her generation. First in history to hold the highest rank at the time of her Ascension, Nereza is renowned as a Purifier not driven by savagery, but by her sheer will and discipline. May her dedication to fulfill the edicts of our dear Sovereign be forever hallowed in our minds and hearts.

Winter loved reading those words. While others fought tooth and claw to become one of the top twenty, Nereza had used her combination of natural skill and discipline to climb through the ranks almost effortlessly.

Whenever Winter felt weary or overwhelmed, especially in the first days following her graduation, she would sneak out of chambers and make her way to the Ascended platform to sit at the feet of her hero, Nereza.

Winter had always felt a deep connection to her. At the conclusion of her trials, the instructors had compared her to Nereza in skill. They said things like: *"Winter is one of those rare, naturally talented Purifiers like Nereza Vossen,"* and, *"What comes to other Purifiers only through years of trial and error, Winter seems to grasp without any problem."*

Winter knew for herself that aside from Nereza, she was the youngest Purifier to ever enter the top twenty rankings. She had tried so hard to live her vocation as Nereza did—not because of savage brutality or a fiercely competitive spirit, but because of her willingness to train her innate abilities and talents. She had noticed early on that her senses seemed sharper than those of other Purifiers. Her reaction time was faster. She was able to recognize hidden signs in plants, the soil, and the air that led her to have more confirmed kills than most others during any single jump.

Winter sighed softly and tucked a long black curl behind her ear.

"I'm still going," she spoke to the silent countenance of her idol. "I'm still doing the very best I can." Her heart felt heavy. "But I *am* tired. It's been . . . a long day. My fighting spirit took a hit. I felt for a moment like we weren't doing any good—like even if I work to my dying breath, that the Blight will still keep claiming lives long after I'm gone." She paused, looking into the crafted eyes of Nereza. "You felt that way, too, sometimes—didn't you? . . . You had too. But you kept going. So I can't stop—I can't let it get to me. I'm going to join you here, and when I do, I'll hold the same rank. I'm going to finish my purification calling as the greatest of my time, just like you did."

She breathed deeply and felt the burdens and cares of the day lift from her shoulders. Nothing had really changed. Day after day, she would train, and go on jumps, and purify their homeland . . . but once again, she felt like she *could* do it to the best of her ability.

Winter bowed her head in respect. "For Sovereign Zeus," she avowed.

She stepped back from the statue several paces before turning to face the arena. The immense structure sloped over rows and rows of simple slab seating to the Hive floor nearly three hundred feet below. A large section of seating was walled off from the rest and boasted an exclusive entrance from the First Tier and individual, cushioned seating for each of the thousands of blessed Elite.

The monolithic dome that covered the enclosure climaxed almost a hundred feet above the highest rows of seats, and at the very top at the apex was the base of the Sovereign Tower on the First Tier.

"Winter!" Eagle Eyes' voice echoed across the Hive.

Winter looked down to the arena floor, which was composed of ten-inch hexagonal tiles from end to end, and saw the tiny figure of her mentor standing there far below.

She slipped over the ledge and dropped to the seating area, then made her way down to the stairs at the lip of the arena floor.

"Took your time." Derrick shook his head with a smile, "Can't be the best if you don't show up."

"I'm here," Winter smirked. "You're the one who insisted that I shower."

"If we're going to train together, then *yeah*, I insisted," he returned playfully and held up his hands.

Winter threw two lazy jabs into his open palms. "Whatever."

Derrick chuckled. "Okay, warm up."

She worked through the exercises with him in silence. Her focus renewed, her energy and intensity at its highest, Winter put everything she had into becoming better—trying to focus not on where she wanted to be but just to see improvement of any kind. She became so engrossed with the work at length that she didn't even notice the smile of pride spread across her trainer's face.

"Good," he said. "Now breathe."

Winter closed her eyes and let her head fall back.

"Relax," Derrick urged. "Let your arms just fall from your shoulders, get the tension out."

Winter exhaled and came to stand up straight.

"Let your head suspend from the ceiling and let your hips sink down. Good," he prompted. "Now, remember what we were working on last time?"

"Open gaze," Winter said.

"That's right. Let your eyes relax and focus on nothing, but see everything." Derrick circled around her. "When you resist the instinct to focus in on any one thing, your mind is free to react to everything." He suddenly jabbed hard at her face from the side.

Barely visible at the edge of her peripheral, the picture changed, and Winter saw the moment he recoiled to strike. She shifted her feet and bent her knees, then stepped in with an immediate but soft deflection as she stepped swiftly forward and circled behind him.

Derrick smiled broadly. "You're getting good!" He laughed with his fist suspended in midair.

Winter couldn't help but smile as well.

"Good shift, nice relaxed reaction, and always moving forward." Derrick shook his head. "I'm such an excellent teacher."

Winter laughed. "No, it's just that all your other students are terrible."

"Cute." He nudged her off-balance. "But no one else has been interested in the old art for years now. All the others want is firearms training."

"Really?" Winter was truly surprised. "Nobody?"

Derrick shook his head. "No, not really. I had some students a few years back—one even who really excelled. But it didn't take. Lost interest. The truth is, even in my generation, no one cared much for it either. Now, in the first days of the Purifiers, it was required learning. Even in Nereza Vossen's time forty years ago, when the surface was still overrun with blighters. Jumps were like open warzones back then." He looked wistful. "Nowadays, we're just the cleanup crew."

"But still," Winter appealed, "you're retiring at the top of your order. That's only been done once before."

"Mm, but with only a fraction of the kills." He shrugged. "I'm afraid my legacy isn't quite the legend I'd hoped it would be."

Winter was troubled at his admission but didn't know what to say. She was astonished by how much the statement stung her personally. She expected him to feel fulfilled and accomplished at the end of such a prestigious line of service. She expected him to say something like he had no regrets . . . and the opposite was not easy to comprehend.

"You, on the other hand," he snapped back to his air of satisfaction. "You're going to join the Ascended as the next Nereza."

"That's the goal," Winter said without confidence.

"You *make* it a reality," Derrick added with gravity. "What have I taught you, Winter?"

"'There are no limits on your performance . . . except the ones you give to yourself,'" she repeated the words her trainer had instilled in her years before.

"And do you believe it?"

"Of course, I do." Winter almost laughed, remembering the day's events. "I even said those exact same words to my initiate today."

The raw intensity of Derrick's eyes was hypnotic. "I want to see you up there with me." He glanced at the Hive's crown of statues. "I want you to take your rightful place in Elysium among all honored and glorified Purifiers. It's where you belong. I know it, and you know it. So *make* it happen."

Winter nodded firmly. She knew that his words were sincere. In all the years she'd turned to him for guidance, he had never steered her wrong. His wisdom and training was likely the greatest contributor to her success as a Purifier. She wanted desperately to tell him how much he would be missed, but bringing emotional vulnerability into a relationship that had been about strength and dignity in service seemed so contradictory in the moment that she couldn't bring herself to speak it. She was also a little afraid of how she would carry on without his advice to rely on. The thought made her stomach feel heavy—the thought that the next time she needed help, she would be on her own. The next time she trained, it would be just her. If anyone else wanted to learn the old art . . . they would have to ask her.

All these thoughts clouded her mind, and Winter shook them off with distaste.

"I'm really happy for you," she said truthfully. Instead of daring to speak her feelings, she reserved all her fears and apprehensions inside— along with her desire to sincerely thank him for all the countless hours of selfless dedication he had given to her. All she could bring herself to say was, "Everything that you'll receive . . . I know you've earned it all."

He beamed. "Thanks." He fell back into a strong fighting stance. "Now, you ready?"

Winter squelched her insecurities and put on her strongest face. She forced herself to smile. "Let's do this."

CHAPTER SEVEN

Bright lights flooded the Hive. Morning brought forth every team not currently deployed on the day's surface jump to the expansive floor. Some of them routinely set out the training equipment while others began lazily warming up.

Having slept no more than three hours, Winter felt anxious to get the training underway. She was afraid that without some stimulation, she would fall asleep again, wasting the day completely. As her team began to appear, Winter glanced around for her initiate but could not see her. She began taking her team through the warmup when Nalara wandered in with the stragglers.

"Alright, Archangels," she spoke in a commanding tone. "Let's get moving."

"You all think you're some kind of slug-faced Guardian?" Wraith bellowed in motivation. "Let's get moving!"

Winter put them all through their paces, taking her position as lieutenant as seriously as everything else in her life. At least in this, if not anything else, her captain trusted her proficiency. Wraith worked and sweated along with the rest of them, snapping at anyone who lagged behind.

Nalara was taking well to her first day of Hive training. She kept pace with the team as Winter led them through drills, she scored average at the range, and her basic hand-to-hand wasn't terrible. In all, Winter was confident that she would find her stride in good time.

Approaching mid-day, Winter stood breathing near the weights, taking a moment's rest before plunging into her strength training.

Suddenly, the floodlights overhead flashed red, causing many in the Hive to start, and a blaring alarm assaulted their senses.

Winter's focus snapped to the massive view screen that stood blank against one wall.

"Emergency deployment . . ." she whispered.

The view screen blipped on, and the stone-set face of Master Purifier Eagle Eyes appeared. "Emergency deployment," he said. "All available Purifiers, to the conference room immediately."

Winter breathed in deeply and exchanged a glance with Wraith before the two of them exploded into simultaneous motion, joined only by a few others of their own initiative.

"Move it! Move it! *Move it!*" Wraith roared.

The sound of frantic footfalls filled the Hive as only the fastest few were able to make it out before the mad scramble. Winter, Wraith, and three others of different teams dashed out the great main entrance and crossed the thoroughfare to the Purifier Quarter.

Emerging from the Hive, Winter squinted in the harsh mid-day sunlight. The citizens of Olympus cheered them on, shouting their team names and callsigns with choruses of encouragement as they sprinted past. Even though several called Winter by name, she couldn't afford to be distracted. Several of the others in her company took the time to smile, wave, or salute for their fans, but Winter was unimpressed. To her, the mission was of the utmost importance; Purifier life was not about fleeting fame.

Winter took a glance over her shoulder as she ran, stealing one last view of her hero up in her stone-cased eternity. Nothing could distract her from her ultimate goal. Nothing would rob her of the glory of Ascension.

The billboards throughout the city lit up with the current rankings and the flashing words *Emergency Deployment.* The excitement was like electricity in the air as crowds gathered in the streets to view the engagement.

They thundered over the threshold of the giant octagonal Deployment Building, greeted by the overhead Purifiers' symbol of the blade wreathed in flame. The empty circular entry room echoed with their breathing as Wraith unlocked the lift with his code. The doors hissed open to the sides, and they all piled in. Lilith 'Razor' Sharpe of the Grim Reapers selected *Purifier Command: Level Four* on the panel inside.

"Go time, little one," she winked at Winter. "Think you'll live through this to face me next month?"

Winter refused to relinquish her focus; she wouldn't take the time or effort to come up with a snide retort. Lilith's taunting green eyes were lost on her. Winter stared immovably at the level display and ignored everything else.

Lilith chuckled and smoothed down her stick-straight blonde hair with indifference. The second the lift opened on the hub floor, she was out and running, followed closely by the others.

Derrick Zinda was the conference room's only occupant. His face was stern and focused. He looked up as the small group flooded into his company.

"What's the threat?" Wraith addressed the Master Purifier.

"Ten minutes ago, we received an emergency aid request from the War Wolves. Their team's pinned down by blighters in a hollow—grid eleven, sector two," Eagle Eyes said evenly. "Our mission is to suppress the enemy and make a clear path to the shuttles." He cut off suddenly as more Purifiers started to pour in. "Get to your hubs, and get to the surface," he ordered the first group.

Winter and the rest of them obeyed immediately as Eagle Eyes continued his instruction. She and Wraith split off into the Archangels' team hub and dove into gearing up.

"Get going!" Wraith barked. "The only Purifiers coming on this jump are the ones who get here before the pilot."

"Yes, sir!" Winter kicked off her shoes and pulled on her tactical suit.

Scorch and Havoc ran in and received the same warning from their captain.

Wraith ignored Viper and Bulletproof as they skidded to a stop inside the gear chamber together. He ducked into the shuttle deck without a word.

The two newcomers looked sheepishly at each other, then to Winter for direction.

Winter pulled on her gauntlets and breathed before responding, "Gear up fast, or stay behind."

They nodded sharply and complied.

Winter summarized the mission once more as she prepared herself for surface engagement. She was fully equipped by the time Savage, Sapphire and Nalara made it into the chamber. She glanced through the window to the bay and saw Wraith already boarding the shuttle.

He really meant to leave without them . . .

Winter pointed at the latecomers. "You gear up and stand by." She trotted out toward the shuttle, followed closely by Scorch and Viper. "Stay sharp and ready in case we need reinforcements," she called over her shoulder.

Piling quickly into the shuttle, Winter took her seat and strapped in.

"Pilot ready," Wraith confirmed.

"Bulletproof and Havoc were right behind us, sir," Winter said.

"No time. Close the doors," Wraith curtly ordered the pilot.

"Sir, we'll get better numbers with more team members," she insisted.

In the moment it took Wraith to glare at her and consider his response, both Bulletproof and Havoc made it into the shuttle.

Wraith quickly turned to the pilot. "Punch it!" He sat and strapped himself in.

Winter felt him staring her down.

The doors closed and the shuttle shot forward into the open air. Winter gripped her shoulder restraints to avoid whipping her head to the side with the velocity of their takeoff. Her teammates were all fired up; they cheered and pounded their fists into their palms as the shuttle dove down toward the surface.

"*Whoo-hoo!*" Scorch howled like a frenzied animal. "Archangels a-comin'!"

"It's blighter wastin' time!" Havoc joined in.

"Let's get some!" Bulletproof roared.

Eyes cold and focused and mind sharp and clear, Winter enjoyed the burning sensation of battle fire in her chest. It was emergency deployments like these that separated the real Purifiers from the pawns. The blighted were easy enough targets to pick off at a distance as Winter was accustomed to doing, but when the mutated horrors flocked together, they were more dangerous than ever. One moment of carelessness could mean the difference between life and death.

Winter could hear the hollow ringing of gunfire as they approached the surface.

"Making a junkyard stop!" the pilot shouted over his shoulder. "The area's too hot!" He switched a setting on his control panel, and a giant glass partition sealed off the cockpit.

"SNATCH AND BAIL!" Wraith roared as the shuttle door opened, flooding the cabin with rushing wind and the harsh pops of gunfire and electric rifle blasts. He grabbed a rifle from the rack and programmed in his security code before jumping out onto the field.

Winter hung back, partly to ensure that her team made it safely to the ground before joining them, but also to take note of any enemy fire that might rain upon them.

Her boots hit the surface; Winter crouched down and sprinted low until she was out of the clearing. She glanced down at her gauntlet display as the shuttle above her whined up and away out of danger. Winter gained her bearings and watched the team beacons fan out through the trees, converging toward the target zone.

She decided to skirt the border rather than charge right in. Keeping her eyes open and footfalls hushed, she managed to ignore the distracting targeting display in her helmet and observe the world around her instead. She circled wide around the target zone until she saw signs of passage through the terrain that didn't match any Purifiers. If the blighters came through this way, it was possible that she could take their flank while the teams focused their fire at the front.

The hollow came into view as she advanced.

It was bad. A swarm of blighters had the high ground, with partial cover under an outcropping of rocks. The War Wolves were truly pinned down in a dell, with dead fallen trees as their only shield from the hailstorm of bullet fire.

It was difficult to discern their exact numbers, but there were scores of them. They were seemingly undaunted by the new arrivals of reinforcements, who could not do much more than take up positions in the woods surrounding.

The Purifiers tried to push forward, but the terrain was such that it forced them to completely expose themselves to gain ground. The blighters had good cover, and they were well-armed. Eventually, the Purifiers would overcome, but not without massive reinforcements and definite casualties.

The gunfire was earsplitting, and the rifle blasts were blinding flashes in the shadowed woods.

Winter breathed and took in the scene.

See everything . . .

The blighters were staggered up the incline; there was no approaching on foot. As the Purifiers pressed in directly to liberate the War Wolves, they would waste precious time. There was no guarantee that more blighters wouldn't show up in that time either. The rock formation was steep on all sides, but not impassable for her. If she could make it to the rocks, she could get at them from a flank they didn't expect. Winter paused a bit longer and tried to look past the hectic readings all over her helmet display. There, in the shadows at the edge of the trees at the summit of the formation, she saw the slightest glint of a reflection. Hidden well and lying in wait, a sentry stood guarding the blighter's escape.

Winter opened the broad channel. "Winter here," she spoke calmly.

"What's your position?" Wraith demanded.

"Northwest of the engagement area," she replied. "I think I can cut through the flank, then box them in. There's an outer—"

"Negative!" Wraith cut her off. "We are not splitting our numbers. They'll run out of ammo soon enough."

Winter clenched her jaw and switched off the channel. "You don't know that," she growled to herself. Wraith seemed to always be about numbers and never about efficiency. Did he consider the time it would take and all the things that could go wrong until then?

Winter gripped her rifle and took off in a low sprint. She needed to reach the outcropping without the sentry noticing her. The battle raged on. Amid the gunfire and rifle blasts, desperate, shouted coordination blared and crackled over the intercom.

Movement swift and precise, Winter achieved her position under the jutting formation without drawing attention. Now was the true test of her grit; if she holstered her weapon and utilized all her limbs to quickly scale the fickle-looking rock face, she would be completely exposed and helpless against attack. Winter took a split-second to analyze her options once more.

Exhaling in silent affirmation, Winter closed her eyes and centered herself. She quickly holstered the rifle on her back and fixed her eyes upon the ascending terrain before beginning her climb.

Unlike her memorized route up the outer hull of Olympus, the unfamiliar course posed the unfortunate possibility of crumbling and drawing attention if she was not careful.

Winter flew up the side of the cliff despite the fact that she was being careful. The natural formations of roots and rocks were tremendously easier to navigate than the exterior of the city ship.

Clinging to the cliff face, Winter hugged her body close against the surface and slowly lifted her eyes up over the summit.

Barely breathing, she scanned the sparse trees and located the sentry she'd spotted from down below.

The hideous blighter was covered in animal hides and weathered burlap. It stood with an eagerly poised firearm trained down at the Purifiers below. Winter almost jumped as it suddenly discharged its deafening weapon and uttered a hoarse, throaty chuckle as it ducked back behind the tree to reload.

Winter took advantage of the shrieking return fire from the Purifiers to breach the summit and crouch behind cover. She waited a moment until the sound of reloading ceased, then quietly drew her rifle and turned to take aim.

With deadly determination in her icy eyes, she peered down the sights and picked off the easy target with a headshot.

Winter grinned.

Snapping to her feet, she switched her rifle to *purify* while sprinting to the carcass. Winter reduced it to ashes with the streaming flames before its disease could permeate further. She engaged her intercom and retrieved the rappel line from its pouch on her belt.

"Winter here," she spoke as she secured the line.

No reply.

"My position is up on the rocks above the enemy," she shook her head as she wondered if anyone was reading her. "Do *not* fire on me," she added for good measure.

It was like Wraith said: if she wanted to break rank, she needed to be willing to accept the consequences. She *was* willing. Completely willing because she knew deep inside that she was right.

Willing to risk her life.

Winter stood on the edge of the cliff's heights and paused.

Tipping forward, then falling fast—her toes curled within her boots as the world rushed past. Winter kept her eyes on the swiftly approaching ground and felt the line bear her weight as she descended. Keeping her feet beneath her, she fairly ran down the face of the cliff as the line zipped and the earth rushed up at her.

Winter locked the line just as the blighters came into sight and snapped the rifle sights up to meet her targeting eyes.

The mutants, all covered in rags and hides, their hideous faces cowled, were so focused on their bloodthirsty actions that they didn't notice her until it was too late.

One, then two headshots rang out in rapid succession and unthinkable accuracy.

The blighters scrambled in panic and confusion to return fire. Winter shuffled, swinging back out of range, and waited for them to pause.

Her distraction worked. It had given her comrades an opening to advance. The teams took up new positions and showered electric blasts upon the enemy while enabling half of the War Wolves to escape from their cornered peril.

At the apex of her swing, Winter crouched low against the rock face and slacked the line a bit to lower her position.

As the pendulum motion reversed, she sprinted low across the cliff and propelled herself forward. Swinging far out beyond the outcropping, Winter took the blighters by surprise once more. She switched her rifle to *purify* and poured blinding fire streams down upon them from above.

Distracted and terrified, the swarm was briefly exposed to the Purifiers' frontal assault. Several of them tumbled about in panic as they were slowly consumed by flame while others fell in bloody sprays from the rifle blasts. The Purifiers below took the opportunity again and pressed in with renewed ferocity. The shrieking mutants fled wildly to escape the inferno.

Winter used the pendulum motion once more and channeled all her strength into running across the rocks. At the height of the swing over the blighter's newly abandoned bastion, she cut the line and curled into a calculated tumble onto the earth below.

She opened the channel once her feet hit the ground. "Push in! Push in!" she urged as her legs pumped, giving chase to the fleeing forms of the blighters as they scattered through the dense trees.

"Secure the area," Eagle Eyes' voice came over the channel. "Good work, Winter."

"Eyes on the blighters?" Wraith demanded.

"North quarter," Winter puffed as she ran. "I'm in pursuit."

A shot rang out, and a tree near Winter shattered, splintering from a bullet's impact. Winter tucked into an evasive roll and dove for cover. Another shot hit the ground near her.

Winter's targeting system pinpointed the origin of the shot and told her where to fire. It annoyed her. The program didn't take into consideration the possibility of multiple threats or return fire.

Two more shots let her know the enemy had her position on lock. Winter held the rifle over her head and discharged a blind shot in the blighter's direction, then gambled that she had a moment to move. She rolled up to her feet and dashed to the next tree to take cover there.

One more round from the blighter betrayed the fact that it hadn't moved. From this position, she could use her eyes instead of the targeting system. Winter took a breath, then fell down into a crouch and leaned out from behind her cover. The split second it took her to find the target felt like an age in slow motion.

Killshot.

Winter sprang to her feet and continued running. The mass of blighters was splitting off into small groups and filtering into the forest. Her gauntlet display showed that her comrades were closing in and combing the area in formation.

Winter saw movement and broke off her current course to pursue the quarry. They came into view quickly as her lifestyle of conditioning manifested.

One . . . two killshots.

She picked them off easily. Ignoring the inane chatter in her com as the teams sorted and organized, Winter's tunnel vision was on the hunt. This was what she lived for—this is why she was created. She felt a rush of validation and purpose as she fulfilled her divinely granted vocation.

Tracking down more fleeing blighters, Winter heard movement and zeroed in. She plunged forward, rifle first.

Through the trees erupted three vicious mutants, one of them roaring savagely and wielding a long, primitive machete. Winter fired on reflex; it flew back in a dead heap.

The other two disappeared running. Winter immediately began pursuit on foot. The trail was simple to follow; easier still was catching up. Winter sprinted madly until she came to an open stretch where she could pause and take aim.

She breathed out and peered down the sights at the running blighters. She slowly squeezed the trigger.

Killshot.

She smiled.

The other didn't stop or pause as its running mate fell dead. It tore through the field into the trees beyond and disappeared from view.

Winter started to give chase again but slowed her gait to glance at her gauntlet display. She was a good distance from the rest of the Purifiers but guessed correctly that her resourcefulness had placed her score well above the rest.

Out of breath, Winter took stock of her surroundings. The thick forest, untouched by man for centuries, grew like a smothering wave over the crumbling remains of a fallen civilization.

Torn, she studied her gauntlet again before looking back at the trail left by the blighter that got away. Protocol dictated her return, but she had already broken protocol today. Winter rationalized that her first act was purely to benefit her comrades. If she continued now, it would only be to gratify her competitive nature.

Winter sighed and swept her eyes over her surroundings before turning around and trotting back toward her team—purifying by fire those devastated in her deathly wake as she went.

CHAPTER EIGHT

W inter regrouped with her team and was met by a chorus of applause. Breathless and sweaty, shaking from the fading adrenaline, Winter smiled wearily and clasped the hands of all those who congratulated her in turn.

Smiling faces all around, damaged armor, light injuries, but no casualties—this was victory in a magnitude rarely seen.

The War Wolves were exhausted, but their faces behind their visors glowed with gratitude as Winter approached.

"Captain Sellers," Winter nodded to their team leader as the stocky man approached her. The word 'BOOM' was painted across the side of his helmet in vibrant yellow.

Hardly tactical, Winter always thought to herself.

Lev Sellers gripped her hand in his and seized her shoulder with the other. His eyes were wide and earnest. "Winter, I . . . I don't know what we would have done. Thank you . . . thank you for saving my team." His stuttered, desperate words were distorted as their shuttle came in to hover.

"All thanks to our Sovereign," Winter said. "How did you get cornered like that, Boom?"

"We were making a sweep through that canyon, and one of my boys twisted his knee." He motioned to the team member and moved to assist. "By the time we reached him, they were all on top of us. Came out of nowhere. Blighted freaks!"

Winter glanced at young Albert, supported under each arm by a team member; his face was contorted, and his teeth were clenched against the pain. Each of them looked at her with humble appreciation shining in their eyes. The War Wolves all boarded their shuttle with only a little difficulty, and it sped off back to Olympus.

Winter turned back to her team, gathered together in a corner of the clearing, waiting for their shuttle to pick them up. They all looked tired, some were also happy . . . but Captain Priest's scowl overshadowed them all.

Winter approached with her eyes down. She knew what her choice would bring. She didn't question in her heart if she had made the right decision and quietly settled into the unavoidable consequences.

Wraith's jaw flexed as Scorch, Havoc, Viper, and Bulletproof all pounded their fists into their gauntlets when she drew near.

"Winter has come!" Scorch whooped.

The team cheered.

"Archangels," Wraith ordered flatly, squelching all mirth, "stay alert and ensure the security of the LZ until all shuttlecraft are dispatched."

Winter drew her rifle without a word and obeyed immediately. Her eyes locked on the view screen and her mind went into blank autopilot as her body began to ache and chill after the exertion.

It wasn't long before the Archangels shuttle buzzed down from the sky to land in the clearing.

Wraith loaded on first and checked in everyone's rifles as they made it through the scanning process. As lieutenant, Winter was the last to embark, ensuring the team was safely on board. The moment she stepped through the scanner, the reprimand began.

"Just who do you think you are!?" Wraith shouted. "Where is your head, Winterton? You think that rank is a suggestion? You think you're above the team—above me?" He scowled deeply. "I cannot believe what I saw today! I cannot believe that any Purifier would go off against orders, split the team, and engage the enemy alone in the most asinine, reckless display I have ever seen!"

Winter silently returned his gaze.

The team members all strapped in silently, trying to avoid the appearance of witnessing the spectacle.

"You're a big celebrity, right?" Wraith continued his rant. "You're invincible because you're, what, special? What makes you think you're too good to stay in formation? What makes you so much better than us, Winterton? Your self-righteous little ego is making some very bad calls, Lieutenant. You think because you're talented, you're above the rules. You're not!" Wraith's voice had risen to a roar. "The next time you endanger my team in the interest of your little quest for time in the spotlight, I will *end* you myself." He touched her forehead and spoke in a lowered, menacing growl. "One round . . . right between those pretty blue eyes."

Winter swallowed back her indignation as her nostrils flared.

Wraith grabbed the rifle from her hands and jerked his head at the seats.

Winter turned away, hands shaking, and strapped in, unable to witness

Wraith's astonishment behind her back when he saw her impressive kill tally.

The team fell into excitedly discussing the surface engagement while Winter and Wraith sat in silence. All harnesses locked, the pilot cleared the ground and began the ascent to their city in the sky.

Winter settled into her quiet mind the way that Eagle Eyes had taught her. The shock and adrenaline of the deployment hummed lower and lower in her awareness as she focused on breathing and emptying her thoughts. She was eager to subdue the burning anger and annoyance at her recent berating at the whim of a man who wouldn't know strategy if it beat him with a stick. She was also struggling to cope with the praises showered upon her by her peers. Appreciation was nice, but it made her feel boastful and presumptuous at the same time. The feelings of frustration and insecurity swelled up in her mind, but she washed them out as she simply breathed and focused on nothing but the still, empty void within.

In good time, they made it back through the barrier, and Olympus swallowed the small shuttle as it passed into the bay. The busy platform was emptying slowly as Purifiers removed their helmets and trudged to the team hubs.

Savage, Sapphire, and Nalara were still sitting on their benches in full armor, waiting to be called in. They stood, obviously uncomfortable from waiting so long, as the combatants entered the gear room.

"Disarm and get to the conference room," Wraith growled. "All of you—just in case that wasn't clear."

Nalara looked like she would ask a question, but Scorch silently warned against it with a desperate face and a quick slicing motion at his throat.

Winter fought to keep her head clear of clouding emotions as she hung up her gear. Back in her training clothes once more, she pulled on her shoes before joining the others.

The boisterous, churning conference room hushed quickly when Eagle Eyes stood at the podium and cleared his throat.

"I have never been more pleased to welcome you back to Olympus," he said thankfully. "The teamwork and dedication I saw today was truly a humbling testament to our Sovereign's power. His wisdom prepared us for today and led us to rescue our friends and comrades. Thanks to your devotion to our great Sovereign and to the vocation he has bestowed upon you, the War Wolves were spared the unspeakable fate of death and defilement."

A wave of exuberance rolled through the room.

"Captain Boom and his team made it to the Medical Quarter," Eagle Eyes continued, "and I've been given word that all will make a quick, full recovery."

Applause and cheers erupted at his announcement.

"Thank you, thank you all." He joined in their enthusiastic clapping and only continued once the applause died down. "Now, we're all tired, and I know we're all looking forward to the bout tonight. So, please, rest up and prepare—you've earned it. And we'll see you tonight. Dismissed."

The instant shuffle of the room banished the thought that Winter was meaning to bring up to her mentor. She shrugged; it was probably nothing. She found that, as his Ascension drew closer, she felt more and more desperate to squeeze as much time in his company as she possibly could. She wished with all her heart that they could simply sit and talk, but she didn't want to appear weak or clingy to him, so she felt the need to always have training questions to initiate conversation.

Several of her team members joined Winter's side as she waited for the next lift. She was secretly overjoyed that they wanted to be near her but also felt the pressure by her position of leadership to remain professional.

"You're fighting Lilith tonight, right?" Viper clenched her fists in excitement.

Winter puffed her cheeks and exhaled. "No, Blight me, I have a whole month to prepare for *that* one," Winter answered. "Thankfully, if I win tonight, I'll qualify to fight her." She shrugged, trying her best to sound impartial. "If not—"

"Pfft! You're *going* to win," Bulletproof cut her off. "I have allotments riding on you." He glanced briefly at Viper.

"Right, so no pressure then." Winter laughed as the lift doors opened.

"Hey, I'd bet on you, too," Scorch held the door as more Purifiers piled in. "If I had any allotments left to spend."

They entered together and rode up with another group holding their own conversation.

"Cafeteria rations for you!" Viper laughed.

As soon as the doors opened, they spilled out into the Second Tier, and

Scorch lifted his eyes to the giant digital board across the street.

"Looks like you're fighting Kurtis Hollins, rank eight, from the Hellhounds." He read aloud. "Nice!"

"Mmmm, lucky." Sapphire hummed as they walked together toward the Purifier's living chambers. "He is so gorgeous. I wouldn't mind trading spots with you tonight, Winter," she half-teased.

Winter pushed her teammate's shoulder in good nature.

"Some of us don't need to grapple a man to keep him around," Viper returned.

Winter caught her flash a brief smile at Bulletproof.

"Don't look at me." Winter shook her head with her hands up in innocence.

"Right, no time for romance." Sapphire rolled her eyes. "Too busy scaling the hull . . . or rappelling down cliffs."

"And being solitary," Viper added.

"And broody," Scorch broke in.

"Broody?" Winter exclaimed.

"The absolute *broodiest,*" Scorch said emphatically. "I couldn't even get you to crack a smile while I was your trainer."

Bulletproof nodded in agreement.

"Maybe you weren't all that funny," Winter returned playfully.

The women laughed.

"Well, obviously that's not true," Scorch balked.

They parted ways at the cafeteria floor with well-wishes for the coming bout as Winter headed to the upper levels toward her exclusive accommodation.

Alone again.

Winter stood just inside the threshold of her room and swept her eyes over the stark, pristine apartment. She looked at the bed, freshly and neatly made, and felt that she should probably rest . . . but it simply held no appeal. The sanitation worker was no longer here, so there really was no excuse. Winter recognized the fatigue in her limbs but figured that falling asleep would cause more trouble than it was worth. She would have to wake up all over again, and then there was the time wasted to consider.

Winter sniffed and set her jaw.

Walking into the bedroom, she kicked off her shoes before falling to the floor and pumping out enough pushups until her arms and chest felt warm. Coming to stand, she began arm circles and stretched to work the soreness from her limbs.

There, amid the silence and solitude, a desperate sort of readiness filled Winter's perception; she felt every breath and every single heartbeat. The emergency deployment was probably the best thing that could have happened today to prepare her for the bout.

Winter's feral, calculating inner predator had been awakened.

CHAPTER NINE

Shoulder to shoulder, crowds filled the enormous archways leading into the Hive. The population of Olympus gathered en masse only once a month, excluding exceptionally rare occasions like Ascension.

"Thanks for walking with me," Nalara raised her voice above the din of the slow-moving throng.

"You're still my initiate," Winter said, though her heightened senses were making her current surroundings a living hell.

"But I know you should be getting ready, and I just really appreciate it," Nalara responded with her doe-like brown eyes pleading for understanding.

"You've only been out of the FMQ a couple days," Winter assured her, "it's alright to be a little overwhelmed. The first few weeks are terrifying for everyone."

"Everyone?" Nalara prodded.

Winter knew what she was pushing at and refused to answer. She pretended not to hear. It was frustrating when people assumed things came easy to her just because she didn't indulge in the self-pity to complain.

The monolithic entry swept up into a long, broad staircase. The light and ruckus of the arena within was perceivable from where they stood, but it was nothing compared to the sight from the top of the steps where the breathtaking Hive gaped out before them like a cavernous maw.

"Wow, it's so different from when we were training!" Nalara exclaimed.

Winter nodded in agreement. It always felt transformed to her, too, having spent so much time alone training within the colossal coliseum. Somehow, when the seats were filled with spectators, when the Hive reverberated with the unintelligible clamor of tens of thousands of Olympian voices, the same familiar place felt alien . . . unreal.

Winter focused on breathing steadily as the noise and confusion around them caused a sharp, stabbing pain behind her eye. All the sectors of the Second Tier sat together, segregated by the various vocations.

"Are you nervous?" Nalara asked suddenly as they slowly shuffled forward through the crowd.

"Sure," Winter admitted with a shrug. "But you can't focus on that, especially when it's going to be you up there soon enough."

Nalara smiled at the thought. "It's got to be great, being able to beat the life out of people who frustrate you once in a while."

Winter laughed. "These events are not about the violence."

Nalara looked skeptical.

"We're teammates," Winter explained. "We're comrades. These events are not a device to create dissension but are another way we manifest the glorious creations of our Sovereign."

The Elite were just starting to appear as Winter and Nalara reached the Purifier seats. The cordoned-off Elite seating, separated by high walls and an entry blockaded by two massive Guardians, was filled with color and luxury. Tables laden with delicacies and seats draped with soft pillows filled the area and distinguished it from the rest of the seating.

"Ooh, they're so . . . so . . . ." Nalara's voice trailed off in awe. "What's the word?"

Winter glanced at the Elites slowly getting comfortable in their exclusive area. Making the rest of sparkling Olympus bland by contrast, the Elites truly were a class set apart. Their lord and Sovereign had given them a tier to themselves to live in his sight, where they enjoyed all the pleasures of life with no toil and no worry.

"Inspiring," Winter said above the din. "Magnificent."

"Yeah . . . yeah, that's it," Nalara agreed with a nod.

"Purifiers are formulated to be superior in strength and agility, but Elites are created to personify the Sovereign's magnificence. You're looking at perfection, Nalara. You're witnessing the Sovereign's greatest works."

"Wow," Nalara breathed.

Winter smiled broadly as she spotted the Grand Elite enter the exclusive seating area. "Look there," she pointed. "Do you see the tall man in the black and gold?"

Nalara paused before answering, "Yes. Dark hair?"

Winter bit her lip and nodded. "*That* is Draven Constantine Rothgard."

Nalara's eyes went wide. "That's the Grand Elite? That's him!?" She bounced a little in her excitement. "Oh, oh, Blight me, he's so gorgeous!"

Winter laughed. "No argument here."

"I had no idea," Nalara gushed.

Watching the striking gentleman as he took his seat, Winter explained: "Draven is the personal subordinate of the Sovereign himself—his right hand in Olympus. Nothing of any significance happens in this city without him knowing. He is *the* Elite among the Elite. Only the Sovereign himself is above him."

"That's amazing," Nalara continued gawking. "Can you imagine what life would be like if you could spend time with the Sovereign every day?"

Winter glanced up at the statues of the blessed Ascended ringing the Hive's top level. "I think about it all the time," she replied quietly, more to herself than to Nalara. She felt the spark of determined ambition swell in her chest. She returned her thoughts to the present. "Hey, I've got to go now. You good here?"

"Stop worrying about me." Nalara hugged her friend. "Go *dominate!*"

Winter grinned before turning away. Not that she was eager to leave her friend, but she was vibrating inside as she was finally able to focus on the swiftly approaching bout. Butterflies danced in her stomach while she quickly made her way through the crowd to the sub-level stairs. She loved the pre-fight jitters. She loved the spurts of adrenaline that shot through her veins as the moment approached.

Every month, only the top achievers of the previous month qualified to enter the bout. All the current challengers were assembled underneath the Hive floor, where they each warmed up in their own way. Some shadowboxed, others lightly sparred, while the rest performed simple exercises. Winter spotted Eagle Eyes in his usual space, sitting in a far corner, quietly observing the others with his sharp, intense gaze.

She knew better than to bother him while he ritualistically studied his competitor—even though she would love nothing more than to sit with him and just listen to any advice he would care to give.

Slow, dynamic stretching was Winter's preferred warmup. It helped her to relax and focus on breathing. It also helped to feel out where the kinks and pains were in her body before going into the fight.

As she pulled her muscles to the extent of their reach, Winter followed her mentor's example and watched her opponent carefully—'Hotshot' Hollins, as he was known; strong and stacked, he clipped out one-arm pushups on the floor like it was nothing while smiling doggishly at the female Purifiers nearby. Winter quickly concluded that his mind was not in the game; however, he *was* a few years more experienced, so she couldn't assume this match would be easy. If she knew anything, it was that experience held its weight. She never saw him train hand-to-hand, but had seen him get rowdy before. He was a brawler—a gritty fighter. Rumor had it that before a fight, he could be found in his quarters, not training, but pounding back as much hard liquor as he could hold. Winter didn't know how much of it was true, but she was not taking any chances.

Muffled by the Hive floor above them, a loudspeaker boomed away with the announcer's voice.

"We come together tonight under the ever-watchful, protecting gaze of our magnificent Sovereign! *Live forever, o glorious king!'* . . . We welcome and reverence his greatest creations: his blessed Elite and his chosen right hand—the Grand Elite—lord Draven Constantine Rothgard! We are honored by your presence. And welcome to all present citizens of glorious Olympus. Gathered here in the spectacular Hive, welcome one and all to the night of the Purifier!"

The crowd above responded uproariously, and all competing Purifiers quickly organized themselves. They stood together in the center of the active space and waited patiently for their introductions. The opponents stood opposite each other, but there was no enmity—just smiles and the burning exhilaration of the moment.

The tiles above their heads rearranged and fell away; the flood of light and cheering washed over them.

Hotshot winked at Winter just before the hexagonal tiles lifted them up to the arena level where the cheering audience greeted them.

"Pretty good crowd," Eagle Eyes commented; he seemed calmly amused.

"Always is," Lilith grinned. "Sure as dying . . ."

Bright lights danced over the floor, and excitement electrified the air. The announcer called out the matches for the evening as three-dimensional holograms of the Purifiers' faces, names, ranks, and stats glowed in pale greens and blues in the Hive's void overhead.

Winter's fight was third in the lineup, right after Lilith and Scarlet.

She was warm; she was ready. The wait was the biggest hurdle. She wasn't nervous about the fight, nor was she concerned about the crowd; waiting was the only thing she couldn't pick up and solve. She couldn't fix it or fight it—she had to just wait.

Once the announcer finished his initial crowd-hyping, the Purifiers all took their places on the raised platforms around the arena. Like silent sentinels, they watched their comrades enter the ring and prepare to fight.

Eagle Eyes was traditionally one of the first contenders. His showmanship and professionalism had built quite a following. Recently, his popularity had grown even more since the announcement of his upcoming Ascension.

The cheering of the crowd built to a roar when the signal was given, and the two Purifiers began their bout. Winter watched carefully—being a visual learner, she took note of every shift and every pivot. She noticed everything and analyzed every move for its purpose and effectiveness of execution.

Larger-than-life holograms of the two fighters danced above the arena, giving even those furthest from the action the ability to see every jab, cross, kick, and strike the Purifiers made.

Even though Eagle Eyes was actively engaged in fighting, he would intermittently glance up at the time counter above the ring.

The audience was eating up the exchange—the back and forth blows and parries.

Winter could see the stalling for what it was.

His opponent—captain of the Dragon Slayers team, Slade 'Specter' Sephiras—was giving his all to the fight, and Derrick was doing his best to keep himself from ending it too soon. The moment the clock reached three and a half minutes, Eagle Eyes moved forward in a blur of motion and finished the fight.

Slade lay on the arena floor looking up in bewilderment, wondering what had happened.

"Victorious and *still* undefeated, uncontested, undisputed!" the announcer boomed. "The one and only, the legend, the Master Purifier—Derrick 'Eagle Eyes' Zinda!"

Eagle Eyes raised his hands to receive the crowd's wild applause. Medical attendants rushed in to help his opponent off the floor. He was not badly hurt; Derrick was well-known for his respectful treatment of bout competitors.

Winter shifted impatiently as the announcer worked the crowd up again for the next fight. The minutes passed like hours as she waited for Lilith and Scarlet to take the arena.

Tension lit the air as the bout began. Lilith's fierce accuracy and devastating strikes made the crowd cringe and cheer. She was strong and vicious, working Scarlet over like a pliable punchbag. Lilith lived for these bouts. She fed off the energy of the crowd and smiled every time they surged in an audible *oooh!* Blood trickled down Scarlet's chin as her defensive techniques gradually turned into blind flailing. The fight climaxed when Lilith took her into a compromising grapple and applied pressure to the shoulder joint. Scarlet screamed in pain as her joint locked up and cracked so loud the audience could hear.

"Ow!" the announcer cried out in mock sympathy. "Even I felt *that* one!"

The crowd went wild when the match was called and the medical team pried Scarlet from Lilith's unforgiving grip. She let go and ate up the energy of the roaring crowd, smiling for them and waving victoriously.

A shock of adrenaline coursed through Winter's veins as the next fight began to be announced over the loudspeaker. She flexed and curled her fingers to get a feel for them and swept her gaze over the whole scene once again. The pressure was real. Winter was as yet undefeated in her short time since qualifying for the bouts, and so was Hotshot. His many years' experience was an asset that Winter wouldn't overlook, no matter his reputation.

One side of Winter's mouth twitched with an inescapable smile as she locked eyes with him from across the arena. Tangible electricity stirred the air as the accentuating voice over the loudspeaker called the boisterous crowd's attention to the Purifiers up next.

"And are we having a good time tonight!?" The Hive reverberated with the roaring response of the crowd. The Elites lightly clapped and looked on. "Up next, for the viewing pleasure of our most gracious lord and lady Elites, we've got a spectacle rarely witnessed on this magnificent Olympian stage. Age and experience and raw strength versus the unparalleled, almost unprecedented talent of our youngest top-ranking Purifier. Who will come off victorious?

"Distinguished Elites and citizens of Olympus, I present to you from the Hellhounds, ranked number eight of the Purifiers, age 26, height 6'1", and weighing in at a jacked 213 pounds—the man, the beast, the machine: Kurtis 'Hotshot' Hollins!"

With his arms stretched up high, Kurtis welcomed the fanfare and smiled. Floodlights swept over the floor as he took the center of the ring and worked up the audience into a frenzy.

Winter's cold, blue eyes narrowed on her target in laser-like focus.

"And his opponent," the announcer continued, "I present from the

Archangels, ranked number thirteen, at only 19 years of age—something not witnessed since the days of the Immortal 'Nightmare' herself—standing at a height of 5'8", and weighing in at 142 pounds of *pure* Purifier muscle—the icy touch of death itself: January 'Winter' Winterton!"

Tumultuous cheers rocked the massive structure. Winter stepped down from the platform and strode forward unassumingly amid the cheering of the riotous multitude. The deafening screams of excitement, the blasting music, the crowd chanting *"Win-ter! Win-ter!"* was all white noise as she approached the center where her competitor stood illuminated by the hot white spotlight.

Consciously keeping her face a neutral slate of indifference, she read her opponent's body composition as he approached.

"Last chance," Kurtis smirked down at her.

His posturing did nothing to rattle Winter's nerves. In fact, his offer stirred her defiant nature, and her concentration settled into dangerous passive awareness.

"Purifiers, ready?" The announcer paused. "And . . . FIGHT!"

Hotshot fell into an impressive fighting stance and flexed his arms tight.

Winter shook her arms slightly to diffuse any tension and raised her hands, relaxed, before her sternum.

Deep breath . . . let it go.

Hotshot danced to the side and came in swinging, his form and bearing all over the place. Winter evaded and moved forward behind him, forcing him to turn around every time before he attacked. Winter shifted, waiting for his movement to dictate her next action while keeping him directly in front of her.

He seemed to be trying to feel out her attack style, but she gave him nothing. His frustration at what he thought to be a humiliatingly unfair match in his favor manifested when he clenched his jaw and shook his head. That was it. Winter recognized the change in posture and knew the fight was on for real now.

Hotshot came in, kicking with his long legs. The fabric of his tactical pants snapped with the speed of each movement.

Move forward.

Winter stepped inside his range. She knew he was a hardened brawler and expected the kick to turn into a knee-thrust as she moved in, but she took him off guard and he was forced to readjust.

He found his footing quickly and double-jabbed at Winter while she moved through his space, but she halted his fists midair with a soft-touch deflection. She came back with a bee-sting jab to his throat and moved around him, forcing him to adjust again.

Hotshot was not impressed; he was irritated, but he put on a fake smile for the crowd. He turned around to face her again; his fists came up in a boxer approach as he coughed and swallowed hard, not recovering well from the unexpected breach in his defense.

That's right, Hollins, use your hands.

Winter smiled to herself.

He was guarded as he came in kicking again. Winter could tell he wasn't trying to land a hit, simply testing her speed. He wanted to see her technique and gauge her reaction.

Winter again gave him nothing, telegraphing none of her relaxed movement as they circled. She remained soft in her deflections. Suddenly, he wound up for a real kick charged with power. Winter lowered her center of gravity and stepped in again, this time catching his knee and twisting him off balance with her bodyweight. He tumbled to the side and rolled on the arena floor before snapping up to his feet again.

Winter knew she could have finished the fight right then, but she held back, following the example of her mentor. She waited for Hotshot to regain his bearings. It didn't take but a moment. Upright again, he spun around with eyes full of shock.

Winter could tell he was getting close to the edge of his patience. She noticed a switch in his posture again and knew to anticipate a leg sweep or tackle.

Hotshot charged in, his arms wide as if he'd take her to the ground. It was always an unsettling sight: seeing a man of considerable size and mass coming in for a full-speed tackle. The second his head tucked down, Winter stepped in—*moved forward*. She sunk her weight down to her core as he came into range. She shifted, stepped forward, and hooked one hand around his jaw. Winter let his own momentum wrench his neck as she stepped past. Again, she could have finished it right there, and if she had wanted, with just a little extra pull at the top of the motion, his spine would have snapped like kindling.

Pain and a little panic sprung to his eyes as the large man stumbled up to his full height and moved his neck around to experiment with the damage. Nothing was broken, but she gave him a good scare.

He was done playing. Swinging full force, Hotshot meant to knock her head off as his fists charged in.

Make the show good.

Winter stung him once, then twice. She tempered her blows and drew out the fight in heightened voltage. She never attacked the core, never struck his strength. Only soft tissue received the stinging force of her strikes.

Like a bolt of lightning, he attempted to catch her in a joint lock, but was baffled when her arm went completely limp and melted from his grip.

He switched instantly and seized her head in both hands, charging his knee up to meet her face. Winter ignored the knee and whipped the back of her hands against his solar plexus, causing him to falter. She twisted into a throat strike and shifted off the line of attack.

Hotshot doubled down on the pain and rocketed his fist around in a wide game-ending haymaker at her head.

Perfect!

Winter seized the opportunity. This was the moment she'd been waiting for.

Breathing steadily, the world melted into slow motion as Winter's focus honed her movement. She tapped his first strike to the side and glanced her forearm off his predictable second swing.

Sliding inside his reach, she stepped with a pivot. Winter brought her arm down, slamming its relaxed, dead weight into the nerve cluster within his throat.

She could see it all in his expression, the fireworks exploding inside his head as his left side went entirely limp. His body crumbled to the blood-spattered white floor. His eyes were still frantically searching for a handle on the churning world around him.

Winter was stifling the urge to help him up when she became aware of the crowd chanting *"End him! End him!"*

It was clear what the majority wanted—thumbs jutting down, crying for blood, demanding satisfaction.

Winter looked over to the Elites in their exclusive seating. Their votes were split.

The Grand Elite of Olympus shrugged passively.

Hotshot struggled to get to his feet. Winter knew he wouldn't recover the use of his left side for a good three minutes.

The crowd didn't care.

Winter stepped directly to Hotshot and struck his face hard. He went down.

The audience exploded in delight.

"Holy Sovereign Zeus!" the announcer's voice resounded. "Elite lords and ladies; citizens of Olympus! What have we been witness to here tonight? A stunning victory by knockout, an incredible feat of speed and agility and power, and a beautiful display of our Sovereign's mightiest creation: *The Purifier!*"

Winter hid the effects of adrenaline well. Though she trained constantly to suppress the unpredictable surge; the rush, the trembling, the pounding in her chest—it was all so powerful. Externally, however, she showed nothing as she stepped over her fallen opponent while the announcer boomed out her name and the crowd cheered on.

CHAPTER TEN

"**C**ome on, Winter!*"

Nalara incessantly begged over the din of the bustling crowd. "Please! I've never been to the Elite tier before, and I can't go without you."

"These parties are just not my favorite." Winter shook her head apologetically. Enjoying the after-party had become a thing of the past since she had qualified to participate in the bouts. The hyperawareness that came with her fighting style was hard to quell after adrenaline had been introduced to the mix. "You should go, though. You'll have fun. And what do you mean you can't go without me? The rest of the team will be there."

"I don't *want* to go without you." Nalara looked over her shoulder at the throng of Purifiers crowding the Grand Stairway up to the First Tier of Olympus. "They said there's going to be amazing food."

"Sure as dying, there always is. But I'm tired," Winter lied; she was still entirely amped up long after her fight.

"You have no excuse, though," Nalara insisted. "You didn't even get hit once!"

Winter sighed. "But . . . I'm tired. I've been on my feet all day . . . smiling and conversing takes so much effort," she pleaded.

Nalara tilted her head slightly, her lips pursing and her brown eyes widening in the most pathetically innocent display she could muster. *"Please . . .?"*

Winter's carefully laid defenses immediately began to crumble. This was a battle she was not going to win. She could face down Hotshot Hollins without breaking a sweat; even the horrific, blighted monstrosities of the surface world paled in comparison to the sight before her now. Nalara's full-frontal assault was overwhelming; resistance was impossible.

"Okay, fine," she begrudgingly gave in. "Just for a little bit."

"Yes!" Nalara triumphed. "This is going to be so much fun!"

"Manipulative brat," Winter whispered under her breath.

Nalara's tongue playfully darted out in response.

The sweeping staircase up to the Elite tier was filled with excited partygoers, but even among the multitude, the beauty of its white marble steps and golden rail was not lost on Winter.

The pillared archway at the top was crafted of intricate purple marble tiles. As they crossed the threshold to the First Tier, their feet passed over a giant golden seal depicting the Sovereign Tower emblazoned in sunlight.

A giant crystal-blue pool stretched out before them across the marbled plaza, adorned by a majestic gold fountain.

The pristine streets were lined with gold light posts, spread among long beds of elegant flowers. Each light post was crowned with decadent crystal fixtures, and their soft glow lit the First Tier with an enchanting golden vibrancy.

"Oh . . ." Nalara gaped, her jaw hanging limp. "Sovereign's blessings. I . . . I had no idea."

Winter ignored her friend's enraptured state. Already, her hyperawareness was on full, but once they reached the Elite tier, it tipped into overdrive as the music, laughter, and movement everywhere became a blurry mass of confusion.

Every pluck of the musical strings, the clinking of ice inside each glass, the scratch underneath the feet of the dancers as they spun on the marble street—Winter's ears caught every single thing. Even the nearly indiscernible buzzing of the lights overhead and every sound and movement around her was noticed as her mind raced to keep track of them all.

Winter swallowed and attempted to block out the extras, but her senses were already strung too tight. The faces of her comrades smiled to see her; their congratulations were heard and acknowledged, but Winter couldn't bring herself to focus on their jovial conversation because her mind needed to keep track of absolutely everything happening around her.

Each month, after the bout, the Elites would open their tier in a special invitation extended only to the Purifiers. Twelve times a year, the fountains, walkways, and gardens of the First Tier would be lined with Purifiers and Elite, laughing and conversing, eating and drinking together. It was a rare opportunity to step up in life and favor with the Sovereign, if only for a night.

Winter remembered the days when she had been just as excited as her initiate was now. She remembered reveling and carousing like the rest of them. But her path had taken her somewhere else. She had found it more and more difficult to spend any time relaxing, or harder still, celebrating these days. Her focus on the future was so fixed that everything else seemed trivial, or even foolish and in the way.

Nalara looked delighted, though. Winter took a deep breath and fought to return to the moment.

Her team was laughing. Everyone was present except for Wraith. Relieved for that at least, Winter guided Nalara over to join them.

"So you and Hotshot agreed on that bout beforehand, right?" Scorch teased and handed Winter a drink from the tray of a passing server.

"What does *he* get out of that deal?" Viper scoffed.

"Oh, you know, the usual." Winter played along for their sake, taking a long drink. "Sore limbs and a really nasty headache for a few days."

They laughed.

"So, tell me," Scorch prodded, "how do you get into the ring with a veteran like Hotshot and come out unscathed? If I didn't know better, I'd say you'd been blessed by the Sovereign himself tonight."

"I keep telling you guys, you need to come do the old training with me after hours," Winter answered quite honestly.

"Psh! And risk crossing the Unifiers?" Sapphire shook her head. "No, thank you."

"What's the old training?" Nalara asked, her interest piqued.

"It's this super archaic art they used back when the surface was crawling with blighters." Scorch rolled his eyes. "Eagle Eyes tried mandating it for a while."

"Right, like I'm going to spend my only free hours practicing slow-motion ballet." Bulletproof chuckled and threw back another drink.

"I've heard that it's actually a type of sorcery." Havoc tapped a finger to his temple. "Mind control and whatnot."

Winter huffed in annoyance. "It's based on body mechanics," she corrected, trying not to be sharp. She was used to being ridiculed whenever the topic was broached, but she still found their ignorance irritating. "It just looks like magic because you don't understand how the body responds."

Suddenly, the laughter stopped and everyone in the group stood up a little taller. Winter turned around as a figure approached her peripheral. The Grand Elite, Draven Constantine Rothgard, drew near to their group, his face swathed in a dashing smile.

He was incredibly striking from a distance, and it was not lost a bit up close. The women of the group beamed and fussed self-consciously with their hair. Winter stepped back to give the Sovereign's right hand his respectful space.

"Welcome to the Elite tier this evening, honored Purifiers," Draven said in a thrumming, velvety voice. His dark hair and attentive eyes were positively captivating.

"Th-thank you, lord Draven!" Scorch uncharacteristically stuttered.

"Yes!" Viper chimed in, clearing her throat. "Thank you so, *so* much!"

"We are the ones who are honored by you, great one!" Sapphire added with a bow.

Draven's stature seemed to feed off their attention. Although he didn't so much as make eye contact with any of them, Winter felt the distinct impression that he was looking for something.

"For your exceptional bravery and faithful service to Olympus, you deserve this reward. Please, enjoy all the luxuries of the Elite tier by the Sovereign's favor tonight. Good evening." Draven smiled broadly and took his leave.

"Did you see him look right at me?" Sapphire cooed after the Grand Elite was beyond earshot, her face flushing red.

"I think I just died and went straight to Elysium!" Savage laughed.

"'*Honored Purifiers!*' '*Exceptional bravery,*' he said." Viper giggled and fanned her face with her hand.

"I can't believe he actually spoke to us!" Nalara squealed, joining in their elation.

"That really was something else." Scorch stepped in and cleared his throat. "But . . . if I were the Sovereign's eyes and ears on Olympus, you girls couldn't keep off me either."

"That's right," Havoc agreed enviously.

All the female Purifiers protested, and a heated discussion ensued.

Winter saw an opportunity and took a discreet step back to test the reaction. She felt secure that Nalara would not notice her absence and was right. Nalara had joined in the debate and was completely engrossed. Winter walked away toward the lift and slowly worked through the mirthful crowd.

Music and laughter filled the perfect, clear night, and a handful of stars shone through the milky barrier. Winter knew the next few days would be completely taken up with training and conditioning in preparation for the next jump. She thought long about remaining with her team and partaking of delights and companionship. She saw Purifiers and Elites scattered around the open plaza, enjoying conversations and food and pleasurable company. She noticed Lilith Sharpe from the Grim Reapers leaving with Draven's entourage. The Archangels team was still arguing and laughing together. They would all be up until early morning and, no doubt, would be late to practice the next day. If Winter stayed, that would be her, too. She shook her head.

The lift was empty, and Winter felt a pang of regret as the doors closed her in. However, the quiet ride down was much appreciated. The gentle hum of the motor got her thinking, and she decided to pay respect to her predecessors before returning to the Purifier Quarter.

The doors opened; Winter was surprised to see the open terrace of the honored Ascended occupied by the leader of their order, Eagle Eyes.

He was alone, looking up at the statues with crossed arms. He turned his head when the lift opened.

"Winter," he smiled.

"Hi," she replied. "Sorry, I didn't mean to interrupt you."

"Not at all. Come, sit with me," he invited. "Weren't you enjoying the party?"

Winter shrugged.

They shared a knowing smile and sat down together on the edge of the terrace, their legs dangling over the high ledge. Silence followed for a moment, but it wasn't an awkward kind of silence. They both appreciated the lack of stimulation for the calm that it brought.

"Tell me what you were thinking today on the deployment," Eagle Eyes prompted.

Winter looked down, her legs hanging free over the sheer drop as they sat together above the Hive. She sniffed distractedly and glanced at the memorials that surrounded them. There was a flood of answers churning in her head, each laden with emotion and charged with passion. She couldn't bring herself to be anything but strong and determined in front of her mentor.

"Just about the job." Winter shook her head, wishing she had the courage to answer truthfully.

"When you put yourself out in front, you become a target."

"You trained me better than that," she smirked.

"I meant from the teams," Derrick returned. "You put yourself out there, someone's going to knock you down."

Winter listened with interest, not sure of his meaning.

"People can't stand to be shown that they're not as good as they could be," he expounded. "We're all made of the same stuff. Purifiers are, by the Sovereign's design, superior to all but the Elite. And even compared to them, we *are* stronger, faster, and more durable. Our vocation—what we do on the surface, how we train—makes us feel indestructible. I learned a long time ago that when you try harder, when you work longer, and then out-perform all the rest, you make them face their own insecurities . . . their own self-imposed limitations."

Derrick looked her in the eyes so she would feel the gravity of his next statement. "It's easier for them to tear you down than it is to face their own weakness."

Winter swallowed. She thought she understood what he meant but had the subtle feeling inside that she really didn't yet.

"So, what do you do?" she urged.

"You make a choice to either stay with the pack and have friends . . . or stand out and be alone."

"Not forever, though," Winter smiled hopefully but felt deep down the foreboding confirmation.

He looked up at her again and raised his eyebrows. "Look around you. Look at our examples."

Winter studied the statues of their predecessors as he continued.

"Olympus has existed for nearly two-hundred-fifty years, but it was not even a hundred years ago that the Sovereign saw in his wisdom to begin the creation of the Purifier class. Every year, dozens die in the service of lord Zeus, while plenty die in training before they even reach initiation." Derrick pointed down the line of stone figures, drawing Winter's gaze to the silent sentinel at the far end. "From the days of the very first Ascended—Jaxen 'Spartan' Waters—until today, only seventeen Purifiers have lived to their day of Ascension. Seventeen . . . out of thousands. Maybe even tens of thousands."

The reality dawned on Winter as she listened.

"How many of your peers get up before daylight to train like you do?" Derrick asked.

Winter had never thought of that before.

"How many Purifiers come to train after-hours in the Hive? Alone."

He paused. "Whether you realize it or not, you stand out. You are alone. Because you put yourself out there, you become a target. And for those who choose to only aspire to mediocrity, someone like you becomes very easy to hate. Believe me."

Winter shook her head. She didn't understand. Was he warning her to stop trying? Her impulsive nature stirred a twinge of rebellion inside her chest.

"Hate?" She was incredulous. "Are you saying that people hate you?"

Derrick didn't answer.

"I don't understand," she confessed. "You're the greatest Purifier Olympus has seen in forty years—ever since Nereza Vossen." She gestured to the massive marble statue of 'Nightmare' down the line from where they sat. "You are only the second in history to reach Ascension while holding the rank of Master Purifier. I don't understand how what you say can be true when people don't hate you. They love you. They revere you."

"You'd be surprised," he quietly replied. "For some, 'love' is a fluid term." His insightful eyes locked with hers. "It's happened to me, and when you put yourself out there, trust me, the same will happen to you. There's not much more that weak-willed people fear than someone who aspires to excellence."

Winter was held spellbound, lost in the immense depth of his gaze. 'Eagle Eyes' he truly was.

"So," she finally asked, swallowing back her apprehension, "what exactly are you saying?"

The rigidity of Derrick's countenance melted away as he smiled engagingly. "Be *immortal.*"

Caught off guard by his captivating smile and words, Winter could do nothing but return the big smile and laugh softly.

"If they'll listen to you," he went on, "do what you can to lift them up to your level. But for those who won't listen—for those who prefer mediocrity, who *choose* it—let them have it. And most importantly, never submit to another person's perception of what you should be, just to make them more comfortable with themselves." He spoke from experience, shaking his head. "Just don't. You're better than that. You deserve so much more than that. You are one that aspires to excellence, so reach out and take it. It's yours."

Winter pursed her lips together, not sure what to say, but feeling deep gratitude for his advice.

Derrick stood suddenly and stretched his arms half-heartedly.

Winter stood as well and gazed down into the Hive where cleaners were mopping blood from the arena floor and sweeping debris from the among the stands.

"Well, that's enough from me." He sighed. "See you tomorrow, kid." He began walking toward the inner stairs to make his exit.

"Hey, Derrick?" Winter called out after a moment.

He stopped and turned at the top of the stairs.

"You know that I don't hate you, right?" she asked sincerely, needing him to understand. "You know that I revere you?"

Eagle Eyes laughed. "That's different," he replied. "*You* are my pupil. Revering me, your mentor, is part of the job description." He held his arms out in a grand gesture.

Winter chuckled back.

With a little wave, Derrick returned to the stairs and continued down.

Winter watched him leave until long after he had disappeared from sight. Her knee-jerk reaction to his declaration of aloneness was, self-evidently, denial. She knew aloneness. Even when she was surrounded by her team, the feeling of disconnection and incompatibility was like a constant bubble—just like the barrier that encircled the city—but instead of protecting her, it isolated her.

For the several minutes she spent standing on the terrace accompanied only by the marble heroes of times past, Winter seemed to feel every moment of aloneness that had accumulated over the year. The nights spent studying alone, the days spent training alone, and all the times she had broken off to stand out in her pursuit of excellence.

How could it always be that way?

Winter shook her head. It couldn't.

She moved to the statuesque image of Nereza and gazed longingly into the eyes of her inspiration. Winter knew she was working toward something bigger and greater than all the loneliness combined. To stand up here with the likes of Nereza 'Nightmare' Vossen . . . Jaxen 'Spartan' Waters . . . Kayla 'Phoenix' Eason . . . Reuben 'Avalanche' Rawles . . .

To be considered an equal with all Ascended in Elysium.

Winter closed her eyes and breathed. That was the ultimate goal, and to achieve that goal, she knew she was willing to pay any price—to make any sacrifice. Even if the road to excellence she was called to walk was a lonely one, she determined within herself that she would nevertheless walk it.

"I won't be alone forever," she comforted herself, smiling up at Nereza, and for the briefest of moments, she felt her hero smiling back from eternity. "I can't wait to finally meet you . . . someday."

Turning from the glorified Ascended, Winter traversed the long stairs down to the Hive floor, exited the coliseum, and turned towards the Purifier Quarter. The streets were all but empty—a stark reflection of the metaphorical path she chose to walk. The dark night swaddled Olympus in its sheets of twinkling, star-studded blackness. The iridescent barrier shimmered overhead in its perpetual opaline presence.

From the shadows, a Unifier appeared and approached to intersect Winter as she progressed toward her Quarter. Their nymph-like build and pale, hairless heads were always a striking sight.

Winter slowed to a stop when it became evident that she was the Unifier's target.

The earpiece on the Unifier's headset lit up and a digital view screen appeared before one eye. "Identify," she ordered.

"January Winterton," Winter complied.

The green scanner confirmed her answer as it played over the Purifier mark on the back of Winter's outstretched hand.

The census worker paused to read the display.

"Heart rate is slightly elevated," the Unifier spoke flatly. "State your current destination."

"My chambers," Winter answered.

A green light blinked. The Unifier checked a box in the air on the digital display. "State the reason for your late return to chambers."

"I was at the celebration with the Elite after the bout."

The Unifier made a note. "How are you feeling today?"

Winter sighed softly. "I feel like I did my best," she affirmed.

A green light blinked. "Staying out late is a sign of delinquency. I have put a note on your short-term record, but no mark as you were ordained by the Elite. To avoid marks on your permanent record and possible reclamation in the future, please consider returning to your living chambers early. Proceed in your service to our Sovereign."

The Unifier's last words were all white noise to Winter; she didn't understand nor care what they meant or to whom they applied. She was simply content to be on her way.

CHAPTER ELEVEN

The next two weeks played out as Winter daily escorted her initiate to and from training at the Hive and accompanied her on the regular scheduled jumps. Nothing so dramatic as the emergency deployment transpired again. The conditioning and marksmanship drills rolled out one after another in uniform routine. Winter put more and more of herself into training as Eagle Eyes' Ascension drew nearer. A strange sort of obsession manifested in her consciousness, and she realized that no amount of approval from him would be enough.

All the hours at the range, every single drop of sweat, every moment where her teeth clenched in determination to excel and push through even harder was nothing compared to the pain and regret she would feel if she didn't show her teacher that she took his training seriously while she still had the chance.

Every strike was her hardest; every individual impact was made to count as the ending blow. Moisture cascaded down her temples as her laser-focused eyes locked on her target immovably.

"Whoa, *whoa!*" Lev Sellers, 'Boom,' held up the padded gloves in surrender. "Blight me! Take it easy!" He laughed uncomfortably.

Winter snapped out of her inner thoughts and looked up at her sparring partner. Her heavy breathing and shaking arms confirmed his objection.

Boom took off one of the gloves and shook the life back into his hand. "Got something on your mind, huh?" he asked with a soft chuckle.

Winter tried to steady her trembling arms, and took a deep breath to collect herself. "Too much," she answered simply.

"Well," he mumbled, "just a suggestion; please don't take it out on me."

"Sorry—I'll lighten up." Winter smiled. "Don't want to damage your delicate hands."

"Hey, now," he warned lightheartedly. "These are the hands the Sovereign gave me."

"I'm just preoccupied, I guess," Winter said.

Boom put his hands back up and Winter returned to sparring.

"You're worried about the Ascension, right?"

"What makes you say that?" Winter evaded the question, jabbing right and crossing left into the gloves.

"It's understandable. It's your first time seeing the Sovereign face to face."

Winter didn't correct him, because she thought he might be right. "I hadn't thought about that," she admitted.

Lev laughed out loud. "Right. I remember the first time I stood before the Sovereign. All I could think about were all my failures, all the wrong he could see in me. Every party, every skipped training, everything I'd ever done was written right there for him to see." He shook his head. "But it didn't matter. The Sovereign saw me—saw *into* me—and accepted me nevertheless."

"What did it feel like?" Winter couldn't help but ask.

"Like his warm eyes saw past the wrong," Lev said in reflection. "Like he saw into my true self and only saw me as his own creation."

"Poetic," Winter quipped.

"You'll see for yourself," Lev countered. "Once you stand before him, you'll understand."

The com above the Hive squealed, and Eagle Eyes' voice came over the loudspeaker as his face appeared on the overhead display. "All teams, report to the conference room immediately. We've got work to do."

Every soul in the Hive quickly packed up their current activity and filed toward the Purifier Quarter.

Winter found Nalara and took up her side protectively.

"What is this?" she asked, her big brown eyes pleading for an answer.

"I don't have that information yet," Winter shrugged. "But it sounds like we're all going to be briefed together."

Derrick Zinda stood at the conference room podium. At his side stood a man from the Science and Technology Quarter, his lab uniform and digital tablet a dead giveaway of his vocation. Both waited in silence until all the teams were assembled and accounted for by their captains.

"Purifiers," Captain Zinda began, "this is Head Engineer Franco Benson of the surface drone team. He's going to lead this briefing." Derrick stepped aside and gestured to the podium. "Benson."

The engineer looked down at his hands and swallowed. "Teams," he began, then cleared his throat. "I mean . . . Purifiers . . . I am honored to be in your presence and to address you today. Thank you for your attention." He shifted nervously in his posture, clearly unaccustomed to addressing an audience of Purifiers. He cleared his throat again. "One of our telemetry outposts has been damaged and the corresponding drone destroyed." He transferred the display from his tablet to the giant screen behind him.

"What's he talking about?" Nalara leaned over and whispered.

"The surface drones," Winter responded quietly, "are unmanned flying scanners that track and record any movement and tell us where to focus our purifying. They also find safe clearings for the shuttles to land." She pointed at a spot on the large screen. "That's a telemetry array. It transmits readouts from the drone it's paired with and relays commands from Olympus."

"The last transmission from the drone was inconclusive," Benson continued, "but it is possible that the blighted may have been involved. All subsequent scans of the area by piloted shuttle have turned up negative, so we can't be certain." The engineer concluded with an apologetic shrug.

Scorch huffed, annoyed. "It was probably just a wild animal."

"A camel, maybe?" Viper jabbed.

"Hey!" Scorch shot her a serious look. "Don't even joke about that."

"The Purifiers have been ordered deployment." Eagle Eyes took the stand again. "Half of you will be dispatched to sweep the last known location of the drone and retrieve it. The others will be escorting the repair team to the telemetry array."

"Blight me, please don't put us on the escort . . ." Winter breathed.

"Grim Reapers, Broadswords, Dragon Slayers, Knight Hawks, War Wolves—your teams are tasked to find the missing drone," Derrick announced.

Winter grimaced.

"Shadow Lords, Iron Raiders, Archangels, Black Ghosts, and Hellhounds—your teams have been assigned to escort the engineering team."

An audible grumble filled the room.

"Don't want to hear it." Derrick dismissed their passive protests with a wave of his hand. "Your pilots have the coordinates and are awaiting their teams. Gear up, and move out!"

Each team captain gave their rallying cry, and the Purifiers dispersed to their hubs.

Winter walked with Nalara and ensured that every piece of equipment was donned correctly. Her big, worried eyes begged for comfort as Winter looked her over.

"You did great," Winter assured her. "Don't worry, this is perfectly normal. It happens often enough, and our assignment is so easy, it's basically boring."

"Not much chance of scoring any points this deployment," Bulletproof grumbled from his alcove.

Winter pressed her lips tightly. She agreed with him.

"Archangels," Wraith called them to order once all preparations were complete. "I don't have to tell you our team is holding the standard on this jump. I expect complete professionalism. I expect you all to embody the discipline and perfection with which our creator and Sovereign has imbued the Purifier class. Our task is not menial; our assignment is not small. The engineers are relying on us to ensure their safety surface-side. Let's get them back here in one piece."

"Archangels!" Scorch thrust his fist in the air.

"Archangels!" they all answered in kind.

Wraith led the way to the shuttle bay where the teams assigned to the search party were already beginning to deploy. The five teams assigned to escort the engineers assembled on the dock and awaited Wraith's instructions.

"Listen up." Wraith looked over the scores of Purifiers and five engineers present. "Each team will leave behind one Purifier and take an engineer in their place." He pointed at Nalara.

Nalara's countenance fell.

"When all teams have landed," Wraith continued, "the last shuttle will fly the remaining members down to the surface. This will ensure the mission's success if we come under fire for any reason. The last shuttle's team members will secure the LZ while the rest of us proceed to the array. Keep track of the engineer in your group, and above all else, ensure his or her safety. You engineers stay with your assigned team of Purifiers, no matter what happens. I expect no one will get creative with my instructions." Wraith looked at Winter pointedly. "All scans have turned up negative, so there's little reason to anticipate an encounter with any blighters, but sure as dying, there's no reason to let our guards down either. As always, let's stay on our toes down there and finish this job."

Winter turned to Nalara and put her hand on her shoulder. "It's up to you to keep the shuttles and the LZ safe." She locked eyes with her in reassurance. "You're supposed to be my initiate for another few days, but I know you've got this."

Nalara nodded, biting her lower lip hard.

Winter jostled her shoulder. "Stay with your group, and keep sharp," she said confidently.

The rest of the Archangels were already loading into the shuttle. Winter joined them quickly and assisted the hesitant engineer to take that daunting step over the threshold.

"First time to the surface?" Winter asked.

"No, I just hate it," the young man responded through the large white bio suit.

"You'll be fine." Winter chuckled, trying to not to laugh at the large, floppy outfit.

"That's what they always say," he responded woefully as he stepped inside and began strapping in. "The surface is not for me. The thought of mutated blighters skulking in the shadows all around me, or that death is literally only a thin layer away. And to top it all off . . . I'm prone to airsickness." He shook his head. "Like I said, I just hate it."

The rest of the team ignored him. Winter had been on several of these escort missions before, and it was always the same. No one bothered speaking to the engineers, as all they knew was numbers and readouts. They never made interesting conversation, and most seemed to prefer silence anyway.

The shuttle shot out of the bay and left Olympus behind. Winter watched the floating city ship grow smaller and smaller as they descended toward the surface. She watched as the next shuttle emerged, and then the next, before her own breached the layer of thick, fluffy clouds. It was bumpy and turbulent as they passed through. The engineer gripped his restraints and squeezed his eyes closed.

Wraith read from the display on his gauntlet. "Surface temperatures are moderate, but the barometric pressure is up. Looks like rain."

"Precipitation . . . perfect." The engineer scowled, his face a shade of green. "Great for repairing delicate machinery."

No one responded to him as the shuttle slowed to land. Wraith checked the rifles, handing one to each Purifier in turn.

Winter took hers and exited the shuttle, sweeping her eyes around carefully as she walked slowly out with the others.

They were in a large clearing, cradled on one side by thick trees and lined with a small stream on the other. Across the stream was a large rock face, possibly sixty feet tall and topped with forest. To the right, the steep barrier extended out beyond sight, but to the left, there seemed to be a steady incline. Winter glanced at her gauntlet display and saw their objective was up above them, into the trees beyond the cliff.

For security, the telemetry arrays were built in secluded, hard-to-reach places like this.

Rifle ready, she cleared the area with the rest of the Archangels.

"We're holding until all teams arrive," Wraith reminded, standing protectively with the engineer.

Winter nodded and returned to surveilling. The dark gray clouds above gave a heavy feeling to the day. She could neither hear nor see much of anything beyond the sheer barrier of her armor and the digital screen of her helmet.

Something felt intensified, but she couldn't put her finger on it.

Her eyes trained on the still, silent terrain. Winter waited while the other teams slowly assembled, the shuttles delivering nine purifiers and an engineer at a time. Finally, the last five had arrived to secure the LZ.

"Alright, teams!" Wraith called everyone to attention. "All together now; our objective is at the top of that hill. Left flank with me, right flank stagger back. We're Purifiers, and we've got a job to do!" He gestured forward. "Move out!"

Winter staggered back with the second group and looked over her shoulder at Nalara. Even with the increasing distance, her nervous and self-conscious posture was visible. Perhaps after this mission was over, Nalara would feel more confident in her abilities.

CHAPTER TWELVE

Water sloshed around her boots as Winter pushed through the stream. The gravel-covered ground on the opposite bank crunched loudly as dozens of armored feet impacted the surface in steady progression. As they passed under the leering coverage of the cliff face, Winter gazed up at the summit, scanning for movement. Her rifle trained and ready, she felt her heart beat a little faster as they moved closer to the incline.

Dark clouds overhead intensified the feeling of tension in the air, but apart from the crunching gravel and the heavy breathing as the engineers struggled to keep pace, everything was completely still.

An eerie nothingness filled Winter's senses, and she couldn't quite grasp what it meant.

She glanced around at the faces of her companions—relaxed, glassy-eyed, and uninterested. They hardly seemed to feel the anxiety that she was experiencing.

Winter inhaled sharply and shook herself. It was nothing but nerves, she thought. Maybe Boom was right, and she was just nervous about meeting the Sovereign face to face. If he could see within her, however, why would she be nervous? She had always applied herself in both training and service. She was happy in her vocation. There was nothing she could be ashamed of. But perhaps that was it—maybe she couldn't see what the Sovereign would see. Suddenly, Winter was terrified that her best was not good enough, and the Sovereign would find her lacking despite her best effort.

Glancing up the incline, Winter noticed that they were turning a bend where the path opened up into a deep, clear ditch leading in a straight shot to the top. She hesitated briefly, but couldn't justify the feeling.

They continued without breaking pace, stepping over a large wet area, possibly accumulated moisture from the last rainfall. It didn't seem right. Winter looked up toward the front of the group, her apprehension swelling into solid concern as she saw the six huge boulders poised at the head of the trail above them.

Wraith's group was far ahead of Winter's, almost halfway up the ditch. He didn't seem concerned in the least.

Understanding dawned like a light turning on in her mind. The quiet, the tension, and now, the path and the boulders—it suddenly made perfect sense. They were walking into a trap. Every instinct inside Winter went off on high-alarm. Desperate to warn the others, she fumbled for the button to activate her intercom, but it was too late.

Shots rang out.

Winter ducked instinctively as bullets struck her companions' armor and exploded into the dirt around them.

She looked to the source above them on the outcropping and trained her rifle upward, reflexively discharging three shots before the screaming on the trail ahead stole her attention.

The gunfire had only distracted the Purifiers briefly, but it was long enough for the blighters to push the boulders off their seating. Winter gasped as the giant rocks began bearing down toward them, crushing a few of the fleeing Purifiers from Wraith's group in their wake.

"Fall back! Fall back!" Wraith bellowed, dragging an engineer behind him.

Chaos ensued as Purifiers and Engineers alike ran to escape the thunderous force of the wild, rolling boulders, while up above, blighters fired down on them from the outcropping.

They were caught in a chokehold.

The blighters fired volley after volley into the frantic Olympians. Purifier armor was built to withstand high velocity impacts, but the hailstorm of bullets would chip away at the diminished energy levels. With the intensity of the enemy fire, Winter calculated that any Purifier who braved the volley would have depleted shields before they reached the front line. Several of her comrades already lay motionless in the path where they had been mown down by the giant boulders.

"Hold your position! Return fire!" Wraith ordered. "Stagger down the incline and secure a path to the LZ."

The Purifiers responded in kind and finally organized amid the chaos. One team returned fire while the others made ground toward the shuttles, then the next team staggered back to provide cover fire while the first team retreated. They made steady distance until they reached the bend in the path.

Between their group and the shuttles, two blighters brandishing flaming torches burst from the trees and set alight the thick line of damp ground that Winter had noticed before. The two were shot down and purified quickly, but the oil roared into flame regardless, cutting them off from the shuttles. Against kinetic energy, their nano-armor was nearly impenetrable, but against fire, it was a different story.

Winter took another hit and grunted against the impact to her armor. She glanced at her gauntlet. Her shield energy level was fading. Wading through that wall of fire would surely take the last of it.

She fired off several blasts with her rifle, desperately attempting to thin the pack of blighters up on the ridge.

"We're going to die!" the engineer who had ridden down in Winter's shuttle cried as he held the sides of his helmet.

Winter glanced back at him to respond just in time to see a bullet strike his head, driving him to the ground. Blood trickled down his blank face. Someone near Winter switched their rifle to *purify* and a stream of intense fire washed over the engineer's lifeless form.

Winter snapped her head back to the front, her eyes wide, struggling to keep a handle on her panic. She swallowed and took a moment to see everything. Another round of immense boulders came barreling down the ditch, and the Purifiers and Engineers hugged the wall to avoid being crushed by their bouncing, tumbling, unstoppable weight.

Winter noticed the gunfire cease and looked up. The cliff was slightly concave, so they were out of the blighter's line of sight as long as they clung to the wall.

"Captain Wraith," Winter spoke over the com, "Scorch and I can scale this."

"Negative, we wait for reinforcements," Wraith snapped.

Winter could see him where he stood by the wall of fire and locked eyes with him.

"Sir!" Winter stared him down with intensity as the deafening volley of boulders continued by. "We can't wait. Our shields won't last that long. The other teams are all spread out in search parties. Give us cover fire, and we can end this now."

Wraith glared at her through the crowd of their peers. A long moment passed. "Black Ghosts, Hellhounds," he spoke at length, "on my mark, you cross the ravine and get to cover in the trees. Lay down heavy suppression fire on the blighters above—keep them occupied while Winter and Scorch scale the rock face. We'll pick them off when they open fire as you cross."

The two teams confirmed his orders with fear and determination in their eyes.

Winter suddenly wondered which of them she would see again once this was over. The gravity of her suggestion hit her as she realized their sacrifices were ensured.

She looked away from their apprehensive faces and switched her rifle to *purify* before holstering it. Scorch joined her by the rock face and did the same. His nostrils were flared, and his lips were drawn in a tight line.

"Gonna get me some today!" he growled through gritted teeth.

"We both will," Winter said, swallowing down her fear as she found her first holds and waited for Wraith's signal.

The break in the rockfall appeared, and Wraith called out, "Go now!"

Winter heard the charging footfalls of her companions and the deafening fire of bullets from above. She and Scorch began their ascent, ignoring the crackling screams pouring through the com. Rifle blasts tore through the air and several mutant bodies fell from above. The red light of flame glowed on their shields as the Purifiers below carried out their vocation in efficient execution.

Arms and legs pumping in coordination, Winter and Scorch made steady progress up the face of the cliff. So far, they hadn't been noticed, but Winter knew she couldn't worry about the blighters on the summit. That was her team's job. She needed to concentrate on getting up there as fast as possible.

Small rocks trickled down from above as excited mutant feet kicked them over the edge when they lined up to take shots at the Purifiers below. Merely ten feet from the edge, Winter could see movement above. She and Scorch waited for the next assault of rifle blasts to drive the mutants to seek cover. The electric volleys ripped through the air and cleared the ledge. Winter and Scorch tore up the last few feet and breached the summit.

One hand still gripping the crest, feet still braced against the rocks, Winter pulled out her rifle and blasted the tree line with streaming flames before the blighters could react to seeing them. All the fury of her fallen brethren manifested as Winter screamed in wrath while torching the blighter's cover.

The mutants fell back, giving the two of them time to take the summit and find their footing. Winter and Scorch split apart and staggered their positions behind tree cover.

Bullets filled the air and shards of wood exploded with each impact. Winter gripped her rifle close and waited for the break.

"Cover me," Winter signaled to Scorch and sprinted forward to the next line of defense. Earsplitting gunfire and bright blasts exploded as she took the opportunity to gain ground. Relying on Scorch's supporting fire, she tumbled into place behind a large turned-up root.

Winter hoisted her rifle over her head and fired off several blind shots before poking her head up to take aim. She picked off two easy headshots and ducked back down before the return fire.

Scorch used her attack as an opportunity to gain ground as well and nodded at his teammate once he was safely in position. From their current location, Winter could see a large group of Purifiers making their way up the straight ditch, picking off the blighters that lined the summit—the ones who'd been barraging them with boulders.

Scorch pushed in as the blighters steadily gave ground. They all seemed to be fleeing in the same direction, which made the distant crack of gunfire in the opposite direction catch Winter's ear. She turned to see its source.

Winter spoke, "Scorch, you good?"

"Oh, yeah!" he shouted sarcastically. "I'm *abso-freakin'-fantastic!* Blight me!"

"I've got something." Winter tucked her rifle close to her body and took off to the right flank of the fleeing blighters. She charged through the trees and found a small group of them unloading bullets into the LZ. The Purifiers there and the shuttles were just out of range, but they couldn't come assist as long as they were under fire.

Winter went down on one knee and took careful aim. She breathed out and took one headshot. The other blighters jumped in surprise when one of their own collapsed in a dead heap.

Another headshot. The second blighter fell.

The last one standing raised its rifle. Third headshot. It flew backward over the ledge in a bloody spray.

Winter ran up to the ridge and looked down at the LZ. Nalara and the other team members looked like little insects down below.

The com crackled while Winter purified the carcasses.

"Winter!" Nalara's panicked voice flooded over the speaker. "Should we come help?"

"Stay with the shuttles," Winter ordered crisply and shut off the flames. "Keep the LZ secure."

Nalara stared at her warrior friend on the summit. "W-we need to h-hold position," she gulped to the other Purifiers guarding the landing zone.

Up on the cliff top, Winter had already taken off into the woods again. She knew Wraith would push straight through to the telemetry array and secure the area there. If she followed in kind, she would be stuck there with the teams, and they would have no eyes on the blighters' movement.

Winter charged through the woods until she could see the clearing with the array: a giant antenna with a metal-shielded base to protect the machinery. She saw blighters fleeing and returning fire as the Purifiers pushed in but veered to the right instead of moving to join them. She pumped her legs hard and circumvented the clearing. A group of blighters breached the tree line from the south, closely followed by Scorch, firing indiscriminately into their midst.

Winter didn't halt her pace, she needed to run twice as fast and be twice as focused to avoid tripping on the rugged terrain or falling behind as they fled. Just as she predicted, Wraith surrounded the array with his numbers and fired upon the enemy from there.

Winter stepped suddenly in a puddle and looked down. It looked like water, but different somehow. The ground was wet, but not everywhere; just in a curving line that seemed to circle the clearing.

A small portion of Wraith's forces were driving the blighters from the clearing while the bulk of them surrounded the array.

Winter ran in an arcing path around the clearing, hoping to cut off the blighters in their escape.

"Wraith, you've got to send some runners around the perimeter!" Winter gasped as she ran.

"Negative," Wraith growled. "We're not pursuing. If they run, we let them. Our mission is the array."

"Our calling is to purify," Winter insisted. "If we cut them off, we can do both."

No response.

Winter's passion rose up in her throat, and her pride got the better of her. She felt like now she finally had a chance to prove to Captain Zinda, to the Sovereign, and to her own insecurities that she was worthy.

Winter circled around to the rear flank of the blighters and prepared to attack.

Suddenly, a fire was struck and the ground set aflame. The inferno took only moments to leap into an uncontrollable blaze and sweep out a swift path in both directions. Winter watched in alarm as the Purifiers were cut off from any chance of pursuit or retreat by a towering wall of fire.

Winter was alone on this side of the fire, cut off from any reinforcements and surrounded by a hoard of blighters.

CHAPTER THIRTEEN

Most imperative over everything else, Winter could not allow them to realize she was alone. She took no time to think at all before blasting several rounds with her rifle, then charging to a new position and doing it again.

Secondarily, she must not let them regroup and advance toward the array. With her comrades boxed in by the fire and terrain, it would be like a shooting gallery.

Winter wound back through the trees to make a wedge between their group and the wall of fire. Her nano-armor rippled wildly as it repelled the radiation damage from the blazing heat. However excellent it was in defense against kinetic energy, the armor's weakness was fire.

Winter squinted and gritted her teeth against the blinding inferno and fired into the mass of scrambling blighters. Their efforts to organize and fire upon the trapped Purifiers were frustrated by the unexpected attack. They started giving ground carefully as she pushed in. Against the backdrop of the fire wall, they couldn't tell how many she was, and Winter continued switching positions to that purpose.

The blighters broke off into groups and fled the area. Winter's pride in her calling surfaced violently as she instinctually gave chase.

She hurdled through the trees, rifle on point, picking off any who lagged behind enough to fall into her sights.

With the blazing wood falling behind her, Winter took a moment to speak into her com.

"Winter here." She received only static in response. "I'm in pursuit northwest of the array."

More static.

The fire must be interfering with the signal, she surmised.

Winter saw the terrified face of that engineer flash before her eyes, shot mid-sentence and purified. She saw the crushed bodies of her comrades lying prone and broken in the straight ravine. She growled with feral vengeance and let loose another shot at the distant forms of the fleeing blighters.

She lost sight of them and began to track. Not a shred of protocol entered her mind. Subconsciously, she was probably actively suppressing it. Her hunter instinct intensified, and she followed the signs of passage deep into the unknown forest.

Their prints disappeared when Winter broke through the trees and encountered a long, clear pathway that might have been part of an ancient road system.

Quiet hung in the air.

It seemed so foreign after the raging firefight that had swallowed her senses just moments before.

Winter looked up and down the overgrown road. Disintegrating vehicles lay in the ditches, covered in rust and moss—almost unrecognizable. She scanned the tree line and scrutinized the various buildings that were still partially intact. She didn't like this setting. There were too many places around from where the enemy could make covered fire. Subtle, deep rumbling from the dark sky signaled the impending rain.

Stepping carefully out into the open, Winter proceeded down the ancient road, following the trail left by the fleeing blighters' haste to escape.

In the utter silence, she hunted—carefully picking her way through the desolate remains of humanity. Faint signs of passage led her deep into the urban terrain where Winter found herself stepping out onto an expansive bridge that crossed moving water far below. Littered with debris and heaps of mechanical garbage, the bridge arced before her in silent testimony to the marvel that was once humanity's civilization. From the center of the bridge on which she stood, she could see another bridge down the river— smaller and almost completely destroyed by time.

Winter continued to the other side, completely engrossed in her hunt. She tracked tirelessly through the dense woods and ancient stone.

She came across a circular structure covered in vines and falling apart with age. Set on the edge of the river, across an open green, its once-white stone construction was columned and stately.

It stood out so poignantly that Winter could scarcely contain her curiosity.

A glint of light inside caught her eye as the dimmed sunlight reflected off an unknown surface. She didn't know if it had been movement within or simply the right angle of light, but something had caught a ray of sunlight through a break in the darkening clouds.

Winter approached carefully, with no other choice than to assume it had been a hostile presence. Crouched and ready, rifle pointed in, she advanced up the steps to the columned entry. There was no movement within the dark, cavernous building that she could detect, but the hanging tension forced her to be thorough.

Rumbling shook the sky as she breached the threshold. Stepping into an immense open room with vaulted stone ceilings, she found the most unexpected sight. Her heightened battle anxiety disappeared suddenly, replaced by a calm sort of reverence that fell over her as she entered the all but empty circular room. The fragile silence seemed disturbed by even the slightest motion of her boots.

The remains of a statue were the circular structure's only occupant. The figure of a man crafted in bronze lay on its side in quiet majesty. Only the feet, broken off at the ankles, remained on the pedestal in the center where the statue had once stood.

Winter was mystified. She had no idea the old world was so much like hers. This man must have been akin to the Purifiers of his time—even akin to the glorified Ascended. Not only had he become immortalized in bronze, but within his own shrine as well. Winter circled the supine statue in curiosity. The workmanship was marvelous. Even after all these years, she could see the detail and care that was put into crafting his likeness. Unable to make out the features, Winter crouched by the head and carefully swept the growth and dust from his face.

His eyes were steadfast, tilted upward. His mouth, though drawn in a straight line, appeared to smile somehow. His features seemed to embody hope and made Winter feel something like courage swell deep within. She touched the edge of the neck; it didn't appear to have been broken but rather roughly sawed off.

Winter looked at the neck of the statue where the head had once lived, then lifted her eyes to the pedestal and noticed words inscribed about the circumference of the domed ceiling.

She stood up and read it carefully while turning in a slow circle.

I HAVE SWORN UPON THE ALTAR OF GOD
ETERNAL HOSTILITY AGAINST EVERY FORM
OF TYRANNY OVER THE MIND OF MAN.

A smile flicked across her lips. She was amused by the inscription. What a funny riddle to carve around the statue of an honored hero.

Her attention was diverted from the strange discovery as it began to rain outside. The light tapping of precipitation steadily grew to a heavy downpour.

Emerging from the structure, Winter cleared the area with a quick sweep and trotted down the steps amid the falling rain. It was pouring so heavily that she could barely make out the road from where she'd come. Winter took partial cover behind an old vehicle and checked her gauntlet display.

She had racked up a respectable six killshots and several confirmed hits in one day. She hadn't received any communication from her team yet. Now that the adrenaline and rage had subsided, Winter was able to think clearly once more. It was doubtful that she would get any more killshots if she continued tracking, and it was likely that Wraith needed help in the fallout of such an attack.

She started backtracking toward the array and opened her communicator channel. "Winter here, two klicks northwest of the array," she spoke as she ran. "Requesting coordinates for regrou—"

A shot split the air and struck her helmet between the eyes.

Blackness.

Shrill ringing . . .

Can't breathe—where's the air? Where . . .?

She felt her body spasm. Winter could have sworn her eyes were open, but she saw nothing. Nothing but darkness—thicker than she'd ever known—enveloped her and smothered her. Panic set in as Winter slowly asphyxiated within her own suit, not for lack of oxygen, but because she couldn't force her lungs to work.

Suddenly, like a shot of lightning, her chest expanded and she was able to breathe fast, desperate gasps.

Her vision began to clear, and Winter found herself dazed and disoriented, looking up at the thick clouds and falling rain. She lay on her back, arms splayed wide. Her first thought was to locate her rifle, but she couldn't move. She felt motion around her, felt footfalls impact the ground and approach quickly.

Move—MOVE!

Her mind screamed amid a high-pitched ringing. Her instincts rebelled harshly against her unresponsive limbs.

A shrouded figure skidded to a stop and towered above her, it raised Winter's own rifle to her face and pulled the trigger just as her adrenaline kicked in, forcing her body to obey. She snapped to the side just as the electric burst exploded into the ground, sending torrents of dirt up into the air.

Winter's screen was cracked, her helmet display flickered madly. The weak signal, damaged equipment, and loud rainfall ensured that she could not make out any words amid the intermittent static issuing from her communicator.

Winter shot to her feet, her head still ringing wildly. As she stepped in to her opponent's space and latched on to the rifle, three more blighters poured from the trees toward them. Two of them fired their guns and hit her body armor. She stumbled back as the nano-tech absorbed the forceful impacts, but the alarm on her view screen told her it was growing dangerously weak. The flickering chaos on her helmet display and the crackling voice on her com added to her disorientation. She was desperate and confused. She tried to wrench the rifle from her opponent, but the blighter dropped one hand and struck her head.

To her absolute horror, Winter felt fresh, cool air puff into her face. She gasped as the liquid armor flickered and disappeared. She felt the cold panic of death grip her heart, but it lasted only a moment before a feral anger took root deep inside and curled her panicked expression into icy cold focus.

Winter had nothing to lose now.

She dropped the rifle and latched onto her attacker's face. While the blighter remained gripping the rifle, she jumped and pulled its face down hard into her knee with a ferocious snarl. Glass shards from its dark goggles shattered in all directions. The rifle went flying to the side as the blighter collapsed in a spray of blood.

No time to think as the others came rushing in, guns first.

The blighters closed in and one of them pointed its gun at Winter's head. Darting forward, she wrapped her arm around the blighter's outstretched limb and dislocated its shoulder. It screamed in pain as she spun around and used it as a body shield to absorb two more shots; simultaneously drawing her own sidearm and raising the sights to her eyes.

She shot one center mass, dropping it to the ground, but the other circled around behind her. The blighter in her clutches twisted and elbowed her in the face, knocking her helmet sideways. Winter knew she was dead already, so she pulled off her helmet with a spiteful growl and threw it at the one circling behind her.

The blighter she was grappling screamed and elbowed her again. Winter fumbled for her sidearm, but she responded by snapping its neck.

The large blighter she'd kneed in the face pushed up from the muddy forest floor and lunged at her with a thick knife. She stepped forward into its momentum, bent her knees and shifted off the line. Drawing her own knife in response as she moved, she ignored the attacking blade and caught the blighter's elbow. Her aggressor's own movement carried the blade all the way down to its bone.

Winter's gauntlet washed over with deep red blood as her blade disappeared into the blighter's flesh. One more shift, and she stepped again, trailing the knife up the arm and through its carotid.

Another gunshot hit the tree next to her. Winter's deathly cold eyes snapped to the last one standing. Without thinking, she charged straight at the blighter, plunging her blade at its heart.

The mutant struck the blade away with the butt of its long gun, and snapped it back to strike her in the face with the barrel.

She pulled back and tucked her elbows into her core, coiled like a spring, and stepped forward cutting toward its neck with the full force of her bodyweight.

The blighter circle-stepped and deflected again with the stock but then dropped it and latched on to Winter's neck from behind. One arm around her neck, the other secured behind her head, her eyes went black as the pressure overwhelmed her senses. She had to act quickly. Winter switched her blade from one hand to the other and stabbed blindly behind her. She missed with the first swing but struck true with the second. A grunt of pain, and her attacker's grip weakened.

Winter felt the give and grabbed its thumb knuckle below the wrist and pulled her elbow down to her center. The gap created gave her the chance to throw its grip off and gain the upper hand with a flying spinning back kick. As the blighter stumbled back, Winter gripped her knife, breathed in deeply, and snapped forward with ferocity. She lunged forward two steps, then jumped into a flying knee strike to the creature's sternum. She rode it down to the earth and landed on top of it, pinning it to the ground.

She held her blade against its neck and panted desperately, rainwater pouring down her face, dripping from her drenched hair.

Its hands went up; it didn't move.

The rain continued to pelt them in torrents.

Winter gasped and breathed the clear, fresh, moist air. Every breath was poison. Every breath was one closer to her last.

I'm dead.

Her laser-focused eyes locked on her prey and Winter snarled as she pushed the drenched hair out of her face, unknowingly streaking her fallen foe's blood across her brow.

"YOU KILLED ME!" she screamed above the rainfall and struck the masked face. "YOU KILLED ME, YOU BLIGHTED FREAK!" She punched again.

She was dead. Olympus would not be her resting place, she would never see the day of her Ascension. Her chest burned with adrenaline and rage. She was going to kill this creature that cost her eternity, but she wanted to watch it die.

Winter gripped the cowl and jerked it off the mutant's head.

Soft amber eyes met hers within an expression of sheer horror.

Winter's heart stopped.

A human face. Fair skin, ash brown hair. It was a man—a human man.

Her mouth fell open.

Human . . . she thought in utter astonishment.

It was not real—it couldn't be. Winter blinked hard, thinking the poisoned atmosphere was toying with her perception. But the face remained the same: strong, clean and alert.

It—no—*he* looked up at her, eyes brimming with fear and horror . . . like she was . . . a monster.

Winter held the blade against his neck, fully intending to end him, but somehow, she couldn't focus. She couldn't make herself do it. This was not what she expected. This 'blighter' wasn't an unspeakable terror; he was just like her.

Stunned, Winter dropped the blade altogether. It splashed down in the mud as she fell backward off of him. She was dumbfounded. This was a blighter; this descendant of what was once human was supposed to have mutated, adapted physiology to inhabit a toxic earth. This was supposed to be a crazed scavenger hideously deformed by the Blight . . . but he looked like her.

Their eyes locked. Winter couldn't have reacted if she wanted to when suddenly he scrambled backward out of her reach.

His horrified eyes reached out to his fallen companions and he pointed with a shaking hand.

"I'm just going to help them," he ventured, speaking her own language. "Please . . . we don't need to kill each other."

When Winter couldn't react to his plea, he carefully rose to his feet.

In programed response, Winter shot to her feet as well and rushed over to her rifle, skidding to a stop in the mud to retrieve it. She brought the sights up to her eyes and clenched her teeth. The man was kneeling by the one she'd tagged with the center mass shot. He was desperately pushing cloth into the wound.

"I got you, don't worry," he said. "I'm gonna get you home! Just stay with me." His eyes darted up once more to Winter, his expression pulled tight with worry and caution, but he continued his work. He stood and slung two rifles over his shoulder, pulling his companion from the clearing by the shoulder fabric of his coat, his eyes fixed on Winter the whole time.

Winter watched him go through the sights of her rifle. Her finger clutched the trigger. It would have been so easy to end him, but she stood frozen nonetheless . . . helpless in shock.

The man and his companion disappeared into the forest.

Winter stood and stared after them for a long and silent moment. Everything was still but for the blood and the sweat and the rain that dripped down her body. At length, she swallowed hard and looked around at the two dead blighters that lay where she'd slain them.

This was a mistake; this was obviously a fluke.

She was seeing things.

She was *hearing* things.

Winter stepped quickly to one of the corpses. She pulled off its mask and looked at the bloody face of a middle-aged man, dark hair, clean-shaven face, slightly overweight . . . broken nose . . . sliced throat. His blank eyes stared off into nowhere.

Winter reached down and turned his head from side to side with a scowl of determination.

No. This wasn't right.

She approached the other and took off its mask as well.

She found no mutant . . . she found no monster. Under the cowl, Winter found only a red-haired woman with pale skin and freckled cheeks—her neck snapped and her body covered in blood from the two bullet wounds.

Winter looked back and forth between the two faces. Their slack eyes were glazed and distant and lifeless. Their bodies . . . so still . . . She turned around in confusion. She couldn't process this. She couldn't.

Sun broke through the canopy in long golden streams as the pouring rain dissipated into a slow drizzle. Winter looked up at the sky, and tears filled her eyes. So many emotions stormed around inside her; it felt like she was being torn apart. She looked at the bodies and then up to the sky once more. Winter's structure couldn't handle the stress and collapsed to her knees, dropping the rifle in her hand. Anger flooded her mind, yet tears streamed down her face.

Every breath she drew reminded her that she was a dead woman. Bitterness and disappointment joined her rage and confusion and made her head swell. She could feel her heart beating in her ears. Her throat burned and ached as her breaths came faster and faster.

In an instant, her mind completely shut out the emotions and switched to cold practicality. She had always been able to rely on her training before.

What did her training say?

If your armor fails on the surface and you are exposed to the Blight—the first and only course of action you must take is to purify yourself. Hail, Zeus!

Winter's eyes darted around at her chaotic surroundings. She located her sidearm and scrambled over to it. On her knees, she sniffed back the tears and checked the fuel cells.

Resolve the infection; purify the Blight.

She swept her matted locks from her face and cocked the weapon. She could hardly see through the tears; her hands shook uncontrollably inside her gauntlets. She quickly raised the muzzle to her temple, finger on the trigger.

Purify the Blight.

Click

Winter exhaled a shaky, panicked groan. The rain and mud must have been playing with the sterile construction of the firearm. She quickly cleared and cycled the chamber once more before pressing it into her temple again.

She held her breath, trying to force her hand to stop shaking, and started squeezing the trigger slowly. She clenched her teeth, tears trickling down her pale cheeks. Her arm shook violently for a moment . . . and then fell.

She slumped and looked up into the sky, letting the tears fall freely. She sobbed, stared up through the trees, and screamed in frustration at her own weakness.

The sunlight reminded her of the home she would never see again. The macabre scene around her reinforced the revelation she could never ignore.

Winter closed her eyes tight against the reality, shutting it all out, and cried.

. . . and cried.

CHAPTER FOURTEEN

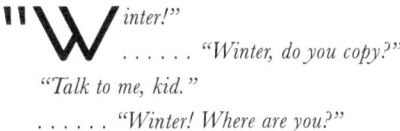

"*inter!*"
. . . . . . "*Winter, do you copy?*"
"*Talk to me, kid.*"
. . . . . . "*Winter! Where are you?*"

Red eyes and dried salt tears on her face, Winter looked over at her helmet where it lay on the soaked earth near the spilled blood and cold corpses. Derrick's voice cracked forth from the com inside.

Her chest hurt, her head throbbed, but she concluded that she didn't have it within her to take her own life. Shivering, soaked through, she got up to her feet and slowly approached her displaced gear.

Eagle Eyes was still trying to hail her as she bent to retrieve her helmet.

She paused before replying. Did she really want to go back and admit her weakness? Wouldn't it be better to stay here and die inside her failure? The thought of slowly being eaten away from the inside out by the Blight flooded her mind. She compared that painful and drawn-out death to a quick and dignified purification.

She swallowed hard and finally replied, "Copy. Winter here."

"Winter! Oh, thank Zeus!" Eagle Eyes exclaimed. "You're way off the grid. Are you hurt? Why aren't you at the LZ?"

Winter swallowed again and glanced at her gauntlet display. It was covered in blood; she couldn't see the screen. After wiping a section clear enough to see the readout, Winter breathed out slowly to steady her voice. "I'm on my way. ETA, ten minutes."

"Just hurry up," Wraith's voice snapped over the channel. "We've got the techs and all our wounded back to Olympus already. You're the only thing holding up the works. Ten minutes, then we're leaving without you."

With a deep breath, Winter accepted her fate. She would just show up, make her report, and let the purification happen. It was how it needed to be.

Resignedly securing her helmet, she was surprised to see the cracked display somewhat functioning again; and when she engaged the armor, to her astonishment, it made a full circuit and sealed at the helmet. The connection was weak—there was no way it could take another single hit— but it was steady.

Winter gathered her sidearm and her knife, holstering both before retrieving her rifle. The eerie death that surrounded her—the pooled blood, the blank faces, and lifeless eyes—all imprinted in her mind. Even when she closed her eyes tight against them, they still stared back at her.

Winter backed out of the clearing, her heart in her boots.

She blocked out the feelings, blocked out the madness. She refused to let her mind catch traction. She could not allow it to start down the path of trying to make sense of it all right now. All she needed to do was reach the LZ, and it would all be over. She just needed to outrun the madness until then.

She held her rifle close and began running. It was difficult, not because she was tired or hurt, but because she had exactly no heart to do it. Every step brought her closer to death, but at the same time, closer to purification.

The rain had finally stopped, and the forest was damp and heavy. The sound of shuttle engines whirred in the clearing ahead, quickening her already racing heart and escalating her inner turmoil until it reached a crescendo.

Her gait slowed again as she reconsidered the option of staying behind. She was surprised to find that she did not fear dying. She had accepted death long ago and embraced the reality of it. Dying was not the thing that harrowed her mind. But deeply, truly did she fear the prospect of the look on her comrades' faces. The face of Trigger suddenly flashed in her mind, then disappeared as purifying flames consumed him and the Blight within him. The thought of them looking at her—of her mentor looking at her—and not seeing a comrade and fellow Purifier, but instead seeing a broken, infected thing . . .

NO! Not like this.

She couldn't let them see her in this fallen, defiled state and then burden them with the responsibility of purifying her. That would haunt their minds, eat away at their resolve, and hinder their service to the Sovereign in their vocation.

She wanted to die with honor like her teammate Trigger had done weeks ago. He was able to perish quickly and painlessly among his fellow Purifiers. This is what Winter wanted for her own death—not to be shot like a blighter, but purified by the Sovereign's fire.

She steeled her resolve and pushed through the last line of trees in time to see the Grim Reapers' shuttle just taking off.

Winter walked past the Broadswords and the Hellhounds teams, both awaiting their shuttles. They all looked askance and bewildered at her appearance.

The Archangels were in the process of loading, so she quickened her gait.

Scorch threw his hands up in the air with jubilance. "Hey, there she is!"

Her team pounded their fists into their palms as she approached in silence. The applause was short-lived as they continued the process of scanning and boarding.

Wraith had that hell-bent look on his face when he spotted Winter. He stalked toward her and seized her helmet in his giant hand, pulling her head roughly as he examined the damage with a furious scowl.

"Seal breach?" he demanded.

Winter breathed once before responding. "I don't know," she lied.

Wraith torqued her head again. He was asserting dominance, not voicing concern, and Winter didn't like it. She jerked away and brushed his hand off.

Wraith was shocked and livid, but he paused; it looked like he was deciding how to react to her insubordination.

Winter was frustrated and impatient. She turned toward the transport and ignored him. She was about to be purified anyway, and it didn't matter.

The first glass shield lifted and allowed her entry. With a deliberate step, Winter entered her death chamber, her countenance stoic and set, her eyes their usual icy steel.

She looked at her team. In a moment, they wouldn't be so jovial. In a moment, the jokes and stories would cease, and they would all endure the endless flight home without her.

The glass descended and closed her in.

Winter could feel the perspiration gathering on her hairline. She would not show it. She refused to let any shred of fear or regret escape her eyes.

The scanners began their sweep. Green lights played over her, and Winter felt her face grow red hot as she imagined the flames purifying her body out of existence. The lights were brighter than usual; the buzzing was louder. She was aware of every inch that they moved, aware of the expressions on her comrades' faces, aware of the pilot fine-tuning the controls while he waited. The sound of her own shaky breathing competed with the thump, thump of her heartbeat.

She was aware of her hands trembling . . .

This is it.

Winter closed her eyes and accepted her fate.

This is my end.

Green.

Ding

Winter flinched and gasped audibly as disinfecting spray filled the chamber, then vented out the floor.

What . . .?

The inner glass partition raised.

. . . was this real?

Scorch noticed her odd reaction and shot a puzzled look. Winter breathed and stepped forward. How was this possible? Were the scanners faulty? She had been fully exposed to the Blight and engaged in close-quarter combat with the enemy for several full minutes. She even had traces of their tainted blood on her suit that the rain had failed to completely wash away.

How could I possibly be clear?

Winter walked blankly toward her seat, trying unsuccessfully to get a handle on the moment.

Wraith entered the shuttle after her and was cleared quickly as well. After securing his rifle on the weapon rack, he snatched Winter's and scanned the data with a sharp scowl.

His eyebrows rose. "Seven?" He looked to her for confirmation.

Winter nodded. *Nine,* she thought to herself. Two unaccounted for by the shot tracing technology—one she had killed with her blade, and the other . . . with her bare hands. She started to shake, feeling physically sick as their dead faces flashed into her mind.

Wraith shook his head. He looked like he wanted to be angry, but he had far too much respect for her numbers at the moment.

"Take your seat," he directed. His expression spoke confusion and suspicion. He studied her armor, her face, her gauntlets. He looked like he wanted to throw her off the shuttle mid-flight.

Winter strapped in and tried to not allow her turbulent emotions to show. Her stomach churned within. Nothing made sense.

A moment ago, her hyper-awareness had been on full strength, but now, it seemed like the entire world around her was fading into a fuzzy blur. The voices of her teammates devolved into a distant white noise. The shuttle engines disappeared into a hum. The lights, the motion—it all became a dizzy, disoriented mass of unfocused turmoil.

The transport bore them up into the sky. Winter didn't look up to Olympus this time; she stared at her boots, covered in the remaining traces of dried mud and blood splatter left from the disinfection chamber.

They arrived in the shuttle port before she knew it, and the weary team disembarked one after the other.

The jump station was filled with sweat-soaked, exhausted Purifiers slowly making their way to their respective gear chambers. Winter stepped down from the shuttle to see Eagle Eyes pushing his way through the crowd.

"Winter!" he called.

She looked up at him as he approached.

"Great Zeus, kid! You alive?" He touched the bullet hole on her helmet, his face drawn with concern. He saw the blood on her face and feared that she'd caught the worst of it.

Winter nodded. Tears threatened to well up in her eyes, but she blinked them back and moved on toward the gear chamber before they could escape. "I was lucky," she choked out as evenly as she could manage. "The shielding took the brunt of it, but a shard must have broken off inside and nicked me pretty bad."

"What happened out there?" he persisted, keeping pace. "I heard you went all commando."

"There needed to be an alternate to planting and shooting," Winter growled, blaming herself for the incidents of the day. "It was the only way to ensure the blighters didn't regroup toward the shuttle." She didn't realize it, but her voice was rising with each word, and she was speaking faster and faster. "We didn't have time to wait for reinforcements because the blighters had the terrain controlled, and our forces only had one accessible route to advance. I flanked the array and cut them off from the teams, but they scattered—"

"Hey—hey! Whoa, just slow down," he cut her off reassuringly. "You did first-tier, kid. No one could have done better. Just breathe." He paused as Winter halted her stride and inhaled deeply. "I'm really very proud of you. I saw you got seven killshots," he said with a smile.

Winter looked at him in surprise. Could he possibly understand how that sounded to her? All she could see were the dead faces looking at her. She didn't know how to respond. She didn't know what to say.

Winter began toward her team hub again, hastening her steps. Her mentor called her name in concern as she practically ran to her team's room, but she couldn't stop.

She felt the panic creep up in her throat as she entered her security code and began disarming. She felt as if everyone in the room was staring at her, like somehow, they knew she should be dead. She couldn't help but feel like she was infecting them all. What if the scanners were really broken? What if she had just infected Olympus? The conflict churning inside her head was unbearable. The scanners detected no pathogen. The Sovereign doesn't make mistakes. She knew she was covered in the evidence to the contrary, but she could not question the validity of her creator's design. She took the time to scrub her gauntlets and boots clean before hanging them up.

By the time Winter was down to the clothes in which she'd arrived, Wraith entered the gear room and stalked directly over to her.

"I watched your blast-cam footage," he said accusingly.

Winter turned to face the giant man, who stood uncomfortably close to her. He stooped slightly to look her in the eyes.

"And what?" Winter matched his gaze, not giving an inch.

Wraith's nostrils flared at her response.

The other Purifiers gave each other significant glances.

"You broke rank *again*," Wraith growled. "The only reason I haven't shot you myself is that you didn't put the rest of us at risk by doing so."

Winter breathed and suppressed her impulse to retort. He was the one putting people at risk by hesitating like he did.

"The fact that you got seven killshots today doesn't mean that you can do whatever fool thing pops into your head. You can't just run off like that. I saw the up-close shot you took. I mean, look at this!" He aggressively grabbed her broken helmet from its place in her alcove. "Do you know how close you came today?"

Winter stared blankly at the bullet hole.

"A fraction deeper and it would have *ended* you." Wraith rolled his eyes.

"Are you even hearing me?"

How she wished she had a leader in whom she could confide. "Yes, sir," she responded softly.

"Answer me, Lieutenant!"

Winter locked eyes with him again. "Yes, sir! I hear you, sir!"

Wraith scowled. "The fact that you made it through the scanner after an encounter that close is nothing short of dumb—*stupid*—luck." He shook his head; his eyes narrowed in suspicion. "Get yourself to the infirmary," he ordered. "I'm sending a wave there now. You're getting looked over again."

Winter's heart fell. "You've got to be kidding me," she protested.

"No, you listen." Wraith jutted his finger into her face. He lowered his voice. "You think you're special. You think you're above the rules, but you're not." He stormed away. "Infirmary—now!" he shouted over his shoulder.

Winter gritted her teeth in anger and punched the wall.

CHAPTER FIFTEEN

The moment Wraith turned his back, the team returned to their own business, trying to hide the fact they had been watching. Nalara cautiously approached Winter, still in her gear. Her eyes were wide, filled with apprehension and excitement.

"What happened?" she asked eagerly. "We stayed at the LZ. Wraith never sent for us."

"I made sure of it," Winter muttered.

Nalara exhaled, her face burdened with pity for her friend. "So . . . what happened?"

"Nothing." Winter shook her head. "It's . . . nothing." She pulled her street shoes out from under the bench.

"Are you okay?" Nalara inquired with genuine concern.

People kept asking her that. Winter sighed in frustration but recognized the sincerity in her friend's eyes and was reminded she was not on the battlefront anymore. She paused to take a calming breath and to steady her emotions.

"Your face is covered in blood . . ." Nalara said timidly, not sure if she had crossed a line. "Your helmet is damaged . . . I just didn't know how bad you were hurt."

"I'm fine," came the fast response. "A fragment of the helmet broke off inside from the bullet impact," Winter repeated the lie, struggling to keep down the panic at her rampant guilt. As far as everyone else was concerned, she had simply been hurt. They didn't know the grim reality of what truly happened on that jump. No one knew it wasn't her own blood. The truth kept creeping up her throat, threatening to explode from her if she didn't let it out in small, controlled increments.

"I . . . I saw something," she whispered almost involuntarily.

Nalara's face contorted in surprise and intrigue. "What do you mean?"

Winter glanced around. "I can't explain it." She bit her lip, immediately regretting saying a word about it. "I can't—it's just . . . I don't know what to think right now."

The others in the room gave her odd glances as she and Nalara whispered together. They carried on and went their ways, but Winter felt their judgment.

She saw disdain everywhere—how much of it was imagined, she didn't know. She didn't know what was real at the moment.

Winter concentrated on relaxing her shoulders and exhaled slowly. "Why don't you come by my living chambers later? We'll talk then. I think I just need to decompress right now."

"Yeah, you do look pretty beat up," Nalara said, gesturing toward Winter's head.

Winter touched her forehead gingerly as if there was a wound there. "Right. Just gear down for now." She stood to leave. "We won't need to go back to the surface until the next repair crew is ready."

"Okay . . . I hope you're not too hurt . . ." Nalara trailed off as Winter walked away.

Winter felt the need to shower before complying with Wraith's order to visit the infirmary. She knew the healthcare worker would appreciate it—aside from the obvious reason of disposing evidence.

Entering the women's showers, Winter peeled off her clothing, stepped inside one of the opaque glass stalls, and punched her preferred shower settings into the touchscreen.

She ached all over. Her body was a little battered, but nothing to warrant the hollow, all-encompassing pain that permeated her frame. The hot water fell over her in steaming rivers and washed away all the evidence of her attack on the surface. The crusted blood on her hairline dissolved, and the dirt disappeared, but no amount of water could wash away what she had seen and felt on the surface.

She closed her eyes to block out the images but found herself remembering the sweet smell of the earth's air. She could almost feel the crisp breeze against her skin as she recalled the sound the trees made when it washed through them. She'd never heard that sound unmuffled before, having always been safely confined inside her air-tight nano-armor. She remembered the vibrant colors of the trees and the underbrush, having never appreciated them from behind her helmet's digital readouts.

Head feeling so heavy, she leaned against the wall and let the water cascade over her to drown out the thoughts.

She should be dead by now. The Blight should have taken her. The scanners should have caught the infection and purified her in the incinerator.

Winter felt so done—done with trying to figure it out.

She pressed the touchscreen and held out her hand to catch the soap as it fell from the materials dispenser, then slid her finger up the screen to turn the temperature hotter. Steam filled the chamber and she drew deep cleansing breaths of the warm, moist heat.

The man's face flickered across her mind again. His wide eyes . . .

Had every single blighter she'd ever put down since initiation looked like them?

Winter jumped as the sound of his voice echoed in her mind.

"We don't need to kill each other."

. . . Had each of them been as scared?

She felt sick.

How could the Sovereign be wrong? He couldn't. If there was a mistake, it was with her. It was her own imagination that they were human, and her own dilution that they spoke her own language. It couldn't be anything else.

It was simply impossible.

After her shower, Winter made her way to the infirmary. Her emotions were somewhat settled by the hot shower, but still the fear that she had somehow carried the pathogen to her beloved community gripped the back corner of her mind.

The check was thorough and brief. Winter was baffled when, other than a few minor contusions, she received a clean report. She could scarcely form words when they discharged her only minutes after arriving.

Could she really be that blessed? Perhaps she was overthinking it, and her encounter, though brutal, was a testament to the Sovereign's power of protection against the Blight's evil?

Passing by the beds of Purifiers who had not been so blessed, Winter took a moment to greet and comfort the conscious ones before noticing the hour. Tonight was the night of Eagle Eye's Ascension, and the time was fast approaching to begin preparations for the celebrated, momentous event.

The streets outside were filled with people coming and going; most of them congratulated her as she passed by. Scoreboards all over the city displayed her name and personnel picture, hailing her as the top achiever of the day's surface engagement. Winter felt dirty even though she had just showered, guilty even though she had only done her job well. She felt traitorous for thinking that there could be a fault in the Sovereign's system.

The quiet ride up to her level brought only heaviness as she walked to her living chambers, her mind laden with doubt.

As she retrieved her dress greens from the closet and laid them out on her bed, Winter studied the dozens of ornaments of distinction that decorated her austere jacket. A large medal for highest achieving cadet of her class hung on the right breast, right above the gold marksmanship and the ruby hand combative achievement awards. Seven black stripes adorned the left shoulder—one for every long-term deployment tour in which she'd participated. The medal she was most proud of hung beneath her name and rank display. Winter was only the second Purifier in history to receive special commendation after her trials down in Tartarus; Nereza Vossen had been the first. A variety of smaller awards earned during her time at the FMQ clustered near her row of kill patches. She remembered every day she had achieved a new one. The ten-kill patch, the twenty-five-kill patch, fifty . . . one-hundred . . . *two*-hundred . . .

Winter's knees buckled suddenly, and she collapsed to the floor. She gasped as the gravity of the lives she'd taken crushed her down, and the tears came again. She hadn't cried this much since her trial days. But she wasn't a little girl anymore; this was maddening. She tried to force them to stop, but the hot tears trickled down her cheeks. She examined herself from within, attempting to put a handle on her emotions.

Why couldn't she stop seeing his face?

The fact of the matter was that somehow, she had escaped a truly awful death. She had breathed the air of the surface, been covered in the blood of the blighted, and somehow remained unaffected herself.

Either she was gifted with immunity as yet unknown to Olympus, or . . .

Was it all a lie?

She sighed and closed her eyes. She didn't dare think what came to her mind next. It was too much . . . no, she couldn't think that.

Winter stood and changed quickly. She obviously had too much time to think.

She looked at herself in the full-length mirror near her bed, picking off a tiny piece of lint from her shoulder and smoothing down the folds of her pristine uniform. She had never before been at a loss for her sense of identity. She had never been unsure about anything in her life, and she had never felt uncomfortable with her vocation. But here, looking at herself in full dress uniform, adorned with all her achievements, wearing the fiery red beret of her Archangels team, Winter felt so out of place.

A soft bell signaled from the door, announcing a visitor.

"Enter," Winter called.

Nalara entered quickly and smiled to see her friend.

Winter was unable to respond to the smile. She looked over Nalara's uniform and only saw slightly scuffed shoes and a careless wrinkling in the shoulders from being hung improperly. She set her jaw and held back her criticism. Any other day, she would have sent an initiate back to her bunk to try again and not show her face until the proud uniform of their team was presented perfectly, but at this moment, her heart just wasn't in it.

"So, are you feeling better?" Nalara asked. "How's your head?"

"It's fine," Winter said. "Head injuries just bleed a lot, even when it's nothing big."

"I'm glad you're okay." Nalara pursed her lips. "Did you want to talk now?"

It was a good question. Did she want to talk? Nalara had always been a trusted confidant, but was this something Winter wanted to share?

Winter raised her chin. "I saw the face of the enemy today," she spoke honestly but without disclosing the truth.

Nalara looked surprised and disgusted. "Really? Was it bad?"

"Yes . . . it was," Winter nodded, again feeling guilt—again seeing his face. "It was horrifying. It . . . changed me, I think."

"I'm so sorry." Her friend batted her sympathetic brown eyes.

The pity was enough to kick Winter out of her slump. It was repulsive, no matter from whom it came.

"But that's why we fight." Winter straightened herself and her collar to perfection. "That's why we exist." She reflexively raised her right hand and formed a fist, limply, the conviction of her high calling drained from her for the first time in her life.

"Don't worry," Nalara beamed. "You're the strongest person I know. And even though you might have been shaken today, tonight will make up for it. You get to stand in the presence of our Sovereign in a little while." Her voiced filled with soft awe. "His gaze will purify—that's what we're taught, right? He'll see whatever's wrong and make you strong again."

Winter felt a cold lump form in her stomach, and her hands became clammy.

His gaze will purify.

The blood drained from her face, and she struggled to swallow the lump that had risen in her throat. She suddenly felt dizzy.

"Oh!" Winter stammered, desperate to hide her horrified surprise. "I . . . I'd forgotten, I guess."

"You forgot?" Nalara was genuinely puzzled. "That's what you told me. Remember? On the surface? The Sovereign's Eye purifies all?"

"Yes. Yes, of course," Winter returned quietly, seeing the fire of the Eye of Zeus in her mind and feeling the heat of the flames on her skin. She felt both cold and hot all over. "I remember."

"You weren't a member of the top twenty the last time there was an Ascension." Nalara smiled. "I'm so excited for you!"

"Right."

"You get to stand with our Sovereign and the Grand Elite during the ceremony. You get to witness Captain Zinda's Ascension in person," Nalara said with more than a hint of jealousy. "I'd give anything."

Winter struggled to maintain her composure as she fought to mask a cold panic, the likes of which she was completely unfamiliar with.

If only Nalara knew.

"Don't worry," Winter eventually said, her voice bereft of its usual confidence. "You'll get there someday."

Chime, Chime

The intercom signaled.

Winter and Nalara fell to their knees in a simultaneous show of devotion as the wall faded to transparency.

The projected face of the Sovereign looked at her from the side of the golden tower, and Winter felt the fear of destruction clutch the core of her soul.

The pledge she had spoken twice daily since she was a child suddenly became an earnest plea for mercy.

Hail to his supreme holiness.

Hail to our Sovereign ruler.
Hail to our living god.
Your name is a light to our path.
Your wisdom guides us through darkness and death.
Your power governs the whole earth.
It is to you and you alone, o gracious lord, that I swear my life, my loyalty,
and my unconditional obedience.
I swear to live for you.
I swear to die for you.
Live forever, o glorious king—for in you, we are granted life.

The intercom chimed again, the visage disappeared, and the wall became solid once more.

Nalara stood.

Winter did not.

"Is something wrong?" Nalara asked, confused when she noticed Winter shaking on her knees.

Winter didn't respond. She was absolutely terrified. Now more than ever, she wished she'd had the strength to purify herself on the surface. Now she would have to face her Sovereign, blighted and shamed. He wouldn't see her as a faithful servant who had given her life to his service, who had given her best effort every single day. He would see a traitor who broke the rules of combat and carried home the wretched disease that killed their race.

Before all of Olympus, the Sovereign would see nothing but a failure of a Purifier.

He would *see* her . . .

CHAPTER SIXTEEN

Winter and Nalara joined the throng of citizens wending their way to the Hive. So many of them wanted to shake Winter's hand and thank her for the amazing feat of combat that morning. Some were thankful for her contribution to the cause of Olympus, but most had made out well on betting allotments.

Everyone was wearing their finest attire, walking together in smiling, excited clusters. Ascension was a rare and joyous occasion. After fifteen years of active service, when a Purifier reaches the age of thirty, he or she is given the highest honor by the Sovereign himself. Of all the thousands of Purifiers that had come and gone over the past century, only seventeen had achieved Ascension. Derrick 'Eagle Eyes' Zinda would be the eighteenth, and all of Olympus would gather to witness and celebrate.

Winter and Nalara passed through the giant arched entrance, joining concourses of people making their way up the expansive steps to the stadium seats. The crowd pressed hard, and the noise was overwhelming. Eventually, they arrived at the Purifiers' seating level. The Hive was filling quickly with citizens from every tier of Olympus.

The teachers and caregivers, the engineers, scientists, and doctors all sat on one side of the top row. The technology and communication technicians sat with the pilots and mechanics around the middle section. The entertainers, the cooks, and the servants for the Elite all sat near the crowning section exclusive to the residents of the First Tier. The core workers, janitors, and waste management all had their own entrance down at the base of the stadium near the Hive floor. They had no seating but stood, barely able to peek over the edge. Their area was cordoned off as well, not because of special status like the Elite, but because none of them should ever associate with the more important citizens.

Guardians stood as imposing sentinels throughout every level of the Hive, with Unifiers stationed at their hip in silent, scrutinizing observation.

Nalara found an open seat and took a moment to observe her surroundings.

"So exciting!" she nearly squealed.

Winter smiled. She remembered when she was an initiate. So immense, so many people. Being out of the FMQ can be overwhelming for some cadets, but Nalara was just happy about everything.

"Look—look!" She pointed.

Winter followed Nalara's outstretched finger to the Elite stand.

"It's the Grand Elite!" Nalara breathed. "I still can't believe he spoke with us at the party."

The striking man looked regal and imposing in his breathtaking silk robes. His dark hair just barely showed flecks of gray, and his focused eyes always looked like they were targeting something. He was currently shaking hands and conversing casually with all the Elite he passed by.

"Yeah, that's him." Winter nodded.

"Wow, he's just so handsome," Nalara sighed.

Winter chuckled but didn't disagree.

"What do you think it's like to be the right hand of the Sovereign?" Nalara asked. "He would see every thought and every flaw. I don't think I could do it."

"That's one thing you never have to worry about doing," Winter said and grabbed her friend's shoulder, shouting to be heard above the din of people finding their seats. It was difficult to grasp the depth of sadness that stung her heart as she wordlessly said goodbye to her long-time friend. "Promise me you'll . . ." she swallowed back the emotional plea and struggled to keep a stern expression. "Promise me you'll go straight back to your chambers after . . ." She shook her head, determined to mask her emotions. "After the ceremony."

"What? I don't get to go to the after-party!?" Nalara protested.

"I . . . I just want you to skip this one," Winter instructed, holding back the tears that wanted to surface. She knew it was hopeless; soon, all Olympus would know her terrible, sickening secret. Soon, they would all see the ugly truth of her failure.

"These celebrations . . . they can get out of hand," she said at length, desperate for any excuse to keep her friend from witnessing that ugliness.

Nalara looked disappointed.

Winter scooped her friend into a tight hug. "There will be more of them for you later, but you're fresh out of the FMQ. I don't want you getting hurt or in trouble. Besides, for now, you need all your strength for training."

"Alright," Nalara relented with a sigh. "Have fun."

Winter forced a bright smile and took her leave, jostling her way through the sea of shoulders. Every step shook her facade further and further from her ability to maintain it. She worked slowly back down the steps to the lower level, where two Guardians stood watching the door that led to the under stage. The large open room was populated with the nineteen other Purifiers that held the highest scores in Olympus, and the one Purifier who would soon take the space left open by Eagle Eyes' Ascension.

Derrick stood a little way off from the rest, fussing over the buttons down the front of his perfect uniform. If anyone could shed some light of clarity on her tempestuous confusion and dread, it was her beloved trainer.

Winter cut a straight line to him. He smiled distractedly as she approached.

"Can't get them to sit right," he grumbled and brushed his hand down the length of his jacket.

Winter timidly offered forth her hands. He nodded in frustration and stood still as she smoothed the center seam. Attention to detail was simply a facet of her personality, but he was the one who'd taught her to pursue perfection.

Eagle Eyes looked her over. "You good?" he asked, a twitch of concern in his eyes.

Winter nodded halfheartedly, feeling nothing but emptiness inside. She withdrew her touch after setting the stubborn seam straight.

"Gave me a big scare today," he reminded.

Winter shook her head. "I just saw a better way."

"Yeah, I know." He paused, admiring for a moment the student who had exceeded every expectation . . . the one who actually pushed and inspired him to excellence.

"And now Wraith is taking your place as Master Purifier . . ." Winter looked over across the room where her captain stood in austere silence. "He's never going to let up."

"Don't worry about him," Derrick said. "Hey, look at me."

Winter complied.

"The only reason he stomps on you is to keep you down. You *are* what he wishes he could be."

She almost rolled her eyes but checked her incredulity before it manifested.

"I'm serious." Derrick lowered his voice and leaned closer.

Winter held her breath and tried to give her full and absolute attention to him.

"Remember what I told you the other night: when you put yourself out there, you make yourself a target for their hate. Wraith is only *one* example of the many you'll have to deal with. Remember, though, he's only got two years left as a Purifier, and he's going to be Master Purifier *only by default*. Now that he's finally on top, he's afraid you're going to overtake him—to knock him off his throne, as it were." Derrick held her gaze in silence for a moment with his intense eyes. "Do it." He smiled broadly, invigorating her with his enthusiasm.

Winter couldn't help but smile back.

Derrick broke into a laugh. "You're going to go even further than me, kid."

Winter didn't know how to respond. His faith in her . . . voicing her inner dream and challenging her to new heights was all she had ever wanted. Unfortunately, at this moment, she didn't even know if she would live through the day. She was so broken inside, she didn't know how to tell him.

"Captain Zinda . . ." she ventured.

His title and the tone of her voice caught him off guard, and he looked up from adjusting his cuffs once more.

"Have you ever seen a blighted?" Winter swallowed nervously, not knowing where she expected this conversation to go. She desperately wished for some relief—some kind of comfort. She felt like she was burning up inside. All the guilt, all the confusion, all the fear of what might happen tonight—it gnawed at her and racked her body with indescribable, intangible pain.

"Sure," he shrugged. "Of course, I have."

He must not have understood. "No," Winter elaborated, "I mean . . . *seen* one—you know, the way they look . . . underneath."

Derrick's visage shifted to serious and grim. He nodded slowly.

"Really?" Winter couldn't believe it.

"It's not something you forget," he said in a low tone. "It changed me."

Winter almost breathed a sigh of relief. Finally, someone who understood. Maybe he could make sense of everything at last.

"Those mangled faces, the misshapen limbs." His face contorted. "The boils . . . the fangs . . ." He cringed. "It was haunting. Still is."

Winter's gut wrenched inside. "Wait, what? Where did you see them?"

Derrick was surprised at her response.

"I mean, you actually *saw* them for yourself?" she rephrased in a more controlled tone.

"Sure, anyone can."

Winter gaped in confusion.

"You should check them out at the Archives," he explained. "Just ask for the files."

Winter breathed, trying to convince her body she was still able to. Her chest felt tight, and her head was foggy. It seemed like there was no air.

They stood together, visions locked for what felt like eternity. He had given his entire life in service of the purifying cause, achieved more killshots than any other in his generation . . . and at this moment, Winter didn't know if she should be proud of the man for his years of honorable service, or mourning for the man who never knew the truth.

Derrick leaned in and, casting an inspective glance around the room, spoke in a low whisper. "Is that what happened to you down there? Did you . . . see one?"

Winter felt a surge of emotion flood behind her eyes, an already cracked dam threatening to burst wide open at any moment. Holding back the cascade of tears, she managed a singular nod. "More than one," she breathed, seeing their dead and terrified, *terrifying* faces all over again. She winced at the memory.

"Oh, January . . ." Derrick whispered as he placed a comforting hand on his student's shoulder.

Winter was caught off guard. She couldn't remember the last time her mentor had addressed her by her real name. She felt the crack in the dam split wider.

"I'm so sorry." He shook his head. "That must have been horrible for you."

She nodded in earnest. "Yes. It was." She desperately wanted to tell him. Her hands shook. "And . . . there was . . ." She opened her mouth and fought for the words, but she couldn't force them to come. Her head fell in defeat.

Derrick gave her shoulder a consoling squeeze. "Hey, listen. This will—"

"Heads up!" Kaz 'Warlord' Warren called from near the main group, cutting him short.

"Showtime!" Nia 'Scarlet' Azlin rejoiced.

Twenty-one hexagonal tiles lowered from the ceiling in a single straight row. The opening let loose a spillway of fanatic cheers from the boisterous crowd, and the quiet chamber filled with the din of excitement.

"This will pass," Eagle Eyes continued, lifting her gaze with a finger gently guiding her chin. "You'll see. With just a little time, I guarantee you'll beat this. You're my greatest student, Winter. Something like this—it's not going to beat you. You're far too strong for that. Just remember my training and I know you'll rise above it."

He winked with a warm smile and squeezed her shoulder one last time before he moved to walk away.

"Derrick," Winter spoke suddenly.

He looked back at her inquisitively.

"Did you ever wonder . . ." She swallowed. "If what we do is right?"

He didn't break pace, but his eyebrows lowered in thought. He didn't get a chance to answer as he was swept away by his excited comrades.

Each Purifier occupying a single tile, they took their places in the line together.

Winter exhaled. She was more conflicted than ever. As she slowly fell into formation, thirteenth from the lead, she looked down to see her mentor's stoic face and intense eyes focused straight ahead, standing at perfect attention.

The platform rose, bearing the Purifiers up and into the heart of the stadium where thunderous applause greeted them as the crowd clapped their hands and cheered the Purifiers' names.

Winter had never been on the floor for an Ascension before. Bouts were different. When she competed in a tournament, she had a mission, and her tunnel-vision focus kicked in. The crowd, vastly reduced in size, cheered for her during her fights and didn't distract her. But at this moment, all the eyes of Olympus were trained on her as she stood at attention with her comrades. She had no task to perform but to stand and be admired—and it wracked her nerves.

The Second Tier citizens all cheered and clapped while the sequestered people of the Third Tier whooped and jumped around. In stark contrast, the elegant Elite smiled their dazzling smiles and clapped politely.

Once the Purifiers were raised up from the under stage, the Grand Elite made his entrance onto the Hive floor from the Elite seating.

The tall, handsome man raised his hands in greeting as the crowd's applause grew to a roar when he appeared. The hexagonal platform on which he stood rose higher than the heads of the Purifiers, and he goaded the cheering crowd with his smiles and his waving.

He touched the communicator in his ear and spoke, his charismatic voice booming throughout the stadium. "Welcome blessed, honored Elite." The throng cheered. "Welcome citizens of Olympus." He reveled in the praise for a moment, then lifted his hands and paused until the cheering subsided. "We gather today as subjects of our mighty Sovereign. All hail to his great name—Antiochus Ignatius Theodosius Zeus!"

The boisterous crowd became chaotic at the full name of their Sovereign.

Draven ran his fingers across the small touchscreen in his hand, taking advantage of the crowd's fanaticism to rearrange the face of the Hive. Various hexagonal pillars raised or lowered to create a walkway in front of the Purifiers.

Winter stood in silent decorum with her comrades. She attempted to keep her mind in the present, though her misgivings about the surface engagement were inevitably in the forefront at all times. She tried over and over to tell herself that there was no way a pathogen could have made it past both the shuttle scanner and the medical examination. Nonetheless, she knew what she had seen and experienced, and the nagging fear and guilt ran rampant through her heart and mind.

When the audience eventually calmed down, the Grand Elite continued. "Our finest Purifiers stand before you today. We owe them our gratitude and much honor. As divinely appointed to do so, the Purifiers cleanse our ancestral home world. They place the future of Olympus above their very lives." He fell silent.

Draven's captivating voice boomed through the stadium as he introduced each Purifier by their name and callsign. "May I present to you our Master Purifier, rank number one from the Grim Reapers—the valiant soldier, courageous warrior, and soon-to-be glorified Ascended whom we delight to honor here tonight: Captain Derrick 'Eagle Eyes' Zinda!"

Winter shifted her eyes, without losing posture, to see her mentor smile with poise and dignity as the stadium echoed his praise.

Clamorous applause followed each name as it was called, and one by one, the platforms on which they stood rose to the same level as the Grand Elite.

"And rank number two from the Archangels—our new Master Purifier: Captain Orrin 'Wraith' Priest."

Captain Priest nodded with a stone face to his cheering public.

"Rank number three from the Hellhounds: Captain Kaz 'Warlord' Warren."

Kaz waved his hand politely.

"Rank number four from the Dragon Slayers: Captain Slade 'Specter' Sephiras."

Slade raised his fists in victory.

"Rank number five from the Black Ghosts: Captain Bobby 'Titan' Hayer."

Bobby nodded and smiled.

"Rank number six from the Iron Raiders: Captain Darren 'Judge' Hannon."

Darren made no motion but accepted the applause with a scowl.

"Rank number seven from the Grim Reapers: Lieutenant Lilith 'Razor' Sharpe."

Lilith smiled broadly and drew a finger across her neck before waving at the people all around her.

"Rank number eight from the Hellhounds: Lieutenant Kurtis 'Hotshot' Hollins."

Kurtis shot finger pistols at the audience and laughed.

"Rank number nine from the Shadow Lords: Captain Victor 'Vicious' Aldren."

Victor raised a fist and shouted, "Yeah!"

"Rank number ten from the Broadswords: Captain Carmella 'Gorgon' Gleason."

Carmella smiled and waved.

"Rank number eleven from the Dragon Slayers: Lieutenant Hector 'Hitman' Rowland."

Hector held his hands behind his back, nodding and smiling.

"Rank number twelve from the War Wolves: Captain Lev 'Boom' Sellers."

Lev howled, joined by the rest of his team in the stands.

"Rank number thirteen from the Archangels: Lieutenant January 'Winter' Winterton."

Winter raised her chin and breathed through the introduction. She glanced around at the stadium full of wildly cheering spectators and realized that she had been one of them not too long ago. She had clapped and screamed just like they did now.

"Rank number fourteen from the Black Ghosts: Lieutenant Sabin 'Raven' Pember."

Sabin waved with a wide grin.

"Rank number fifteen from the Hellhounds: Dorian 'Chaos' Valker."

Dorian clapped with the crowd.

"Rank number sixteen from the Knight Hawks: Captain Nia 'Scarlet' Azlin."

Nia pointed at her team and gave a shout.

"Rank number seventeen from the Broadswords: Lieutenant Samuel 'Sentinel' Wilde."

One of the youngest in the top twenty, Samuel simply smiled, showing off his dimples.

"Rank number eighteen from the Grim Reapers: Damien 'Checkmate' Reznick."

Damien saluted the crowd and stood at attention.

"Rank number nineteen from the Shadow Lords: Lieutenant Morgan 'Midnight' Rowe."

Morgan stood still and stared down the crowd with a thinly veiled smirk.

"Rank number twenty from the War Wolves: Lieutenant Kenna 'Scarecrow' Crew."

Kenna shook her head and chuckled as her team, including her captain, all howled in unison.

"And soon to be joining the top-ranked Purifiers, we introduce tonight from the Iron Raiders: Lieutenant Pierce 'Paladin' Latham!"

The young man smiled and waved, unsure and unprepared for such an honor.

Draven fell silent and the crowd settled quickly.

The Grand Elite spoke once more, his robust voice flooding from the loudspeakers. "The Purifiers are the hand of Zeus, and with his power, they work every day to sweep the surface clean of the unholy blighted. From the time a Purifier is formulated, they are trained and molded to be the Sovereign's executioners—the most effective, the most deadly. No monster can stand before them as they carry out the will of our great creator!" Wild cheering broke out again. "And when a Purifier has completed his mission, when he has given his all for fifteen long years of service and reached the end . . . alive . . ." His voice fell into reverence. "He is given what all lower citizens dream of. He is gifted with *Ascension*. He is raised from his lowly mortal state to become an Elite in the life to come."

Reverence fell over the crowd as the Elite clapped politely.

"As you well know," he continued, "for those of the third-tier in this world, if they are found worthy, they are allowed to remain third-tier in Elysium. Those who are first-tier, our chosen and blessed Elite, remain first-tier forever. Those who are second-tier, likewise only if they are found worthy of Elysium, remain second . . . except . . . those few, extraordinary Purifiers who reach the Age of Ascension—who, through their countless sacrifices and great many bloody struggles, have earned the singular honor to ascend from second to first."

Gesturing with a hand to the seventeen giant marble statues that ringed the top level of the Hive, the Grand Elite continued, "Only a handful of Purifiers have achieved this magnificent honor since the beginning. Only the choice, rare few can survive the horrors of the surface for so many long years. Only the finest can outlive the bloodthirsty hordes of mutant blighted. For these few—for their bravery, for their sacrifice, for their unwavering devotion to our Sovereign, they are immortalized."

Winter glanced up at the statues of the Ascended. She saw her idol, Nereza Vossen. It was almost like she was looking down at her, saying goodbye. Winter hurt inside at the thought that she would never ascend to be with her. She would never meet her hero in Elysium. She would never see Eagle Eyes again, because she knew she would not live past this day.

The moment was coming.

Brilliant light suddenly streamed down from the domed ceiling above the Hive, and the crowd hushed instantly.

The stark quiet was broken only by a subtle hydraulic hiss that issued from the very pinnacle of the dome, and utter silence ensued as a single hexagonal disc slowly lowered from its place, beginning the descent of the Sovereign from his throne within the crowning tower of the Elite tier above to the thronging masses below.

With agonizing slowness, the hexagon descended, drawing out the desperate expectancy of the crowd. Every neck craned and every eye strained to catch the first glimpse of their holy god. When the hexagonal disc finally dropped low enough for the Sovereign to come into view, the crowd lost all control. Even the Elite dropped their pretense and began screaming and clapping and waving their arms. Winter and her comrades stood at attention and waited as the platform lowered to their level. The uproar was so deafening that Winter cringed at the noise. It physically hurt as the echoes throughout the stadium split her ears.

Finally, the plate descended far enough that Winter could see the Sovereign for herself. Her heart leapt and her stomach twisted as both a thrill and a chill ran through her body. Once before, she had attended an Ascension ceremony and witnessed his presence from the stands, but here . . . he was right in front of her.

This was it.

CHAPTER SEVENTEEN

Death.

It seemed so familiar now. This feeling of utter terror—still and helpless. Winter's heart beat faster than she could believe. The fear, not only of death, but of something much worse chilled her blood. Her Sovereign, her creator, stood not fifty paces off. He walked down the line of Purifiers, congratulating and greeting them in turn. Each took his hand and kneeled in thanks.

The audience was completely silent. Every soul in attendance was awestruck with the sight of their living god right before their eyes—each wishing they were blessed to live as a Purifier; the only class given the opportunity to ascend from one tier to the next. They were the only class allowed to interact with the Elite and attend their functions. The Purifiers were truly a favored vocation—the chosen class—the ones who could stand before their god and touch him with their own two hands.

Winter felt sick. With every step her god took, it brought him closer to her as he made his way up the line. She could almost feel his purifying gaze already. Her stomach felt hard and hollow at the same time.

Her head fell as the Sovereign greeted Raven beside her. Raven fell to his knees, grasping the Sovereign's hand in tender reverence.

Their god's voice was soft and dignified. "Congratulations on your advancement," he spoke, sending thrills through the veins of all who could hear. "Olympus smiles upon you. You have made me very proud."

"My life is yours, great lord," Raven spoke in deep adoration.

Winter couldn't breathe. Beads of perspiration gathered on her hairline. Her hands were cold and clammy. Her mouth was dry, and her lips trembled as she faced her death. As her head hung, she watched the Sovereign's gold and diamond encrusted shoes come to stand before her.

She gasped.

This was it!

Her face was so hot that she could almost feel the purifying flames consuming her.

Winter fell to her knees and closed her eyes. She could feel his gaze upon her and cringed as she anticipated the power of her Sovereign washing over her, purging her unclean, marred self from existence.

She breathed her last breath . . .

. . . and waited to die . . .

"Congratulations on your advancement," the Sovereign repeated. "Olympus smiles upon you. You have made me very proud."

Winter opened her eyes in surprise and looked up. For the first time in her life, she studied his face—not just to admire and idolize, but to really *see* him.

The elderly man who looked down extended his hand for her to take. His face showed some deep wrinkles, and his eyes were gray. His white hair and beard had only flecks of black remaining. The hand he held outstretched showed age spots and was crossed by a web of blue veins. Each finger was adorned with gold rings crowned with glittering gemstones.

Winter locked her eyes with his, expecting to see within their depths the evidence of his omniscient sovereignty. However, she saw no enlightenment, no penetrating perception, and no judgment—nothing at all but passive, emotionless, distant observance.

She slowly took his hand . . . his cold, mortal hand—which held a pulse—and kissed it gently.

"Th-thank you, my lord Z-Zeus," she stammered.

The Sovereign moved on indifferently, congratulating Boom in identical kind beside her.

Winter steadily rose to her feet, jaw slack. All the stress and terror that had consumed her all afternoon suddenly melted away and was replaced by astonished disbelief.

"He . . . he didn't see me," she whispered to herself as her limbs went cold.

"January Winterton." The voice of Draven Constantine Rothgard, the Grand Elite, drew her from her thoughts. He had followed closely behind the Sovereign, adjusting the ranks of the Purifiers, and now he stood expectantly before her.

Winter couldn't hide the bewilderment in her eyes.

Draven's piercing gaze locked on to hers, and his brows furrowed, but he continued with the ceremonial rank adjustment. "Congratulations on your advancement." He changed the rank displayed on her uniform. "You are now ranked number twelve. May Olympus continue to smile upon you."

Winter bowed in silence, unable to speak. Her voice was struck from her; she was so astonished at her realization.

While the Sovereign and his Grand Elite made their way down the line, congratulating and adjusting ranks, Winter watched in quiet astonishment.

It was a lie.

How could he be a god? This man . . . was mortal.

She had witnessed for herself that he could neither see nor purify the supposed Blight that she carried. She felt for herself the pulse in his cold hands. If he had been an omniscient god, he would have seen.

There was no way he couldn't have seen!

"This Purifier," the Sovereign's voice came over the loudspeaker; he stood at the end of the line with one hand upon Derrick Zinda's shoulder, "has achieved what only the chosen few can. He has reached the Age of Ascension and gained favor in my eyes. As he ascends to become one of the Elite, we celebrate his life and his sacrifice. Rising to immortality, my son . . ." he spoke directly to Derrick, "you have made me very proud."

The Sovereign turned and walked to the platform where Draven raised a plate to stand a meter above the rest. Derrick followed them up to the pedestal and stood calmly behind it as Draven pulled another tile up from the floor. Upon it rested the holy blade called 'Ascension.'

The crowd cheered wildly at the sight of the divine blade. Forged in Elysium by the Sovereign himself, the magnificent single-edged sword was curved, gilded, with a crimson grip, and studded with fourteen precious gemstones, seven on either side: a pink ruby, a green emerald, a red garnet, a blue sapphire, a yellow topaz, a black onyx, and a white diamond.

Winter had never seen it so close before, only in digital displays during lessons at the FMQ, from a distance during the last Ascension, and, of course . . .

She glanced down at the Purifier mark on the back of her right hand—the blade wreathed in a ribbon of purging flame—the chosen symbol of the Purifier class, the symbol which embodied and inspired all of her vocation. Ascension was the material representation of who she was created to be, who she driven and trained to be, who she could ever hope and aspire to be.

It represented the pinnacle of Purifier achievement and potential, and up close, seeing the real blade, it was truly breathtaking.

The raucous clamor of the wild crowd drowned everything out. Winter's ears hurt, but her focus was on the pedestal where Derrick knelt and lay his head. His eyes were passive, his posture relaxed.

Taking up Ascension, the Sovereign raised it high for the chaotic crowd to see.

Winter couldn't breathe.

The masses cheered and screamed in exultant jubilation as the Sovereign held the blade over his head and approached Derrick.

Winter's mentor for the past four years knelt calmly, his face turned away from the crowd. He didn't look at Winter; he didn't know she was watching in horror.

His sharp, eagle-like eyes closed gently.

"Ascend, Derrick Zinda!" the Sovereign cried out. "Ascend as an Elite!"

With great speed and force, the Sovereign swung the sword, severing Derrick's head from his shoulders with one strong, clean stroke. It hit the Hive floor, bounced once, and rolled to a stop.

Eagle Eyes stared blankly into empty space.

The audience went wild.

On stage, the Purifiers jumped up and down and hugged each other, cheering and clapping. Their pride and joy for their comrade was palpable.

Winter watched in silence, her eyes wide in stunned disbelief. She had known all her life that this was the path to Ascension—the very destination she had desired and fought and sacrificed to achieve with her every breath. *This* was what she had always wanted for herself.

Inside, the dam broke. Tears rushed to fill her eyes and ran hot down her cheeks.

The Sovereign plucked up the severed head from the platform and held it up for the whole crowd to see. Blood dribbled from the head and splashed off the hem of his white robes before pooling on the tiles below.

During the last Ascension ceremony, Winter had been one of the screaming fanatics in the stands. She had celebrated the passing of the last Purifier from mortality into the next life of Elitehood. She remembered the conviction with which she had believed that he had taken his place as one of the blessed Elite on the other side. She remembered watching the same ceremony in rapture and joviality as his blood spilled across this very stage.

But now, seeing with new eyes, horror gripped her frame. Horror and regret.

The Grand Elite touched his controller to bring up a sizable slab of hexagonal tiles, bearing from below three large vats; one filled with actively boiling acid, one filled with molten gold, and the other waiting and empty. With the vats stood a handful of attendants, waiting with their eyes to the ground and their hands folded before them.

The Sovereign dropped the disembodied head into the boiling liquid. It disappeared into the effervescent, hissing acid. The smaller, empty vat, he placed under the gushing neck and caught the spilling red blood as it slowly issued forth. As the vat steadily filled, Draven toggled the commands so that a large section of floor gave way for a twelve-foot statue to rise slowly from the floor. It only came up high enough to be eye-to-eye with the Sovereign.

Blurred by the tears, Winter could see Derrick's face 'immortalized' in stone; his left hand outstretched before him like all the other Ascended, his right hand placed dutifully over his stone heart in a silent, never-ending salute.

A nearby attendant handed the Grand Elite a pair of large tongs. Reaching into the vat, he used the tongs to fish through the boiling acid to retrieve the late Derrick Zinda's now pristine skull. The white bone glinted under the bright lights of the stadium as Draven handed the tongs to their Sovereign.

The living god dipped the skull into the molten gold and spoke as the hot metal encompassed the remains and drenched very crevice with the liquid sunset metal.

"Arise forth, my son," he bade tenderly. "Live again in my sight as an immortal Elite in the realm of Elysium." He lifted the golden skull and turned it several times until the gold ceased dripping, then set it upon the statue's open palm.

He handed the tongs off to the bowing attendant and lifted his arms high and wide. "Go now to join all the Ascended!" He gestured grandly to the seventeen statues crowning the top terrace of the Hive. "Welcome him, honored Elite Purifiers! Live forever in my sight!"

The Grand Elite raised the statue to its full height. At the bottom was a plaque beneath the feet. Draven retrieved the vat of Derrick's blood and poured it carefully into a small port on the top of the plaque. As the blood emptied into the opening, crimson words appeared on the plaque that read:

THE GREAT LEADER DERRICK 'EAGLE EYES' ZINDA

His diligence and perseverance brought him to lead the most successful team of his generation. Attaining the Age of Ascension while holding the first rank of the order was merely the crowning achievement of many in his lifetime. His example of excellence will live on forever.

The Sovereign walked back to the center tile of the stadium, and suddenly, the entire audience fell silently to their knees.

Winter followed reflexively, but as the voices of thousands of citizens and Elite lifted their vow of loyalty to the Sovereign, Winter found herself unable to join in. She simply couldn't bring herself to utter the words.

Hail to his supreme holiness.
Hail to our Sovereign ruler.
Hail to our living god.

Winter tried to speak anew with every phrase, but her voice failed her. Her lips refused to move. Every day of her life, she had repeated this prayer once in the morning and once at night—every single day throughout training, through long-term deployments, and through stays at the infirmary—but for the first time, now, Winter simply listened to the words.

Your name is a light to our path.
Your wisdom guides us through darkness and death.
Your power governs the whole earth.

She listened with a stillness in her soul that allowed her to hear the words and feel the meaning under a new light. She listened with an understanding that there was nothing immortal about their Sovereign at all.

It is to you and you alone, o gracious lord, that I swear my life, my loyalty, and my unconditional obedience.

She listened with a mind open to the possibility that this was simply a man who had power only because these people believed in his lie.

I swear to live for you.
I swear to die for you.

She listened with a heart broken for all the lives she had taken in his name . . . and for all her fellow Purifiers who had given their lives for his conquest.

Live forever, o glorious king—for in you, we are granted life.

As the prayer ended, the Sovereign's disc slowly began to rise. The whole of Olympus—third-tier citizens, second, and first alike—were on their feet, wildly waving their arms and crying out, as if begging their god to remain with them for only one sweet moment longer. The Sovereign continued his ascent towards the massive domed ceiling, where he disappeared once again.

"Blessed Elite," Draven's voice boomed out across the Hive once the Sovereign had gone. "Citizens of Olympus. Let the celebration . . . BEGIN!"

With a resounding cheer, the audience began to spill out of the Hive and into the streets.

The Grand Elite took a long last look at the Purifiers on stage before making his exit.

Sanitation workers approached the platform. Some began cleaning up all the blood, while others pulled the headless corpse into a sealing bag.

All of the Purifiers began to make their way to the exit, talking excitedly among themselves; but Winter couldn't contain her curiosity. She approached the sanitation workers and addressed them—directly.

"Where do you take the body?" she asked, hands shaking with a mixture of rage and disgust.

The sanitation workers all looked away, refusing to make eye contact. A few of them stepped backward in fearful respect.

"Answer me!" she commanded.

One of them bowed almost completely in half and spoke softly. "R-Reclamation, honored and r-revered Madam P-Purifier. The body goes to Reclamation. P-please forgive me."

Winter ignored his stuttered plea and moved on without another word. Her burning hunger for answers had made her irritable and impatient; her inner conflict and confusion had melded into an overwhelming sadness that felt like a veritable weight around her neck.

She wearily climbed the steps where the entrance to the highest level was left open. Standing up there with the silent statues of the Ascended, she could view the entire middle tier of Olympus. The sea of color and music and movement down below sat as a noxious vision deep in Winter's stomach. Entertainers were scattered about everywhere, playing lively music and dancing in mesmerizing choreography. The cooks and servers were all out in full force, delivering delicacies and drinks to the Elite and any lower tier citizens who could afford the indulgences. She spotted a few members of her team, laughing and reveling together near a fountain in one corner of the square.

Winter turned away from the edge and walked to her hero—'the Nightmare.'

Tears in her eyes, she lifted her voice to the stone face. "It wasn't supposed to be like this." She gulped, scarcely able to hold the flood of sadness at bay. "How can anything be real now? How can I exist?" Winter shook her head. "You didn't die for Olympus' future—none of you did!" she shouted down the line of lifeless statues and let the tears fall. "You died for him," she sobbed softly, "and none of you even knew who he was." She sniffed, then flinched as the dead faces of the humans she'd killed on the surface flashed into her mind. "None of you even knew what you were doing."

A new thought suddenly entered her mind. She gave it a voice. "Or . . . maybe some of you did." She probed the thought further, deeper. "And maybe you didn't even care."

For a long moment, Winter cried softy in silence, letting her loneliness and emptiness swaddle her in its heavy clutches.

At length, four bulky Guardians broke her solitude as they lumbered slowly up the steps, bearing the statue of Derrick Zinda on their shoulders.

Winter dried her tears on her sleeve and watched them set the new statue in its place as the eighteenth Ascended, then straighten it to perfection. She remembered suddenly his exhortation to check the files at the Archive and see for herself the images of the blighted.

Something like hope pricked her heart, and she rallied at the thought of receiving some miraculous correction that would set her right. Perhaps Eagle Eyes, in his wisdom, was looking out for her even after his Ascension. Maybe she still couldn't see the whole picture like he could. It was possible that there, at the Archive, lay the answer that would allow her mind to rest back into life as she knew it.

There was no choice in the matter. She had to see for herself.

CHAPTER EIGHTEEN

The crowded streets were filled with smiling people and clamorous music; the chaos was heightened by the swirling dancers and the loud, rambunctious Elite—quite transformed from their austere, superior demeanor before the reveling began.

Winter worked her way through the throng as fast as she could, ignoring the frequent entreaties to linger and celebrate. She had a mission locked in her mind. She knew what she had seen on the surface, she simply had no context for it, and this lack of context was, no doubt, what had caused her to throw shadows on all that she was raised to believe. After all, what was more likely: that she had become the first person in the history of Olympus to stumble on a truth of this magnitude, or that her fears and doubts were rifled up somehow by a lack of all the facts? She had to believe deep in her heart that she would find the answers she needed to put her beliefs and truths back in place at the Archive like Eagle Eyes had said.

She eventually came to the Science and Technology Quarter, a place she had only visited a few times before. Here also, the dense crowd pressed tightly in their merrymaking. Winter actually recognized some faces of the technicians who had survived the treacherous jump that morning. They were so transformed in their drunken euphoria from the survival-bent countenances she knew that she almost didn't notice them.

The Archive was a small building near the base of the Biological Research and Development Lab. The doors hissed open to the sides, and Winter entered the dimly lit room filled with rows and rows of data storage. Behind a desk to the right of the entry sat a bored and sour-faced archivist.

Winter looked her over quickly, noticing her bitten nails and also her red, sagging eyes that testified to just waking from sleep.

"I don't have a bathroom for you to use," the woman snapped before Winter could say a word.

"I don't need one," Winter said in surprise. "Why aren't you in the city enjoying the Ascension festival?" she inquired with a cock of her head.

"What is your defect?" the archivist retorted crudely. "I'm working tonight, obviously. Some people are blessed by the Sovereign to be created as Purifiers that work once a week their whole lives and then get to become

Elite in the next. Others are made into archive slaves who sit alone in an empty warehouse day after miserable day until we *die.*"

Winter was shocked by her tone. She had never experienced a lower citizen talk to her in such a disrespectful manner. She glanced at the archivist's name badge, then leaned in closer and spoke gravely. "Archivist Kara—you *will* address me with respect, or would you like your superior to find out you were sleeping on your shift?"

The woman straightened in her chair and rubbed the blurriness from her eyes. She blinked, then gasped audibly. "Oh! Madam Purifier!" She gulped as her hands started to shake. "Forgive me, honored Purifier Winterton, I didn't recognize you! Please—a thousand, *thousand* apologies for my rudeness!" She bowed her head low to her desktop. "How may I be of service to you?"

Winter breathed out the tension, willing to let the matter drop now that she'd been appropriately addressed. She was too close to getting the answers she needed to concern herself with one ill-mannered, insignificant archivist.

"Give me the image files for the blighted," Winter ordered directly.

Kara's face contorted. She asked in tangible aversion, "Why would you want to look at those?"

"Quicker would be best," Winter deflected.

"Yes, yes, of course!" With a bow, Kara disappeared down a row. She rummaged for only a moment before returning with a file case in hand. With another bow, she silently handed it to Winter and returned to sit back behind her desk.

Winter took the file case to a projector dock and plugged it in. A touchscreen appeared, and she entered her security code. The projectors on the ceiling blipped and turned on, creating a holographic life-sized image of a blighted surface mutant, complete with stats and titles in floating text around it.

Winter cringed. The displayed creature was truly more hideous than she could have imagined. It was just like Eagle Eyes had said. The creature projected before her was grotesque and nauseating. Its melted face and jutting fangs were hard to look at. The long, mutated limbs were covered in rot and boils. It was hunched and inhuman.

"Gross, right?" Kara prodded suddenly.

"When was this image captured?" Winter asked.

"These are originals from soon after the creation of Olympus—some two-hundred years old, I would think," the woman replied as if she expected a big reaction.

Winter gave her none. She scrolled to the next image. Same title, different stats . . . same horrific appearance. This mutilated, burned and hideous, unrecognizable thing was nothing like what she had seen. She scrolled to the next image, and the next. One after another, the holographic blighters rolled past, each more stomach-turning than the one before.

"You know . . ." Kara interjected carefully. "I'm just so grateful that you deal with these monstrosities so that people like me don't have to. Thank you, Madam Purifier."

Winter ignored the woman's obvious and pathetic tactic to regain her good graces.

She continued scrolling through the nightmarish images until she came to the last one in the data file and stared into the slit-eyed horror before her.

There were two realities: the one she had been taught and the one she had seen for herself.

One reality dictated that the surface was a poisonous place populated by inhuman monsters that needed purification. It taught her that she had been created by a god who had given her abilities to fulfill this purpose, and that if she did, she would be raised to immortality at the age of thirty.

The reality she had seen for herself was a beautiful surface world, inhabited by creatures—no, by *people*—who looked just like her. The reality she had seen for herself was a mortal man raised to god-status by nothing more than the blind worship of zealots. What she had seen was a friend and mentor murdered on stage for nothing more than the carnal appeasement of a roaring crowd.

Winter stared at the image. She stared at it the same way she would stare down a nightmare in the dead of night when she was a child. She knew it wasn't real. She knew it couldn't hurt her. She knew she had to find out the truth one way or another.

She left the image on and turned to walk out of the Archive building, paying no attention to the questioning archivist as she went. Her emotions were far too high-strung to interact with anyone now.

The boisterous middle-tier inhabitants where still celebrating the

Ascension of their hero in chaotic mirth. If it was anything like the last Ascension, Winter knew it would last all night long. As she made her way slowly through the crowds toward the Purifier Quarter, she recalled her own merrymaking with her comrades not so long ago. Dancing and drinking, senses dulled and heightened at the same time, the warm surge of sick ecstasy filled her memory. Her stomach lurched inside, and her head pounded as she moved faster, trying to escape the feelings that seemed to chase her. She was appalled that when last a man was slaughtered for the entertainment of the masses, she had been one of these reveling idiots in the streets, partaking of substances, behaviors, and actions that in her right mind she would never have considered.

Drawing closer to the living chambers, Winter began to recognize the faces around her. Mixed in with the entertainers and the servers, now she saw her teammates and comrades. Only *they* were considered worthy of the company of the Elite, and several inhabitants of the First Tier engaged with the Purifiers in their festivity. Their faces were all contorted in drunken delight; they were scarcely in possession of their senses.

Someone grabbed Winter's hand as she pushed through the masses. It was an Elite that she didn't know. His handsome face and striking features were locked onto Winter's with a lustful smile.

"You're a pretty one," he moaned and touched her hair, his words an inebriated slur.

Winter recoiled from his touch and slipped her hand from his grasp. She struggled to keep moving forward to her safe haven, weaving in and out through the pressing, suffocating throng.

She finally reached the living chambers, and Winter entered the lift where she finally had a moment to just breathe. The lift moved swiftly and the doors opened, revealing an empty corridor, save for a couple kissing in the hallway.

Winter ignored their giggling antics as best she could while entering her security code. The moment the door closed behind her, she drew the curtains to drown out the light from the city.

Now that she was alone, she could finally think.

Winter fell on her bed, full uniform, and closed her eyes. She rolled on her back and chuckled ironically, thinking about her beautiful home. The sardonic laugh carried confusion and frustration, ending in a little sob.

She had always loved the imagery of her city floating in the clouds above the danger and poison of the surface. She breathed the recycled, sterile air of her bedroom and remembered the soft, clean air of the surface. The vibrant sensation was marred by the accompanying flash of dead faces and dead eyes penetrating her mind once again.

Winter clenched her eyes against the images and attempted to rub it out of her head by squeezing her temples with the tips of her fingers in slow, circular movements.

The faces wouldn't go. They stared at her in steadfast, lifeless accusation.

When once only the Sovereign's face had occupied the forefront of her mind, now, all she could see was the blank stare of death.

Exhaling sharply, Winter stood from the bed and walked to the bathroom, where she splashed her face with cold water. She gazed blankly at her reflection and slowly unbuttoned her formal coat. She removed it carefully and hung the symbolic item in its place, smoothing out the shoulders and straightening the hem to perfection. Finally, she took down her hair and ran her fingers through the length of its silky strands.

Everything in her life—even her hair—was modeled after her hero, Nereza Vossen.

. . . *The greatest.*

Winter attributed her high marks in the Formulation Quarter to her idol's inspiration. It had been Nereza's strength offered from Elysium that had empowered her to survive the hellish depths of Tartarus, to even accomplish what only 'the Nightmare' had before her. She gave all credit to Nereza's guiding example throughout her entire service. Winter's driving goal in life was to become worthy of Ascension in her time—as the greatest of her time—just like Nereza . . .

And just like Derrick . . .

To achieve Ascension—to see her hero in the next life, to look her in the eyes and gain her approval. Winter had imagined it many, many times.

Her fingers slipped out of her hair and fell to her sides. She could no longer feel the hope. It was gone from inside her, and it left what felt like a gaping wound deep in her chest. What had once filled her with courage and purpose now filled her with a knowing, biting sickness.

The feeling seemed to suck her down, almost as if it were a vacuum, and any good thought or feeling she tried to have was inevitably doused by the endless vortex within.

Her friend and mentor was gone. It hurt so badly, even though it was still so surreal. She could feel the pain of loss but, at the same time, could not quite manage to believe he was dead at all. Her mind confirmed the permanence of his state, but her bleeding heart almost hoped it had been imagined.

No.

Eagle Eyes was now gone. His wisdom and guidance that molded her adult life had been extinguished. Just like that, he would no longer be her safety net . . .

. . . never again.

CHAPTER NINETEEN

Blinding white light surrounded her.

Winter stood in the center of eternity with the Sovereign and with her mentor, Derrick. She was vaguely aware of every single person of her acquaintance staring at her, but they all seemed so distant.

Winter reached for Derrick, but he only drifted farther away. In horror, she watched as he kneeled at the Sovereign's feet and bowed his head. Her heart began racing as the Sovereign raised the blade overhead.

She fell to her knees—struggling, crawling, fighting to move toward him, but to no avail.

No!

The blade fell.

Winter screamed.

Derrick's head was severed cleanly.

Please no!

The head hit the floor with a hollow thud and rolled toward her. His body collapsed in a heap, and everything and everyone disappeared into darkness, but the head rolled slowly closer and closer, trailing blood all the way, until it finally stopped right in front of Winter, facing her.

She stared at the severed head of her beloved mentor, shock and disbelief and agonizing regret welling up inside of her.

I could have stopped this. Winter sobbed. *I should have stopped this!*

Suddenly, Derrick's eyes snapped open.

Winter started in fright.

The intense eyes of the bloodied head stared directly at her.

Derrick opened his mouth to speak, but no sound came forth.

Instead of a voice, Winter felt the words in her mind, and his warning pierced right to her soul:

"Open gaze, Winter. See everything."

Sunlight burst over the cloud banks, dousing Olympus in golden hues. The sleepy city was quiet throughout, recovering slowly from the revelry of the previous night.

A blade of light slipped through a tiny crack in the curtains of Winter's bedroom. The blinding shaft fell across her face and made her jump violently as she awoke.

Drenched in sweat and shaking with fatigue, Winter buried her face in her hands and took a moment to shake off the vicious nightmare.

She inhaled a cleansing breath, and the terror of the night slipped away as fast as the shadows from her bedroom.

Morning brought clarity. Morning was the reset for everything. It washed away the sadness of the night; it chased away the shadows and reaffirmed that life did indeed go on.

Winter's eyes opened, slowly adjusting to the new light. She sat up and swept the cascading black hair from her face. She breathed deeply, suddenly feeling like everything she'd experienced on the surface was now a series of events that could be categorized.

She hadn't set up a wake-up alert last night, knowing that all Purifiers were given a standard day of rest following an Ascension.

The extra sleep worked in her favor. It was something in which she seldom indulged, but it felt good to have a body fully rested and a mind that was clear and fresh. Winter suddenly realized that she couldn't remember the last time she *hadn't* awoken early to train.

She was also surprised to find that everything hurt less. Not just physically, either. The pain of losing her friend and mentor . . . she had expected to fall asleep crying and then waking herself with tears. But although the pain of loss was still poignant and tangible within her heart, she found that the sorrow didn't take precedence the way she thought it would.

The unnerving dream did leave her feeling uncertain.

Winter felt the need to *do* something.

Stretching her limbs slowly, she made the time to take stock of her feelings before emerging from her blanket. The sunlight filtered through the opalescent barrier and lit up her room with a comforting, soft vibrancy as she walked to the window and pulled back the curtain.

She looked over the city down below and could almost feel a mental curtain begin to slide apart as well. It was impossible to justify the notion of her surface encounter being imagined. Her mind was far too objective to seriously consider such nonsense.

She trusted her eyes. She trusted her mind.

As a Purifier, self-reliance is truly the only option.

Her cascading raven locks rippled as she pulled them over her shoulder and thoughtfully threaded her fingers through the morning-matted strands.

Her mind was not so foggy now. The confusion had left, and now, she could objectively sort what she knew.

She began categorizing the things she knew for herself and the things she had been told were true throughout her lifetime as she changed clothes. She slipped into her athletic gear and soft-soled shoes before strapping on her chalk belt. She exited her living chamber to find some sleep-deprived comrades chatting outside in the hall.

Winter nodded politely as she walked past them. Carmella 'Gorgon' Gleason was standing there outside her room with a man from the Bio Lab. Their cordial smiles disappeared and their conversation ended at Winter's arrival.

Winter didn't pause, not knowing what had brought on the awkward silence.

As her back turned to them, Gorgon snickered, "Bloody Winter off to train." She and her companion chuckled.

Winter didn't stop but looked over her shoulder with confusion.

Gorgon and her partner laughed before returning their attention back to each other in an amorous end to last night's celebration.

Winter was used to being teased for her overachieving nature but was confused at the new need to add 'bloody' to her name. She thought again of her teacher's warning of becoming a target and shrugged off the jeer as he had advised before continuing to the lift.

The doors opened to reveal city streets strewn with the remnants of festivity. The only sign of life was the dozen or so cleaners pushing brooms and carrying bags of discarded rubbish to and fro.

Winter walked directly to the Engineering Quarter, barely noticing the sanitation workers, or that they bowed very low with their eyes to the ground as she passed. Their existence was meaningless to her. As members of the lowest tier, they had no worth, no value, and afforded no acknowledgment from a Purifier.

Inside the Engineering Quarter, Winter smiled to see the reactor vents pluming thick streams of quivering hot air into the sky. Olympus was like a living, breathing entity to her. She loved walking through this quarter because it was like the heart of the city—the place that pumped life to every quarter. Even though it served as the very lifeblood of Olympus, the Engineering Quarter was considered the lowest station of the middle tier. But Winter loved the rugged charm of it all. She felt like there was intricate beauty in the work done there.

Winter approached the utility lift: a huge, flat platform lined with safety bars that operated to every single level within the core of Olympus. The utility lift was mainly used for transporting large equipment to the lower levels, but personnel often used it as well. It was the fastest way to gain access to the base of the city ship. Without it, the only other option was to traverse a dozen small lifts scattered across thousands of hallways through hundreds of floors one at a time.

A large number of workers gathered on the utility lift as Winter approached, each of them dragging heavy tool chests or carrying boxed parts or digital boards.

When Winter came near, the lift operator whistled loudly for attention. "Hey! All you clear off!" he shouted.

Every worker present looked up in confusion until they spotted Winter, at which point their faces turned to surprise and understanding before they quickly performed as commended.

The lift operator removed his protective hat and smiled before bowing graciously. "Madam Purifier Winterton, what level would you like?" he asked once Winter had stepped onto the lift.

"Base level," she replied without eye contact.

A loud warning alarm announced the impending lift movement and the operator paused to check all sides before initiating the slow, steady descent into the belly of the ship.

The tired, dirty faces of the workers standing together on the street were lost on Winter. Did she cause a delay in their workday? Irrelevant. All eyes locked on the lone Purifier as she was lowered out of view, but she hardly noticed that they were even there.

Winter loved watching each level *whoosh* upward as they fell. It was a stunning reminder of the immense majesty that was their monolithic home.

The air below Olympus' topside was stale, mechanical. Familiar. She breathed it in and smiled. Memories—most pleasant but some causing revulsion—of the Formulation Quarter flooded her mind. Fifteen years she had spent in the depths of Olympus, developing and learning and training for her vocation. It was difficult to believe that four years had already passed since her commencement, since passing the trials and being instated as an active Purifier for the Archangels.

Living topside had made her memories of the FMQ fade, but they always returned each time she breathed the stale air again.

"Congratulations on your recent victory on the surface, Madam Purifier," the operator mentioned politely, drawing Winter out of her inner nostalgia. "I'm betting all my allotments on you in the next bout."

"That's very kind," Winter replied flatly, eyes straight ahead.

The operator stifled the urge to praise her more and let her stand in silence for the remainder of the ride.

The giant opening at the top level was barely a pinpoint of light by the time the lift ceased its movement. Winter glanced upward briefly to admire the staggering view before exiting onto a metal catwalk. This was as deep as the utility lift could descend, but there were seventeen more levels to the very base of Olympus where the city's core glowed steadily—the path to reach it made up of catwalks, winding metal stairways, and mechanical corridors.

Core workers were never allowed up in the city except for special occasions, and even then, they were only given admittance to their designated section of the Hive. They exited their Formulation Quarter as children and entered the core to live, serve, and sleep in the sunless interior for their entire lives.

Winter worked her way through the corridors, knowing the way by heart, not affording any of them a single glance.

Each level of the base had an access door to the outer hull where intake fans needed regular cleaning and maintenance. She wheeled open the manual airlock on one of these access doors and gasped as the open air puffed her hair back in a sudden gust.

She remembered the first time Scorch had taken her out here—the fear and excitement of it all.

This was once his favorite recreational pastime—back when she was the initiate—and he used to climb every single morning like Winter did now. But he had since grown complacent in his practice.

Winter stepped out onto the grated balcony and looked down into the forever of cloud. It made her toes curl inside her boots to see the earth's terrain thirty-thousand feet below. The skyline was brilliantly lit with the radiating glow of morning, and everything was still and silent.

She closed the door behind her and wheeled the airlock secure once more before sweeping her hair up into a firm braid that she tucked inside her shirt. The narrow wrap-around balcony on which she stood hugged the hull in a complete circumference of Olympus' base. The intake vents, humming softly, sat just above her eye-level in twenty-foot increments from each other.

Crystalline blue eyes looked up at the convex metal surface that towered up overhead until it disappeared over the curve. Winter felt, as she always did at this moment, a tingle of trepidation and adrenaline stir within her heart. It was at this very moment before every single climb that the decision had to be made.

Was this the day she backed down?

Was this the day she felt too tired or too afraid to make the climb?

Once she started, there was no going back. Once she was out there, relying on herself, she could not change her mind or afford to grow weary. It was not so much the strength in her limbs but the steel of her mind that made the difference between life and death.

Winter gripped the edge of the intake vent and stepped up onto the railing. Her feet left the rails, and she began her long climb up the hull of Olympus.

Her toned arms and conditioned legs worked synchronously as she slowly progressed upward. Vents, seams, and fasteners served as the only means to climb. She focused on her practiced route and anticipated every difficulty, following the faint traces of chalk seen traversing up the concave metallic structure.

Her mind was completely occupied now, and her heart thumped with work instead of emotion. The clarity and simplicity made her feel like, once again, she was in control of her whole life, and nothing could take it away.

She loved Olympus, her beautiful home in the clouds. It gave her a purpose; it gave her meaning and hope for the future. She was blessed with a vocation that gave her the opportunity to carve the way for significant progress.

But now, she was faced with the reality that the beautiful future and progress for which she was raised to give her life was based on an ugly conflict of facts.

Yesterday, she was too close to the problem, far too emotionally involved to make any rational judgments. Today, as the open, filtered air filled her lungs, and her muscles throbbed with the ecstasy of exertion, she could see the problem for what it was.

As her fingertips finally crested the edge of the city ship's outer gardens, Winter felt she knew what she must do. She pulled herself up to sit on the railing and dangled her legs over the open space. She peered down at the clouds far below as they parted here and there to give little glimpses of the surface far below.

She did want her people to return to the surface; she wanted with all her heart to bring to pass the day that they could rebuild civilization as it once was. But she also needed to understand the reason for the lie. What was the basis for their continued onslaught? Was *all* of the surface no longer toxic? Were *all* of the inhabitants no longer affected? Or was it just in certain areas?

Most painfully of all, Winter needed to understand why a man—who was clearly mortal—would claim to be a god and dictate such things.

She turned to look over her shoulder at the city and pondered upon all the inhabitants who followed every word the Sovereign spoke . . . implicitly and without question. From the day of her formulation up until yesterday, she had been one of them. She had never thought to question; she never had the urge to divert. Not once. Not until her eyes were opened by a single truth . . . then the rest seemed to follow.

She smiled suddenly as the image of the broken statue, the ivy-covered walls, and the faded wording flashed to the forefront of her mind:

I have sworn upon the altar of God eternal hostility against every form of tyranny over the mind of man.

The feeling that gripped her heart at the thought of those words was incredibly distinct. Winter's chest began to burn inside. Her throat swelled and triggered a surge of emotion so strong that, as it swept up her frame, it culminated in producing small tears that rimmed her eyes. But these were not the frustrated, desperate tears of which she had become so weary over the recent past; they were soft, comforting tears of conviction.

Her brows furrowed in thought as she struggled to understand why it stuck so poignantly in her mind—why it caused her entire being to react.

If lord Zeus were truly an immortal, benevolent, omniscient being, he would know that the surface was no longer toxic, and if that were the case, then why were they hunting disease-free surface-dwelling humans when they could be busy building their new civilization? But if lord Zeus did not know that the surface was no longer toxic, then there was no possible way he could be a god. A truly omniscient being could not be ignorant to a truth that affected the fate of his creations. So, if the Sovereign truly did not know, the only possible conclusion was that he was not omniscient . . .

. . . that he was not a god.

No matter how she turned the tables, he was unavoidably no more than a man wielding complete power over the minds of an entire civilization for his own purposes. What those purposes were exactly, she didn't know. But in every case, both Purifiers and surface humans would continue to die in pointless droves if something did not change.

Winter breathed deeply. The tyranny was the problem. It grated sharply against her lifetime of indoctrination, but she knew by the feeling in her chest that it was right. She had always been able to trust her instincts and judgment. Now more than ever, she felt the urgency not to second guess them.

CHAPTER TWENTY

The orientation in the conference room two days later was short. Winter had been on edge since the night of the Ascension. Her training, apart from the mandatory Hive drills, had been alone late at night, running the empty streets. Her newfound rebellion of the mind since been strengthened, and she had steeled her resolve and thoroughly prepared herself for this day.

Nalara was finally ready to be an independent Purifier. Even though she still had trepidation written upon her countenance as they geared up, Winter was confident that she had trained her exceptionally well. Nalara would be fine without her now . . .

All around, her teammates quipped and teased, and Winter enjoyed each familiar voice to its fullest. Her mind flooded with memories, good and bad—all surrounding her highly regimented life there in the Purifier Quarter. The first few team members began exiting the hub to the shuttle bay in anticipation of the launch. Winter was close to follow, but she paused at one of the alcoves and stared at the illuminated name.

Ashton 'Trigger' Cross.

His name sparked a pang of bitterness in Winter's soul. At the time she'd reentered the shuttle after being exposed to the surface air, she had known without a shadow of a doubt that she would be purified just as he had been. But fate had reserved for her that moment to be spared. Surviving that moment as he had not been so lucky to do made her conviction to find answers all the more reinforced in her mind.

Why had the Blight been detected in Trigger and not in her?

Why had she lived and he purified with fire?

She shook her head in frustration. Nothing made sense.

Master Purifier Orrin 'Wraith' Priest emerged from his office and noticed Winter paused there among the others.

In her musings, Winter didn't notice her captain approach until he was leering down at her.

She snapped to attention. "Captain Priest, sir!"

"Forget which one is yours, Lieutenant?" he rumbled.

"No, sir. I was just . . . no, sir." Winter faltered through her swirling thoughts and emotions.

The newly ordained Master Purifier's eyes flitted briefly to the name display as he righted his posture. "Being a Purifier means accepting the prospect of death every time you enter those doors." He gestured to the shuttle bay entrance where two more of their team members were passing through. "Hammer knew it. And Trigger knew it, too."

"As do I, sir," Winter replied with conviction. "I know it, and I accept it."

"We don't waste time regretting the past," he asserted, straight from the cadet training curriculum. "We don't split our focus from the Sovereign's mission. Reminiscing about the fallen is a distraction we cannot indulge." He took that moment to poignantly erase Trigger's name from the display.

The screen sat in heart-rending blankness, pulling at Winter's conscience. She closed her eyes and watched Trigger's once-smiling face turn to ashes and disappear.

"Yes, sir. I understand, sir." Winter knew it was what Wraith wanted to hear. She turned and finished with her jump preparations.

Walking with the Archangels through the shuttle bay to board their craft filled her with nostalgia. She savored each scratch on the hull, every sound the engine made. With her newfound creed to discover the deeper truth, everything could change.

Winter breathed steadily and concentrated on keeping her expression neutral.

In silence, they descended to the surface, and in her own mind, Winter said goodbye to each of her teammates as they were dropped off at their respective zones. She pored over every memory she shared with them and kept it all inside.

Captain Priest had been a pillar of strength and fortitude from the very first day. He was the first active Purifier she'd met out of the FMQ. She remembered feeling like there was too much air surrounding her—like the open space and noise of life on the Second Tier was actively drowning her, but then there was Captain Priest, towering over her.

"Sit down, cadet," he'd said when she wandered into the orientation room. *"Never show a moment of fear."*

Scorch had been her trainer—he'd been late that day. He appeared halfway through gearing up and gave no excuses for it. He was smiling and aloof. Winter remembered thinking maybe the Formulation Quarter was harder than the vocation itself if this was her trainer.

"Hey, you ready?" he'd asked excitedly. *"Wow, look at you—you're already better at gearing up than I am!"*

Winter smiled inwardly at the memory.

When it was Nalara's turn to disembark, Winter stifled the urge to look at her childhood friend at all, fearful that she might inadvertently give herself away. They had been through too much together. Their shared past and pains had formed something deeper than bond. Years apart had done nothing to diminish the emotional connection they had forged through tears and fire.

The shuttle poised for a drop once more, and Wraith called Winter's name. He checked out her rifle and handed it to her as she approached. She looked him in the eyes and swallowed down her twinge of paranoia.

Wraith spoke nothing as she exited the shuttle.

Winter hit the ground and cleared the area quickly, making her way to cover just as her training dictated. Until the moment the shuttle was gone from sight, she kept up pretenses. Once it was gone, however, she dropped the point of her rifle and stood erect to study her gauntlet display.

After scrolling for a moment, she saw the ancient road she'd discovered on the last jump. It intersected three of the current active purifying zones. She watched the movement of her team members on the map and predicted their search patterns.

It would be tricky, but she was confident in her skills.

Winter struggled internally, suppressed all training and protocol, and holstered her rifle. She exhaled slowly as all the alarm bells went off in her head, screaming the dangers and disciplinary actions she would incur.

She attempted to slow her breathing, slow her racing heart, but the moment was too imperative. Her entire future—whether it led to death or to liberty—came down to this moment.

Once she took this action . . . there was no going back. All the regret in the world could never undo it.

. . . Was this the moment she backed down?

Winter took in a deep, steadying breath.

No.

She disengaged her armor and immediately felt the sensation of cool air wash over her, entering into her helmet at the unsealed neck. She held her breath, dreading the consequence of her own action. When she couldn't physically hold it any longer, Winter let it out and shakily breathed the fragrant and refreshing air in desperate little gasps.

Her heart raced. Her face flushed hot.

Too late now.

Filled with fear but unable to go back, Winter removed her helmet and opened the small panel that held the com. She looked up at the sky, sudden trepidation rampant in her stunning blue eyes, as if somehow, her Sovereign could see her actions. She could almost feel the searing heat of the Eye of Zeus upon her. She swallowed hard and forced herself to focus on the plan. She fished out the com device and removed the power pack, severing her connection with Olympus and the rest of the Archangels.

"Archangels, Master Purifier Priest. Do you copy?" the voice of a Flight Control technician crackled over Wraith's earpiece.

"Wraith here," he responded, confused at the sudden and inexplicable intrusion on his thus far quiet sweep.

"Requesting a team status report, honored Master Purifier."

"All accounted for." He paused in his steps and put a hand to his helmet, waiting for an explanation.

At length, the technician expounded. "You have a team member whose communicator has ceased transmitting."

Wraith looked down at his gauntlet display and searched the positions carefully.

"Please supply a team status report," the control tech repeated.

Wraith clenched his jaw in frustration and opened the broad channel. "Archangels, status!" he ordered briskly.

"Scorch reporting, all clear."

"Viper here. My zone is clear so far."

"Sapphire, sir." The com crackled. "Nothing to report."

"Bulletproof, sir. No activity."

"Savage—*aaaand* nothing exciting!"

"Havoc reporting here. I'm good, sir."

"Hi—uh, Gressen—s-sir. Um . . . so far so good."

Wraith's scowl deepened as he studied the markers. "Winter, report immediately," he snapped. "Winter!" He growled to himself and opened the broad channel once more. "January Winterton, I swear—does anyone have eyes on Winter?"

All responses were negative as he feared they would be.

"Control, this is Master Purifier Priest."

"Go ahead, Master Purifier," came the response.

"Requesting coordinates for Lieutenant Winterton's com."

Pause.

"Negative. Her com is offline."

"You can't track the signal?" he almost shouted.

"Negative. There is no signal to track. Her com is offline."

Wraith cursed audibly and stomped. His fury-filled voice echoed through the hollow: "Blight me, you defective trash-gene, Winterton!"

Carefully monitoring the team activity on the gauntlet display, Winter moved through the forest as quietly as she possibly could. It was remarkably easier now that her nano-shielding was disengaged. It had been nearly impossible to hear anything besides the intercom while sealed inside the sterile bubble.

She passed through Havoc's assigned zone with plenty of margin for error and found the ancient roadway. This was it—this was as far as her plan went. She was fully aware it was weak at best . . . but nothing compared with the torment of not trying at all.

She needed answers like she needed to breathe. The tangible yearning pulled at her mind with an urgency she had never before known.

Winter looked up and down the overgrown road as far as she could see and shrugged before picking a random direction. As she walked, she was careful to keep an eye on the movement of her team, frequently checking the gauntlet display to ensure she didn't accidentally intercept one of them.

It didn't take long before she came into Sapphire's grid. She was dangerously close to the road, so Winter decided to veer away into the woods a bit and slow her gait to avoid arousing interest altogether.

Once inside the woods, she was fascinated to find what appeared to be a rudimentary path of obvious current use. Having stumbled upon it completely by accident, it looked like it was frequented by heavy boots and animals. She decided to embrace the happy coincidence and follow wherever it might lead.

Surely, sooner or later, it would take her to the answers she sought.

Miles away from where Winter currently paved her rebellious course, Nalara stood in complete uncertainty and borderline panic. Hours had passed since the alarming report that Winter was missing, and no updates had reached her com.

With nothing but her training to fall back on, Nalara continued her sweep and hoped that everything would be sorted out by the time she returned to the LZ.

Her hands felt sweaty inside her gauntlets, and the air inside her armor was stifling and heavy. She felt neither prepared nor ready to be a full-fledged Purifier. How could anyone feel ready while standing in the shadow of the amazing January 'Winter' Winterton? Janey had always stood out in excellence, but seeing how far she had widened the gap since their time together in the Formulation Quarter, Nalara had no hope of ever feeling sufficient.

Not only that, but the simple fact that she had now been on several jumps to the surface and had yet to score a single killshot—at least, one on her own—weighed very heavily on her waning self-esteem.

Winter had racked that point *for* her on her rifle, but it wasn't the same. She appreciated the gesture at the time, but now, it just felt like the final say in the accusation of insufficiency.

Her gauntlet display lit up and Nalara caught her breath, hoping for good news, but the hope was extinguished somewhat as she realized it was only a reminder of their Loading Zone coordinates being relayed by their pilot.

Nalara sighed heavily, both in frustration and relief, having completed her first grid sweep on her own with no engagements.

She saw all the markers of her teammates begin to move toward the LZ on her gauntlet. With one final glance around, she turned in her tracks and headed back as well.

The clearing where the shuttle lay idling was just beginning to fill with Archangels members when she arrived.

Even within the obscuring helmet, it was obvious that Wraith's face was redder than usual. He stood by the shuttle door, his finger thrust forward at Scorch's face.

Scorch looked both afraid and angry—not a common look for him. His complexion was white and flighty, his posture defensive.

Everyone was on edge as Nalara drew near.

"You." The Master Purifier pushed Scorch aside and zeroed in on her arrival. "You know, don't you?" he accused forcefully. "What's Winter trying to pull here?"

Nalara froze in fear, terrified of the giant man domineering over her.

"I don't care what kind of nonsense this is; I'm ordering you to disclose it now."

Nalara's brown eyes were wide with terror, and she gripped her rifle for security. "She . . . she didn't tell me anything, sir," she whimpered, struggling to keep her voice even. "Honest."

"Where is Winter?" he demanded. "Why did she disappear off the grid?"

"She didn't say anything, Captain. I swear! I don't know where she is." Nalara looked to her teammates, her eyes pleading for help.

"Winter said nothing, sir." Viper shook her head. "To any of us."

Scorch stepped forward. "Sir, it's true. We're all in the dark here. Something must have happened to her. We should be searching right now, not speculating."

Wraith's jaw set firmly, and his scowl sunk deeper. He switched on the broad channel for all to hear, pausing for a moment to choose his words. "Winter, if you can hear me . . ." He shook his head and laughed. "We're leaving. You understand?"

The team looked shocked and crestfallen.

"We are *leaving* you here," Wraith repeated. "I never thought I'd live to see the day a Purifier put herself before the edict of Olympus, you selfish, showboating *nothing* . . ." He paused as only silence reigned on the channel. "Enjoy your grave."

Tension filled the air as the Archangels watched their captain turn and enter the scanning chamber, stone faced and more serious than ever.

He had just pronounced Winter's death sentence, and not one of them could do a thing to change it.

Nalara turned away from her teammates and cried.

"Janey . . ." she breathed, her eyes scanning the trees. "Where are you?"

CHAPTER TWENTY-ONE

Two days later, the hazy glow of daylight faded slowly into the western canopy of ancient vegetation. The warm afternoon melted into the cool of evening. Something felt heavy in the air as Winter stepped steadily forward down the almost indiscernible trail littered with fallen blossoms of pink and white. At this point, she was not sure that she was following anything more than her own footsteps in a long circle. At several points, the trail had branched, but no matter how many times she deviated, she always seemed to end up on familiar ground once more.

Her eyes burned and ached as she struggled to keep them open. Her parched throat made it hard to breath, and the agonizing gnawing of her empty stomach made it nearly impossible to concentrate on anything else.

She remembered this feeling, every bit of it, including the swimming head and throbbing feet. The dark memory of her trials flooded into her mind in sporadic bursts. It caused her heavy, labored breathing to become tight, panicked gasps—the pain, the blood, the sheer terror . . . alone in the dark with nothing but her own ability to preserve her survival or prove her demise.

Winter's vision tunneled as the panicked breathing robbed her already taxed frame of much-needed oxygen, and she stumbled heavily on her dragging feet.

She tried to catch herself but was unaware of exactly how weak she'd become in the days she'd spent away from Olympus, with sleep deprivation and malnourishment taking their toll. Her helmet rolled away out of reach as her face met the hard earth; Winter groaned—in frustration more than pain. She tried to push up off the ground, but her strength was exhausted. Rolling instead to her back, she looked up through some blossoms at the tiny glimpses of sky between them as the branches moved softly in the breeze.

The ground was cold . . . there were still tiny patches of snow clinging to existence in the deep shadows. The filtered sunset through the pink hues was mystifying; Winter could almost feel the earth move beneath her.

So much life all around. The tiny insects, the growing grass, the moving trees—it all testified to a place thriving and growing—not poisonous and deathly as she was taught.

Or . . . when her eyes closed . . . would it be her last?

Winter exhaled her exhaustion. Her frame relaxed into the hard ground, and gradually, her eyelids felt heavy and dense upon her face.

Crisp chirping broke the silence, and suddenly, Winter's eyes snapped open. She was instantly aware of movement around her. Birds flitted from branch to branch above her head, but something unseen crunched softly behind the thick cover of trees.

Winter twisted to her front and pushed up from the ground before sweeping the matted hair from her eyes. Her breath was steady and her heart calm as her senses honed in on the direction of the unknown approaching entity.

She couldn't believe her own eyes when the trees parted and a face emerged—a face she knew so well. It had haunted her for days and nights; every waking moment was spent trying to focus on something other than him. His features were burned into her subconscious like a brand.

Chin-length brown hair framed glittering hazel eyes that spoke volumes of sadness without him uttering a word. Winter could see in his eyes a lifetime of hardship and loss; it was so poignant that she almost looked away. His overwhelming soulful gaze was riddled with caution, however, as he stepped carefully from the undergrowth cover. The grungy tactical clothing he wore was patched and frayed. His equipment appeared piecemeal, and his rifle looked aged but well cared for.

Winter made no move—she scarcely breathed. Already, she had exceeded her wildest expectations in that she hadn't been killed at first sight. She consciously turned slowly in a circle with her arms out and came to face him once more. She closed her eyes tight and carefully removed her rifle, placing it on the ground. She did the same with her sidearm and knife as well before stepping several paces back.

A tense moment passed, and she swallowed apprehensively. She was determined not to be the one to make the first move but take dictation from his actions. If he was going to take her prisoner, or even execute her, she didn't want to cause any panic either way. There would be no more pain or terror here caused by her actions.

To her sheer surprise, the visitor crouched slowly and laid down his own rifle.

Winter was shocked. *Was he here to talk?* After witnessing her murder three of his companions, then nearly being decapitated himself . . . he wanted to communicate.

He stepped to the side away from his rifle a few paces. Winter knew he was still close enough to reach it with ease. Just because he wanted to talk didn't mean he was letting his guard down.

Winter's heart beat faster and faster. She didn't understand the burning, nervous feeling inside. Perhaps just seeing a surface human face to face again was causing her distress—she couldn't tell.

Those penetrating eyes . . . his sorrow and trepidation manifested within them as he scanned her features in disbelief.

He scoffed in irony. "I told them you were human," he muttered to himself.

Winter's lips parted in shock. "So, you *do* speak Olympian," she said neutrally.

He fairly jumped out of his skin at her words. He looked like he didn't believe his ears. "I . . ." He paused, and his brows knit together. "Um, we call it English." They stared at each other for a long silent moment. "Are you . . . do you call yourself *Olympian?*"

Winter nodded slowly. "Olympus is our home." Her expression contorted in curiosity. "How is this possible—how can you know the tongue of the gods?" The final word stuck in her mouth like bitter gall, feeling the poignancy of everything she was discovering to be untrue.

"It's always been what we speak here," the man replied, equally shocked as she. He paused, seemingly at a loss for words. "You mentioned your 'gods' . . . can you tell me about them?"

Winter felt a deep hollow pulling in her chest. "Our Sovereign," she recited slowly and painfully, "is our creator. He formed Olympus from the ashes of the old world. He gave us life and purpose. To purify our ancestral home, we sacrifice our lives to him. We're taught that in his wisdom, humanity will thrive in paradise once more."

Her words hung in the air.

The surface human looked as though he were carefully considering how best to respond. "I can understand the power of purpose," he finally said with a short nod, "to live with hope in the promise of a better world. If you ask me, life without that hope is no life at all. But I was always taught to pay very close attention to the one that's making the promise. If it's the wrong person, then there's always a high price to pay for their version of 'paradise.'"

"I've seen for myself what that price is," Winter returned softly, her heart swelling with inner pain at the thought of her comrades and predecessors— all the Purifiers who'd ever given their lives to the service of the Sovereign's cause. The memory of dead faces invaded her mind, and she flinched as she recalled the thousands of surface humans who were victims of the Sovereign's genocide. " . . . And Olympus isn't the only one paying it."

"Where is . . .?" he began to ask when a light of recognition suddenly came on in his eyes. Winter could see his mind flooding with thoughts and emotion. He glanced up at the dark object hovering distantly in the sky, visible only through breaks in the clouds. "Is that what you call it? We've never known."

Winter's lifetime of conditioning made her uncomfortable with the question, and beyond that, she was still unsure how to answer.

He waited silently.

Winter looked up and pointed ambiguously. "Yes. Olympus is a city ship. It's our home. It's existed for almost two-hundred fifty years."

The man remained silent.

She had so much she wanted to ask him, so much she wanted to say, but she couldn't force the words out of her hot, swollen throat. She felt mortified to stand before the representative for her victims, but she desperately wanted to know the whole truth.

"How long has the surface been habitable?" she finally ventured.

His eyes narrowed.

Winter lowered her gaze to the forest floor. She didn't want him to see the shame and guilt she felt.

"Always," he replied at length, then posed his counter question: "Why are you here?"

She swallowed hard as she recalled the sight of Derrick Zinda's blood spilling across the Hive floor. She could start at the beginning and explain the entire thing, or she could start by apologizing for the systematic extermination of his people. Her mind was a foggy blur, and she couldn't believe she was at a complete loss for words—here, now when she finally had a chance to gain clarity.

She spoke slowly the only real explanation that came into her tumultuous mind: "I have sworn upon the altar of God eternal hostility against every form of tyranny . . . over the mind of man."

He looked surprised and confused.

Winter half-shrugged as emotion rang though her chest. "I saw those words the day . . . the day I first saw you . . ." she trailed off.

"I know those words. I know them very well," he commented.

"I don't know what they mean . . . not exactly," Winter attempted to explain. "But after I saw what I was . . ." she took a steadying breath, "what I was sent to purify . . . it made me think that maybe my mind was under tyranny. I needed to come learn the truth for myself." She swallowed hard again as her throat began to burn. She felt her cheeks grow hot and her eyes well with tears.

A long moment of silence passed again. He looked pained and conflicted when he asked, "What did you *think* you were . . . purifying?"

"Diseased, mutated remnants of our race," she answered quickly. "We're taught in formulation that the surface is toxic—poisoned with a man-made virus called the Blight that destroyed the old world. We didn't know it had changed."

"What do you mean 'changed'? It was never that way." He shook his head poignantly. "Is that why your people are trying to kill us? Why they incinerate our crops? Our animals?"

A tear escaped Winter's eye. "I don't know," she admitted. "I really don't know at all."

He passed his hand over his stubbled chin, looking truly distressed as he struggled to keep his emotions in check.

"I just want to know the truth," Winter almost whispered.

"You . . . and your people," he started calmly, his voice attempting to mask the roiling emotional storm just beneath the surface, "have been coming down here to hunt and kill us for generations . . . and none of you ever bothered to ask why?"

"We are *taught* why," Winter tried to explain. "We're created to purify the surface. From the day of my formulation, I was trained to exterminate the Blight and all those infected by it."

"What do you mean by *formulation?*"

Winter was confused. "Well, formulation is . . . you know, when I was created," she answered uncomfortably.

"You mean when you were born?"

"When what?" Winter returned. "I don't understand."

His head cocked to the side. "How exactly were you created?"

"In the Sovereign's Formulation Quarter, where genes are engineered to create individuals with specialized traits and abilities specific to their tier and vocation," she recited from her childhood lessons. "I was formulated as a high-ranking citizen of the Second Tier . . . as a Purifier."

His face twisted in confusion. "Well . . . that's . . . that's something . . ." His voice trailed off. "What about your parents?"

Winter shook her head. "I don't know that word."

"There are no parents on Olympus?" He looked bewildered.

Winter shook her head again. She assumed not. They were speaking the same language, but she fully understood that there must be some discrepancies in the terms used. She was surprised to see his expression suddenly change to pity. She didn't like it; the feeling of being pitied sat like sour bile deep in her gut.

"So, you were created," he began, "and all you were taught your whole life is how to kill people on the surface . . . because it's toxic here?"

Winter felt ridiculous and guilty.

"Will your people stop if they know it's not true?" he asked hopefully "Will you tell them?"

"It's not that simple. Our Sovereign gives us life and purpose—" she felt sick just saying it, " . . .and he dictates that the surface *must* be purified. You don't just contradict that. Not even in thought. The consequence for . . . for what I'm doing now . . ." She looked down at her boots in momentary silence. She clenched her eyes shut and fought back the uncontrollable urge to scream. "The Sovereign is powerful," she began again once the moment passed. "You mentioned your crops being incinerated. *He* does that. And for what I'm now doing here, if he knew, he can and probably would do the same to me."

The man cringed visibly. "Sounds like the Antichrist, if you ask me." There was distinct and clear venom in the tone of his voice.

Winter didn't understand. "The what?"

He dismissed her question with an apologetic wave of his hand. His soulful eyes held hers in silence, seemingly searching her soul. "So, this 'Sovereign,' as you call him—is he the tyranny of the mind that you're trying to escape?"

Winter felt the knee-jerk shock and abhorrence that accompanied any such accusation against her lifelong deity. But her righteous rage subsided as she breathed out the programmed response and breathed in liberty. "Yes," she answered truthfully. "I saw your face and that you weren't what I expected—what I was taught you were. And I wasn't poisoned by the air. When that happened, I knew there had to be a lie somewhere. Once I let go of what I was told, suddenly, all of it became a lie.

"But," she continued, the memory of Trigger being reduced to ashes burning in the forefront her mind, "at the same time, there's so much that doesn't make any sense. You say the surface has never been toxic—that it's always been habitable. But I've *seen* people die from the Blight. I've seen the pathogen detected in our scanners. If the surface has never been toxic and the Blight doesn't really exist, then . . . I just don't know. It's like everything conflicts . . ."

He waited to see if she'd say anything more. When nothing came, he quietly ventured, "It's sometimes difficult to know where a lie ends and the truth begins. As long as you recognize that there is a lie present, that's at least a good place to start."

Winter's gaze narrowed, intensifying the cold blue of her eyes. "I *know* there's a lie. I just don't know how far it goes or even why it's there to begin with."

"Does anyone else on Olympus know?"

"No . . . at least, I don't think so."

" . . . Will you tell them?"

"I don't know," Winter replied honestly. "I don't know if I will even be allowed to go back."

The sadness in his eyes intensified. "I'm sorry," he whispered.

Winter was astonished by his response. "Why?" she couldn't help but ask.

"If you can't go back home, that's terrible, and I'm sorry for you."

She heard nothing but sincerity in his tone, but somehow, the pity infuriated her. "I killed your team," she reminded him.

He appeared troubled by her statement, but pity still overwhelmed his features.

"I was going to kill you," she growled. "I almost did." There was no way he could look at her like that and mean it. He had to think she was a monster. If he'd killed three members of her team, she would hate him with every fiber of her being. She would assuredly have killed him on sight had the tables been turned.

"You had no knowledge of the truth. You were taught to kill. I can't hate you for something you did in complete ignorance." His statement was unequivocal.

"Yes, you can," she almost snapped.

"That's true. I suppose I can, but I refuse to." He shocked her to silence with his abrupt correction.

Winter searched his eyes and found nothing but sadness and pity within. There was no deceit; there was no manipulation. When he spoke, it was with authority and conviction.

"You can't tell me that some part of you doesn't want to kill me for what I've done." Winter's statement nearly sounded like a plea. Why couldn't he just hate her and let her be the monster? Why couldn't he just reach for his rifle and end her right now? She suddenly realized that if he were to make the attempt, she wouldn't try to stop him.

She detested feeling like the victim.

He shook his head in solemnity. "We're all led in the wrong direction sometimes," he stated firmly, then added softly, "I'm guilty, too." A shadow of discomfort crossed his visage.

Winter felt something inside her break at his words. A glass shield she had no idea even existed, shattered and fell into nothingness deep within. A foreign sort of softness touched her heart, and she almost smiled. The burning pain in her chest subsided, and she could veritably feel a physical burden lift from her shoulders.

" . . . I'm so . . . so sorry," she spoke more earnestly than she'd ever felt in her life.

He appeared as if he could tangibly feel her anguish.

"I can't explain how sorry I am," Winter teared up again.

His lips pursed, and he said nothing.

"I wish I could go back and change it all." A single tear rolled down her cheek. "I would take it back if I could." Her eyes fell to the woodland floor in shame. "But I can't."

A moment of silence passed as tears streamed her cheeks.

"You're right," he offered at length. "You can't ever go back and change the beginning. There was a time when I would have given anything to go back and change what I'd done. Living with my own actions was . . . unbearable. But I realized that wishing to change the past was only me trying to avoid the bitterness of having to live with what I'd done. Moving on and changing course from where you are right now is the only way to reconcile yourself. Trust me. You may not be able to change what you've already done, but you can always change what you do and where you go from here."

Winter looked up to meet his gaze.

"Now that you know the truth," he explained, "simply change course."

Winter sighed softly. "How? I don't know how."

He let out a long, controlled breath before responding. "I can't pretend to know what it will mean for you. But . . . one day at a time," he spoke with a small shrug, and a faint smile crossed his lips.

A long moment passed as Winter witnessed an eternity of thoughts pass through his eyes.

He slowly and carefully extended his hand. "My name is Joshua," he said softly.

Winter couldn't believe this moment was happening—standing there in a sunlit forest, free of her weapons, her armor, speaking with a surface human. It was all completely surreal. If she shook his hand, would she wake up? She didn't know if she wanted to. She paused and took stock of her convictions. She was here to learn the truth. That was her only priority.

This was not the day she was too afraid to go on.

She stepped forward and removed her gauntlet. "Winter," she said as she took his hand. In his grip she felt the calluses from a lifetime of hard labor; she felt a steady heartbeat; she felt warmth and strength.

His glittering hazel eyes held hers with respect and confidence. "Winter, huh?" He looked amused.

"It's actually—" she stopped short, thinking better of telling him her full name. "Yes. Winter."

Joshua smiled softly with a little shrug.

Winter was fascinated that his face could smile while his eyes still appeared so sad.

"Okay then. Winter it is." He gave her hand a gentle squeeze.

In the blink of a moment, she saw his eyes fix briefly on the Purifier mark on the back of her hand, though he said nothing of it.

"Thank you, Winter, for talking to me," he said simply.

She felt she should say something, but the silence was so comfortable.

Waves of thought and emotion coursed through her mind. The question of what to do now bore so much gravity, it was dizzying. She knew she had no choice but to go back and try to spread the truth. But the countless variables that accompanied the realization were overwhelming.

She let go of his hand suddenly.

"I want to bring an end to the purifying," she stated, hardly believing the words herself. It felt like she was stabbing herself in the back. "My people have to know that there's no more need for bloodshed." She paused and studied his penetrating, sad eyes.

"Be careful," he cautioned. "History is full of societies like yours. If they are anything alike, you should choose very carefully who you tell." His face turned in a captivating half-smile. "I want to be sure I can talk to you again."

"If I return to this place, will you be here?"

"I can't make any promises." Joshua shook his head. "It'll be cold wrath and hellfire as it is when I tell 'em about this." His eyes twinkled as if he'd said something funny. "But I'll be around."

Winter stepped back. "I'm going to try to find my way home. But I've been lost out here for so long, I don't know how successful I'll be."

"Oh, that's because you stumbled into our travelers trap," Joshua smirked. "We made this intricate set of intertwining pathways to mislead intruders from our farming grounds. It spans several miles." He paused. "I could show you the way out."

Winter was surprised by the offer. "You would?"

Joshua shrugged. "Sure. Wouldn't be right not to show a girl her way back home."

For the first time since Derrick Zinda's Ascension, Winter smiled . . . and meant it.

CHAPTER TWENTY-TWO

Miles away from the place where she and Joshua parted ways, Winter reassembled her communicator and placed the helmet back on her head. Opening to the broad channel, she was pleasantly surprised to hear voices but was careful to maintain silence on her end. She retraced her steps until she reached the clearing where she'd been dropped off for her zone several days previous.

She felt a twinge of betrayal as she activated her armor. Even though it was second nature, she couldn't help but wonder: what would she become if she brought an end to the Purifiers?

Looking up at the clear blue, sunny sky, Winter breathed deeply her last breath of the sweet surface air before the nano-armor sealed. Above her, she could see the dark ship in the clouds—her home. Once so majestic to her, it now seemed small and insignificant in contrast to the vastness and beauty of the surface world. She did feel guilty about betraying her comrades in a way, but if she could show them this place and bring her people back to their ancestral home without bloodshed . . . they could be free. They would have the freedom to grow as a civilization. They could be free to pursue other assigned vocations and passions that were not so dangerous. They could be free to choose whether or not they die for a cause that was not their own.

Joshua's handsome face entered her mind. She closed her eyes and pictured his brown hair, his deeply sad hazel eyes. She smiled as she imagined him smiling at her, seemingly assuring her that the path she was on was the right one. She felt a wave of confidence wash over her as the nano-armor fully engaged and sealed her in.

Winter flinched as the view screen on her helmet flashed and blipped in its constant analysis of her surroundings. She had been so long without it; now, it seemed intrusive to her senses. The purified, recycled air made her feel sick. A small headache began to swell in the corner of her temple.

The gauntlet display outlined the Loading Zone for the current team in the area. Winter stretched her aching limbs and pushed the pain of hunger and fatigue to the back of her mind before taking off at a steady pace toward the LZ.

Her body objected violently to the abuse. Her hunger and sleep deprivation, her stress and grief had all come to a head now. But it didn't matter. Winter's tunnel-vision focus wouldn't allow her to indulge in weakness at this point. She had a mission. No gnawing hunger or pangs of muscle failure could sway her from her course. She pushed through and forced her body to respond.

Monitoring the chatter on the channel, Winter knew the coordinates and ETA of their shuttle. She slowed to a stop when she heard its engines up ahead. As the craft landed, and while the Purifiers were assembling to embark, she looked over her equipment and armor pieces. She knew the deception was weak, but she wanted to make certain there was no damning evidence upon her person.

Winter moved forward with a giant lump in her stomach, completely filled with trepidation about what would follow. She didn't know if this moment would separate her from Olympus forever or if it would be the end of her life. She didn't know if they had purification orders for her or how they would respond to seeing her at all.

She could hear their voices now through the trees, and she continued to approach steadily. Before their loading began, right in the middle of their headcount, Winter emerged from the trees.

The shuttle lay idling in the clearing with the War Wolves team assembled in its shadow. They didn't see her at first, but when she drew near, they all looked up in shock. Some of them reflexively trained their rifles on her, others simply gaped in disbelief.

Captain Sellers stepped forward with an expression like he was seeing a ghost. Through his helmet's visor, his face twisted with confusion and disbelief but then slowly curled into gratitude and relief. He approached Winter with his arms wide.

Winter stepped toward him, her chest tight and breath coming hard, her stomach sinking into her boots. Everything seemed to slow down as butterflies of apprehension flurried within.

"You're alive!" Boom exclaimed. "I . . . I can't believe it! It's so good to—"

"Sir! Our orders," one member of his team reminded.

The captain stopped short as a light of recollection entered his eyes. "Wait, Winter, you need to stop right there. Our orders are to consider you blighted."

Winter continued forward and spoke loud enough that the team could hear. "I'm not." She maintained confidence in her voice, though her insides lurched with fear. "I'm not infected."

Boom stepped back and somewhat reluctantly drew his rifle. "No, seriously, Winter. Stop! You disappeared for three days. Your com was offline."

Winter halted at his order and thought carefully about the consequences of telling the truth, even though there was nothing she wanted to do more. If they were already given purification orders for her just for going offline, trying to convince them of the truth would certainly result in her instant death . . . then no one would learn the truth.

"I was hunting a pack of blighters," she lied. "They were hiding in some dense forest miles from here—it was too deep for a signal."

As the team looked to their captain for direction, Winter counted herself lucky that she didn't happen upon the Loading Zone for the Grim Reapers or any of the other high-ranking teams who didn't ask questions.

Safe amid his team now, Captain Sellers was able to collect his thoughts. "Just . . . disarm," he commanded at length.

Winter complied and put down her rifle, sidearm, and knife before raising her hands. It was like encountering a surface human all over again. She tried to be patient, understanding how hard it must be for them to even slightly go against orders.

"I'm not trying to hurt anyone," Winter spoke clearly. "I just want to go home."

"You've been out here alone for three days," Boom repeated as he attempted to wrap his mind around the situation. "No orders, no long-term team deployment. Just you, for *three days!* No one knew where you went or what happened. You just disappeared. And now you want me to, what, just *ignore* the directive? Your brain's been scrambled."

"Just take me home," she took an unconscious step in his direction. "I promise I—"

"Not a chance!" he snapped. "Come any closer, and I swear I will end you right here!"

"Lev," Winter addressed him evenly, "I'm sorry I caused so much trouble. That was not my intention, and I don't even want you to give me a pass. All I want from you is to let the scanners decide," she said as she pointed at the shuttle.

Boom lowered the point of his rifle and took a long moment to think. He looked bitterly disappointed. "Winter . . ." He took a long pause. "You were the best Purifier I've ever known. You singlehandedly rescued my team—you're the reason all of us are alive today."

His team members slowly relaxed their rifles downward.

His expression was doleful, as if he was giving a eulogy. "I've always respected you, and I always will. You deserve better than to be shot like some blighter." He holstered his rifle. "You deserve the respect of dying like a Purifier." He shook his head mournfully. "I'm sorry that it's come to this, but I pray that our Sovereign will take you quickly."

He ordered his team to load up and led the way through the scanning process.

Winter didn't move a muscle as, one by one, they entered the chamber. She pushed her insecurities down and maintained her confident posture and expression despite her utter exhaustion. She knew the scanner would come up negative and grant her entry . . .

. . . at least . . . she *hoped* she knew.

The mystery remained insoluble as she reflected upon Trigger who, not long ago, had been incinerated upon entry, not to mention the countless others before him who had fallen victim to the indiscernible process. There was a tingling doubt in the back of her mind that refused to give way to logic, and she could do little but hope that she was right.

Once the team was safe on the other side of the glass, Winter retrieved her armaments from the ground and slowly approached. Stepping inside the scanner was more difficult than she'd anticipated. The sheer force of will that it took to make it inside was unexpected. Her fear would not get the better of her, however, and though she felt shaky and incredulous, she stood confidently amidst the horrified and confused eyes trained on her from inside the shuttle.

The glass slid to seal behind her, and the green beams began their sweep. Winter concentrated on keeping her breathing even in the nerve-wracking moments that followed.

She closed her eyes and pictured Joshua's smiling face again. As the scanning lights splayed over her body, Winter smiled back at the pleasant image—noticing that simply imagining his face had a discernible effect in settling her nerves.

Green.

Ding

The noxious disinfectant spray spilled into the sealed chamber, obscuring the faces with mouths agape inside the shuttle, then it hissed out the vented floor.

The inner glass raised.

Winter didn't move. The War Wolves were terrified—at a complete loss for procedure. The inside of the shuttle was completely silent; the only sound was the engines warming up.

Captain Sellers' face was drawn with concern. "Take us up," he said flatly to the pilot, not taking his eyes off Winter. "Contact Control. Tell them what's happened."

Winter looked at each face—her friends—they all looked afraid of her. They couldn't understand this betrayal. The sickness they were certain she bore—she knew they all felt it. The terror and sense of treachery within the shuttle was poignant and tangible.

Hoping beyond anything that this was contributing to a greater cause, Winter simply gripped a ceiling strap and held on as the shuttle moved off the ground. She looked straight ahead and said nothing for the entire ride back to Olympus.

CHAPTER TWENTY-THREE

The Grand Elite, Draven Constantine Rothgard, straightened his collar as he obsessed over his image in the gold reflection of the Sovereign Tower's outer wall. Sunlight glinted off the immense structure, which loomed overhead in lustrous majesty.

The flawless skin of his perfectly clean-shaven face pleased him. He smiled in self-satisfaction before turning to face the approaching Guardians.

The two enormous officers said nothing, their countenances stoic, as they came to a halt with their small charge walking between them.

"Blessings to you, young Elite," Draven greeted cordially, forcing his face into a half-amiable smile as he addressed the little boy.

"Thank you, lord Draven. Sovereign's blessings to you, too," the blonde-haired boy recited with a bow.

Draven motioned for them all to follow before turning away and leading them under the vast archway that served as entry to the cavernous foyer of the Sovereign Tower.

"You must be excited, young man," he spoke over his shoulder without turning around. "Only *special* boys such as yourself are chosen to enter here."

The shy boy said nothing. Lord Draven shook his head to himself as he entered his personal security code on the keypad to the lift. He couldn't help but notice that this child's delicate features and curly hair would fetch him quite a bit of favor in his near future.

The face of innocence . . . he was always reminded of what it looked like on these little introductions. Somehow, he could never quite forget what it was like before.

As they waited for the lift to arrive, he broke the silence.

"I remember being your size," he smiled neutrally with uncomfortable nostalgia. "The first escorted trip away from the Elite Formulation Quarter—all a little overwhelming, isn't it? Perhaps . . . a little frightening?"

The little boy nodded.

Draven straightened his collar. "When I was your age, the Grand Elite—a striking man—Atherton Alistair Travers. He was so . . . refined. I remember looking up at him and thinking: 'I want to be as tall and handsome and remarkable as him someday.' And, in time . . . it happened." His attempts to goad admiration fell flat. "As Grand Elite, I spend hours every day with our Sovereign. I am his eyes and ears among the people." He looked to the boy for a reaction but received only, *"Yes, my lord,"* in reply.

"My influence is felt all over Olympus," Draven boasted. "Perhaps someday, you'll be the Grand Elite yourself, where you'll be granted the authority to wield all the massive power and influence that I do now."

Again, he didn't get the reaction he was hoping for and fell silent. He was beyond annoyed at the lack of awe.

The doors opened. Once they were all within the lift and riding up to the citadel, Draven spoke again. Dropping all pretense, he commenced the orientation. "You have been well prepared for this day," he frankly lied. "Coming to *know* the Sovereign is the first big milestone in your blessed life—in your journey to becoming a true Elite among those of . . . lesser quality."

In truth, Draven thought to himself, this is the only part of a male Elite's life they are *not* prepared for.

"Try not to speak unless you are commanded to do so," Draven continued. "And do not look his Greatness in the eyes, unless, of course, he commands it." He swallowed and fussed with his collar once more. Something inside him felt off every time he brought a new boy up, but he always pushed the uneasy feeling aside. The sickly, heavy feeling deep in his chest had grown easier to ignore as the years passed.

Draven stood up taller as the lift slowed to a stop. He cleared his throat before the doors hissed open.

The brilliant white chambers were beyond pristine. The vaulted ceilings were covered in an elaborate painting of sunbursts through thundering clouds. Each wall was alcoved with intricate gold arches. Lush ivory drapes adorned the giant windows and reached down to the warm marbled floor with grouting that was fixed with lines of tiny diamonds. A large sweeping staircase with gold railing led up to the lavishly draped bedchambers beyond a purple and ivory marble archway. The giant balcony above the staircase was crowned with a gold and crystal chandelier that refracted the pouring sunlight into a thousand tiny rainbows throughout the entry.

Draven led the party through the hallway. Not a speck of dust in sight, everything shined and polished to perfection, the sterile entry was filled with mirrors framed in rose gold—nothing growing or living, no sign of any plants or servants.

At the base of the stairs, the path split in two. A door to the right led to an opulent conference room where sunlight poured through the floor-to-ceiling windows. A giant silk-draped archway to the left led to a shimmering parlor with plush sofas and majestic paintings.

Movement within the parlor made Draven stand up even a little taller. The Guardians lowered their eyes. The young Elite kept his head bowed to the glittering floor.

Sovereign Zeus appeared from around the corner, his steps slow and soft. His golden silk robe hung loose on his bare chest, and his naked feet made no sound as they traversed the luxuriously carpeted floor. His salt-and-pepper hair and beard were groomed perfectly like a soft waterfall of snow. As he emerged slowly from behind the silk veil, Draven bowed before looking up into his strong, yet wrinkled face. His eyes looked tired.

Lord Zeus extended a bejeweled hand to his Grand Elite.

Draven took his hand softly and kissed it with respect and gratitude. When he looked up at his Sovereign, however, he found his eyes not trained on him as he would have liked, but rather fixed upon the child.

"Magnificent lord Zeus," Draven spoke, hoping to draw his gaze. He was disappointed. "May I present your new consort," he introduced them, stifling his frustration at not being noticed.

"And what is your name, sweet boy?" The Sovereign smiled reassuringly at the young lad who stood nervously before him. "You may look upon me."

"Weston Blaine Adderly, great Sovereign," he recited, looking sheepishly up at his god.

"Lord Zeus," Draven broke in. "May I humbly request a mere moment of your precious time before I go?"

The Sovereign looked irritated as he glanced up at his Grand Elite, knowing Draven would never be satisfied without having his moment. "Very well." Turning again to the boy, he pointed through the marble archway and instructed, "Wait for me in there, my dear Weston." He smiled and touched the boy's face before turning away. "I shall only be a moment."

"Please forgive me, my lord," Draven said as he bowed.

"Never mind. Come." He led the way to the conference room and took the time to seat himself in the large throne at the far end of the table before exhaling slowly.

The conference room had a firm, austere feel to it with the obsidian and gold walls. The long walnut table and tall winged chairs that surrounded it were the room's only furnishings, aside from the enormous, plush throne that crowned the arrangement. Made of pure gold and inlaid with diamonds, the throne's high arching back framed the Sovereign like a golden halo.

Draven walked to the wall-sized window as he waited to be addressed. The city far, far below, glittered underneath the iridescent glow of the barrier. It was beautiful. He loved Olympus for the adoration it gave him. Every citizen down below revered him for his looks and charisma; he could positively feel their adoration as he looked down upon them from the lofty heights of the Tower.

"Speak, young man," Zeus commanded at length. "Tell me, how fare my children?"

"Olympus thrives, great king." Draven smiled, happy to have some personal attention at last.

"And your reason for desiring an audience?" Zeus tapped his fingers softly on the long table.

"My lord, the people still rejoice every day in the glory and splendor of their god and your beautiful city."

"Yes . . .?"

"Yet your Unifiers report that many are restless to know more of the conquest to reclaim the surface world."

The god's nostrils flared. "I see . . ." He paused. "Close the doors."

"It's not that they're unhappy with their lives in your sight—" Draven continued as he obeyed as bidden.

"Simply that they have been infected with the idea of leaving," the Sovereign finished with a growl.

"They don't appreciate the world you've created for them," Draven spoke as he made his way back to the window. "How could they? I remember my ignorance before being initiated as your right hand, my lord. Those who live in paradise can't appreciate its perfection. Apparently, perfection is lost on lesser minds." At some point during his sentence, Draven was distracted by his reflection in the window and was no longer looking at the streets. He sighed in satisfaction.

"What is to be done then?" the Sovereign inquired, curious to know his right hand's state of mind.

Draven reluctantly turned from his reflection in the window to face his god. He bowed his head toward the throne. "In this, I plead to your benevolent omniscience, my lord," he pandered. "I am nothing more than a pale vessel for your glorious wisdom—a humble flask asking to be filled by the ocean of your magnificence.

"The Elite are duly entertained by the Purifiers and distracted by the delectation of their noble class. We publish the images and opulence of their celebrations and lifestyle to the lower classes. The Third Tier is, of course, of no concern whatsoever. They have no time to indulge in fantasy, and honestly, no capacity for imagination. Your genius has engineered the perfect workforce. They question nothing and are content with the distractions we give them . . . and they don't live long enough to spread much to the younger generations." He paused and lifted his eyes to the Sovereign. "The middle class, however, is another story. The Second Tier is where the true problem lies. Their intelligence leads some of them to question, their strength leads them to live longer lives, and their proximity to the Elite leads them to desire better things."

"And this is the problem for which I have yet to find an adequate solution." The Sovereign stroked his beard in frustration. "I require intelligent workers for the middle tier but frustratingly cannot yet isolate it from these pervasive longings of the soul. Here on Olympus, for over two-hundred years now, I have tried." He eased back, reclined his head on the cushion of his opulent throne, and sighed. "Know this, my child: the fundamentally flawed nature of man—his innate desire for freedom—is truly a troublesome beast to put down."

"Even still, my lord, as has been guided by your wisdom, your Unifiers have performed their tasks well and have consistently been able to root out any deviants at the first sign," Draven reassured. "That, at least, has stemmed the tide."

The Sovereign was silent for a moment, his face stern and unmoving as he considered his next words. "You are to encourage my children to focus their energy on the betterment of their vocations. Let everyone who dreams of returning to their ancestral home work doubly in his calling, thereby hastening the work to progress and earning them even higher accords in Elysium." He paused. "And also orchestrate a second Purifier bout this month. Some entertainment will return their minds to the present.

They are to be continually reminded of the pleasures of the here and now. If sufficiently implemented, such pleasures serve to dull their senses and drown their inner voices."

"Truly, lord Zeus: *'Your wisdom guides us through darkness and death.'*" Draven bowed low. "I will perform as you have commanded. Purifiers have become quite the center of our society in the recent past."

"They do indeed serve their purpose—as I intended."

"We all strive to, my lord. I do believe the citizens will be suitably distracted by the extra diversion."

"Very good." Zeus leaned forward in his chair, placed his elbows on the smooth tabletop, and rested his chin on his thumbs as he intertwined his ringed fingers. "There was a time when my children were content with their vocations—a time when they needed no . . . diversions to keep their minds from dangerous paths. It was a simpler time."

"I remember when I was a boy . . ." Draven spoke, attempting to spark a memory that would rekindle some favor. "You spoke of the genes growing weak."

"Corroded," Zeus glowered, ignoring his subordinate's plea for attention. "The unfaithful corrode the weak and leave traces of devastation in their wake long . . . long after they are gone."

Draven considered his words. "What may I do to aid you, great Zeus? Your wish is my will."

The Sovereign sighed slowly. His eyes truly looked exhausted. He paused before answering, "The weight of eternity weighs heavily upon me."

"Eternity pales to you," Draven flattered.

"Eternity is nothing but an empty void," he grumbled, uncharacteristically grim. "No matter how long you gaze into it, it stares back at you with unblinking eyes."

"If there is anything under the sky that I can offer," Draven pounced on the opportunity, "I would give anything of myself in your service—anything at all to aid you, Sovereign Zeus." He didn't mean to, but inadvertently, his eyes shifted to the far wall where a solitary keypad lay dormant.

The Sovereign smirked and looked up at the ceiling. "Oh, Draven," he said and shook his head. "You always were a curious one." Zeus stood and walked over to the keypad. "And persistent."

Draven followed briskly, almost daring to hope. He could just see the seam in the wall where the vault door would open. He wanted so desperately to be shown again.

Zeus dragged his hand down the seam in deep thought. He looked at Draven with a condescending smile. "Even when you were a child, you were insatiable." He stroked Draven's cheek.

"Lord Zeus, my only desire is to be the help you need," Draven spoke emphatically, feeling as if he was not being taken seriously. "Let me have more responsibility so that you may rest more. Permit me, my lord, and I will gladly take some of the weight of eternity from you."

"My dear Draven, you are not yet ready." Zeus shook his head and walked away from the wall.

Draven stifled the surge of rage that welled inside. His fists clenched until his knuckles were white, and his vision blurred almost black as he bit his tongue physically to substitute pain for rash action. He released the tension and controlled his voice. "How long, lord Zeus?" he asked impulsively.

"You may never be ready," the Sovereign said flippantly. "That is your burden to bear . . . and bear it you shall."

This chafed Draven's ego in a way he was not equipped to handle gracefully.

Luckily, the Sovereign's back was turned, and he could not see the Grand Elite's facial struggle.

"As Grand Elite," he sputtered, "I should be afforded all the power—"

The Sovereign slammed his hand down on the desk. "Enough!" he growled. "Don't think for an instant that you are not as completely replaceable as that boy out there." He pointed to the door. "I crafted the stars and formed the world millennia before I brought you into existence!"

Draven was stunned to silence. "Of course, lord Sovereign Zeus. Forgive my pretentiousness." He lowered his eyes and bowed low, barely stifling his rage. "I will go now and perform as you have commanded."

"I am not to be troubled with any trifling news," the Sovereign ordered. "Understood?"

"Perfectly, great Zeus. I will see to it." Draven bowed again, unlatched the door behind him, and backed completely out of the room before turning to the lift where the two Guardians still stood in silence.

Draven's hands shook as he entered the floor level on the keypad. His vision was growing blurry once more, and he could feel the hot wrath boiling up his throat.

The doors closed and the lift began to descend.

Turning in unbridled rage, Draven struck one of the Guardians with a balled fist three, four, five times in a fit of blackout fury.

The outlet didn't satisfy his impassioned state, and Draven kicked hard, buckling the knee of his silent victim. Another kick broke it, and the giant creature fell with a grunt.

The other Guardian looked on in silent compliance, having been conditioned for such things since formulation. Interceding wasn't even a thought as the Grand Elite pummeled and kicked his associate with complete impunity.

Knuckles bleeding, Draven struck the Guardian's face again and again until he could no longer clench his own hand into a fist. He screamed at the bloodied brute and drew a dagger from his robe, stabbing it deep into the man's torso three times before exhaling in exhaustion and dropping the blade. The Guardian's eyes rolled back into his head as his heavy mass first tensed then relaxed into a lifeless heap on the floor.

Draven backed away to the other side of the blood-spattered lift and breathed heavily as he wiped his fingers clean on the other Guardian's sleeve.

The lift doors opened at the base of the Tower, and Draven straightened his collar.

"Make sure that gets cleaned up," he ordered over his shoulder as he exited the lift and walked away.

Near the bottom of the steps, below the massive gleaming tower, Draven was approached by a Flight Control technician. The worker fell to her knees, face down near his feet.

"What is it?" The Grand Elite was curious. He wasn't addressed by workers often.

"Lord Grand Elite," the worker said. "Please forgive my imperfection."

Draven couldn't help but smile in self-satisfaction at being addressed in a manner so befitting his proximity to the Sovereign. "Go on," he bade.

"We've just received communication from a team returning from the surface. My lord, the War Wolves have recovered the lost Purifier, January Winterton."

Draven's smile disappeared. "Recovered her body?"

"No, my lord, she's alive and on board the shuttle."

"Who authorized that?" Draven demanded, his mind racing with a flood of potential disasters.

"Captain Lev Sellers, great one."

Draven fell silent, his mind generating dozens of solutions and scenarios and projecting the fallout of each. The Sovereign had just finished telling him the danger of corrosive influences. If this Purifier survived the surface for the better part of a week, the people might get the idea of colonizing again. He needed time to formulate a plan that would limit the possibility of upheaval. He needed to stall.

"Have a medical team isolate her immediately upon arrival," he commanded. "Remain in contact with me for further instruction. Dismissed."

"Yes, lord Grand Elite," the worker responded, rising quickly to her feet. With a bow, she turned and took off running.

CHAPTER TWENTY-FOUR

When the shuttle came to dock, the War Wolves all unstrapped in haste and exited the craft like they were running from a fire. Lev stayed behind, his eyes red, as if he was holding back tears. He gestured to the door with a face so tragic, it hurt Winter to see.

Winter took the invitation and walked to the shuttle door to disembark. She turned back. "Thanks, Lev," she said softly. "Everything will make sense soon."

Lev's sad face held a twinge of contemplation.

Winter stepped down from the shuttle and paused as a medical team dressed head to toe in biohazard suits swept in to take custody of her. They threw a thick, crackling canvas suit over her and topped it with a glass-shielded helmet.

The eyes of the other Purifiers disembarking their shuttles were all trained on her. Their faces shocked and confused—Winter recognized the fear in their eyes, the betrayal in their expressions. Maybe they would understand; maybe they wouldn't. Their faces swept past in blurs of emotion as the medical team laid hands on her and whisked her away.

"Do not allow her any contact with her team," the Grand Elite had ordered.

When they approached the Archangels' bay, chaos broke out as Captain Priest and the rest of Winter's team all crowded in. The medical team would let no one interact with her or speak with her. They blocked them from even seeing her as they rushed by. Wraith was shouting something, Scorch was pushing through, trying to speak, and Nalara's voice rang out with surprise and concern, but they were all indistinct noise to Winter. The mad rush to get through the bay, the sterile gloved hands that pushed her along, the giant white suits that surrounded her all blocked any reasonable thought.

Winter tried to say that she was alright—that she wasn't poisoned—but the din of confusion drowned out her voice completely.

"Limit her exposure to any eyes on Olympus," Draven's command continued, "and ensure that only the necessary medical staff have access to her once she's confined."

When they made it to the lift, half the medical team broke off to stay behind, blocking any Purifiers from following. Winter's breathing became a bit panicked as the rush and chaos of it all began to erode her focus. The lift halted and the doors opened, and her stomach fell to find a crowd of citizens gathered outside to see the spectacle. The medical team authoritatively escorted her through the onlookers, ensuring that no one came into contact with the tainted Purifier.

Winter couldn't help but think that her cooperation with these people was purely voluntary—that, at any moment, she could decide to resist, and there would be nothing they could do, given her advanced genetic build, strength, and lifetime of training. When she thought of it that way, it seemed quite ridiculous. But if she was going to show all of Olympus that the surface was safe, she needed to be as cooperative and collected as possible.

Once inside the infirmary, Winter was escorted to a sterile room where they stripped her gear and jumpsuit before throwing them into a contamination bin.

While one staff member swabbed her arm with alcohol, another shone a bright light into her eyes, and a third checked her blood pressure. Before she knew it, someone was taking her blood, and someone else was wheeling in a scanner.

Winter breathed deeply, subduing the urge to resist as they pushed her to a horizontal position on a gurney. The big scanner swept over her and hummed loudly, competing with the chatter and bustle of the room.

After a moment, it finished, and as quickly as it had all begun, the blood vials, equipment, and scanner disappeared as the team exited the room, locking Winter inside . . . alone.

The quiet washed over Winter, and she felt the pressure of circumstance build inside. The magnitude of her actions began to sink in. Everything began to feel polluted with fear, like a dream wherein nothing is tangible, nothing is distinct, but somehow, it feels intensely frightening. It was like a nightmare of falling from an unmeasurable height and not realizing it in time to wake up. Winter felt indistinct, yet poignant fear.

She felt the free-falling.

Did her foot slip on her upward climb towards the truth?

No . . . not slipped—jumped—with eyes wide open.

Winter had jumped off a ledge no one had ever seen before. She had become one of a kind in the whole history of Olympus. There had been long-term surface team deployments before—even ones she had participated in. But never solo. Never alone. She was now the Purifier who had disappeared on the surface for three days and returned alive. She didn't know what life would be like after this. Obviously, it couldn't be as it had been before. It would never be normal again.

Winter held fast to the idea that she was bringing Olympus to the truth. If she held on to that, she wouldn't fall forever.

She couldn't fall forever.

Voices outside the door came and went. Sometimes, it was large, excited groups; other times, only two soft voices. Time passed without perception. Winter had no idea how long she would be there. Now that she had no distraction, her stomach felt like it was eating her alive. The cold, sterile room, the processed air, the emptiness around her all felt so alien. Even though this was her home, even though she had been in rooms like this countless times as a Purifier, she couldn't stand the feeling.

The isolation itself was maddening.

Finally, the door unlocked and opened, revealing a Unifier. Her high cheekbones and completely neutral face were somewhat off-putting. The white suit was perfectly pressed; the smooth, hairless head was ornamented only by the small earpiece and view screen exclusive to their vocation.

The emotionless woman came to stand directly in front of Winter.

"How are you feeling, January?" the Unifier asked in a smooth, even voice.

Winter was taken aback by the unusual break in the Unifiers' standard routine. Her intuition told her something was off. "Hungry," she replied, "and thirsty."

"I understand." The Unifier studied the readouts on her display. "Can you remember how you got here?"

"Yes," Winter spoke slowly, wondering the point behind the question. "I found the War Wolves' shuttle, and they brought me home. When we got to the shuttle bay, a medical team brought me here to the infirmary."

A green light shone on the display, and the Unifier might have smiled a little.

Winter sat patiently.

"State the reason for your intercom malfunction."

Winter paused and considered how to answer truthfully. "The signal was prevented from transmitting."

Green.

"State the reason for your failure to report to the specified Loading Zone."

"I encountered a surface inhabitant and was detained by the engagement," Winter said carefully, needing to speak the truth, but trying not to pause or sound as if her mind was racing for a solution.

Green.

A long moment passed.

"You are very dehydrated," the Unifier said. "It would be understandable if your experience was riddled with hallucinations." She switched off the scanner—something Winter had never seen before—and looked her in the eyes. "I would be very careful with the words you choose to share with the Unifiers that follow."

Winter was confused by the suggestion.

The Unifier walked out without another word.

The door had barely closed before it opened again, and a healthcare worker walked in with a tray bearing food and water.

"The doctor says to eat slowly," he cautioned. "Your body needs to recover." He exited quickly.

Winter was flabbergasted by the treatment. This was nothing like what she expected. The very suggestion that she had been hallucinating was offensive to her. If that was in the official report, it would throw incredulity on anything she said in the future.

The water was cool and refreshing, and Winter could feel it travel down her throat into her empty stomach. She tried to take a nibble at a time of the simple nutrition blocks, but they were so unsatisfying, and she was so ravenous. As she continued to eat, a strong feeling stirred inside, but she passed over it as recovering from starvation.

It wasn't long before the door opened again, and another census worker walked in. He was tall and thin and wore the signature headgear and uniform of all Unifiers. His large eyes were somewhat unsettling as he approached.

A green scanner projected from his headgear and played over Winter's

Purifier mark. This was the routine she was accustomed to, throwing an even more mysterious light on the previous visit.

"Steady resting heart rate of fifty-two," the Unifier spoke.

Winter shifted uncomfortably and finished her mouthful.

"Identify," he said with profound disinterest as he monitored the readings on his view screen.

"January Winterton," she answered. "A Unifier was already—"

"State your position," he cut her off.

"Purifier, Archangels' lieutenant." Winter tried to settle her rattled nerves.

"Baseline established." He switched his gaze to Winter. "You were recently deployed to the surface with your team."

"Yes," Winter replied in programed compliance.

"You completed your surveillance of the assigned area that day?"

"Yes."

The view screen turned red.

"Signs of deception detected," the Unifier stated.

Winter cursed internally before correcting herself. "I . . . I was sidetracked by signs of blighters." Her head began to swim.

The display switched to green.

"State the reason for your intercom malfunction," he repeated the question from the previous Unifier.

Winter paused but answered in kind. "The signal was prevented from transmitting."

Green.

The Unifier nodded and continued. "When your communicator lost its signal, why did you ignore protocol and fail to return to your drop point?"

Winter's mouth felt dry and unnatural; she swallowed and picked her words carefully, struggling to keep her voice even. "I was determined to find the blighters in the area."

"And did you locate them?"

"Yes."

"Did you neutralize them?"

"Yes." Winter winced when the screen flashed red again.

"Signs of deception detected," the Unifier stated again.

"I didn't use my firearms," Winter added quickly.

The screen switched to green once more.

The Unifier's brow furrowed. "Heart rate is now seventy-four." He paused and followed the readouts before continuing at length. "Do you believe you were exposed to the Blight in the time you were stranded on the surface?"

Winter caught herself in time to keep from chuckling. "No," she answered quite honestly. She fought to keep her eyes open as a sluggish feeling washed over her.

The green light held steady.

A moment of tense silence followed. Winter almost jumped when the Unifier turned suddenly and exited without another word.

Left alone once more, Winter fought the heavy fatigue that began to set in. It felt forced and unnatural. She struggled to stay awake but could barely hold on to consciousness, even when a doctor and two large Guardians came in.

Winter was partially aware of the doctor explaining they were there to escort her back to her living chambers, but her head was swimming heavily and the world seemed to melt before her eyes. She couldn't have resisted if she tried as the Guardians scooped her up under her arms. Her breath became labored as they approached the lift, and the surroundings began fading to darkness. Her feet felt like heavy weights hanging from her torso, and all of a sudden, she could have sworn she stumbled but . . .

Throat burning, eye aching, Winter slowly awoke in her own bed. The evening light flooded in through her open windows, and everything looked completely perfect.

Surreal and glowing, the room seemed more like a set stage and less like a place of living.

Winter stood up with difficulty and stumbled to the bathroom, where she drank several glasses of water before washing her face. The overall muscle weakness and bleariness in her mind was more than she could bear. She melted to the floor of her bathroom and spent several minutes simply propped up against the counter.

Everything seemed heightened and intensified. It was somewhat dreamlike being in her apartment again, in her own clothes again. Of all the scenarios she imagined, she never expected this.

Something was very off.

Hungry more than anything else, she leveraged herself by propping an elbow on the toilet and hoisted herself up. After testing her legs and finding them stable enough, she moved slowly to the kitchen and fixed a practical snack, trying to remember that her stomach needed to adjust. Her mind was flying and coasting at the same time. Every thought imaginable raced through, but with such speed and incoherence that it was impossible to make sense of anything.

Something about her living chambers was increasingly bothering her.

Everything was immaculate, like she always kept it, but almost *too* immaculate. Some small things were not where she normally left them. The furniture was slightly . . . off.

Her door chimed and then opened before she could respond.

She was happy and surprised to see Nalara walk in, but her friend bore a stoic face. Winter smiled anyway.

"Don't speak," Nalara cut her off before she could begin. "Just go get into your dress greens and follow us."

"What do you mean? I just—"

"No, you can't speak," Nalara insisted. "They barely let me come as it is." She turned away and exited the apartment but whispered over her shoulder, "I'm glad you're safe."

Winter caught the glimpse of a smile before Nalara walked out.

She sighed heavily. Blocking her mind from generating possibilities for which she had no context, she switched her mind to utter practicality. She had made this what it was. She was the one who had diverted from her training and thrown Olympus into a situation for which they were completely unprepared. Now was the time for patience and composure. She needed to show that she was capable and sane; she needed solid credibility before announcing to the city that everything they knew was wrong.

Courage was difficult to muster as she donned her uniform once more. This time, it was not to receive medals and honors; it was probably a disciplinary council where her fate would be decided.

Winter shook her head as a physical signal to cease the conjecture. Truly, she had no clue what could be in store. She didn't know what to expect.

She brushed her ebony hair carefully and fashioned it into an attractive bun, then pulled on her beret, making sure not to move a single hair out of place.

She looked perfect—she looked like a model Purifier, just as she needed to appear. Whoever saw her needed to believe that she was the best of the best. They needed to believe her words. She felt the weight of responsibility on her shoulders. She felt in her heart that nothing in the universe was more important than bringing the truth to her people.

Not only for the sake of her people, though. Joshua and all the surface inhabitants, whether they knew it or not, depended on her for survival as well. If their extermination was to be avoided, it was up to her. She couldn't help but think about the potential progress and cooperation of the two sides and what they could accomplish together.

Finally, Olympians had a chance to return to their ancestral home—a goal that had seemed unreachable for so many years.

Finally, Joshua's people could stop living in fear.

No more bloodshed, no more waiting.

Winter felt a warm calm fill her heart as she locked in her purpose.

She was ready.

CHAPTER TWENTY-FIVE

Somewhere down on the surface, Winter knew that a man stood alone. His sanity was being called into question, no doubt, as he told his people about a face-to-face encounter with a stranger from the sky—a hunter who had mercilessly and singlehandedly killed hundreds of them. He felt uncertainty, maybe thought of keeping it to himself. But somehow, he found the courage to share with his people that he had opened a dialogue with the enemy. Perhaps he was telling them right now that up there in the clouds somewhere was a woman who was standing up to her people. And for the first time in the history Olympus, there was a voice against thousands telling the truth about the surface. Perhaps his extermination-ravaged kindred were now feeling hope for the first time.

Winter latched on to this thought as the lift descended, carrying her in the midst of four enormous Guardians, as well as Nalara, down to the floor level of the Purifier's housing building. The stoic, silent Guardians fixed their blank eyes straight ahead and didn't move a single over-sized, swollen muscle.

Nalara fidgeted a little as she struggled to keep her gaze forward. Winter could tell she was nervous, but she also looked excited somehow. A playful smile kept struggling not to manifest on the corner of her lips.

The doors opened, flooding sunlight into the lift as they stepped forward and exited the building. Winter's eyes adjusted quickly to the outside light for the first time in—she realized she didn't know how long. The busy city street was filled with citizens smiling and clapping, all of them looking at her.

Surreal.

It didn't seem like it was really happening; she felt almost as though she was a third-person observer. The iridescent sunlight filtering through the barrier, the smiling faces all around, the ambient clapping . . .

She felt like she was walking in a dream.

A Guardian's subtle but firm nudge from behind reminded her to continue forward. Winter complied in a silent daze. She couldn't quite place this new development into context.

Their six-person convoy made a direct line through the throng of cheering citizens gathered across the Second Tier of Olympus. After eventually reaching the Hive, they left the crowds behind as they ascended the Grand Stairway to the Elite tier. Glittering diamonds set into every white marble step, the immaculate Elite paradise came into view as she progressed upward. When the long climb ended, they veered toward the Sovereign Tower where a massive congregation was assembled.

Brilliant shafts of sunlight came glistening through the barrier and glinted off the monolithic structure. Every single initiated Purifier in Olympus was present, wearing full formal dress greens and standing in perfect sequential rows. Each team stood by rank at perfect attention, their eyes held fast toward the Tower's arched entrance where stood the Grand Elite himself: Draven Constantine Rothgard. The handsome man with his striking eyes and chiseled features stood on the top step beneath the arch. He was arrayed in the very finest silk clothing, fashioned to resemble militaristic uniforms, but with the embellishment of dazzling jewels and bright gold chains adorning his chest where medals and honors would have been.

The exuberance of the Second Tier was entirely absent here. Here, it was so silent; Winter could hear her own breathing. Their footsteps seemed like echoing hammer falls amid the utter stillness.

Small groups of Elite had gathered here and there in casual interest and stood at a distance to spectate.

Led by Nalara, the Guardians walked Winter up the center of the gathered Purifiers and ascended the steps directly to the Grand Elite.

Winter sighed, trying to break up the tension building in her chest. This was unnerving, not to mention completely unexpected. The Grand Elite looked directly at her as she approached and steadfastly held her gaze. His charismatic eyes sparkled with some hidden emotion while his face remained neutral. The Guardians led Winter to stand before him, then broke off to the side with Nalara.

Suddenly, Draven opened his arms and pulled Winter into a full embrace. She stifled her immediate defensive reflex as she consciously allowed his arms to close around her. She remained motionless as his hands pressed into her back, pulling her up against him for a long moment before letting go. He held her shoulders and smiled warmly.

"Welcome home, brave Purifier," he spoke with projection for the whole assemblage to hear.

The Purifiers ruptured into hearty applause as Draven held Winter's hand up in victory in a fantastic display of showmanship.

Winter's wide eyes could not mask her confusion. She looked at Nalara, who beamed and clapped and bounced with full sincerity and pride.

Was this a joke?

Was this even real?

Draven smiled, but the look in his eyes sent shivers of discomfort down Winter's spine.

"Welcome home," he repeated to her once more before turning to the quieting throng. "January Winterton of the Archangels shall forever be remembered as a Purifier like no other. Her bravery and proficiency has been a brilliant reflection of our Sovereign's glory since her very first days in the Formulation Quarter. Our creator's favor has been seen throughout her life in her dedication to his unfailing wisdom. All of you willingly put your lives on the altar of Olympus' future. Lord Zeus is pleased with his Purifiers. But here today, he specifically honors January Winterton for her unparalleled resilience and combat prestige—for surviving three days on the surface, alone and unafraid, completely cut off from her team, battling the Blight-affected mutants day and night in the most memorable display of righteous resolve to never submit!"

Winter's mouth dropped involuntarily.

This really is happening . . .

Draven turned to Winter and produced a small polished box. "January Winterton," he spoke fervently. "I remember the day you returned from your trials—from the hellish pit of Tartarus—having accomplished what only the great Nereza Vossen had been able to before you." He chuckled a little. "I knew from that day that you would be a Purifier for the ages." He opened the box, revealing a brilliant gold chain. "And here, I find myself again, holding yet another award for you. January Winterton, for your bravery, for your fearless service of our lord Zeus' great cause in the face of isolation and death, I present to you: The Survivor's Award." He clasped the chain to each of her shoulders as the Purifiers all exploded into applause.

"Congratulations, January! Olympus truly smiles upon you," Draven opened his arms again and moved in for another embrace, but Winter flinched back instinctively.

Draven's expression melted suddenly, and amidst the din around them, Winter saw the truth behind his eyes. The cold wrath that he'd kept hidden boiled to the surface for only a fraction of a second, and he glared at her in utter loathing.

His lapse lasted only a moment before it was drowned out by an expression of love and concern. He whispered something to the Guardians before joining with the crowd in smiling and clapping.

The Guardians moved in, and two of them seized Winter's wrists and elbows in a firm escort position.

Winter complied, not wanting to appear violent or unbalanced. She struggled a little, but she knew they would not relinquish their hold without a real fight.

"Each of you," Draven continued to the assembly as Winter was escorted away, "should reapply yourselves to your vocation with renewed fervor. Make your efforts double, just like our hero that we honor here today. Each of you is a hero when you complete your given tasks. By so doing, you bring glory to our creator and pave the way for a brighter future! The Blight may be an unrelenting, uncompromising enemy, but with heroes like you and January Winterton, we cannot fail!"

At the end of his speech, his voice was replaced by roaring applause, and Winter felt suddenly as if the lie of the surface had become a living entity that was smothering her in a hateful wave. The truth became her lifeboat, and she clutched on to it desperately, repeating it over and over in her head, trying to tread water in the drowning pool of the loathsome falsehood.

Walking down the middle aisle of the throng, Winter caught sight of her team and reflexively pulled against the Guardians that held her arms. She called to her companions, but they either didn't hear amid the applause or didn't understand. She saw Captain Priest, his glowering face a mixture of emotion she'd never seen in him before.

Almost the size of a Guardian himself, Wraith stalked up to their procession and walked with them.

"Pull yourself together," he hissed, walking fast by their side. "Show some dignity; if not for yourself, then at least for the team's sake."

"Captain Priest, I didn't—" Winter began.

"I don't want to hear it," Wraith cut her off. They were far enough away from the crowd that now, his voice carried more gravity. "You got what you wanted; you got all the attention in the world. Now, let it go."

At the bottom of the stairway, Winter planted her feet and set her jaw. "You're wrong about me."

With their genetically enhanced size and power, the Guardians alone could compete with her considerable strength, and they prepared to do so.

"You're dismissed," Wraith waved the Guardians away.

"The directive from the Grand Elite is to escort this one to living quarters," one of them grumbled firmly in the signature otherworldly low voice of the Guardians.

"I am the Master Purifier, Orrin 'Wraith' Priest," he pointed out firmly. "Concerning *my* soldiers, I am far more capable than you in fulfilling the Grand Elite's commands. Now get lost."

The Guardians looked questioningly at one another, then begrudgingly relinquished their charge before walking away.

Winter and Wraith each stared holes into the other's skull. A fire could have spontaneously ignited in the air between them.

"Walk," Wraith ordered harshly.

"You think I disobeyed you on purpose for the attention," Winter accused but complied immediately. She was still his second, and insubordination would gain her nothing.

"That's the only reason you do anything," Wraith snapped, his patience gone. "Eagle Eyes is dead now, and you have to find another way to get your . . . *ego* stroked."

"That's a lie!" Winter returned, edgy at the disrespectful mention of her teacher. "I'm trying to help Olympus."

"Everything you do is to help yourself!" Wraith growled. "You've never cared about your team; you constantly disregard rules and orders—all to gratify your own interests. You've always been out of control, Winter, but this last one takes the prize. I know you broke off and hid somewhere for three days and made up this crazy story about surviving."

"I didn't make up anything!" Winter insisted. She looked down at the gold chain draped across the top of her chest—her 'Survivor's Award.' It seemed like such a joke. She scoffed bitterly. "And I *never* said anything about 'surviving.' I was . . ." her voice faded as she attempted to reign in her frustration. She paused to breathe, forcing her haze of thoughts to come into focus. "Please, Wraith. You have to believe me," she begged. "What I did was for Olympus."

"No." Wraith almost laughed. "I checked your weapons. They were never even fired. Not once. But still, you're the celebrity no one can get enough of."

"Can you even hear yourself?" Winter shook her head in disbelief, her frustration returning like a tidal wave crashing. "I have been the model Purifier my entire career! I have achieved faster than anyone I know. I'm already ranked in the top twenty, and it's only been four years since my initiation. Why can't you believe that maybe I knew what I was doing? Why can't you trust me?"

Wraith stopped in his tracks in front of the Purifiers' living quarters doors and leaned forward to get right in her face. "Why can't I trust you?" he repeated. "Because you've always been, and always will be, nothing more than a cheap, showboating, little attention *whore.*"

Winter was stunned to silence by the unbridled show of raw hatred.

The utter lack of any kind of respect, the complete loathing that she saw in his eyes was almost frightening. He looked like a predator, cold and vicious.

"I'm trying to help," Winter insisted, not giving an inch.

Wraith opened the door to the lift. "I don't care." He motioned her through.

"How?" Winter couldn't help but ask as they entered the lift together. "How can you *not care?*"

"I don't care because, like it or not, you are *not* a god," Wraith retorted. "We gain direction from the Sovereign—not you."

"Wraith, I'm a good Purifier," Winter tried to reason with him as they arrived at the third level and walked down the empty hall. "I always have been, you know that. You have to believe that I did what I did for a good reason."

"No, I don't," he said flatly and entered his code into her door pad. Having regained his composure after his outburst of rage, he gestured to the open door.

Winter stepped inside, obedient yet frustrated beyond belief.

"Winter, I'm putting you under forty-eight-hour solitary quarantine." He entered the specified programming into the touchscreen. "This is a gift from me to you. Get your head straight." He gazed at her with cold aversion. "If you *want* to be a good Purifier, think more about how your choices affect your team—and less about how to stay in the spotlight."

"But—" Winter protested in desperation.

The door closed.

She couldn't believe it.

Footsteps retreated from her threshold, and she tried to open the door. The pad turned red and denied her.

Winter growled and punched the door. The release felt satisfying, so she punched it twice more in anger.

This hadn't gone as she anticipated at all. She wasn't able to share the truth because it had been drowned in a popular lie. Now—especially after days of confinement—her voice would never be heard over that of the Grand Elite's.

Everyone loves to see their heroes win.

CHAPTER TWENTY-SIX

Draven turned away from the cheering crowd of Purifiers and pressed his fingertips into the space between his eyebrows, massaging the skin in a little circle. His facade of a smile disappeared as he retreated into the shadow of the Tower's arched entrance.

Finally, that was over.

His code was accepted on the lift keypad, and Draven felt his headache intensify as the lift ascended to the Sovereign's living space. A spark of fanatic jubilance caught in his throat as he rationalized that his was important enough news to interrupt the Sovereign after he'd specifically commanded to not be disturbed with trivialities.

Draven sighed with enthusiasm at the opportunity to share his cleverness in solving the unique problem with the Purifiers. This was the extra responsibility he'd asked for, and he was eager to share his success and receive praise.

The doors opened into the opulent chambers, and he instantly heard the sound of soft laughter. The Grand Elite followed his ears into the conference room where sunlight flooded the area and bathed the Sovereign in a godlike glow.

The familiar sickly, heavy feeling sank deep in Draven's chest when he saw the little boy there with him.

What was his name?

Draven shrugged internally. This child would be nothing to the Sovereign soon enough.

A gentle twittering and flapping filled the room as the two of them played with a tiny bird near the vault door, which stood conspicuously ajar.

The Sovereign's laughter faded as he looked up to see his Grand Elite, and a subtle neutrality took over his features.

"May I be permitted to enter, merciful lord Zeus?" Draven requested with a short bow.

"Enter," the Sovereign replied and returned his attention to the boy.

Draven obeyed. "I see this young Elite has been gifted his first pet."

The little blonde boy held up his new bird, and the colorful little thing chirped again.

Draven feigned a smile of approval, which quickly melted into a sardonic smirk as he remembered being that small and seeing a living creature in person for the first time. What a waste of time his gift had been.

"This had better be important, Draven," the Sovereign said without looking up, a sharp edge to his voice.

"It is, lord Zeus," Draven replied quickly. "An urgent matter with one of your Purifiers."

Lord Zeus bent down to the boy's ear, "Go play in the bedroom."

With a nod, the child took his new pet and quickly complied.

The Sovereign closed the vault and smiled at his Grand Elite. "And I trust that this 'urgent matter' has been resolved?"

"It has, great Sovereign." Draven beamed with pride. "I resolved it brilliantly."

The Sovereign offered his hand. "I knew my trust in you was not misplaced. You have pleased me greatly, my son."

Draven drew closer like a praised dog and took his master's hand, kissing it eagerly.

"You always were my favorite," Zeus stroked Draven's face softly before moving away toward the throne at the head of the chamber. "It's been a long age since my creations malfunctioned. I had hoped the formula had finally been perfected this time." He sighed and sat down.

"Everything you do is perfect, great king," Draven fawned, enjoying the attention.

"Dissension is the natural tendency of mortals."

"What can be done then?"

"Take up any shred by the roots and burn it," was the Sovereign's immediate, grave reply. "Leave no traces of dissent, or they will continue to taint the minds of others." He seemed to be talking to himself now, but Draven noticed his knuckles turning white as he clenched and fussed with his fingers. "The weak, malleable state of a mortal's mind will forever be a frustration to perfect. I cannot stress enough to you, my right hand, the importance of eradication. Your resolution to dissent must be swift and final—every time."

Draven bowed. "Thank you, my lord. Your wisdom is, to me, an unfailing light. I knew that following your example would lead me to success." He took an eager step forward. "Would you care to know how I conducted the correction?"

The Sovereign waved him off. "I trust your judgment in the matter." He arose from his golden throne. "Please, take your leave, my son. I feel that a long afternoon enjoying all the pleasures Olympus can afford—" he glanced out toward the bedroom—"is what *you* should go and seek."

A little bitter at being dismissed without having shared with the Sovereign his genius solution, Draven nonetheless bowed and exited the conference room quickly to ride the lift back down into the city.

On the streets, Draven couldn't help but feel connected to everything he saw, almost like Olympus was his arena, and everyone there existed just for him. His crowd-pleasing smile was on full display as he walked through the highest tier of the city like a peacock that owned a garden.

The Elites there wandered in aimless, perpetual, pleasure-seeking luxury. A large number always seemed to gravitate toward the immense fountain, where a marble rim provided easy seating as they conversed and laughed together. Mid-ranking second-tier citizens, specially formulated to function as entertainers and servants for the Elite class, tended to their needs and whims in silent obedience.

Many of the young Elite men were accompanied by their various and assorted pets as a show of their favor with the Sovereign. A snake draped over the shoulder or a tiny dog in arm was fairly common. The few with larger pets would have a lower citizen there to care for them, like the gentleman with a servant walking a tiger on a leash or the boy with a falcon on the arm of his handler.

On his way home, Draven circumvented a mélange of plush cushions scattered about a small orchestra that performed solely for the entertainment of the Elites who lazily reclined around them, jovially sipping fine red wines and chortling at the freshest gossip.

Even as a younger man, before his divine appointment as the Sovereign's right hand, Draven would have never joined them. He had always found such pleasures tedious and unsatisfying. His refined palate demanded . . . *more*. But especially now, as Grand Elite, he was elevated far above even those of his same class—as high as the eagle flying above the pigeon. They may be Elite, but he was Grand. It would be beneath him to waste time with the frivolities of those truly undeserving of his presence.

One of the sculptural estates that was given to Draven as the Grand Elite was separated from the general population by a manicured lawn with bordering hedges and giant marble pillars lining a stone courtyard and perfectly kept gardens. A well-groomed servant of the middle class stood erect, waiting for him at the palace's open door. Draven couldn't have distinguished one servant from the other; he neither knew nor cared to learn their names. It was a gift enough for them to serve in his presence.

Draven removed his coat and shoes and left them with the nameless man at the door before moving into the spacious, gold-laden lounge where warm sunlight passed through scarlet linen curtains.

He walked directly to a giant deep oak cabinet and poured two glasses full of dark liquor. Lifting one glass to his lips, he drank deeply, savoring the burning sensation as it washed down his throat and filled his stomach. He closed his eyes to enjoy the release and painkilling effect. He could feel the stress of the morning begin to relax from his shoulders. He glanced at the bottom of the glass and thought about putting it away. He considered the frugality of rationing himself briefly, but then filled the glass again and drank it down.

Toned arms with soft skin passed under his armpits and clasped across his chest.

"There you are," a woman's voice cooed.

"Have you been here since the ceremony?" Draven asked with slight disinterest, gazing again into the empty tumbler.

"Came right here, just as you commanded, master . . . great one . . . gracious lord Grand Elite."

Draven smiled broadly. He loved hearing those words. He turned and looked into the sharp greens eyes of his most recently favored consort. "I appreciate the obedience," he commented, looking over his guest. She wore nothing but his own red silk robe.

"I appreciate the opportunity," she smiled wryly and tucked a short blonde lock behind her ear.

"You're welcome." He handed her the untouched glass he'd poured, then asked directly, "Did you tell me your name already?"

"Lilith," she stated, taking a sip of the golden honeycomb bourbon.

"Mm," Draven grunted offhandedly as he turned to approach the hallway. "It must be very exciting for you," he spoke over his shoulder as he walked, "being in the presence of the Grand Elite—here in my own home."

"Very exciting," Lilith agreed readily in languid tones. "I truly hoped I would be invited back."

"Well, I prefer Purifiers over Elites," Draven shrugged. "Unlike you, their lifestyle makes them . . . soft and fragile. They tire easily . . . and break even easier."

She raised her glass in thanks and took another sip.

Draven's countenance shifted as they entered the lavish bedroom. "The citizens *like* Winterton?" he stated, though it was a question.

Lilith shrugged. "She has a fair amount of followers."

"More than you?"

Lilith showed her indignation, but answered honestly, "Yes." She took a long drink. "But her status is purely sensation over her age." Her lips curled into a sneer. "It will pass soon enough."

Draven reclined into one of the soft, cushioned chaise lounges in his room. His companion followed and draped herself across his lap. "I made the right choice then," he said, nodding introspectively.

"Why do you care?"

"Lord Zeus is showing increased confidence in my abilities. He put this matter fully in my hands since he was . . . otherwise occupied."

"I don't understand why you didn't just assign her to reclamation," Lilith muttered into her glass.

"The people love seeing me." Draven shifted in his seat and ran a hand along her thigh toward her pelvis; he dug his nails in slightly, leaving red lines across her skin. "Award ceremonies are fun to watch, they get everyone excited   and no one asks questions. I could have just as easily ordered her death, but then the questions and the mystery would never end. This way, it's out there where everyone can see. Hiding in plain sight—always the best place to hide."

Lilith moaned and leaned into him. "I think you did it just so you could watch me kill her myself at the next bout."

"Well . . ." Draven chuckled and wrapped a controlling hand around her neck. "You know how I love to watch."

CHAPTER TWENTY-SEVEN

Winter fell to the floor with sweat cascading down her face. Her muscles swelled with exertion as she pumped her arms, completing fifty pushups in well under a minute before jumping to her feet once more. She jogged in place as she waited for the rest of her team to finish their sets before leading them around the Hive arena in an all-out sprint. Not stopping for a rest after their completed lap, Winter guided the Archangels to the stairs lining each of the countless rows in the immense coliseum.

"Aww, man!" Scorch whined in agony.

"Push it!" Winter yelled and began charging up the stairs, two steps at a time. Once they reached the platform of the Ascended, she turned them all around, led them back down another flight, then raced right back up again. The third time up, she made them jump squat each step; the fourth time was side steps facing one direction on the way up and facing the other direction on the way down; the fifth time was sprinting backward up the steps and high knees on the way down.

"Murder!" Scorch cried out, panting wildly. "You're a *murderer!*"

Winter's mouth went dry as she struggled for a lung-full of air. A heavy weight settled in the base of her gut as dead, staring faces appeared in her memory. *All too true,* she thought sickeningly, shaking her head to drive their empty-eyed faces from her mind.

"We're done," she relented at the base of the stairs and began stretching the burn out of her legs as her companions collapsed to the floor wherever they stood.

"Oh, thank Sovereign!" Nalara gasped in relief, her chest heaving violently.

Sounds of physical labor filled the vast arena as five of the ten Purifier teams performed their conditioning training. An obstacle course fashioned from the hexagonal platforms took up the center of the stadium, while a running track circled the perimeter. Strength training stations filled some spaces here and there, but nothing was used more than the firing range. Digital targets were set at twenty-meter intervals, cordoned off from the rest of the training areas by a high wall of hexagonal tiles. There was always a large group of Purifiers taking impatient turns with the training rifles.

There were only a few team captains that took physical training as seriously as they did marksmanship, and those teams were always the top achievers.

Captain Wraith, genetically built more like a tank than a man, rode his team hard every single training day, stressing strength and agility.

"Everyone on your feet!" Winter commanded. "Three kilometer run for your cool down!" She took off at a relaxed jog so the team could catch up once they stood.

Eagle Eyes had impressed the same focus and drive for physical superiority with his team. Winter remembered him with painful fondness as she led her team through finishing the run. Derrick had wished more than anything that his team would have the desire to learn the old way, but he said they seldom showed any interest. Even when he had mandated it as part of their training, they hadn't seen the value.

Winter was thankful for the lifelong-honed ability to channel her emotions into training. Before the death of her teacher, the only time she had been swept up in emotion the way she'd been over the course of the last week was during her trials, and the reminder was not pleasant.

As beads of sweat soaked her brow and trickled down the small of her back, Winter was able to think clearly. The physical exertion took up all the extra energy needed to feel frustrated or confused and left only enough focus to level out one thought at a time.

She rounded the final bend and slowed to a stop, her team gasping and wheezing as they trailed in behind her. Most of them doubled over and leaned on their knees. Winter was exerted, most definitely, but this was nothing compared to the free-running she practiced on her own late at night.

"Five minutes," Wraith barked, his massive frame drenched with sweat as he brought up the rear of his team. He always ran in the back to berate stragglers.

Shaking with fatigue but still composed, Winter took a few paces from the group. None of them knew how to behave around her right now.

"Bloody Winter off on her own again." Sapphire shook her head and rubbed her sore arms.

"Hey, she's been through a lot. Give her a break already," Scorch chided lightheartedly.

"You always defend her," Viper derided. "Just 'cause she was your initiate."

"You should, too," Bulletproof reminded solemnly. "Don't discount all she's done for us just because she's wrapped up in some weird stuff right now."

"Exactly," Scorch cast a glance in Winter's direction. "What she needs now is our understanding. Whatever she went through, I'm sure it took its toll."

"Come on, Seth," Savage accused. "Even *you* have to be freaked out about her showing up at the LZ with the blood on her."

"Yeah, man," Havoc said. "I mean, seriously! What was that all about?"

"And I heard the medical worker cleared her with just contusions," Sapphire added. "Does that sound right to you?"

"And then on top of all that, just suddenly disappearing for three days." Viper released an exasperated sigh. "Look, I know the Grand Elite honored her with that Survivor's Award and all, but still . . . something's just really off with her."

Nalara remained silent through the conversation but listened in rapt interest.

"Aren't you guys forgetting something?" Scorch reminded with a smile. "Winter's an Archangel. We're on the same team here. More than that, she's our lieutenant. Got it?"

"Yeah, but so were you, not too long ago," Havoc scoffed.

"And there's a reason I'm not anymore," Scorch snapped in uncharacteristic severity. He sighed sharply, glanced around at his teammates, shook his head, and walked away.

Nalara had never seen Scorch upset before. Even under fire, he always seemed to be above it all. "Didn't Winter just pass him up in numbers?" she couldn't help but ask once he was out of earshot.

The team exchanged significant looks with one another.

"Oh, sweetie." Sapphire shook her head.

"Don't ask," Viper warned. "That kind of drama ruins you."

"You guys heard what Gorgon told me about Winter, right?" Savage goaded.

When urged, Carmella 'Gorgon' Gleason of the Broadswords team jogged over and began to spill her gossip. Nalara felt awkward and didn't like the direction of the conversation. She turned away before hearing any of it, confident that none of them would even notice her leave.

She trotted after her friend and joined her near the weight racks. "Winter!" she chirped happily and held out her water bottle in offering.

Winter held up her hand, declining gratefully.

"What're you doing over here?" Nalara asked after taking a long, gulping drink.

Winter looked over her friend's shoulder at the rest of the team and sighed softly. "They searched for me," she said at length. "They grieved for me, and now, I'm back leading them through drills like nothing happened. I can't imagine the bitterness they're feeling right now."

"You took some time off," Nalara offered but knew perfectly well that Winter was accurate in her assumption. "It's not like they haven't had time to come to terms."

"*Mandated* time off," Winter muttered as her eyebrows twitched in annoyance.

"Still," Nalara shrugged. "We're just happy that you're back. Seriously. The Grand Elite himself even gave you that award and everything."

Winter descended into a slow stretch. "Mm. That ceremony sure wrapped up the whole thing nicely, didn't it?"

Her sarcasm was lost on Nalara, who simply cocked her head in confusion.

Winter paused, considering her words. "The only reason I got an award is because they wanted to keep the whole incident from going in any direction other than where they wanted it to."

"What?" Nalara's perplexed look deepened. "'Where they wanted it to?'"

Winter stopped herself from answering.

Nalara's expression turned to pity. "It sounds like you just feel guilty for surviving," she said softly.

She was a good friend, Winter recognized that, but the ignorance with which she spoke kindled an anger inside of her that she couldn't ignore. She cleared her throat and tried her best to douse the feeling. "Maybe you're right," she stated simply before retrieving some weights from the rack.

Nalara followed her.

"In the meantime, I'll just give them some space," Winter said, attempting to conclude the conversation.

"I don't think they need space," Nalara countered. "I think they need to hear what happened down there from you. They're your team; you should talk to them. Clear out all these rumors that are flying around. They'll listen to you; they'll believe you. They just need to hear it from you."

"They do . . . or *you* do?" Winter diverted while loading the bar.

" . . . I'm one of your team, remember?" Nalara sounded hurt.

"Mm."

"No—I *am* one of your team," she insisted defensively.

"I know you are," Winter reclined on the bench and spoke through her set, "which is why you need space, too."

"I don't need space; I need my best friend to open up to me," Nalara corrected, hoping she didn't sound clingy.

Winter was frustrated that having a friend like her meant having someone who could see through her barriers, no matter how many she cast up in defense. Winter adhered, however, to the cold detachment that had kept her alive for so long.

"Well, I'm not going to," she responded flatly.

Nalara put her hand down on the bar, using her Purifier strength to prevent Winter from lifting it again. *"Whhhyyyy?"* Her deep brown eyes glared with an insistence and immovability that Winter had rarely seen.

Annoyed, but touched nonetheless, Winter relented a little. "I'm not going to talk to you about it . . . not yet," she answered softly. "Not until I can see the whole picture. I can't make assumptions . . . I have to see everything." She recognized that Nalara was not satisfied and was a little worried that she wouldn't let her out from under the bar until she was. Winter's arms began to burn and shake. "As soon as I do . . ." she tried her best not to strain her voice, "I'll tell you everything. But until then . . . *I* need the space."

Nalara fixed her searching gaze for a moment longer, then let go of the bar and crossed her arms. *"As* soon?"

Winter struggled to rack the bar and breathed out in relief. She sat up on the bench and locked eyes with her friend. "The minute." She nodded.

"The *very minute?"*

Winter couldn't help but smile with a little chuckle. "Blight me, yes! The *very* minute!"

Nalara huffed. "Fine." She fluttered her lashes and rolled her eyes.

"Brat," Winter snipped.

"Shrew," Nalara returned before walking away with a masked smile.

Winter gaped in comic surprise for a moment before returning to her set. She had just finished another when Wraith called the team back together. Everyone but Nalara seemed to gravitate away when Winter approached, and Scorch trotted up in owned tardiness with a singularly forced smirk.

"Alright, Archangels," Wraith called their attention. "We've known for a few days that next month's bout was rescheduled for this weekend."

The team muttered in understanding.

"Could be a walk in the park," he continued, "could be a spectator position; and it could be that you get stomped by a nobody who just trained harder than you."

Winter was caught in his glare momentarily. Wraith hadn't spoken with her since the moment he confined her to her room three days previous. Ever since her forty-eight-hour quarantine, all instruction had been given through indirect orders and generalized statements.

"The latter is unacceptable!" he shouted. "Just in case that wasn't clear to everyone already, you lose this bout, and you can consider yourself banned from active team service until you prove to me that you are *anything* more than a weak nothing who doesn't deserve to breathe Olympian air."

The team was silent and looked around awkwardly.

"Uh, sir?" Scorch spoke willfully.

"What is it, Scorch?"

"Question: aren't you and Winter the only ones competing?"

"Once more through the course!" Wraith ordered, pointedly ignoring him. "Then fifty rounds on the range—each. We have a jump tomorrow, so skipping curfew is not optional tonight."

Groans of compliance followed as they all filtered off to make their way through the assignment.

Winter hung back and waited for the others to go first. She knew she could lap them on the course, but she didn't want to draw any more unwanted attention today. She kept a stoic face, though her cheeks burned with embarrassment as Wraith brushed past her in fierce aversion.

She understood that her captain was a man with neither fuse nor filter. If he was being passive-aggressive, she knew from experience that it was because he didn't want to release the kind of unbridled rage you can't come back from.

She breathed through the swelling emotions and focused on the task at hand.

Eagle Eyes had once told her that watching her fly through the obstacle course made him feel like all Purifiers should have wings. She remembered how proud it made her and wished more than ever that she could talk to her mentor just once more. She never realized how much she relied on his wisdom until now. All of a sudden, as she worked hand over hand across a rope, she felt completely robbed—like she had been cheated out of time with someone she desperately needed. Winter gritted her teeth against the feeling and channeled it into fuel to get through the workout.

More than anything, she felt the need to keep an even keel at this time. She knew that any more unusual behavior would surely not escape scrutiny. And if that meant bottling her emotions and suppressing her words, that's just how it had to be.

After completing the course, Winter didn't take long at all to fulfill the fifty-round quota on the firing range.

Physically tired and mentally spent, she resorted to the only thing that could come close to compare with Eagle Eye's advice. Trying to escape notice, she climbed the steps to the blessed Ascended. The statues were all newly cleaned, and they glistened under the glow of the barrier.

Winter stood at the feet of Derrick Zinda and looked up at the golden skull resting in the statue's hand. She looked down the line of statues, each of them holding the plated remains of Purifiers that were murdered in their prime of life. The chilling reality sent shivers down her spine as she imagined each of them sacrificed to the glory of a tyrant wielding ultimate power over the minds of an entire population.

She advanced down the line and came to a stop at the marble figure of Nereza 'Nightmare' Vossen. Her hero—the pinnacle of Purifier perfection—stood still and silent. She gazed at the skull in the statue's hand, seeing it for the first time as the face of a murdered woman. The intensity of the moment swept her up and Winter's tunnel vision could not break from the skeletal features. Nereza may have been a hero . . . an athlete . . . a marksman . . . a warrior.

But in the end, she was no more . . . than a *victim*.

Winter gasped suddenly, realizing her chest had grown very tight, and she had stopped breathing. She glanced around her immediate surroundings and steadied her breath before parting her lips to speak.

"I'm sorry," she admitted to the idol of stone. "I can't help but be . . . just sorry. As long as I've been a Purifier, I've promised to strive for your level of accomplishment. As long as I can remember, I've pushed myself so that I'd meet you in Elysium someday and that you would be impressed with me . . .. that you'd see me as an equal." Winter hung her head and laughed ironically. She turned a full circle with her arms outstretched to the sides. "But who's impressed now?" she called out, then soaked in the silence that followed. "Not me," she added remorsefully. "I was going to *be* you . . ."

Winter gazed at the statue in cold disconnection. The neutral face and perfect features seemed so lifeless now. Winter used to speak with this piece of stone, believing it could hear her. She once listened to her own thoughts as if they were answers coming from her hero, as though Nereza's essence lived on in effigy like they were taught in the FMQ.

The stone eyes, her hip-length hair captured in a perpetual imaginary breeze . . . Winter had admired her for so long. She pulled the tie from her own hair and let it fall down her back. Running her fingers through the dark locks thoughtfully, she shook her head.

"I was willing to make any sacrifice to stand up here with you. I was willing to do anything to be immortal, and if you could give me just one reason to continue as I once was . . ." she admitted, "I would do it." The realization hurt. "Even now, with all that I know, I would turn my face from the truth in a heartbeat if you could give me even a shred of a reason." Winter smiled against the pain. "But you're not going to." Her words sounded empty and pointless as the soulless statue stared on. "Because you're not really there . . . are you?" Her voice fell to a trembling whisper. "You never were."

All was silent.

There truly was nothing there.

Winter returned to the feet of her mentor's statue and placed a hand gently on the polished stone. She looked up into the blind eyes. Derrick's once intense, piercing eyes had been replaced with the blank, empty stare of oblivion. He who had been 'Eagle Eyes' in life, whose striking gaze alone could both command and inspire, was just . . . gone.

"Open gaze. See everything," Winter whispered the words of her beloved mentor. "That's what you were teaching me." She scoffed bitterly, angry that she had failed to see the truth until it was too late. She closed her eyes, and a small tear escaped from her lashes. "I'm sorry, Derrick. I'm sorry I didn't see." Her hand slipped from the smooth stone. She turned her back to the silent statue. "And I'm sorry you didn't see either."

Winter mournfully bowed her head.

Goodbye.

Leaving the place that had been her haven for so long, in that moment, Winter intended to never return. Deep inside her heart, this was now a monument to her foolishness, to her blindness. This place was a tether now—an anchor that held her mind face down in a pool of lies.

It made her hate the place.

It made her hate herself.

Long ebony locks trailing behind, rippling and shimmering in the sunlight, Winter put Ascension behind her and walked away.

CHAPTER TWENTY-EIGHT

Lovely Olympus sat in prestige and glory in the clouds above the surface world. Sunlight bathed the towers and streets of every quarter.

Winter walked through the gardens after her climb with a steadfast burning in her heart. The jumps since her sojourn on the surface had been routine and professional, though she had purposefully avoided any contact with the few surface humans she came across. Having no killshots from their previously top-achieving teammate made the rest of the Archangels fairly unhappy, but Winter was as yet still unable to find the words to explain.

She didn't know how much longer the avoidance would fly. It was awkward and unsustainable. She knew that sooner or later, she would have to face the hard choice. She dared to hope that her example would be enough to make others question their own actions . . . but that was farfetched, and she knew it.

The Second Tier manifested several Purifiers on their way to the conference room for the morning's pre-jump orientation. Winter was not met with smiles or greetings much anymore. Her comrades mostly averted their eyes and quickened their steps.

Nalara was always the exception, though.

"Janey!" her sunny voice hailed as she approached to walk with her friend.

Always jarred by the reminder of her childhood name, Winter smiled. "Good morning."

"You seem okay," Nalara said.

"And why wouldn't I be?"

Nalara winced. "Did you see the scoreboard?"

Winter's face twisted in confusion as she looked up to the digital display above the street. She didn't notice anything upsetting at first—until she saw her name ranked number *thirteen* once again. The Black Ghosts' Sabin 'Raven' Pember was ranked *twelve* above her.

Her heart sank, but she quickly reminded herself it didn't mean anything. It wasn't like she was going to start killing surface humans again to get her rank back up.

Nalara monitored her friend's reaction with concern.

Winter shrugged a little half-smile. "Raven's been working hard. He deserves it."

"Blight me *sideways!* Captain Priest won't feel that way!" Nalara blurted.

Winter knew she was right.

The moment the briefing was over, the rant began, and Wraith tore into Winter's lack of performance with passion. It was almost white noise to her by this time. It was all trivial anyway . . . it didn't matter. He could disapprove as much as the day was long, but she would still not kill any more surface humans. It wasn't some competition like all the Purifiers were raised to believe. She hoped she could find a way to show them that, but until she did, the interim felt like living death.

The shuttle ride was quiet. Winter was torn between anger and calm. She fought against her very nature to not be crushed by the news of the rank adjustment. She felt she had no footing whatsoever—no mentor to guide her actions, no hero to confide in. She felt like she had been thrust into a scenario with no preparation and no training, and she was expected to lead and find her way at the same time while not having the slightest idea where she was going.

The shuttle lurched heavily to the right, and she could see the surface looming up through the ports. The rambling sector almost looked like a tousled network of veins, with the ancient roads partially concealed by tall trees and crumbling buildings. Large waterways seeped and pooled in clusters throughout the terrain.

Winter saw for just a brief moment the columned building where she had encountered Joshua for the first time.

"The dome between four bridges . . ." she whispered softly.

Seeing Joshua again was not on her mind as a possibility for the day at the time she'd entered the shuttle. But now that she had bearings and the idea struck her, she couldn't get it out of her head. She knew it was outrageously unlikely that she would actually find him in the vast wilderness. But simply the idea of trying was tantalizing and impossible to ignore.

An excited hope sprang up in her chest, and Winter gripped the restraints eagerly.

"We each have huge zones to clear today," Wraith's voice rose over the sound of the engines through the com. "Our glorious Sovereign wants to move Olympus to the next sector by the end of the month. Get your heads right and tough through it. We can't afford any babysitting today." He glanced at Winter with no sign of discretion.

One by one, the Purifiers were dropped off in their zones. Wraith checked the rifles and handed them out.

When Winter's zone was called and the shuttle came to a stop, Wraith stared her down with only a crisp, "No messing around," to send her off.

Winter stepped off the shuttle and scanned her surroundings in every direction while she ran toward the tree line.

As the sound of engines faded into the distance, Winter slowed her gait and looked up to watch the shuttle move on. How quickly she had fallen back into her training. Her eyes were up and alert, her posture crouched and ready. She watched her view screen as it analyzed and identified everything around her.

She lowered her rifle and relaxed her posture. She was weary of being *told*. Everything in her life was controlled input. Everything she learned in the Formulation Quarter, everything she trained for, even her surroundings down here on the surface were filtered through the lie.

She exhaled a long, soul-cleansing breath. Glancing up at the sky one more time, she disengaged her armor and removed her helmet. The clean, fresh air caressed her face and filled her lungs with vitality. She felt her limbs become energized, and a smile crossed her lips.

She would never get away with disconnecting her com from the power source again. After giving it some thought, she spent the better part of an hour tracking back and forth across her designated zone, creating movement for Wraith to track later. Once she had established a suitable search pattern, she found a thick tree in which she could securely hide her helmet. She was satisfied it would not be found easily but fully acknowledged the folly of her intentions. It was nothing short of foolhardy, but she didn't have the willpower to deny the burning desire in her chest.

Winter took off, chiding herself with each step as she made a direct line toward the river she'd seen from above.

The journey was not too long, but Winter worked hard, careful not to leave a trail that could be followed. She took her time, monitoring the movements of her teammates in their assigned grids. She was so focused on her passage that she almost missed seeing the world around her. But it was not altogether lost. The trees moved synchronously in the wafting breeze—

something she'd never experienced on Olympus. The air was sterile there, and completely stationary. The air here, blowing against her face, triggered an unexpected euphoric response from deep within.

A sweet and tangy smell, altogether unfamiliar to her, swept past in a warm breeze. She couldn't help but take a moment to locate the origin of the enchanting scent. Following her nose, she came upon some white blossoms hanging low on some swaying branches.

Magic.

She enjoyed the moment and drank in the smell before moving onward.

As the river came into view, she could see where the tributaries winded toward each other, and she spotted one of the crumbling bridges through the thick forest. Using it as her compass, she worked her way slowly forward through the dense brush near the water and soon found herself on a tiny plateau looking down on an open patch of land. Her heart stopped on reflex when she spotted a blighter there below.

Her danger instincts raged to full-alert before she could remind herself that it was a human and not a bloodthirsty mutated beast.

Not 'blighter,' she reminded herself.

Human.

She had never paused and taken the time to observe a surface human before. Moving painfully slow, making certain not to rustle a single leaf in passing, she was able to come within ten meters of the surface dweller without being noticed.

Winter perched in curiosity.

The activity was fascinating. Crouched there near the herbage, it pulled up leaves and roots by the handful, moving methodically and quickly forward.

The simplicity spoke to Winter in a way she couldn't describe. She had noticed the harvest drones at work over the rows of cloned produce pods on Olympus. It was completely unremarkable. But here, she witnessed a person gathering what it needed from a living plant that gathered what *it* needed from the earth itself.

The human paused and took a knee before scooting up the giant goggles and pulling down his face mask. Winter's heart jumped to her throat when she recognized Joshua. He was taking a moment to test the quality of one of the plants he'd pulled.

Winter didn't want to alarm him and certainly didn't want to alert any comrades he might have in the area. She stooped and retrieved a small stone from the earth and tossed it gently in his direction.

The soft impact it made was enough to supercharge Joshua's alertness. He silently, swiftly backed into the bushes nearby and readied his weapon.

Winter stepped forward, eyes steadily fixed on his position. She was so nervous, fearing their previous conversation was a one-time event.

"Winter," Joshua spoke in surprise as he emerged, rifle down. "You came back."

She tried not to show it, but she was secretly elated that he would talk to her again. "I wasn't sure I'd be able to," she admitted.

"I remember. So, you were allowed back on Olympus?"

Winter nodded. "It was strange, though."

"How do you mean?"

"Nobody wanted to know why. No one questioned how. I can't explain it . . . it's like they swept it all aside like I never left, really."

Joshua could tell she was deeply troubled. "Tell me more," he said.

"It's become a strange reality to me somehow. I can't feel the same as I used to, but nothing *there* has changed." Winter sighed. She could talk about her frustration all day, but the prospect made her weary. "What is it you're gathering here?"

Joshua looked down at his small satchel half full of leaves and roots. He'd abandoned it when he heard the noise, and it lay where it had fallen. "What, these? We use some of these for medicine." He rifled through the satchel. "Or stew . . . some are good for storage. Oh, here." He produced a cloth handkerchief tied in a close knot. "Do you have raspberries on Olympus?" he asked with a little smile as he untied the knot and held out the offering.

"Yes . . . but they don't look like that." Winter shook her head at the deep, rich color and the wrinkled, dry shape.

"Try some," Joshua offered before popping one in his mouth. "These were from last year's harvest. Dried out for preservation but still really good."

Winter experienced a knee-jerk trepidation at the thought of consuming anything from the 'toxic' surface. But swallowing her fears, she pulled off her gauntlet and retrieved one single piece of fruit.

A sweet and tangy, earthy taste filled her senses as the chewy, fragrant raspberry filled her mouth with sensation.

She couldn't hide the smile that spread across her face. "That doesn't taste like raspberries on Olympus." She almost laughed.

Joshua chuckled and ate another.

"Why are you here?" Winter asked suddenly.

Joshua returned her steady gaze. Winter thought she saw the answer there in his soft, sad eyes.

"I've been hunting and gathering around here all week, kinda hoping you'd return." He gave a little shrug.

"It's dangerous," Winter cautioned but smiled in spite of herself. "Another Purifier might find you." Saying it out loud reminded her to glance at her gauntlet display. There were still no Purifiers in the immediate vicinity, but the reminder was enough to put her back on edge. Her voice lowered in grave warning. "If I had been anyone else—you would be dead."

Joshua smiled and calmly waved off her concern. "In all fairness, I should already be dead from our first encounter. But I'm not. So, I guess it's just not my time."

Winter felt her stomach knot up. This was a matter of life and death, and yet Joshua seemed so unconcerned about it. Serene even. How was that possible?

She desperately wanted to change the subject.

"What is it you hunt?" Her curiosity was sparked, feeling her Purifier instincts take hold.

"Deer mostly." He half-shrugged. "Every now and then, a nice big herd of elk wander through. I even bagged a bear two years ago. Now, *that* was fun! Good food for a good long time."

"'Bagged?'" Winter cocked up one eyebrow curiously.

"Yeah," Joshua responded, "you know, 'bagged.'" He waited to see if there was any recognition in her eyes. When none came, he continued, "Uh, that is, I 'killed' a bear. 735-pound grizzly, actually." He lovingly ran his hand down the aged wooden stock of his rifle. "Yep! Took five rounds to bring that ole-boy down."

Winter grinned at his moment of self-satisfaction. She couldn't explain it, but something about Joshua put her completely at ease—his calming voice, his inviting smile, and those eyes that strangely remained kind and comforting despite the reservoir of sadness walled up behind them.

She suddenly felt the impulse to move in with a friendly jab. "Five rounds because he was big or because you're a bad shot?" She grinned.

Joshua was taken aback. "The Purifier from the city in the clouds actually has a sense of humor." He grinned back and shook his head in bewilderment. "I honestly didn't see that one coming."

"I couldn't resist," Winter said with a shrug. "I reserve it for special occasions."

"And *this* is a 'special occasion?'"

"Well, yeah. It's not every day I get to talk with . . ." Winter's voice suddenly died as the words failed her.

"*Wiiiith,*" Joshua revived it, "a—let's see, how did you describe us?—a 'diseased, mutated remnant of our race,' I think it was."

"I *wasn't* going to say that," Winter protested, eyeing him sharply.

Joshua put up his hands to deflect her criticism. "I know, I know." He winked. "You're not the only one with a sense of humor—for special occasions, of course."

Winter felt her face flush warm. She smiled and looked away, pretending that something in the trees had caught her attention.

"Your turn," Joshua invited, bringing her back. "Do you have any animals on Olympus?"

Winter recalled the images of the giant livestock formulators within Olympus' lower levels. She nodded. "Yes, but they don't 'wander through,' though. I know that some special Elites are given pets, but most animals never leave the Nutriment Quarter."

Joshua half-smiled. "I'm almost afraid to ask, but what's the Nutriment Quarter?"

"It takes up several levels of lower Olympus," she explained. "Modular animals are grown there in pods and remain inert throughout their lifespan until they're harvested."

"Grown . . . in pods?" Joshua looked repulsed. "Harvested?"

Winter suddenly felt defensive. The comfortable atmosphere between them disappeared as quickly as it had come. "All life on Olympus begins that way."

A light entered his eyes. "Ah—that's why you don't understand what *parents* are." He seemed to be speculating out loud. "There really are . . . no parents on Olympus."

Winter shook her head.

"Well . . ." he paused to clear his throat. "I guess it would be kinda hard to explain to you." His voice lowered to a whisper as he mumbled, "Birds and bees and all that."

"You spend a lot of time hunting?" Winter less-than-subtly changed the subject and began casually walking.

"Not so much," Joshua replied, taking the hint and following her. "We're able to keep most of the animals we need." There was a moment of silence. "In pens!" He clarified. "We keep them in pens where they live and grow until they're . . . you know . . . 'harvested,' I guess."

"Sounds messy."

"It is, but we make it work."

"Oh, so you have cleaners and reclamation workers, too," she surmised.

"We all work, really."

Winter paused. "I thought you were a hunter and a soldier."

"Yeah, I am." Joshua blinked softly as if the truth of the answer hurt him. "But I'm also a scout, a sentry, a cook sometimes—when things get really desperate—a gatherer, a cleaner. I've even acted as a field medic a time or two. I am whatever the situation calls for me to be. I try to help out as much as I can wherever I can, to do whatever is needed to support my family."

"Family?" Winter asked inquisitively.

"Oh, right, that again." Joshua breathed and looked up at the sky. "My *people,* I mean."

Winter smirked. "In our society, cleaning workers are the lowest degree of the lowest tier—below even the core workers who never see the sun in their lifetime."

Joshua listened carefully to every word before responding. "In my society, we help each other."

"You sound a little condescending," Winter observed.

"No more than you," he returned. "I'm sorry." He shook his head quickly. "I don't mean to be. It's just different—and difficult—to think that you could give more worth to one life over another."

The thought was completely foreign to Winter. "But . . . we *are* worth more than them. Purifiers are engineered to be the pinnacle of physical achievement," she explained, attempting to process the new thought. "But

I'm still just of the Second Tier. The Elites are of the First Tier. They are the embodiment of genetic purity and perfection. Their beauty and intelligence are meant to reflect the Sovereign's magnificence. They are the only First Tier citizens.

"Other Second Tier citizens like the Purifier class would include the Unifiers, the Guardians, pilots, technicians, physicians, and formulation trainers. Unifiers are specially designed as surveyors and analysts. Guardians are designed for their size and brute strength. Pilots have superior reflexive abilities. Science and engineering technicians and several other classes are designed to process data and retain great amounts of knowledge with accuracy."

She paused. "And then there's the Third Tier." Her voice lowered in noticeable disdain. "They all live within the lower levels of Olympus. They take care of the menial labor. They're farmers, gardeners, cooks, various maintenance personnel, like core workers. Core workers are created to be resilient and small. And those designed for waste and reclamation management have virtually no special attributes whatsoever. They're the equivalent of genetic trash." Winter cocked her head quizzically. "But you're saying that your people would believe that their lives compare in value to the Elite? How is that possible?"

Joshua narrowed his eyes and smiled. "Do you remember the saying you repeated to me the last time we met?"

Winter nodded.

"That saying was carved into stone surrounding the man who spoke those words," Joshua explained. "He lived a long time ago and was one of the wisest men of his generation in Earth's history."

Winter listened carefully, fascinated at the chance to hear this lost knowledge.

Joshua continued. "He also wrote the words: *'We hold these truths to be self-evident, that all men'* (that is, all 'mankind,' all 'human beings'), *'that all men are created equal'* . . . Of course, not everyone agrees, but I know that all human life—big or small, weak or strong—is imbued with intrinsic value that cannot be tarnished or lessened by time, ability, or circumstance. Just because I might be a faster runner than someone else, or I can jump higher, swim farther, or even if I'm smarter than they are, that doesn't mean I'm *worth* more than them. The same thing goes for whether I'm young or old, tall or short, beautiful or ugly, or whether I work as a physician or a farmer or anything else. I know that all are 'created equal'."

Winter shook her head. "That doesn't make any sense," she admitted.

"It might not to someone from Olympus." Joshua drew his lips into a half-smile. "But it's what I believe. And I think you don't realize it yet, but you feel very close to the same."

"How so?" Winter was intrigued.

"Think about it. Why did you care that you had murdered humans?" he asked bluntly, sparking pain in her eyes. "You didn't know they were human before—at least, you didn't know they were just *normal* human beings and not some kind of mutated monster—and you killed indiscriminately. Never bothered you before—you probably never gave it a second thought."

Winter knew he was right about that.

"Now," he went on, "after seeing that we're not what you were told we were . . . how many of us have you killed?"

Winter's lips parted, taken aback by the faith he put in her nature. "None," she said quietly, even though they both already knew the answer.

"Why?" Joshua asked pointedly. "I mean, if you're so superior to us, and we're nothing but worthless creatures—human or not—who cares if you kill us? You're superior, right? So, who cares if you kill off some . . . 'genetic trash?'"

His questions hung heavily in the air between them. Winter suddenly felt sick to her stomach. Joshua's sharp eyes felt like daggers that pierced her heart and his words like iron weights that sank deep in her gut. His questioning made her want to run and hide, but she knew there was nowhere to go, nowhere she could avoid the truth that now seized her in a vice-grip.

"You obviously did," he finally pointed out, smiling slightly. "But why? Did you ever stop to ask yourself why you cared?"

Winter looked inside herself and realized the truth was there. "Because you weren't a monster. You were just like me . . ." She paused, slowly seeing the hidden truth materialize before her as if a door had been cracked open into a darkened room to let in a shaft of light. "And my whole life, I was told the lie that made you that monster. My eyes were opened to the truth when I saw your face. On Olympus," she continued, forcing open the door all the way in her mind, "the lie is that some lives are worth more than others. But just like here, we're all human, and because of that . . . we're all equal."

Joshua's smile widened. "You see: 'Self-evident'."

Winter smiled broadly at the realization. She breathed in the unexpected truth and breathed out liberty—sensing one additional shackle of tyranny over her mind suddenly unclasp and fall away.

"So," Winter began, attempting to find and see all the puzzle pieces now illuminated in this previously darkened room, "I think I see what you're saying about being equal, but if you perform all those tasks, what exactly are you then?"

"What do you mean?"

"I mean, what *are* you?" she repeated more insistently, annoyed at the language barrier that apparently existed between them. "For example: I am a Purifier, the lieutenant of the Archangels team. What are you?"

Joshua shrugged his shoulders. "I don't think of myself in those terms. I just think of myself as being me," he stated plainly. "I might perform the tasks of a hunter and a scout and a cleaner, but those are all things I *do*. I choose to do those things, but they don't define who I *am.*"

Winter's brow furrowed. "You choose to clean up after animals?" She failed to keep the disgust out of her voice.

Joshua laughed. "Someone has to do it. Might as well be me." He stopped walking, bringing Winter to a halt as his eyes, filled with that strange and persistent sadness, met hers. "At least I can say I get to choose."

Winter felt a cold chill race down her spine as she realized the sadness in his eyes was for her.

"Is that what that tattoo means?" Joshua asked, pointing to her right hand.

Winter lifted her hand and looked at the mark of the Purifier—the blade called 'Ascension' wreathed in purifying flames.

"I noticed it the last time we met," Joshua explained. "I wasn't sure what it was, but now I have a pretty good idea. It means you're one of these 'Purifiers,' right? Sent to *purify* the disease-ridden surface world?"

Winter swallowed down the dryness in her throat, feeling a wave of guilt and remorse overtake her. She nodded silently.

"That's what your 'Sovereign' made you to be." He waited for a long moment before asking: "Did you ever think you could choose to be something else?"

Winter's jaw went slack, shocked that her entire life's story suddenly manifested in the mark on the back of her hand. It truly did define her. Every moment of the nineteen years of her life, from her formulation to her training, trials, and four years of active service—all of it was to be a Purifier and her ambitions to be the very greatest Purifier. She had fought and bled and killed hundreds for this mark.

She thought of the lifeless statues of Nereza Vossen and Derrick Zinda, and of the gilded skulls resting in their left palms and their right fists placed over their hearts in dutiful, silent veneration to their god. Her hero and her mentor, among countless others, had been murdered for this mark and for the man who had given it to them. She had always before seen the mark as a symbol of life and noble purpose, but Winter's stomach now roiled sickeningly as, for the first time in her life, she saw the mark for what it really was: an image of death—thrust upon her.

Fighting back tears and a sudden surge of raw anger, she shook her head. "No. I've always been a Purifier. Nothing else was ever a possibility. Not even a thought." She dropped her hand and looked into Joshua's eyes. The depth of sadness within them was overwhelming. This time, there was no holding back her tears. "At least, not until I met you."

Joshua gave her a quizzical, doleful smile. "Do you hate me for that?"

"Hate you?" Winter wiped at her eyes in an attempt to clear her vision. "No, of course not. How could I?" She chuckled hollowly and sniffed as another tear filled the corner of her eye. She brushed irritatingly at it and looked away, no longer able to hold his gaze. "You're the one who's supposed to hate *me*. I killed your team, remember?"

A deep silence draped the forest as the surface human and Olympian Purifier stood together—two inhabitants from distant and very different worlds trying to find their footing on uneasy ground.

Joshua leaned in after a long moment. "Not all of them," he said quietly.

Winter looked up, confused but suddenly hopeful. "But . . . I—"

"You killed two and *shot* one." He recalled the awful scene. "The one you shot is still in serious condition, but we're hopeful that he'll make it."

Winter blinked in disbelief. "Really?"

"Really, truly. I checked on him just this morning."

She smiled in relief as a ray of sunlight broke through the dark clouds in her heart. She closed her eyes and saw the dead faces of the man and woman she had killed staring at her with unblinking, judging eyes. "What were their names?" Winter asked with a lump in her throat, filled with a sudden, desperate need to identify her victims.

Seeing her need, Joshua complied. "Joel and Alyssa were the two you killed. Zack is still alive."

"Joel . . . Alyssa . . . Zack . . ." she repeated the names in a whisper with her eyes still closed. "I'm so sorry," she pleaded earnestly with them. She wished she could know the names of the hundreds of others she had killed as a Purifier so that she might say the same to them. Before they had fallen into the crosshairs of her rifle, who had they been? She would never know.

"It's like I said the last time we met: change course," Joshua said reassuringly. "Just change your course, Winter, and you'll make it, too." He reached out and playfully jostled her shoulder. "Besides, you're strong, right? All that . . . how did you put it? 'Purifiers are engineered to be the pinnacle of physical achievement,' or something like that."

"Yeah," Winter said with a smile, feeling lighter at the news of Zack being alive than she had in what seemed like an eternity. "Something like that."

Joshua grinned broadly. "I'm curious. You wouldn't be willing to put that to the test, would you?"

Winter lifted an eyebrow suspiciously. "What kind of test?"

"Oh, just a simple, all-in-good-fun test of strength." He looked around and, spotting a large fallen tree nearby, said: "Ah! Here." He moved to the far side of the log, lowered himself to his knees, and placed his right elbow atop the wood's moss-covered surface. "Care for an arm-wrestle?"

"A what?" Winter asked, moving closer.

Joshua looked shocked. "You've never been challenged to an arm-wrestle before?" He shook his head incredulously. "Listen. It's really easy. Just kneel down on that side facing me."

Winter followed his instruction, still skeptical.

"Okay, now with your elbow on the log like mine, take my hand."

She did so, feeling the many years of hard work in his rough grip.

He grinned again. "Alright, here are the rules. Without lifting your elbow off the log, push against my hand as hard as you can and try to get the back of my hand to touch the log—like this." He guided her hand to illustrate. "Now, at the same time, I'm going to be pushing against you as hard as I can," he guided her hand back in the opposite direction, "to try and get your hand to touch this side of the log. Whoever gets the other person's hand to touch first wins. See? Simple, right?"

Winter was intrigued. Throughout her years of Purifier training, she had participated in many similar strength tests, but this was new to her. She gave him a nod in agreement. "Seems simple enough."

"It is," Joshua replied, then gave her a boyish look that contradicted his age. The sadness in his eyes pleasantly disappeared. "But winning might not be. I'll count down from three, and we go when I say 'go.' You ready?"

"Are you sure about this?"

"Yeah, I'm sure. You ready?"

Winter nodded and tightened her grip as Joshua tightened his.

"I have to warn you, though," Joshua said with that same youthful grin. "I'm really good at this."

"Consider me warned."

Joshua locked his gaze on Winter's hand and shifted slightly in his position. "Okay, here we go. Three . . . two . . . one . . .."

Winter flexed her muscles and tightened her grip further.

"Go!"

It happened so fast, Winter was unsure if she had done it wrong. The second their strength engaged, she easily put his arm down to the log so forcefully that it split the bark beneath. Joshua gasped in alarm and pain as he toppled over the other side.

"I'm sorry!" Winter quickly exclaimed. "What happened?" She leapt over the log and bent to help him back up.

Joshua stumbled over his own feet, but Winter braced him up. He sat down in a daze, then gripped his shoulder and winced in pain. "Holy prophets! What was that!?" he cried out in disbelief.

"I'm really, really sorry!" Winter apologized again. "I thought you'd offer more resistance, so I kinda went . . . all out."

Joshua blinked and tried to slow his breathing, all the while gently massaging the tender muscles of his shoulder. "All out, huh? That was . . . unbelievable." He looked up into Winter's blue eyes, his face pleading for an explanation. "And all Purifiers are as strong as you?"

"Well, no, not exactly, not *all*. I train a lot more than most. But there are some who are stronger than me, like my team's captain. His name's Wraith, and the guy's built more like a Guardian than a Purifier. In terms of raw physical strength, he's probably two or three times stronger than me."

Joshua looked dumbfounded. "Three? Times? Stronger?" He shook his head and winced again. "Consider *me* warned." Rising to his feet while still nursing his shoulder, he suddenly looked perplexed. "Wraith? What kind of a name is Wraith?"

"It's his callsign," Winter clarified. "His name is Orrin Priest. 'Wraith' is something he earned. Just about all Purifiers have them."

"Oh . . ." Joshua turned and started walking away, but then stopped and turned back to Winter. "So, wait . . . Does that mean that 'Winter' is your name, or is that your callsign?"

Winter swallowed and cleared her throat, suddenly feeling both embarrassed and uneasy. "It's my callsign, but it's become more of my name than my actual name is."

"So . . . what is your name then?" Joshua asked sincerely.

She was silent for a moment, considering how she should answer. She took a deep breath and decided to open up to this surface human further. "January. January Winterton."

"January," he repeated, smiling satisfactorily. "That's really pretty. Were you born—" he stopped to correct himself, "I mean, were you—you know—*formulated* in the month of January?"

She nodded. "Actually, yes. I was the first of my generation to complete my formulation. It takes just over three months to formulate a Purifier, and I was finished on the 17th of January. I was assigned the name 'January Winterton.' That was nineteen years ago, but for the past four years, I've only gone by 'Winter.' I prefer it."

Joshua rubbed his shoulder one last time, then nodded. "Fair enough. Winter—the very, very . . . *crazy* strong Purifier—it is then."

"I really am really sorry about going 'all out' on you like that," she apologized for the third time. "I hope I didn't hurt you too bad."

"No, no, I'll be just fine," Joshua assured her. "My pride was hurt more than anything else. But, hey, it probably deserved to be hurt."

For a moment, they enjoyed a lighthearted laugh together, but the moment was cut short by a blip from Winter's gauntlet display.

Shaken, she took the gauntlet out from the crook of her arm and studied the readout. The screen showed that Havoc had logged a killshot three klicks west of her location.

"What is it?" Joshua looked concerned.

A wave of guilt suddenly washed over Winter's heart. She felt terrible for keeping it to herself, but she simply could not bring herself to tell Joshua what it was.

"I have to go," she sighed.

"Is something wrong?"

"No, I just need to get back to my beacon," she deflected. "It's been stationary too long; I don't want Wraith to get suspicious."

"Yeah, a guy like that, I wouldn't want him to get suspicious either," Joshua admitted frankly. "I'm sad you can't stay longer, though. Learning more about Olympus has been . . . enlightening."

"And I want to learn more about you and your history," Winter said with conviction. "But I'm coming back. The next time I'm on the surface, I'll come toward the four bridges again. I need to learn more about you. I think I can start to bring the truth to Olympus if I just have the facts."

"I know you can," Joshua replied.

Winter felt deep gratitude for his confidence. She paused only a moment before nodding in farewell and turning away to start her return trek.

Running fast, she passively enjoyed the warm feeling of comfort in her chest. Even though her life on Olympus was beginning to deteriorate, she was able to feel good about what she was working toward.

She barreled into the grove where she had hidden her helmet and quickly retrieved it from the tree. She paused to catch her breath and brushed some white blossoms off its surface before placing the helmet on her head.

She reactivated the armor and took out her rifle. Falling back into engagement protocol, Winter resumed the satirical facade of sweeping her zone. If she kept up pretenses, with a little luck, she could fake her way long enough to gain the knowledge she needed.

Hopefully, this wasn't the day her luck ran out.

CHAPTER TWENTY-NINE

I t was amazing to feel like everything was going to be alright. It had been so long; Winter almost didn't recognize the feeling. Not only a hope for the future, but she also felt a lightness in her chest that settled her into a confident calm. It was the best she had felt since Derrick had died. It was the first time since then that she emerged from her living chambers with anything more than firm apathy.

Joshua had opened her eyes to a whole new truth, and today, she could feel nothing but enthusiasm for the tasks ahead of her. It really seemed possible.

Winter smiled to herself as she traveled down in the lift to the floor level on her way to the much-anticipated, expedited bout. She knew that most of the Purifiers had gone ahead already, trying to beat the crowded madness to find seats, but she figured she would take a side trip to Nalara's unit to see if her friend wanted to walk with her again.

After exiting the lift, Winter veered to the right and entered the hallway that led past the cafeteria to the garrison units.

She paused in her tracks, surprised to see someone sitting alone in the empty dining hall. Winter wouldn't normally have given it a second thought, except it was obviously Scorch. She glanced down the empty hallway and thought better of it.

Nalara was probably at the Hive already anyway.

"You skipping out on me?" Winter asked, approaching from behind.

Scorch turned and smiled broadly. "What are you doing here? You should be at the Hive already, preparing to crush your opponent and whatnot."

"I'll crush *you* if you don't join me." Winter slapped his shoulder as she crossed the table and sat down.

Scorch chuckled sarcastically. "Bloody Winter . . ." he muttered into his mug before taking a drink.

She smelled the alcohol and heard his sardonic jeer. His smile had slipped momentarily, but by the time he put the mug back down, it was back.

"You better watch out," he warned. "Captain Sharpe's as cold and efficient as they come. After you beat her tonight, don't start turning into her."

Winter chuckled. "I don't think I have it in me."

"Well, you're going to be captain of our team soon enough." He downed another gulp. "I can see that: You, one day, overtaking Wraith. Captain of the Archangels—Master Purifier Winter . . ." His eyes stared off into empty space. He nodded with a smile. "Yeah. Has a real nice ring to it."

Winter had known him long enough to recognize the masked pain in his tone. Scorch never let anyone see it. He was probably trying to think of a way to flippantly push her away.

"You better get going." He cleared his throat. "I spent my last allotment on this eighty-proof, so I'm not rushing it."

" . . . You feeling okay?" Winter asked directly.

"Oh, sure." He smiled at her but looked away quickly.

She pursed her lips. *"Really* okay?" she insisted gently.

He lifted his eyes, softly dewed with emotion.

She was silent, waiting for him to speak.

"Just . . ." Scorch started, then paused to stare into the dark liquid swirling the bottom of his mug. He took a deep, trembling breath. "It's just that you're someone who works as hard as you possibly can. You have that fire and drive that's so rare—even among Purifiers. If there's anyone who deserves to succeed, it's you." He took a lengthy sip. "And then you disappeared . . . and it felt like that nightmare with Samantha was happening all over again." He leaned over, his knuckles against his lips, and fell silent.

Winter reached out and placed her hand over his. "I came back," she spoke softly.

"Sam didn't." Pain and regret laced his words. He brought the mug again to his mouth, then paused and lowered it without taking a drink. He sighed wearily. "It seems like her death was so long ago. I really thought I had gotten over it. But then, when you disappeared, it all just . . . came rushing back, you know. It hit me harder than I ever thought it would."

" . . . I'm sorry," Winter whispered with sympathy. She was surprised, though. Scorch almost never mentioned Samantha. The years of loneliness and grief seemed to well up all at once behind his typically jubilant eyes.

At the mention of Samantha, Winter momentarily allowed herself to recall the faces of the Purifiers she'd served with throughout her fifteen years in the FMQ, through her trial in Tartarus, then through her last four years of active service. There were too many to see any of them clearly. They flew through her memory as distant shadows—disembodied shades of forgotten companions and lost friends. She fought to bring several faces into clarity, suddenly annoyed with the unexpected difficulty of the task. She honed in on those she considered as her closest companions, but try as she might, she couldn't keep them from fading back into the haze.

Purifiers were raised and trained with the prospect of death. They courted it every day of their lives—until it strangely became more familiar and more of a friend to them than the flesh and blood it stole away. Purifiers were conditioned—numbed even—to the pain of loss. But it was still always there, scratching restlessly on the door of their hearts and minds, begging to be released.

Winter felt her throat tighten as she recalled one of them shriek out her name from the depths of Tartarus:

"Janneeeyyyy!"

Winter closed her eyes and lightly shook her head to dislodge the horrifying memory.

"All for the Sovereign's glory," Scorch spoke at length, raising his mug.

His words struck Winter like a punch to her heart. She knew he was perfectly sincere—and that's why it hurt so much. The presence of the lie was everywhere. It was pervasive. It was relentless. She hated seeing it choke the life out of her friends.

Literally.

Winter bit her lip to keep from saying what she wanted to say. She was desperate to bring the truth to Olympus, but she still floundered in the dark as to the surest and safest way to do it.

After a long pause, all she could manage was another heartfelt yet pathetically inadequate: "I'm sorry."

"Don't be." Scorch sat up straight. "I'm glad you made it home." He smiled. "Olympus just wasn't the same without you."

Winter's heart broke. His pain was tangible, yet he worked so hard to make sure no one ever saw it.

She shook her head in agonizing frustration. "I wish I had the words, Seth. I really do. Please, just know that I'm here for you . . . anytime."

He squeezed her hand, then withdrew his.

Winter was still and silent, willing to sit there with him all night and miss the bout if that was what he needed.

He growled and stretched. "Blight me! Can't a guy just drink alone?" he teased. "Go on, get out of here. Go bury the Razor." He jerked his head at the entrance. "I'll be along soon enough."

Winter smiled softly and stood. "You know I'm always up late training if you want to talk," she reminded.

"Yeah, like I'm going to fall for that one," Scorch scoffed. "You'd just make me work out with you—like more stadium running. Thank you, but no, thank you. I get enough of that kind of torture as is, Lieutenant."

Winter nearly laughed but kept her composure. "But, you know," she insisted.

"Yeah, I know," he said, raising his mug to her before taking another drink.

She paused just a moment longer, then took her leave.

Music echoed across the Hive in heart-pumping rhythm. Fanfare flooded the air and riled the spectators into elation. The uproar was so extreme that even below the arena, Winter could feel the music pulsing in her throat. The very walls shook with the noise and excitement of Olympus' citizens.

All twenty top-ranking Purifiers stood facing their assigned opponents, waiting in stillness and patience to be raised to the Hive arena.

Winter could hear the announcer's muffled voice through the arena floor as he built up tension for the spectators' entertainment. She didn't listen to the words; she couldn't be distracted. Her tunnel vision was focused straight ahead, staring into the eyes of Lilith Sharpe, the new captain of the Grim Reapers since Eagle Eye's Ascension.

Lilith had never yet been her opponent, but she had seen her fight many times before. Her technique was very methodical. Winter understood the necessity for caution. She knew Lilith preferred to tire and play with her opponents, then strike hard and relentlessly once their defense slacked. With her opponent's level of proficiency, Winter knew she couldn't simply barrel through Lilith like she did for other defensive fighters.

These bouts were rarely appreciated for their technique anyway. They were there to entertain, not destroy. If it were merely a question of killing her opponent, Winter would be untouchable. The old way, taught to her by Eagle Eyes, was incomparable when used in these settings, but it was far too efficient—far too lethal to utilize to its full extent in a friendly bout.

The people wanted blood, they wanted brutality, but they did not want to see their heroes kill each other.

Winter didn't blink. She breathed steadily. Her face was neutral, just as her mentor had taught her. Eyes slightly narrowed, nostrils slightly flared.

Lilith's lips betrayed a hidden smile as she did the same.

Their platforms rose to the Hive floor level and the stage was made ready. Winter's fingers twitched with anticipation as the first fight was called up.

"Revered lord and lady Elite, and our most blessed Grand Elite Rothgard!" The announcer took a deep bow to the Elite in their cordoned-off, posh seating area, then turned with his arms wide to the chaotic, cheering crowds. "And all present citizens of glorious Olympus! We begin this evening's entertainment with a match that'll shake the very foundations of Elysium itself.

"I present to you from the Archangels, ranked number one of all Purifiers, age 27, standing at a towering 6'4", and weighing in at a rock-solid 243 pounds—he's unstoppable, he's unbeatable, he's the Master Purifier himself: Orrin 'Wraith' Priest!"

Wraith stepped forward into the bright lights and deafening clamor of the arena, his perpetual scowl set firmly in place, his unblinking eyes locked on his opponent obscured in the shadows.

"And the challenger," the announcer went on boisterously, "from the Black Ghosts, ranked number four, age 25, height 6'0", and weighing in at a shredded 192 pounds—he's lean, he's mean, he's a blighter-killing machine: Bobby 'Titan' Hayer!"

Titan stepped out of the shadows, bouncing lighting on his toes and throwing a fierce jab, cross, and hook into the air.

The announcer raised his hand high. "Purifiers, ready?"

Wraith tilted his head to the side till his neck gave an audible *crack*.

Titan pounded his fists together and gave a quick nod.

The hand dropped. "It's WAR!"

Wraith and Titan circled each other before exchanging fierce blows. Titan was as athletic and stacked as the next top-ranking Purifier, but Wraith's tank-like build outweighed him by an impressive margin. After only a moment, blood splattered the arena floor as their brutality surged into full force. Muted blue-green holograms of the two warriors filled the Hive's cavernous void overhead, capturing every move and pummel in immense detail.

As she watched in passive silence, Winter suddenly and inexplicably felt deeply sickened. She averted her eyes from the fight and attempted to settle her nerves. The offsetting feeling surprised her, and she couldn't quite put an explanation to it.

Winter found her gaze resting on the core workers within their cordoned area. Their eyes barely visible over the rim of the floor, they all enjoyed in rapt fascination this exciting diversion from their lives down in the belly of Olympus.

She had always known they existed, but she had never so much as looked one in the eye before. She saw them there, wide-eyed, pushing to get closer, plain jumpsuit uniforms . . . they bore excitement and hope in their eyes. They spoke to each other with emotion and passion. When their favorite fighter struck a point, they cheered; when he was injured, they cringed. Having never seen core workers as human beings before, Winter suddenly could not stop looking at them, marveling that they existed just as she did.

Wraith dominated the drawn-out battle, and the crowd cheered or howled respectively as he took the stage in a victory lap. Titan knelt in a pool of blood, his face disfigured beyond recognition.

The Elite's cries of displeasure filled the air. They waved mercilessly from their cushioned seating and jutted their thumbs down, demanding their final ounce of violence.

Wraith didn't pause for a moment. To satisfy their calls for blood, he stepped straight to Titan's kneeling form and tucked into an all-out bloody pound that drove his face into the Hive floor, rendering him completely unconscious.

The crowds roared, and the Elites cheered in delight before returning to their conversations, their drinks, and their delicacies.

Winter bore witness with new eyes.

That was it?

The Elite demanded blood, and they received blood. They wanted more food, and they received more food. If they wanted to walk in the sun, they simply did so.

The core workers had training and skill; they toiled every day of their lives. They never saw the sun; they weren't even given allotments like the middle-tier citizens. Everything in their lives was rationed and controlled by the ruling power.

The Elite suddenly shifted in Winter's perception. They seemed to serve no function on Olympus whatsoever—only to create a system of inequality. They existed solely to establish that some lives were more valuable than others. Because the Sovereign needed mindless workers, the Elite were given a life full of luxury and gratification.

Because he needed slaves, he created gods.

"A brutal and satisfying victory to our Master Purifier!" the announcer congratulated as medical crews lifted Titan's limp body onto a stretcher and hurriedly ran him out of the arena. The announcer wasted no time and began fomenting up the audience for the next match.

Winter didn't hear him. She couldn't focus on anything other than the revelation that she was practically one of the Elite. She lived a life of favor and luxury compared to others on Olympus simply because the Sovereign told her she was worth more. Over the blaring music and the thunderous babel of the crowds, one voice spoke loudest and clearest in her mind.

Joshua.

Winter closed her eyes, pictured his handsome, weathered face, and willed herself to hear his words again:

"Self-evident."

Winter suddenly realized that her name was being spoken over the loudspeaker.

"As I said," the announcer repeated himself. "January 'Winter' Winterton!"

Winter's perception snapped out of her roiling inner thoughts, and she noticed the Grand Elite looking down at her from his pedestal. The crowd laughed and cheered. Lilith was already on the Hive floor. She was staring at Winter expectantly, her arms held out to the sides in a prolonged shrug.

Winter stepped down almost in a daze. She tried desperately to get into her fight mentality, but there was nothing there to access.

The hype mounted, and her crystalline eyes floated to her team in the stands. Nalara was there cheering—an innocent child, forced to put on a uniform and murder other human beings. Scorch was there—a man who'd lost so much in the name of a ruler who didn't know that he even existed.

The announcer called the start of the round, and Winter pulled her guard up . . . but could not stop looking back at the core workers down in their sequestered cavity.

Her spirit was crushed. She didn't want to be a part of the system that created such division anymore.

"I don't want to fight . . ." she voiced, and consciously lowered her hands moments before Lilith's fist impacted her face.

Suddenly time sped into fast-forward as the full force of genetic engineering came crashing down on Winter. Lilith unloaded her deft volley of attacks. In a matter of seconds, she blasted Winter's face and torso in a vicious pounding combination, then spun around and landed a ferocious spinning kick to the side of her head.

Winter was sent careening off the arena floor.

The crowd cringed and fell silent as her slack body hit the ground and rolled to a stop.

No one knew how to respond. The announcer, probably for the first time in all his vocation, was speechless. Many of the Elite, including the Grand Elite, were on their feet. Lilith trotted to the side of the ring and looked down at Winter in utter amazement and confusion.

Winter squeezed her bleary eyes and tried to gather her strength after the stunning blows. She managed to push up off the floor, but one by one, the crowd began to *booo* until the Hive echoed with their wildly animated disapproval.

"Does that count as a win?" Lilith's voice drifted through the mounting uproar.

"Uh," the announcer stammered. "C-citizens of Olympus, and our honored Elite lords and ladies . . ." His voice wavered. "V-victory . . . to Lilith 'Razor' Sharpe—captain of the Grim Reapers!"

The audience ignored him, intensifying their onslaught of heckles and jeers.

A medical team rushed to Winter's side and began checking her over. The announcer continued his vain attempts to pacify the tumultuous crowd. The Purifiers all looked to each other for explanation. No one had seen Winter lose before, let alone give up altogether. Nobody could believe their eyes.

A bright scanner temporarily blinded Winter's vision.

"No concussion," the medical worker said, looking baffled.

"I'm fine." Winter pushed him away and attempted to stand.

The medical team tried unsuccessfully to stop her.

"Wait, you really shouldn't stand, Madam Purifier!"

"We don't know what happened yet."

"For your own safety, please lie down!"

They all excitedly cautioned at once.

The announcer again called out the winner, and Lilith successfully whooped the crowd into a frenzy, diverting their attention away from Winter.

As the medical workers continued to try laying guiding hands on her, Winter spoke firmly over the din. "I didn't want to fight."

She failed to notice some of her team assemble in concern, close to where she stood. She didn't notice them or the handful of citizens who heard her statement over the applause.

"I don't want to fight my friends—my comrades." She winced through the building pain from the recent beating. "It's crass, it's insane! Why should I stand down here and take a beating—or inflict pain on someone I serve with—all for *their* entertainment!?" She pointed an accusing finger at the Elite stands before shaking her head and turning away.

The workers and Purifiers who bore witness to the statement were stricken speechless.

Winter pushed through the pain and marched to the stairs where she made a quick exit to the room down below the Hive. She wanted to gather her things and go back to her living chambers. She was so frustrated, and her face and ribs throbbed and burned. Her programmed instincts rebelled against her own actions, but she felt in her heart that what she did was right. She refused to comply anymore and fight just for the sake of conformity.

She vaguely heard footsteps behind her, and she felt internal alarms arise, but she didn't turn around. She could never have foreseen the folly in her single-mindedness to get back to her chambers. The sick feeling in her gut as she entered the empty ready room beneath the stage heightened when she heard the door at the entrance close and then lock.

Winter turned at the sound, just in time to see Wraith's gigantic form barrel into her. He shoved her back with the full force of his bodyweight and drove her hard against the wall.

The wind was driven from her chest, and her head exploded with fireworks. She barely had time to get her hands up as Wraith seized her throat and pinned her against the wall. She clutched desperately at his wrist and struggled, but the pressure building in her head was too great as he squeezed.

"What were you thinking!?" Wraith struck her face twice with his balled fist and lifted her feet off the ground.

Winter kicked him hard in the thigh, then the knee, but his immense build and his raging fury seemed to make him momentarily impervious to pain. She swung at his neck as her face turned purple, but his arms were too long.

Wraith knocked her head against the wall with each word. "You *pathetic! Attention! Whore!*"

Winter's spinning head notwithstanding, she brought her elbow down on his arm with all the strength she had left in her, but the impact didn't loosen his grip even a little. She struck it again to no effect. Panic set in and she writhed frantically to get air.

"W-what—are . . . you doing?" Winter forced out with the last of her breath in a barely audible murmur. She sank her fingernails into his forearm in one last ditch survival effort.

She could only see his wrathful face, twisted in hate, so close to hers. His eyes were filled with unreasoning murderous intent.

The room began to go black and Winter's form began to relax just before Wraith released her neck, but before she could fall, he pinned her up against the wall with the length of his other arm across her shoulders, pressing the whole side of his body up against her with such force that she was unable to move her torso or legs even slightly.

Winter wheezed and struggled for air. The room spun sickeningly.

"You're a member of *my* team!" he shouted in her face.

Still dazed and disoriented from the assault, Winter desperately pulled down on his arm and pushed against him, trying to get off the wall.

"Your failure to perform is an embarrassment, Winter! I've put up with your nonsense and your showboating for too long!"

"Stop!" Winter gasped as she shifted to kick his knee, but his sheer size made it impossible.

"The only reason I tolerate you is because you *score.*" He pressed against her harder, controlling her movement even more. "But you haven't racked a single kill in weeks—you've actually fallen in rank! First, you pull that ridiculous stunt on the surface, and now *this!?*"

Winter pushed against him and struggled to get free, but that only made him angrier. He grabbed her wrists and crossed them on her chest. He pinned her hard against the wall and turned his torso to the side.

"You've failed my team. You've failed Olympus. You're an embarrassment to our vocation and an insult to our Sovereign—and you know it!"

Winter shifted and wrenched her arms to no avail. Wraith's face was inches from hers and his full strength and bodyweight held her against the wall while his unforgiving vice grip strangled the blood from her wrists.

Fear flooded Winter's mind as she simply could not discern if he was crazed to the point of killing her outright, here under the stage, with his bare hands. "You're psychotic," she hissed, refusing to give into his fear tactics.

"And you're defective," Wraith spat. "I'm done putting up with your insubordination. You're going to start obeying my orders," he spoke through clenched teeth. "You're going to start making points again just like the rest of us, or I will beat you into formation."

A hollow terror gaped open inside Winter's chest as Wraith lowered his voice and spoke slowly, his face almost touching hers.

"I will *beat* you," he repeated. His menace and hatred, his size and strength made her feel small and powerless. These foreign feelings clutched her heart as Winter suddenly struggled to keep in control of her fear.

A timeless moment passed as they stared at each other in complete mutual abhorrence.

Wraith released her and stepped back. His disgust brutally apparent, Wraith shook his head and snapped, "Get your head straight!" before he turned and exited the understage.

Winter remained propped up against the wall and slowly slipped down to sit after her captain had gone. Wide-eyed, her hands shook violently, though she didn't cry. Her face throbbed and her throat burned in the aftermath of the attack. She felt a cold chill creep over her skin and fought to keep her breathing steady. The shock that set in removed her from any coherent thought as she sat there, alone.

Absolutely alone.

The muffled sound of cheering was lost on Winter, as above on the Hive floor, the entertainment endlessly and mindlessly continued on into the night.

CHAPTER THIRTY

The numbness in her soul was overwhelming.

Winter lay in bed long after the sun had risen, even though she'd awoken as usual before dawn. Her face throbbed with pain, but it was the only thing that anchored her to the moment. Everything else felt ethereal and distant, but the pain reminded her that she actually existed.

She was not exhausted or sleepy. She had no reason to stay in bed, except that she knew the moment she set foot on the floor, she would have to be strong again. She knew that if she got out of bed, she would need to put on that facade—the one where she looked and acted dauntless, while inside, she only wanted to cry for help.

Why did she need to get out of bed anyway?

It would just be to train . . . for jumps . . . to kill . . .

It felt pointless, especially since no one could appreciate the truth she was trying to bring to them. How odd it felt that her entire life, her whole existence, was pointless . . . Everything she'd ever wanted and worked to attain, in a matter of a few weeks, was stripped from her and a new reality put in its place . . . Nothing felt real except for the certain consequences that awaited her should she decide to venture forth. If she stayed in bed and just ran away from the terrifying eventualities, who would stop her?

Her answer came in the form of the mandatory wake-up alarm. Winter jumped in startle when her room suddenly lit up with blaring lights and sound. It was so loud and raking on her ears, she had no choice but to move to escape it.

She sighed heavily and moved her sore limbs. The noise was maddening, and it filled her whole apartment. She swung her legs to the side and escaped her bed. She cast about for her athletic training apparel and gear through the relentless alarm and pulled on her shoes in haste. Deciding she had neither the time nor patience for breakfast, she breathlessly ducked out of her apartment.

Out in the hallway she found herself alone. As the door closed behind her, the alarm automatically ceased.

Winter breathed deeply. It had been many years since she'd been so late as to incur the mandatory wake-up call. That noise was just as irritating as it had been in her first days as an initiate, and the recollection was not pleasant. None of the other top twenty Purifiers that shared this level emerged from their rooms. She knew it was because they were already out and moving.

Letting go of a long, exasperated sigh, she began the walk of shame. The lift ride was made in solitude, giving her a chance to comb fingers through her tangled ebony locks and tame them somewhat before emerging at the base.

As the lift doors opened and she exited the building, Winter caught sight of her reflection in a window and was reminded of the events of last evening. Her bruised face was healing quickly, thanks to her advanced genetic build, but the sight was still unsettling as it brought the memory of her defeat flooding into the forefront of her mind—both at the hands of Lilith and beneath the force of her rage-blinded captain.

Winter's heart beat faster, and her face grew hot. She flushed the feelings of inadequacy from her mind and refused to let the darkness take precedence. She was working for something more important than her pride.

The Tower chimed, signaling the call for the morning devotion. Everyone in the streets fell to their knees.

Winter embraced the burning rebellious fervor that leapt up in her chest. It told her to stand her ground and personify the change she wanted to see. But somehow, she couldn't fight the gravity of conditioning and paranoia that bent her knees and forced her to the ground.

As yet unable to rebel in body, she could not be forced to utter those words—not since the Ascension where her teacher was taken from her by the hateful despot to whom these people prayed.

> *Hail to his supreme holiness.*
> *Hail to our Sovereign ruler.*
> *Hail to our living god.*

The overwhelming oppressiveness of it all . . . Winter couldn't fathom how she had been so blinded by the propaganda that suffocated her city in ignorance.

> *Your name is a light to our path.*
> *Your wisdom guides us through darkness and death.*

Your power governs the whole earth.
It is to you and you alone, o gracious lord, that I swear my life, my loyalty,
and my unconditional obedience.

Glancing around at the people she served, all of them kneeling before their god, all of them reciting in perfect compliance, Winter's passion for her self-appointed duty was rekindled.

I swear to live for you.
I swear to die for you.
Live forever, o glorious king—for in you, we are granted life.

Winter looked up at the projected face of Olympus' Sovereign just as it faded from the four sides of the Tower. The people rose to their feet in concert and robotically returned to their predetermined vocations. She painstakingly stood, her ribs throbbing with the movement, and cursed the overpowering fears that drove her to her knees in the first place.

Under her breath, barely audible, she swore a different oath:

"I will see my people stand before that *man.*"

The morning continued, and Winter joined the other Purifier latecomers on their way to training. Their progress was hindered further by the formation of a line at one of the census checkpoints.

A Guardian standing near moderated the passage of citizens while a Unifier questioned each of them in turn. When it came Winter's turn, the Unifier scanned her Purifier mark and spoke: "Identify."

"January Winterton," she answered.

Voice analysis waved across the Unifier's view screen.

"Heart rate, excellent," the Unifier stated. "Physical condition, excellent. How are you feeling today?"

"I'm well," she stated as neutrally as possible.

A yellow light blinked on the Unifier's screen. "You've been flagged for further questioning. Have you been serving in your vocation to the best of your ability?"

Winter knew she couldn't get away with lying. "No," she admitted.

The light turned green. "State the reason for this lapse."

The Guardian standing close by shifted and flexed, staring at her in immovable scrutiny.

She breathed and clenched her fists, "I'm still experiencing difficulty after an incident on the surface."

The green light blinked. "State the reason for this difficulty."

Winter's temper flared, but she held it in check. "I was traumatized," she stated truthfully.

Green.

"Casual effort is a sign of incompetence in your vocation. I have put a mark on your permanent record. To avoid further marks and possible reclamation in the future, please consider reapplying yourself to your vocation and giving full effort to the best of your ability. Proceed in your service to our Sovereign."

Winter took off without another word, brushing past the Guardian in cool disregard.

The Hive was filled with the Purifier teams already well into warming up. Winter accompanied some of the lowest achievers in their late entry and shared in the group heckling they received.

This was a first for her.

She joined her team directly and took up position to lead them in training. On her way past, she shared a visual exchange with Captain Priest that sent a shiver down her spine.

An awkward silence set in.

"Brutal loss," Viper said as she joined them in their warm-up.

"Yeah, not my best day," Winter shrugged, breaking the tense eye-contact with her leader.

"Kinda nice to know that you're actually human, though," Nalara said lightheartedly, a clear attempt to lighten the mood.

"We're all human," Winter almost snapped.

Nalara looked shocked and contrite, but Winter was far too frustrated to spend any time on the topic.

"Hey, Archangels!" Scorch trotted up with a young man in tow. "This is our new initiate, Mason Howell. Say 'hi,' Mason!"

"Hi . . . everyone." The newcomer smiled meekly with a timid wave.

Winter was taken off guard. "I'm sorry." She approached and shook his hand. "I wasn't informed I had a new initiate."

"Because you don't," Wraith interjected, stepping in between them. "Howell is Scorch's initiate. *Special* circumstances and all," he added with emphasis.

At a complete loss for words, Winter watched as Scorch cleared his throat and offered her a little apologetic glance before taking over the introductions.

The awkward moment passed as Winter swallowed her pride once more and stepped back.

"Alright, here we go," she called out in forced steadiness and began leading the morning's exercises. She was still the lieutenant, and she was determined to continue as an example of excellence.

Despite the acute pain from yesterday's beating—first at the hands of Lilith . . . and then Wraith—Winter willed and pushed herself to outlast and out-lift her teammates. But all day long, she was haunted by the all-encompassing thought:

What now?

The Archangels killed themselves trying to keep up with her on the track. She schooled them in sparring—for none of them had nearly as much hand-to-hand training as she did. But despite her aptitude, there would never be a day when Purifiers ceased to be ranked by their number of killshots.

Everyone participated in the day's exercises—everyone except Wraith. The Master Purifier silently marched along the sidelines, scrutinizing her every move and command with hawk-like observance.

Winter tried to ignore him, but no matter how hard she worked to push him out of her mind, she could feel his eyes on her. She could feel the immense weight of his body pressing against her, his big hands gripping her throat.

She hoped it was just the bruised ribs, but something was making it very difficult for her to breathe.

What now?

She knew that if she started openly spreading the truth, everyone would immediately accuse her of heresy against the Sovereign. No one contradicted his decrees. It was unthinkable. Heresy against the *living god* of Olympus was a road that abruptly ended with a cliff.

It was the point of no return.

Being an excellent Purifier meant killing surface humans. That fact was inescapable. What she needed to do was change the entire viewpoint of Olympus—and to do it without publicly contradicting the Sovereign.

But was that even possible?

She feared not.

The Sovereign's rule was unquestionable, and his tyranny over the minds of her people absolute.

So . . . what now?

Winter buried her face in a towel and exhaled, feeling the beautiful release of excess energy and stress as her body descended into exhilarating exhaustion following a long day of proving to herself that she had power to accomplish whatever she put her mind to—no matter how formidable the task.

There was hope. There *had* to be.

She forced herself to believe in a hope she currently could neither see nor grasp.

" . . . Hey."

Winter turned to find Lilith standing behind her. She was still wearing gear from the shooting range.

"Hey," Winter echoed, not sure what to expect.

"What were you thinking last night?" she demanded. "Do you have any idea how embarrassing that was for me?"

Winter wasn't about to apologize.

Lilith read her expression. "I heard the others talking." She narrowed her eyes. "You really planning on not fighting in the bouts anymore?"

Winter's mouth fell open. She hoped that was a rhetorical question, but Lilith stood there, waiting for an answer. She could hear her heart beating as the silence of expectation smothered everything else. The tension was tangible.

Winter had to decide in this moment if this was the day she didn't have the nerve to keep going. Was this the day she backed down?

Always move forward.

She got up to her feet and met Lilith's gaze, flipping the towel over her shoulder.

"Yeah," she said evenly. "I don't plan on participating anymore."

All the Purifiers within earshot made various reactions of disbelief.

Lilith smirked and glanced around briefly. "You think you're good enough on the surface not to boost your numbers with bouts?"

Winter's inner fire sparked. "I think it's degrading being *told* to fight each other. I have too much respect for the people I serve with to inflict pain on them—all for the sake of entertainment."

Lilith looked blown away. She couldn't wrap her mind around the concept and couldn't seem to form a comeback before Winter turned away toward the exit.

The exchange was viewed by many, and an excited discussion followed in its wake.

Nalara trotted to Winter's side. She studied her trainer's expression and hurried to keep pace. "I'm sorry for what I said before," she offered at length. "I guess it was bad timing."

Winter slowed her gait and breathed. "No," she answered. "I'm sorry about how I reacted." She bumped shoulders with her friend and came to a stop.

Nalara half-smiled. "But . . . something has been up with you, right?" she prodded carefully. "I mean . . . you really think . . ."

Winter glanced around. "Come with me." She quickly exited the Hive to escape all the gawking. She turned and led the way toward the gardens lining the outer rim of Olympus. "I need to just speak for a moment. And I know it's not going to make any sense, but if you could just listen and let me get it all out . . ." Her voice tapered off and she shook her head before doubling her speed.

Nalara gave her full attention, though Winter didn't say another word until they reached one of the footbridges crossing the expanse between the Second Tier main and the gardens.

"There are some ideas . . ." Winter started with difficulty, not knowing what would come of this moment of truth. "Some teachings . . . here in our society . . . that I've come to understand in a different way." She gauged her friend's response.

"Like what?" Nalara looked around nervously as they descended from the bridge into the garden. "And should we even be out here? You told me these gardens were for the Elite." Her voice trembled slightly. "I don't want to get caught loitering."

"Don't worry about it," Winter said, her voice brimming with anger. She was exhausted by the pervasiveness of the lie and frustrated beyond measure that she had helped to spread its infection—even to her closest friend.

Winter walked to the garden's edge and leaned against the railing. The opalescent barrier shimmered in the late-afternoon sun. Staring out over the vast expanse of the world far below, she exhaled her frustration and again wondered if the damage of their indoctrination could ever be undone.

She turned to her friend who stood beside her, patiently waiting. Winter's mind raced to find the words, when finally, she spotted a third-tier gardener fifty feet away. She pointed. "Okay, listen." She seized the opportunity to peel away some of that indoctrination. "You see that man over there, the one working in the flower beds?"

Nalara nodded, but only after searching and following the line of Winter's direction.

"Yeah, what about him?" she asked flatly.

"Look at him," Winter urged, hoping she would see with new eyes.

Nalara's mouth twisted in confusion. "I *am* looking at him."

"No," Winter tried again, biting down on the aggravation rising in her throat. "I mean *look* at him." She directed her friend's view. "He may be thin, he may be dirty—"

"He's a worker," Nalara finished for her, still not taking more than an impassive glance at the individual.

"He's a *human,*" Winter accentuated. "He's a human—like you and me."

Nalara's confused expression persisted, but she at least continued observing and listening.

"He was raised in a Formulation Quarter like us," Winter explained. "He was initiated in his vocation. He was scared just like you were on your first day. He has friends, people he works with. He has a place he sleeps and eats. He has feelings. He has doubts, just like you and me."

Nalara scratched her head. "Wait. Are you saying you know him?" Her voice lowered to an incredulous, careful whisper. "You mean . . . you talked to a worker?"

"No, I haven't talked to him. I don't *know* him," Winter tried to explain, struggling since she had no basis for this conversation. With a little panic, she felt this first opportunity to reach someone with even a glimmer of truth slipping from her grasp. "But I *see* him. How many times do we look beneath our vocation?"

"Never." Nalara almost laughed. "The lower tier citizens look up to us."

"But why?"

Nalara shrugged. "Because the Sovereign made us in a form superior to theirs."

Winter clenched her fists, feeling the anger flare inside. She took a deep breath to allow the anger to ebb, reminding herself that she would have said the exact same words only a few weeks ago. How she desperately wanted Nalara to see with the new eyes Joshua had given her, but she would have to exercise patience. If she failed to get even her closest friend to see, what hope had she to open the eyes of Olympus?

"This is what I'm getting at," Winter summed up after taking another steadying breath. "We are human. Purifiers, Guardians, pilots, techs, medics—even the Elite. We're all human." She pointed again to the gardener as he gingerly placed a vibrant purple flower into the dark soil. "And *he* is, too. We all are—First Tier, Second, and Third. And just because we're not all equal in ability doesn't mean that we're not all equal in value. That man is worth just as much as we are."

Nalara lifted an eyebrow in confusion. "Say . . . what?" She shook her head. "That sounds . . . a little bit crazy."

Winter's heart sank as her hope shattered like glass. She swallowed and waited patiently to witness the fallout of her confiding.

"Well . . ." Nalara giggled. "I'm not really sure what this all means to you. Maybe I'll understand someday." She smiled. "I trust you. You always looked out for me in the FMQ, and I know if you're working through something right now, you wouldn't do anything to lead me wrong."

Winter smiled and hung her head. The moment had passed. The door had closed. That same darkened room that Joshua had been able to open for her—to allow the beautiful light of truth to shine in—would remain closed for Nalara.

Winter tried, at least, to garner some comfort in that she had seized the opportunity and given it her best, as woefully pathetic as her 'best' was.

Mocking laughter caught Winter's ear, and she turned her gaze to the direction it came from.

"Is this really what's been . . .?" Nalara trailed off and followed Winter's line of sight to a group of young Elites crowding around the gardener.

Winter didn't hear her friend's question; the disturbance in the garden held her attention.

The young men stood around laughing hysterically while one of their number shoved the landscape worker into a hedge. When he emerged, they continued their abasement by pouring buckets of soil and fertilizer over his head while he groveled at their feet.

"You enjoy the dirt, maggot!" one Elite dressed in white with gold trim, the group's apparent leader, mocked. "You feel right at home, yes?"

"Yes, sir! I do, sir! Thank you, sir!" the gardener responded quickly, remaining on his knees, his eyes firmly fixed on the ground while other Elites upset his tools and kicked them around.

Winter reacted on instinct and made a direct line to the group.

"Uh . . . w-wait!" Nalara protested.

Winter didn't respond. Her laser-focus had found its target.

The Elite in white stood heckling and sneering, then began kicking the worker's ribs repeatedly and laughing.

With each blow, the worker cried out: "Thank you, sir! Thank you! Sovereign Zeus bless you, sir!"

"You dare sully his great name!" The Elite gave him another solid kick. "A filthy maggot like you, speaking the name of our god!"

None of them had time to react as Winter cut through the midst of the gaggling youth and walled herself between the Elite and his victim. Her face a dangerous warning, she clenched her jaw and stood immovable.

"What's this? Move, Purifier," the annoyed Elite commanded offhandedly. "You're interrupting my entertainment." When she did not comply, his annoyance turned to indignant disbelief. "Just what do you think you're doing?" he demanded in confusion while his cohorts laughed at the sight.

"This is wrong," Winter answered evenly, though her heart pounded in her chest. "You shouldn't hurt people, especially when they could never defend themselves."

Nalara ran up to stand on the sideline, eyes wide with dread. The disturbance was gathering a growing crowd of strolling Elite and random workers alike.

"Are you *defective?*" The ivory-featured young man winced in disgust. "Go back to your quarter where you belong and . . . do some pushups or something." He turned to receive the supporting laughter at his jeer.

"I won't let you touch him again," Winter returned in cold, uncompromising conviction.

The young Elites standing around their leader *ooohed* mockingly, yet made no motion to join in.

The Elite took a half-step toward Winter and raised up on his toes to inch closer to eye-level with her. "You will . . . *let* me do whatever I want to do to this maggot." He pointed down at the man covered in filth. "Isn't that right, maggot!"

"Y-yes, sir! You're right, sir!"

"That I am. I always am." The Elite sneered and kicked a small pile of fertilizer into the gardener's lap. "And maggots like you need to eat, right? So, eat up!"

"Yes, sir! Right away, sir!" The gardener grabbed the clump of fertilizer and obediently moved it towards his mouth.

"DROP IT!" Winter shouted without taking her icy eyes off the Elite standing one foot from her. Out of her peripheral, she saw the worker stop dead and remain motionless, clearly unsure with what to do. "Do *not* obey what he tells you to do."

"What impertinence! Such disrespect!" the Elite snapped. "Do you know who I am?" He squinted at Winter in patronizing loathing. "I am Remington Adolphus Blackburn, you defective worm! You . . . you arrogant, miserable working-class baggage!"

One of the Elite's cohorts, a blonde-haired young man with striking features, stepped forward and placed a hand on Remington's shoulder. "Come along, Rem. This is growing tiresome."

Remington shoved his friend's hand away and stuck an accusatory finger in Winter's direction. "I'm not going anywhere until this Purifier *excrement* has apologized for her despicable insolence!"

Winter didn't respond but turned away from him and tried to offer her hand to the landscape worker. The worker, clutching tightly to the clump of fertilizer as if it were a lifeline, looked up at her with fear and confusion rife in his wide eyes.

"You dare turn your back to me!?" Remington raged. "You *listen* to me when I speak, you wretched Purifier! I am a chosen, blessed Elite of Sovereign Zeus—Remington Adolphus Blackburn!" He spoke his name louder, as if it would mean more the second time. "Did you hear me!?"

He pushed Winter roughly, but his puny strength did little but draw her attention in annoyance.

She turned to him and met his gaze, astounded at the thought that she once deified these people. *The Elite*. Right now, he looked so small and pathetic in his squalling. Their title and vocation now seemed more like a joke than anything else.

"I won't stand for this insubordination!" Remington shouted in her face, flecks of spit spraying her skin. "I can have you sent to reclamation, you third-tier piece of genetic trash! I'm going to report you to your supervisor! I'm going to tell the Grand Elite himself!" He saw his threats made no effect and became even more impassioned. "You will respect me, and you will regret this day!" His face flushed red as he shoved her again, only able to budge her slightly.

Winter stood her ground and clenched her jaw. She narrowed her focus.

Stepping deeper into her space, he raised his voice again and screamed, "I am an ELITE! I am SUPERIOR! Granted glory and honor and POWER by the Sovereign himself! I am Remington! ADOLPHUS! BLACKB—!"

Winter shifted into a cold, deft strike—hard, into the pit of his stomach.

The laughter ceased instantly. A shocked silence gripped the area as her sudden and immense force drove the wind from the young Elite's lungs. Remington doubled over Winter's fist, hanging his entire weight on her and gaping comically.

The crowd gaped, too, astonished and dumbfounded as Winter bent over to speak in his ear. "I'm sorry, what were you saying? I didn't hear you."

Remington made a strange wheezing noise in response.

"I thought so." Winter dropped him, where he lay curled in the dirt, clutching his stomach and desperately searching for air.

Every soul that stood witness was horrified and stunned to motionless silence. Winter ignored them all, though inside, she was feeling the first effects of the gravity of her action.

Treason in its purest form.

With a giant lump in her throat, she did the only thing she could think of and turned to the worker whom she'd defended.

She bent down to his level and looked him in the eyes. "Are you alright?" she managed to ask through the rising terror in her chest. She offered her hand once more. "It's okay. I'm not going to hurt you."

The worker's eyes were filled with an ocean of dread. He held her gaze only for a moment before glancing down at the wheezing Elite lying in the dirt near him, the white and gold of his once pristine clothing now stained with brown muck. Remington's face was turning a shade of blue as he still battled for a single breath.

The worker's entire body began to shake uncontrollably. He glanced around frantically, looking for cues from the mortified Elite gathered around.

Winter extended her hand toward him further, but at the gesture, he suddenly spun around, scrambled to his feet, and took off running like a frightened animal. She let out a sigh as she watched the third-tier worker race away until he had disappeared out of sight.

She turned to look at Nalara, who'd witnessed the whole thing. She looked bewildered and terrified, her mouth bunched together in a frozen question that couldn't make it past her lips.

Winter didn't know what to say. This was unprecedented ground. She didn't have procedural guidelines. She didn't have training to draw from. She was making her own rules now. She was forging a new path—a dangerous path.

Slowly, she rose to her feet and looked around. All attention within a hundred meters was fixed on her as if she'd just murdered someone in cold blood before their very eyes.

Glancing down at the childishly weeping form of the curled-up Elite at her feet, again she found herself asking the same question:

What now?

Was this the moment she backed down?

Or had her footing just slipped?

. . . Free-fall.

With dignity in every deliberate movement, she breathed out steadily and lifted her chin before stepping over the sniveling, pathetic Elite and walked off alone.

She'd passed the point of no return. Her only choice now:

Move forward.

CHAPTER THIRTY-ONE

What falls cannot fall forever.

W   A surge of emotion grew in Winter's throat as she approached the Purifier Quarter and saw two massive Guardians waiting there. She knew her actions would have consequences, but the gravity was hard to accept.

Stone-faced, she stopped at their bidding.

"January Winterton," one of them spoke in the signature slow and otherworldly deep voice of the Guardian class. "You will come with us."

Winter nodded crisply and gave no sign of resistance. She and her escorts turned toward the Hive.

She had always been able to rely on her instincts. She had always been able to trust them. She didn't regret her actions; if anything, she felt more liberated than ever. Now that she had put action to her new understanding, she felt like it was the true step-off point towards a different future for her people. Everything had built to this inevitable moment. Acting on the truth seemed to solidify it in her mind. She had known it was true before, but now that she had acted on it, it took root in her heart, and she couldn't see how she had never understood it before. Now, the directive was clear, and she could start working her way up to the ultimate goal of opening the eyes of Olympus. She could finally bring an end to the pointless bloodshed.

A little intimidated by the unknown, Winter, nonetheless, followed her escorts with confidence as she knew whatever happened would be better than the ambiguous limbo she'd been stuck in since her own eyes had been opened.

To her chagrin, the Guardians walked her directly to the Hive's ready room under the stage where, less than twenty-four hours ago, she'd been brutalized by her own commanding officer. She involuntarily stayed her feet before the threshold. A fluttering discomfort stirred in her chest; it was a feeling that she needed to physically swallow down before she could enter that room again.

The Guardians split at the door; one followed her in, the other broke away toward the Hive floor.

"The hearing will be in two hours," the Guardian at the door stated before closing them in.

"So, I'm just supposed to wait here?" Winter objected.

The Guardian by her side looked askance down at her.

Winter sighed and settled into standing at attention, a posture she maintained in silence for a long while. Her training had such a hold on her actions. She pondered on the fact that she could resist, she could rebel right now, but her programmed behavior made it unthinkable.

When she decided to speak again, it was physically painful to deviate from her conditioning.

"What's your name?" She looked up at the Guardian towering over her. The break in silence and protocol split the air like a bolt of lightning.

His neck was so thick that it seemed difficult for him to turn, but the Guardian looked down at her with a confused expression, as if he was trying to understand her motivation.

When he didn't answer, Winter gave a little shrug. "I've never really spoken to a Guardian before. Other than . . . you know, *guarding* . . . I guess I don't know much about your vocation."

The massive man shook his head in disapproval and turned back to face forward in silence.

"It's strange," Winter mused aloud, trying her hardest to break procedural norm. "I've seen hundreds of Guardians throughout my life—maybe even thousands. Ever since I was a child in the FMQ, I remember seeing Guardians. I remember thinking how enormous you all were. But . . . I don't remember ever talking to one." She switched gears and plunged into raw honesty. "I never cared before. I never really . . . *looked* at Guardians or anyone else before. I had no reason to. But now that I am, I'm learning a lot about what's actually real from what we're just *told* is real."

The Guardian looked down at her again, puzzled by the one-sided conversation. "The hearing's in one and a half hours. Until then, you're not supposed to speak."

Winter cocked an eyebrow. "Why not?" she prodded rebelliously. "Will I get in even more trouble if I do?"

He grumbled in annoyance, then returned to stand at silent attention once more.

Winter decided to try one last time. "I just want to know your name. You do have a name, right?"

He remained motionless, as still and fixed as a statue of an Ascended.

This was going nowhere. She never got any answers from the Ascended; apparently, she wouldn't have any better luck with a Guardian.

Winter huffed and reluctantly fell back into her Purifier conditioning to wait out the interim in agonizing silence. She didn't want to conform anymore. She didn't want to adhere to her training. But if she appeared erratic or defective, no one would give her a second thought. She needed to be collected and professional to have any credibility—so that's what she would be.

Petrified, Nalara stood in shock as Winter exited the garden. She was torn between following her training or following her trainer. Winter didn't slow or even pause. Nalara desperately wanted to support her friend, but she had just crossed a line that she couldn't bring herself to follow.

The simpering Elite that lay prone on the garden walkway was refusing to stand, even with the insisting help from his friends.

"No, no, NO!" Remington cried, pushing their hands away. Hot tears streamed down his face and wet snot drained out his nostrils into his mouth. "They're broken! I know they're broken! That miserable Purifier broke my legs!"

"She never touched your legs, Rem," the blonde-haired young Elite from his group was quick to point out.

The handsome Elite suddenly looked up at Nalara. She was terrified he would blame her for the incident since she was the one standing there, but instead, he almost smiled. His gaze drifted over her shoulder, however, and his smile disappeared.

Nalara followed his line of sight to the bridge where half a dozen Guardians and a Unifier approached in stoic formation.

Many by-standing Elite shuffled off in disinterest.

The Unifier's scanner did a quick capture of all the hand marks in the vicinity.

"All witnesses to the incident have been logged," the Unifier spoke to no one in particular. "Your statement is required evidence at the hearing for the sentencing of the Purifier, January Winterton."

Nalara's heart sank.

"That's the one!" Remington shouted in disgust. "That wretched Winterton tried to kill me!"

The workers present bowed their heads and silently obeyed the Unifier's command, following a Guardian who herded them into a single file.

Nalara had no choice but to follow as well, compliantly shuffling into line with the workers from the garden, each being questioned by the Unifier in turn.

The Elite young men declined and waved the order off.

A Guardian was finally successful in helping Remington to his feet.

"Careful, you mindless brute!" he shouted, kicking and slapping at him in a tantrum. "You're hurting me!"

"My sincerest apologies, Elite Blackburn." The giant Guardian bowed in humble obeisance to the Elite less than half his size. "I meant no disrespect, sir."

Remington sniffed and furiously wiped at his dripping nose. "Barbaric monstrosity!" He kicked the mountain of a man in the shin—a pebble knocking against a boulder—then limped off with some of his friends in tow.

"Honored citizen—" the Unifier called after him "—I require your statement."

Remington either didn't hear or simply ignored him.

Nalara waited patiently for the Unifier to make his way to her, knowing the procedure and what was expected of her.

"Identify," he commanded when it came Nalara's turn.

"Nalara Gressen," she stated while the scanner recaptured her hand mark.

"You were present for the incident involving Purifier January Winterton and Elite Remington Adolphus Blackburn?"

"Yes . . . I was."

The voice monitors analyzed her response. The Unifier watched the incoming data carefully as he continued. "In your own words, relay the incident as it occurred."

Nalara gulped nervously. "Well, uh . . . Winter and I were walking in the gardens when she saw the group of Elite harassing a landscape worker—"

"We weren't *harassing* him," a voice behind her interjected. "We were just having a bit of harmless fun."

Nalara jerked her head over her shoulder to identify the speaker. It was the blonde-haired Elite. She was confused by his interruption but also distracted by his heart-stopping looks and sparkling blue eyes.

"Go on," the Unifier ordered.

"W-Winter tried . . ." Nalara turned back to the Unifier, not sure if protocol dictated she give the Elite his due respect or obey the Unifier's command. "She tried to get them to stop just by talking to them, but the Elite—uh . . . Elite Remington . . . he got angry, and he was yelling at her, and then she . . . she punched him. She punched him in the stomach." Nalara stepped closer and hurriedly added, "Honestly, it all happened so fast, I'm really not sure what happened! But I'm sure Winter meant no disrespect. I know that she loves and honors all the Elite of our Sovereign. She's . . . she's just been going through . . . *something* lately."

"Define 'something,'" the Unifier pressed.

"I really don't know," Nalara spoke truthfully. "It all started when she was attacked by some blighters on the surface. That was on the deployment to fix the array. She was attacked and she seemed really traumatized by it, and then afterwards she disappeared on the surface for three days. But then she was given the Survivor's Award by the Grand Elite himself! And—and—and then . . ." Her voice trailed off into silence. She paused to catch her breath and clear her thoughts. "Please. I don't know everything she's been through, but I know that she's been having a really hard time lately, and I know that she would never, *ever* normally do something like this."

The light remained green and the Unifier snapped his unsettling eyes to her. "This inquiry has been submitted to incident report. If you wish to know the results of January Winterton's hearing, you may request it from any Unifier immediately afterwards. Your presence at the hearing is neither required nor allowed."

The Unifier turned to the blonde Elite standing behind Nalara. "Please identify, sir."

Nalara had never heard a Unifier use the words 'please' or 'sir' before.

"Decline," he waved it off casually.

The Unifier neither scanned nor questioned him. "As you wish, honored Elite." He gave a short bow. "If you desire to attend the hearing, please report to the Grand Elite's Administerial Hall in two hours' time. Thank you, and may our Sovereign's favor ever be upon you." He moved on to the next subject for questioning.

Nalara glanced again at the handsome Elite but moved on quickly toward the bridge to cross back over to the Second Tier. Her heart raced in her chest, and she desperately wanted to cry. This was her friend's most fateful time of need, but she was powerless to help.

There was nothing to do . . . but wait.

CHAPTER THIRTY-TWO

Winter waited patiently for her hearing to begin from the center of the round, towering council room. She'd never been inside the Administerial Hall before; for that matter, no Purifier she was aware of had ever stood here. Adjacent to the Sovereign Tower, the massive domed structure was the center of all orders of governance on Olympus—where the Grand Elite, Draven Constantine Rothgard, led the ten members of the Elite High Council in their administrative duties.

Gold wrapped, intricately carved marble columns ringed the rotunda and held aloft the ceiling more than three-hundred feet overhead. The light of the setting sun shone through high arched windows and splashed the dome's white stone with brilliant hues of red and orange.

Winter strained her neck as she gazed upward at the awesome spectacle. The scale and design of the architecture was truly stunning, but standing at the center of the immense, opulent structure, she couldn't help but feel small and vulnerable.

At the apex of the dome, chiseled directly into the stone and plated with rose gold, a single eye amidst carved-out, silver-plated clouds stared in unblinking judgment down upon her.

The Eye of Zeus.

The iris glinted bright red in the light of the evening sun, dusted with thousands of ruby gemstones.

Winter felt a cold shiver race down her spine. She had the sudden dread of drowning come over her and fought to stave off the fear as the weight of the Sovereign's lie bore down upon her like an ocean of oppression.

It would be here, in this hall, with the Eye of Zeus upon her, that her fate would be decided. Perhaps, it would be here that the fate of Olympus would be decided.

Winter closed her eyes and inhaled a long, calming breath. She exhaled slowly and felt the tension recede from her body. It was the hope for a brighter future for Olympus that she clung to—her one and only lifeline that kept her head above the threatening waves. Her programming told her she had committed an unpardonable crime, but having learned to rebel against the conditioned response, she was at least hopeful that her action against Remington would be the needed catalyst to bring the truth to her people.

She breathed in that hope and breathed out her dread.

A side door opened, and the ten members of the Elite High Council, dressed in flowing silk robes and with sparkling rings adorning their fingers, slowly filed in and ascended the stairs to their seats in the elevated stands behind dark wooden podiums. They spoke casually with one another as they got comfortable in their seats.

Accompanied on one side by her statue-like Guardian escort from before, as well as a dozen extra standing nearby, Winter waited in focused silence.

A single Unifier entered the hall and called out: "All rise for the mighty Sovereign's right hand—the glorified Grand Elite of Olympus, Draven Constantine Rothgard!"

All members of the High Council arose, and everyone in the hall stood at attention.

Winter, willing to play along solely for the sake of professionalism, stood a little taller.

The Grand Elite, dressed in black and gold, then entered and took up his exclusive and high position at the head of the stand where everyone was angled to see him.

The Unifier positioned himself below Draven in placid stasis.

"Chosen Elite of the High Council," Draven's authoritative voice echoed throughout the stone hall. He sat and eased into the back of his throne-like judgment seat, where he paused with a subtle smile on his lips as he surveyed his audience. "You may be seated," he finally said.

The High Council obeyed, and the rigidity in the room relaxed.

"The child of Zeus may now enter," Draven announced and motioned with his hand.

Two Guardians opened wide the double doors at the back of the hall, and Remington Adolphus Blackburn entered with several of his friends. His entourage of companions departed and found seats in the surrounding stands, leaving Remington alone on the floor, standing opposite to Winter. He pointed his sour expression and crossed arms at her in dramatic displeasure.

Winter kept a stone face, not willing to show even a hint of emotion—

despite the fact that seeing Remington again made her stomach churn in disgust.

Draven cleared his throat and the room settled instantly.

"Welcome, blessed Elite." The Grand Elite gestured to the High Council seated below him, five on either side. "You are here for the sentencing for an incident of violence involving one of your own honored citizens." He paused as the Council members muttered. "Son of Zeus," he spoke and indicated to Remington, "step forward and speak."

The young man took a step toward the Council stands but kept his glaring eyes locked on Winter. "My walk in the garden today was interrupted when *this* Purifier—" his voice trembled with emotion as he pointed accusingly at Winter "—for no reason whatsoever, viciously attacked and brutalized me in front of my friends. She humiliated me. She victimized me!" His voice grew to a hostile shriek. "She's clearly defective! I demand she be publicly stripped of rank and honors and sent to reclamation immediately!"

Winter's hyperawareness on point, she noticed several members of the High Council roll their eyes or wince at his shrill demand. She took in the whole picture and saw everything. The High Council appeared bored and distracted. Draven himself was not looking at the accuser; he seemed to be gauging each councilman and woman.

"A Purifier using her Sovereign-gifted powers to assault a citizen of the First Tier," Draven spoke neutrally, watching the various reactions. "What say you, Council?"

"Purifiers are too dangerous to leave their quarter!" Remington screeched out of turn, but his wailing seemed to fall on deaf ears.

"What I fail to understand is the motive for such an attack," a councilman stated.

"Agreed," a councilwoman said. "Purifiers are designed and trained as soldiers, after all. They are built for combat. But for one to exercise her abilities unprovoked—and against an Elite, no less . . ." She shook her head and didn't finish her thoughts.

"It certainly is," another councilman chimed in, *"odd* behavior, to say the least. I for one have never heard anything like it." He turned towards Remington. "And you say this was done to you for 'no reason whatsoever'?"

"Yes!" Remington cried. "No reason whatsoever! Her only desire was to humiliate and bully me! To turn me into a laughing stock."

Winter clenched her teeth behind pursed lips. It was becoming more and more difficult to maintain her professionalism being suffocated by such lies.

"Unifier," Draven ordered abruptly. "Step forward and offer the testimony of witnesses."

"Yes, lord Grand Elite." The census worker promptly obeyed. "Incident report. In the case regarding Elite Remington Adolphus Blackburn and Purifier January Winterton—all twenty-one witnesses confirm the two parties were present in the east gardens earlier this day, where an altercation took place. All witnesses confirm that Lieutenant Winterton intervened on behalf of a landscape worker of the Third Tier interacting with the Blackburn party. Some witnesses claim the landscape worker was being harassed by the Blackburn party. All witnesses confirm that Lieutenant Winterton did, in fact, strike Elite Blackburn, and based on witness testimony, it was a single punch to his stomach."

"You see!?" Remington blurted out with his arms held wide. "As I said: *No reason whatsoever!* She's nothing but defective, third-tier putrescence!"

Half the Elite Council shook their heads in disdain, while the others seemed strangely amused.

One of the Council members leaned forward in his seat. "Come now— may we see a reenactment?" he goaded sarcastically, inciting a sudden round of laughter from the Council.

Remington turned bright red in rage and embarrassment. "This is not acceptable!" he screamed and attempted to assert control over the situation. "You *will* listen to me! I demand—"

Draven dropped his fist like a hammer atop his podium. Remington startled visibly and immediately fell silent. A grave hush fell over the hall as the Grand Elite stared him down. "Careful, young man." His voice was a terrible warning. "You may be a child of Zeus, but you will remember your place in our presence—in *my* presence. Understood?"

Remington's shoulders slumped in defeat. He hung his head low and began sobbing quietly.

"Now . . ." Draven relaxed once again into the back of his throne. "Has there ever been an incident such as this recorded? Unifier."

The bald census worker snapped to attention.

"Bring forward any previous incidents of violence against Elite citizens."

"Processing your request, lord Grand Elite." The Unifier paused as images began to fly across his tiny view screen. "Olympian archives record a rash of violence perpetrated against members of the Elite by one: Nathaniel Callum Archer—82 years, 3 months ago. A total of nine separate charges were brought against him over a two-week period. The charges include multiple beatings and two cudgeling attacks with a blunt instrument. One of the Elites he attacked was very nearly killed."

Several of the Council began talking amongst themselves. Draven detachedly observed their dialogue.

"Archer? I've never heard of him."

"Not surprising, considering how long ago that was. But how is it relevant?"

"It can't be considered relevant. That was clearly an Elite name."

The Unifier spoke up. "Nathaniel Callum Archer was, indeed, an Elite citizen of the First Tier, my lords and ladies."

"Well now. That's entirely different. We're discussing Second Tier today, not First."

"But what would have been the motive behind those attacks? An Elite attacking fellow Elites, nearly killing one? It's madness."

"Forgive me, my lord." The Unifier offered a humble bow. "The records offer no explanation as to Elite Archer's motives."

"Out of curiosity, what was *his* sentencing?"

"According to archival records," the Unifier answered, "Elite Archer was offered the chance by the Grand Elite of his day, Chandler Augustus Darrington, to renounce his behavior and offer suitable recompense . . ." The Unifier paused. "Elite Archer refused. He was then sentenced to forced expulsion from Olympus."

"As in . . . he was banished to the surface?" a councilwoman asked.

"In a manner of speaking, my lady," the Unifier clarified. "He was tossed over the side."

A long, stunned moment of silence swept the hall.

Winter dug into herself for courage and took a deep breath. She let it out slowly and expelled every insecurity inside.

"Honorable Grand Elite and all Elite members of the Olympus High Council," she chose her words deliberately, forcing herself to dredge up a disingenuous respect for their acknowledged authority.

Draven and the ten Council members turned wordlessly to the Purifier standing before them at the center of the massive rotunda and waited.

"I hope . . ." she continued carefully, "with all humility, Elite lords and ladies, that you will please forgive this breach in protocol, but I cannot hold back any longer. I plead with you to allow me to speak."

With the 'open gaze' Eagle Eyes had taught her, Winter observed Draven and all ten members of the Council simultaneously. No one moved to stop her; they seemed more fascinated at her audacity than angry at her nonconformity.

Swallowing down the sickening feeling rising in her throat, Winter was confident she could go on. At least she had their attention. It was now or never.

"My heart is so full of possibilities. I know we have a well-established way of life here, but I ask you: For how long? The order is set; the tiers are established. We all love our home and the order and peace it brings, but I *know* that there is not one of you who does not yearn for change."

Eyes open. The High Council was listening.

Move forward.

"The Purifiers were created to cleanse the surface of the Blight, so that we may reclaim our ancestral home—so that we can return to the organic, living world below. But to achieve this, growth must happen first, and it must happen here. We will never progress as a society, not even with the entire world free and clear to live in—not until we can accept each other as living human beings.

"Every one of us . . ." Winter's breath fluttered, and her knees began shaking. She fought against the surge of adrenaline in a desperate battle to remain in control. "We all put everything we have into our vocations. All of us want to be our best. But none of us will accomplish anything if our only focus is to gratify our base impulses—especially at the expense of those who work hard and have done nothing wrong."

Winter's cold gaze fell on Remington.

The young Elite eyed her with raw contempt.

"It's true what some of the witness testimonies claim," Winter went on without looking away. "He and his friends *were* harassing the landscape worker, a man who was only magnifying his vocation to the very best of his abilities. But they thought nothing of him. They treated him spitefully and hatefully. They did not see him as human nor treat him with the basic respect all Olympians deserve."

Winter turned back to face the High Council. "I, and several others, witnessed them mock the worker, pour dirt over him, kick him, and even try to force him to eat manure . . ." She paused to examine the Council's expressions. Most were stone-faced and unreadable; a few leaned forward with seeming rapt attention. "When I saw this injustice, I couldn't stand by and do nothing. I love Olympus too much to allow such crimes to occur. My one and only reason for striking Remington was to defend a fellow Olympian who couldn't defend himself."

Winter took a steadying breath in order to finish strong and confident. "This hearing's purpose is to ascertain my punishment for a crime of violence against an Elite. But I say that it is Remington that is guilty of the true crime: a crime against Olympus itself. I say I was acting in the best interests of Olympus by putting an end to his destructive behavior. And that, lord and lady Elite of the High Council, is my witness." She forced herself to bow in a gesture of sincerity. "Thank you."

Hoping beyond anything that the smallest amount of truth reached their hearts, Winter waited as the High Council whispered among themselves. For a long moment, she kept her head bowed. When she eventually raised her eyes, she found the Grand Elite staring at her from his high position. She was off-put by the lack of malice and saw in its place dispassionate calculation.

Winter truly didn't know what would come of her testimony, but she felt a strange liberation after speaking her mind. She, a Purifier Lieutenant of the Second Tier, stood in the presence of the highest-ranking Elites of all Olympus, those who counseled with Sovereign Zeus himself, and she had spoken the truth with competence and conviction.

The disturbing image of Elite Archer being thrown over the edge of Olympus and disappearing into the clouds far below lingered in her mind. Winter acknowledged the very real fear of her own 'forced expulsion' to the surface being present, but she was genuinely surprised by how little weight it carried. The true weight—the weight of her own uncertainty and the agonizing stagnation she'd been carrying for weeks—was pleasantly gone.

She failed to notice the Guardian escort at her side staring at her in singular interest.

Draven suddenly arose from his judgment seat at the head of the stand. The High Council fell silent as all eyes turned to the Sovereign's Grand Elite.

"Honored High Council." Draven's voice was even, calm. "Continue in your deliberations as I have a private word with the accused."

Draven's announcement spurred animated discussion among the stands, and the cavernous room echoed with conversation.

A new, sickening weight settled in the pit of Winter's stomach. She remembered the hidden truth she had seen behind the Grand Elite's eyes when he had presented her with her contrived 'Survivor's Award.' She remembered his look of cold wrath and utter loathing.

The memory made her shudder.

She focused on steadily breathing and remaining professionally composed as Draven made his way down the stands. She stood tall and kept her eyes fixed forward as he approached.

"Follow me," he commanded, motioning towards the side door he had entered the hall from earlier.

Winter's internal alarms went off, but her mind willed her body to obey.

With a snap of Draven's fingers to her Guardian escort, the silent giant fell in line close behind.

They dutifully followed the Grand Elite through the side door and down a long stone corridor. Draven led them through another door, entering into a spacious assembly room lit by brilliant crystal chandeliers. At the head of the room was a dark, glossy oak table, a single gilded chair behind it, and ten smaller chairs before it. Along the far wall hung enormous framed paintings of magisterial figures dressed in black and gold attire. Before each painting stood a life-size idol of pure gold.

Winter counted the paintings and golden idols—a total of seven of each of them. She scanned the names engraved into the base of the frames.

Marius Andrew Devonshire

Virgil Julius Bloodworth

Magnus Hamilton Mendenhall

Dorian Piers Kingsley

Chandler Augustus Darrington

Atherton Alistair Travers

Winter's breath stopped short as she came to the seventh painting and golden idol. She recognized *him*.

Draven Constantine Rothgard

All who had been appointed to the high position of 'Grand Elite' throughout Olympus' long history lined this one wall. Winter knew where she was. This room was the administrative office of the Sovereign's right hand official.

She had entered the heart of the Olympian government.

Her throat tightened as she felt the eyes of seven Grand Elites and an entire history of lies bearing heavily down on her. Even though her sentence had not yet been decided, simply being in this room made her feel like a defective dissident—a rebel of Olympus and a traitor to their Sovereign.

Draven snapped his fingers again and indicated to the open door.

The Guardian wordlessly obeyed, closing the door behind them and taking up his position as sentry.

Winter was led to the oak table, far enough from the Guardian to be confident that the Grand Elite's 'private word' with her would remain private.

Draven turned, and his dark eyes washed up and down her figure. A little smile twitched in the corner of his mouth.

Winter suddenly felt the need for a hot shower.

This man's eyes looked hungry.

"January 'Winter' Winterton." He shook his head. "You really are one of a kind among Purifiers."

Winter shifted as he circled her slowly but held her gaze steady.

"I've known about you for a long time now," he admitted. "The youngest of the top-ranking Purifiers. The only other Purifier to accomplish what the 'Nightmare' herself accomplished in Tartarus. A Purifier destined for Ascension . . . for greatness . . . for immortality."

He stopped his circling and leered at her with those ravenous eyes. "And you just keep drawing my attention, don't you?"

Winter swallowed and said nothing.

The Grand Elite stared at her in silence for a long while, before finally saying: "You're fortunate that his greatness, our dear Sovereign Zeus, has other things occupying his time right now. If he were even remotely interested in your hearing, I know what his solution would be." He leaned closer. "He would simply *burn* you." He chuckled. "Quick . . . efficient . . . *permanent.*"

He paused and smiled. "However, neither he nor I are without a degree of mercy."

Winter could see he thoroughly enjoyed playing the part of the benevolent power.

"That was quite the speech you gave," Draven changed subjects. "I don't know what exactly you're hoping to accomplish, but I doubt very much that this has anything to do with lowly third-tier detritus . . .. No. It's something else."

He mused for a moment, eyeing her suspiciously. "What are you truly after, January Winterton?" he finally asked. "What is it you truly want?"

Winter straightened and spoke evenly. "I only want what is best for Olympus."

"I decide what is best for Olympus," he said quickly, his tone sharp and deadly. "Not you."

Winter felt her confidence take a staggering blow. She could now plainly see that her testimony before the High Council had been meaningless. They would not hear. Yet again, her efforts to bring the truth to Olympus had failed.

"Whatever your true desire may be," Draven went on, his voice again exuding benevolence, "I assure you that appealing to the High Council's better nature will get you nowhere." He almost laughed. "Elites live in a world far beyond your limited comprehension. Their world is an existence of perpetual indulgence. From formulation to reclamation, they are catered to in every desire . . . every whim. Nothing is paramount to their own gratification. Extravagant luxuries and unbridled pleasures—beyond imagining." He inched close enough to whisper on her neck. "And . . . it could be yours."

Winter's eyes widened, and her skin crawled as his hot breath bathed her neck and bare shoulders. She still wore her training outfit from the day's exercises in the Hive. She suddenly felt naked and exposed. Vulnerable. She desperately wished she had been allowed the time to change into her formal dress greens.

Her urge to run was nearly impossible to keep in check.

"Right now," the Grand Elite continued, "the High Council is undoubtedly fussing over precedence and repercussion. They may deliberate and squabble, January, but make no mistake—your fate *is* in our hands . . . in *my* hands." He moved away to face her. "But . . . if you held the favor of the Grand Elite, your fate would belong to you."

Goosebumps prickled all over Winter's skin. She knew instinctively that there was nothing about her that he found appealing, save for the vulnerable position in which she now found herself. The possibility of having her beg for help seemed to arouse him in some narcissistic way.

One thing was certain: her fate was in his hands. If she was to survive this day, she begrudgingly accepted that she'd have to play a role in his sick game—at least to a degree. Perhaps an opportunity to escape would somehow present itself.

She swallowed down the nausea and forced a shy smile. "You would do that for me?"

Draven flashed a toothy grin. "Of course, I would. This would be my gift to you. At my word alone, your life would transform," he snapped his fingers, "just like that. You'd no longer toil among the basest of creations, but true immortality would be within your reach." He took her hand softly. "I have the power to give it to you. Such is the favor of Zeus. I would take you into my protection, and you'd live in peace and indulgence and pleasures without limit."

His buttery, condescending tone made her stomach churn. Winter's instincts loathed him and his offer, but she again forced an expression she knew he desired. "And what would be expected of me, lord Grand Elite?"

"A world of perpetual indulgence for you . . . as you cater to every desire . . . and every whim . . . for me." Draven's hand traveled up her arm.

Winter was repulsed to her very core. Even though accepting his offer meant saving herself from almost certain death, she couldn't betray her own integrity or self-respect like that. She could never turn her back on the truths she'd learned. While her practical mind couldn't help but weigh the benefits of Draven's offer—the promise of peace and luxury, a life free of turmoil—it was an inner voice that spoke the clearest truth of all:

There are some fates worse than death.

It would be impossible, even if she tried, to ignore the warning of that voice.

Winter now knew that the High Council would never accept nor act upon her testimony. That much was evident. To have ever believed that they would was the height of foolishness. No, they would never listen. If there was any hope of bringing the truth to Olympus, she would have to change her tactics, and to do that, she would need to be alive.

Accepting the Grand Elite's proposition was out of the question, but also, refusing him was out of the question. His will was the Sovereign's will. If she outright refused him, she wouldn't have to wait for the Council's verdict. She will have pronounced her own death sentence.

She would have to lie—convincingly. She suspected that if she played her role just right, she could give Draven what he really wanted, and do it without becoming his newest trophy. It was a gamble, but even death was better than embracing this man's *mercy.*

She shrugged away from his touch and bowed in feigned humility. "Gracious and benevolent Grand Elite, I thank you with all my heart." She made every word drip with sincerity, ignoring the bitter taste the lie left in her mouth. "You are kind and generous, and your offer is . . . overwhelming. But I could never be worthy of your greatness."

Winter paused to let her words sink in, then lifted her chin to face him. His expression spoke volumes—all that she had hoped for. Not only was he listening, he seemed mesmerized by her gushing.

"You're the Grand Elite, after all," she pressed in further, seizing her only chance to save herself and the truth she knew, "the right hand of the Sovereign himself. And I am just an inferior Second Tier citizen. More than that, I have committed a terrible crime against Olympus and against *you.* There's nothing you could ever hope to see in me. To even be with me would be a terrible stain and a dishonor to your grandeur." She bowed again, lower this time. "I am not worthy of you."

Silence.

Winter remained bowed. She shut her eyes and wetted her lips. All she could do was wait and hope she'd chosen the correct . . . possibly only escape route.

Strange, she thought. *Forced to lie for the preservation of the truth.*

It was a long time before Draven spoke, but when he did, his voice seethed with disgust. "You're right. You're not."

Winter looked up into his eyes. The hunger for her was gone, replaced by the more familiar utter loathing—oddly, the more preferable of the two.

Draven wasted no time. He signaled to the enormous sentry standing at the door. "Guardian."

The Guardian obediently and silently approached.

"You are to take this Purifier and wait outside the Administerial Hall," he ordered without looking at Winter. "You'll be called upon when the High Council has reached its decision."

"Your will be done, my lord." The muscular giant bent over and took Winter by the arm.

Winter was guided back to the door, where she breathed out a sigh of relief to be leaving Draven's suffocating presence.

As the Guardian escorted her out, she hoped to never again step foot in this room.

CHAPTER THIRTY-THREE

In many ways, Winter felt that waiting for the High Council's decision was the worst fate of all. She had been formulated as a Purifier, designed for physical activity. She had worked all her life to be the greatest in her vocation—Hive exercises, after-hours trainings, surface deployments, competition bouts. All her physical training and mental conditioning demanded the one thing her mentor had so deeply instilled in her above all else:

Move forward.

But now she was required . . . to wait.

How much time had already passed?

Sitting on a cold stone bench outside the Administerial Hall, Winter stretched her aching muscles and stared out through the corridor's towering windows to the glittering First Tier of Olympus and to earth's horizon far beyond. The last traces of sunlight had long since vanished.

If the High Council's verdict didn't kill her, she was sure that any more waiting would.

And that was the most agonizing part of all: what was it exactly that she was waiting for? Waiting for the High Council to bind her and lead her away to the edge of the city, where her own sentence of 'forced expulsion from Olympus' was sure to be carried out?

Winter closed her eyes and imagined the falling, the freezing rush of wind, and the surface world fast approaching . . .

Would that be her end?

Standing next to Winter was her silent Guardian escort. Several more of the enormous, muscular sentries stood nearby.

She was well aware she could overpower them. Certainly not in brute strength, but in speed and utilizing the old art Eagle Eyes had taught her, she knew that even a dozen Guardians wouldn't be able to prevent her escape.

She admitted that it was a tantalizing thought.

But escape . . .? Escape to where?

There was nowhere to go.

Winter felt ashamed that the thought had even crossed her mind.

Fleeing from her self-appointed mission to bring the truth to her people meant condemning them to a lifetime of the Sovereign's lie. More than that, it meant condemning Joshua's people below to more generations of slaughter at the hands of the Purifiers.

No, Winter decided resolutely. She could never attempt escape. Too many lost lives already weighed heavily on her conscience. She couldn't bear the weight of any more.

So . . . she would wait.

Winter was suddenly aware that her statue-like Guardian wasn't acting like a statue anymore. Was he fidgeting? He seemed to be shifting nervously.

She watched from her peripheral as the giant of a man took a deep breath and let it out as his broad shoulders relaxed. His head turned to face her. She looked up inquisitively.

"I have to know," the Guardian whispered in his characteristic deep, gravelly voice. "Do you really believe what you said in there? What you said to the Elite High Council?"

Winter's eyes widened as she felt her tiny spark of hope burst into an inferno of light. She tried to contain her excitement, but it was impossible to keep from grinning. She nodded earnestly. "Yes, I do. Every word."

The man eyed her suspiciously and gave a shrug. "Why?"

"Because—" she started excitedly but stopped herself. She had already failed to open the eyes of Nalara, perhaps because she had pushed too quickly. She was determined to not make the same mistake with this Guardian. She would instead be composed, go slower, and choose her words very carefully.

"Because," she started again, forcing her grin to disappear, "I've seen things that have made me question our society on Olympus."

"What have you seen?"

Careful, Winter cautioned herself. *Be careful.*

She breathed in and spoke the only words that came to mind: "The truth."

Winter waited for his reaction. The Guardian's expression didn't change. She decided to continue as delicately as she knew how. "I've learned that there are some things on Olympus that are not the way they should be. Like . . . the differences between the First, Second and Third Tier citizens. I don't think it's right that some are considered to have more worth than others simply because of their personal abilities. I'm now thinking that everyone was meant to be created equal." She leaned in closer. *"That's* the truth that I've seen."

The Guardian blinked. He seemed to be considering her words.

Winter tilted her head playfully. "You gonna tell me your name now?"

The bulky man paused before finally answering. "Drake Rowan—First Lieutenant of the Elite Guard Order."

Winter smiled warmly. "Drake," she quietly repeated. "That's a good name. Sounds like a very . . . strong name."

"I *am* strong." Drake flexed his muscles to bulge out his uniform. "All Guardians are strong. We are blessed by the Sovereign with names to match our strength."

"Right . . ." Winter whispered, trying to not be insulting. "You know, it's funny, but I've never learned the name of any Guardian before. Not once. I've always thought of you as just . . . just Guardians."

"We are Guardians."

"Yes, I know," Winter said. "But what I'm saying is that was the *only* way I thought of you before. The truth is you're much more than just a 'Guardian.' You're Drake Rowan. The fact that you have a name proves that you're unique—different from everyone else. I know that now. Before, I had always looked down on everyone below my vocation. I always had seen them as less than me—less important, less significant." Admitting the truth of who she used to be made her feel sick. She swallowed down the feeling and finished her thought. "Of less worth."

Drake seemed unfazed by her admission. "Of course," he agreed nonchalantly. "We may be of the same tier, but Guardians are lower ranked citizens than Purifiers."

"No. No, you're not," Winter insisted urgently, feeling her lose some of her composure. She struggled to find it again. "Drake, what I'm saying is that I now know that I was wrong. I was so wrong to think that you were less than me. I would now much rather think of you as my equal than as an inferior. And the same goes for anyone, no matter what *tier* they've been assigned to. I want to start thinking of all Olympians as equals instead of something . . . less." She breathed to steady herself. "And that's why I defended the gardener today."

Drake's eyes narrowed, and his wide brow furrowed. "You struck an Elite—the chosen class of the Sovereign."

"But that's just it. Why are they chosen? What makes them any better or of more worth than you, or me, or that gardener?" Winter felt like she was losing the battle, but she refused to give up hope. "I did what I did because I couldn't stand by and watch an equal being so cruelly mistreated like that."

"An equal?"

"Yes. *Equal,*" Winter emphasized. "Not in ability or strength or even intelligence. That's not what I'm saying. I'm not talking about equality in outcome. I'm simply talking about equality in worth. Equal because we're all human."

The huge man silently stared at her.

Maybe it was because of Winter's failure earlier to reach Nalara, but she felt that she needed someone—*anyone*—to understand what she understood. Whatever the reason, she needed this man, Drake Rowan, to see what she saw.

She decided to try another approach. Maybe the same line of inquiry Joshua had used with her would succeed where all else failed.

"Can I ask you something, Drake? Something . . . personal?"

He gave a short nod, his thick neck muscles flexing.

"I know you were designed to be a Guardian, but have ever asked yourself if that's what you want to be?" Winter waited while Drake mulled silently. When he didn't respond, she approached from a different angle. "What is it that *you* want to do, Drake? Have you ever wanted to be something other than a Guardian?"

Drake's eyes suddenly became hard, unpleasant. He straightened his posture and lifted his right hand clenched in a fist.

On the back of his big hand, Winter took note of the mark of the Guardian class: a shield emblazoned with the fiery Eye of Zeus at its center.

Drake shook his head once and again flexed his massive muscles. "No." His voice was firm and unquestioning. "I am a Guardian. Drake Rowan— First Lieutenant of the Elite Guard Order. I was created by Sovereign Zeus as a Guardian, and I have *never* wanted to be anything other than what I am."

The Guardian lowered his fist and turned his face away from her to stand at full attention.

Just like that, Winter's statue-like escort had been revived, and the blazing inferno of hope within her died.

Her body slumped heavily into the back of the stone bench.

Another attempt. Another failure.

She didn't know how much more of this she could take.

A few silent minutes—or maybe an hour—later, the large double-doors to the Administerial Hall swung open, and two Guardians stepped out. They signaled to Drake.

Winter stood and locked eyes with her giant.

Drake indicated to the open doors. "It's time."

"Gracious Elite of the High Council."

The Grand Elite, Draven Constantine Rothgard, stood at the head of the stand and indicated to the ten council members before him. All eyes in the great hall were fastened on him.

Winter stood at the center of the massive rotunda, alone. Utterly alone. Even her Guardian escort, Drake Rowan, had fallen back and assumed a sentry position by the doors with a dozen other silent giants.

From her peripheral, she noticed Remington and several of his Elite cohorts snickering quietly in the shadows. She observed Remington draw his finger menacingly across his throat. She ignored him as best she could, but the battle to keep herself from drowning beneath the endless tides of failure and despair was becoming increasingly difficult to fight.

Winter focused on her breathing as Eagle Eyes had taught her. She inhaled slowly and imagined all the fear and anxiety in her body being forced into her lungs. She then exhaled and visualized the fear being expelled and driven far away.

Even in death, it seemed like Derrick was still there for her.

His words suddenly came to mind:

> *"Whether you realize it or not, you stand out. You are alone. Because you put yourself out there, you become a target. And for those who choose to only aspire to mediocrity, someone like you becomes very easy to hate. Believe me."*

Winter again exhaled her tension. The predicament she now found herself in was obviously very far from what Eagle Eyes had meant at the time. Knowing that, she wondered if he would have stood with her, if he were still alive.

Or was she truly alone?

"We gathered here this evening," Draven went on, "for the sentencing of the Purifier January Winterton, in the crime she committed against an Elite citizen. Having listened to the testimonies and heard the body of evidence, and having concluded our deliberations, have we reached a unanimous decision?"

"We have," all members of the High Council spoke up in unison.

"And do we find Purifier Winterton guilty?"

Winter's heart stopped.

"We do," came the clear, united answer.

Winter clenched her jaw as she heard Remington's gleeful chortling from the sidelines.

The Grand Elite lowered himself into his judgment seat and eased into its high back. "January Winterton, you have been found guilty of a most egregious crime by the Elite High Council. You must, therefore, be punished."

Winter again imagined herself being tossed over the side of Olympus. The rushing wind . . . the falling . . . the surface world growing closer and closer . . .

. . . *and then her end.*

Strange how the one thing she detested the most was the fact that Remington would surely be there to witness it. Would the sinister cackling of this obnoxious youth be the last thing she would hear? It was a sickening, repulsive thought.

"And for punishment," Draven announced loudly, "it is the determination of this Council that you are forthwith stripped of your rank, titles, and all awards. You will resume your active service as if you were a newly initiated Purifier."

What? Winter thought hopefully.

"WHAT!?" Remington shouted angrily. "You're letting her go!? She's defective! Destroy her!"

Draven shot the young Elite a silencing glare.

Remington cowered and buried his face in his hands.

"January Winterton," Draven turned to face Winter. "During the four years you've served as an active Purifier, you have, by your own merit, gained sizable notability and prestigious accolades. We, here, have certainly enjoyed your prowess in the bouts. Your feats of skill and past accomplishments are renowned, and these facts were not ignored as your fate was determined. We have also determined that—as misled as your motive was—your primary desire was to protect the interests of Olympus."

Draven leaned forward and lowered his voice threateningly. "But know this, January: any repeat offenses against the chosen citizens of Zeus, and you will find yourself in a very, *very* different situation."

He again leaned into the back of his seat. "We will miss seeing you at the bouts," he added dolefully, as if that were the real tragedy. He picked up a golden gavel and announced, "This case is now closed." He brought the gavel down atop the wooden stand, and a loud *crack* echoed throughout the hall.

The Elite of the High Council nodded in satisfaction, then began to mingle and disperse.

Remington threw up his hands and stormed off in a fit of rage, with his entourage of friends trying to keep pace.

Drake Rowan marched up to Winter's side and nudged her toward the doors.

Winter, dumbfounded, turned wordlessly and followed. At the doors, she glanced back into the round chamber and saw Draven still sitting in his judgment seat, staring at her from across the room. His expression was cold and wrathful.

She shook off the chills and gratefully exited the hall—free.

CHAPTER THIRTY-FOUR

W hat a strange feeling it was to lose everything that she had worked for in her lifetime . . . and to not be completely crushed by it.

Winter stepped outside the main building of the Administerial Hall and looked about the lazy First Tier street. The cloudless sky above was filled with stars glinting through the milky barrier. A working citizen was meekly lighting floating candles and setting them adrift in a nearby giant crystalline pool. Elite in their silken evening gowns and elegant robes were sparsely scattered throughout the plaza, followed closely by servants holding trays of decadent food or handling their exotic pets. Tonight, they were speaking of fashion and entertainment; tomorrow, they would be jovially discussing her scandalous demotion.

Better that than my execution, she mused.

Drake led her along the marble path to the diamond-encrusted Grand Stairway descending from the lofty, immaculate heights of the First Tier down to the lowly, dimly-lit depths of the Second.

A sad sort of acceptance settled into Winter's chest with each step down from the glittering Elite palaces and hanging gardens. She realized she truly had let go of her old way of life. There would be no more achievements, no more popularity, no more benefits. The Grand Elite had even opened a door and beckoned her into paradise, but she had made the decision to shut it, lock it, and forever throw away the key.

That door would never be opened again—thankfully.

"You're free to go," Drake mumbled as they reached the base of the stairway.

Winter looked up at the Guardian who'd been by her side for the past several hours. "Thanks, Drake."

The gigantic man gazed off in a disquiet silence, refusing to make eye contact. Just as it looked like he would say something, he suddenly turned without a word and lumbered up the immense stairway.

Winter watched him go until he'd disappeared over the glowing rim of the Elite tier.

"Bloody Winter prevails again."

Winter turned to see Lilith Sharpe approaching, clapping slowly.

Winter's hyperawareness took in everything all at once. Lilith was wearing leisure clothing that hadn't been washed. Her eyes were slightly heavy as if she hadn't slept much, and both wrists bore bruises that had yet to color.

"Seriously, why do you call me that?" Winter asked, annoyed. "Why is everyone calling me that?"

"Isn't it obvious?" Lilith scoffed. "Your famous rescue . . . showing up at the LZ all bloodied with a bullet-hole between your eyes." She shook her head. "You know, you should have died that day. No one's ever come that close to the blighters and lived to tell about it."

Winter was in no mood for any further confrontations. She'd had enough for one day. "Well, I did," she asserted firmly and began moving towards the Purifier Quarter. "Just let it go already."

Lilith stepped into her path and blocked her way. "Not so fast. You've got some explaining to do."

"Not to you, I don't." Winter brushed passed her and hurried off, hoping it would end there.

Lilith kept pace. "Bloody Winter . . . untouched by even death itself." Her scowl deepened. "What exactly do you think you're doing? First, you play hero saving the War Wolves; then you go off solo against a group of blighters at the array. Next, you disappear for three full days, and then you pull that stupid stunt during our bout. And now *this!*"

Lilith seized Winter's arm.

Winter wrenched herself free of Lilith's vice-like grip and stood to meet her harsh gaze.

"Punching an Elite . . ." Lilith recited Winter's latest crime incredulously. "What were you thinking?"

"I'm just trying to make a difference," Winter defended herself, feeling the blood pulsing in her temples as waves of adrenaline rushed through her.

"Because you've always got to be in the spotlight," Lilith raised her voice.

"That's not true!" Winter shouted above her, exhausted by the constant accusations of showboating. "Everything I've done—*everything*—is for Olympus! I've spent my entire life sacrificing myself for her interests. I wear myself out every single day, and I have never asked anything, not a single thing in return for *my* blood—*my* sanity! And no one cares!"

Winter suddenly realized they had both instinctually assumed a fighter's stance. They tensed their hard muscles as their eyes locked in combat. She wondered if they'd end up finishing their bout right there.

After several unnerving seconds, Lilith finally blinked and backed off a step. "I just don't get it," she said with a shrug.

Winter breathed and cautiously relaxed her stance. "What don't you get?"

"After all you've done . . . even now . . . you still act like you're untouchable."

Winter noticed Lilith grip her own arm like a safety barrier. The bruises on her wrists were fresh—less than six hours old.

"Blight me!" Lilith cursed angrily. "We Purifiers have a good life! We are a chosen class, empowered by the Sovereign to purify the surface world. Why do you always have to push it? You say you're just trying to 'make a difference,'" she raised her fingers to make quotations in the air, "but do you have to do it in a way that creates problems where there aren't any? Isn't our vocation difficult enough without you making things harder for us?"

Winter dropped her guard and straightened, confident that their bout would wait for another day. "You think that my actions somehow reflect negatively on you?"

"Yes! I do," came Lilith's accusing response. "With all the stunts you've been pulling lately, it makes us all look bad, especially after today. You think the Elite will want to socialize with us now that you've assaulted one of them?"

Winter lowered her eyes and focused on Lilith's wrists, when she remembered seeing her walk off with Draven's entourage during the post-bout celebration. She suddenly felt a pang of sorrow for Lilith, realizing that the same door Draven had invited her to step through was one that Lilith must have entered before her. It was a door that led only to his version of *paradise*.

Winter sighed, again thankful that she'd had the mind to shut that door for good.

She pointed to the bruises. "And how's that . . . *socializing* working out for you, Razor?"

Lilith licked her lips in discomfort and smirked sardonically. "No one's untouchable, Winter. You can't stay innocent forever."

"None of us are innocent," Winter jabbed and turned to walk away.

"And where are you going now?" Lilith called after her.

"To take a long shower!" she called back without slowing.

Nalara watched as Winter hurriedly moved away from the captain of the Grim Reapers, leaving her alone, and she thought that now, she would finally be able to see her friend. Waiting for hours for the results of the hearing had left Nalara's nerves frayed and rattled.

She took off at a jogging pace and moved to intercept Winter's path. Her focus was only on being there for her friend after that devastating demotion. She started to close the distance, but a tall figure stepped in her way.

She stumbled to a halt and leaned back to look up at the towering Guardian.

"Are you the Purifier, Nalara Gressen?" he asked deeply.

Nalara swallowed. "Uh . . . y-y-yes. I am."

"His greatness, the Grand Elite, demands your immediate presence."

Her mouth fell open. "W-what?" Her lips quivered. "M-m-me? The Grand Elite, D-Draven . . . he w-wants to see me?" Her whole frame began to shake uncontrollably. "B-b-but I d-didn't do anything. I-I only saw—"

"You will follow me. Now," the enormous Guardian cut off her stammering and turned towards the Grand Stairway.

Nalara's mind hesitated, stunned and terrified at the notion of being summoned, but her body mechanically followed the giant man to the stairs. With each step in their long ascent to the Elite tier, Nalara recalled the first time she'd climbed these stairs following the bout. She had been so excited then—elated to ascend to the First Tier and mingle with the glorious Elite. The Grand Elite had even directly talked to their team, addressing them as 'honored Purifiers.'

Nalara recalled that the rapturous experience had seemed like a taste of Ascension itself.

But now, a deep chasm filled with dark horrors had opened wide within her.

Her mind desperately, frantically raced for an answer.

What could the Grand Elite possibly want with me? Is he angry with me? Have I failed him in some way?

Yes! Another voice in her head shouted angrily at her. *You've failed in your vocation. You failed to prevent Winter from hitting an Elite. You can't even get a single killshot yourself. You needed Winter to do it for you. You're pathetic. You are a failure of a Purifier!*

As they crested the shimmering rim of the Elite tier, Nalara felt her doom being sealed. But still, one foot after another, she dutifully followed the Guardian as they wound their way around sparkling fountains and cackling clusters of Elite to the entrance of the Administerial Hall.

They're all laughing at you. You know that, right?

Nalara's stomach knotted up, and her face grew hot as she followed the Guardian inside. The building's interior was even more opulent and beautiful than its exterior. Her head swiveled madly as she was led through the luxurious halls full of giant paintings of unknown men and women wearing extravagant suits and gowns. The rich surroundings of polished marble, gold furnishings, and crystal chandeliers seemed to grow around her and swallow her inside. She couldn't believe her eyes.

Her heart lurched up in her throat as they suddenly stopped by two immense doors.

The austere man pointed to a nearby stone bench. "Sit. And wait there."

Nalara nodded and moved hastily to the bench, grateful to sit for a moment. She thought that maybe sitting would keep her from fainting.

The big Guardian eyed her for a moment, then opened the doors and disappeared inside.

As the enormous double-doors eased shut, Nalara buried her face in her hands hopelessly.

What am I doing here? I don't belong here.

She felt like crying from both terror and exhaustion and longed for the warmth and comfort of her bed. She desperately wished she could close her eyes, fall asleep, and then wake up to find this whole day had been nothing but a terrible nightmare.

It couldn't possibly get any worse.

"Good evening," a soft, velvety voice spoke nearby.

Nalara's head shot up.

A handsome young Elite wearing a pristine black suit, white gloves, and glossy shoes stood only a meter away, smiling at her with playful blue eyes. She hadn't even heard him approach. His beautiful blonde hair was combed to one side; not a single strand was out of place. His teeth were perfectly white and straight, and his face glowed in the golden light of the chandeliers.

Nalara's jaw went limp. She immediately recognized him as the blonde-haired Elite from earlier—one of Elite Remington's friends.

So . . . so handsome . . .

"I know you from somewhere, do I not?" the Elite asked, his voice like warm butter.

Nalara fought to regain control of her wits. "Uh . . . no," she lied, shaking her head nervously. The last thing she wanted was to be remembered as Winter's criminal accomplice. "No. I-I don't think so."

Don't let him remember me, she prayed earnestly. *Please, please don't let him remember me!*

"No, I do. I swear I do." The Elite put a finger to his chin in contemplation. "Give me but a moment, and—" His eyes glittered in recognition. He snapped his gloved fingers. "Ah! That's it! You were the Purifier that was there when Remington was attacked."

Blight me sideways! Nalara thought as her heart sank. *This day just got worse.*

"O-oh. Right," she admitted despairingly. If only there was a dark hole somewhere deep enough, she would crawl into it and hope to be forgotten. She shook her head apologetically. "I'm really so, so sorry about that. I have no idea what Winter was thinking. I-I just feel so terrible—"

The Elite waved off her apology and grinned broadly. "Please, think nothing of it. In truth, I'm *thrilled* that it happened."

"You . . . y-you are?" Nalara was dumbfounded.

"Quite. It was without question the most sensational event to happen in a long time!" He laughed and moved to sit down next to Nalara.

Nalara's heart began racing and her mouth went dry.

An *Elite* was sitting next to her!

"The look on Rem's face as he lay there in the dirt—his face turning a shade of blue as he struggled to breathe . . ." The Elite laughed again.

Nalara forced a half-hearted chuckle, although it came out more like a whimper.

"I must admit," the Elite went on, "at the time it happened, it was all too overwhelming for me to find much amusement in it. But upon reflection . . ." He sighed longingly. "I only wish such exhilarating events were more frequent. Unlike many of my peers, I personally welcome such unexpected vicissitudes—anything to help break up the exhausting tedium of daily life."

Nalara was speechless. He spoke so fast and with such big words. She didn't even know what *vicissitudes* meant.

The Elite smiled again with those perfect teeth. "Don't you agree?"

"Oh. Sure, o-of course." Nalara tried to smile back. "Yeah . . . I mean, I know I always like *vis-i-ne-tudes.*" She felt her face flush red.

The Elite's perfect smile held. "Were you here to attend your friend's hearing?"

"No," Nalara admitted sheepishly. "I wasn't allowed to. Did you?"

"For the first half, yes. Your friend, Winterton . . ." He gazed off in reflection. "She certainly had a few things to say. Very . . . intriguing things . . ." He paused. "The Grand Elite pulled her aside privately as the High Council entered deliberations, and I left soon afterwards. I only just heard about the Council's decision to demote her." He clicked his tongue regretfully. "It's such a shame she won't be competing in the bouts any longer. True, true shame."

Nalara—not sure what else to do—nodded in agreement.

The Elite locked eyes with her and extended a gloved hand. "It's a pleasure, miss . . ."

Nalara got lost for a moment in the deep blue of his eyes. "Oh! Uh . . . I'm N-Nalara. Nalara Gressen, lord Elite." Unsure what protocol dictated, she swallowed nervously and took his hand with trembling, limp fingers.

The young Elite lifted her hand to his lips. "Alexander Sterling Belmont." He pressed his lips to her skin with a gentle kiss.

Nalara's eyes bulged. What started like a horrific nightmare was now turning into a strange euphoric dream.

Elite Alexander lowered her hand and released. Nalara's arm flopped involuntarily to her side.

"You are quite charming, Nalara," he said engagingly. "You must join me at the Equinox Festival."

"Th-the what?"

"The Equinox Festival," he repeated. "Only the most extravagant event of the season. The Spring Equinox is tomorrow, after all." He rose from the bench and looked down on her. "You will be my guest."

Nalara found herself nodding and grinning stupidly up at him. " . . . Y-yeah. Okay."

Okay . . .?

She licked her lips and tried again. "I mean . . . Yes. Yes, I would like that very much, Elite . . . Alexander Sterling Belmont. Sir . . ."

"Wonderful." He flashed another white smile. "Tomorrow evening, in the main plaza. I will see you then, Nalara."

Without another word, Elite Alexander gracefully turned on his heels and walked away.

Nalara's wide eyes followed him down the glistening hallway. His beauty made the rest of the building seem dull by comparison. She stared after him long after he had disappeared from sight.

"Gressen!"

Nalara jumped up from the bench and spun to see the tall Guardian standing at the open doors.

"His greatness, the Grand Elite, will see you now."

The dream ended, and the nightmare returned.

Nalara, feeling sickening despair wash over her again, tried to breathe evenly as she walked to the doors. She turned and entered an enormous circular room with a soaring domed ceiling. She forced herself not to gawk at the splendid architecture, as someone even more splendid demanded her attention. A solitary figure in black and gold stood in the light at the center of the rotunda: lord Draven Constantine Rothgard.

So handsome . . . so tall . . . so powerful . . . so perfectly perfect . . .

Looking right at her.

The heavy doors closed shut behind her, leaving the newly initiated Purifier alone with the Sovereign's Grand Elite.

Nalara approached and bowed herself in half, fighting to remember proper procedure and etiquette. "Nalara Gressen r-reporting as commanded, g-great and mighty Grand Elite."

"Purifier Gressen." The Grand Elite's voice was calm and soothing. "You were Winterton's last initiate. You've been close to her for the past several weeks."

"Yes, great one."

"And you were present with her in the gardens today," he stated flatly.

Nalara shut her eyes tight and remained bowed over. "Yes . . . great one."

"I'm deeply concerned by Purifier Winterton's behavior . . ." The Grand Elite paused. "I've decided to give you a special assignment."

Nalara's eyes snapped open in surprise.

Special assignment? Me?

"Listen carefully, Purifier," he said, lowering his voice to a severe tone. "Your assignment is to watch Winterton at all times. You've been close to her, and you will remain close to her—in training and on the surface. Observe and make note of her every action, never revealing the nature of your assignment to her or to anyone else. Only your team leader, Master Purifier Priest, will be informed. If you require, he will aid you. This assignment supersedes all other tasks, duties, and obligations. It is of the utmost importance. Do you understand?"

"Yes, lord Grand Elite," Nalara answered, her voice growing in confidence. She could now see the reason why she had been summoned: the Grand Elite had such genuine concern for Winter's wellbeing that she was being assigned to aid in her friend's recuperation.

Given the opportunity to help, Nalara suddenly felt gleeful.

"You will report directly to me every evening without fail. I want to know who Winterton talks to, where she goes, what she eats, when she sleeps. Everything. You will report here after she's gone to quarters. Is that clear, Purifier?"

"Yes, lord Grand Elite. Perfectly clear, my lord."

"Then you're dismissed." He abruptly turned and left the rotunda, exiting out a side door.

Shocked by the sudden end to the conversation, Nalara paused for a moment before awkwardly straightening her posture.

She nearly laughed as it slowly dawned on her that the nightmare was over. There had been nothing to be concerned about from the beginning. The Grand Elite only wanted to help Winter, and she had been chosen as the instrument of his benevolence.

Special assignment. Utmost importance.

Nalara beamed and nodded in satisfaction. Finally, she had an assignment only she could fulfill; finally, she had an opportunity to contribute to the glory of Olympus. She sighed in relief as the overshadowing weight of inadequacy lifted from her shoulders.

Before leaving the hall, Nalara took just a moment to take in the splendor of her surroundings. She arched her back as her eyes followed the intricate gold filigrees and towering marble columns to the high domed ceiling. The ceiling was lit by soft white light, and there, in the center of carved silver-lined clouds, was the sparkling, ruby-encrusted Eye of Zeus staring down at her.

Her jaw went slack as her knees instinctively bent to the floor.

"Hail to his supreme holiness," she prayed with tears filling her eyes. "Hail to my Sovereign ruler. Hail to my living god." She bowed until her forehead kissed the floor. "Thank you, Sovereign Zeus. I promise . . . I *promise* I won't fail you."

CHAPTER THIRTY-FIVE

Winter heard the chime of her door as she soaked in the regenerative heat of her personal shower. She would miss this: her own living chamber, her own kitchen, her own bathroom and shower. Soon, it would all be taken away, and she'd be bumped down to the lower levels with all new initiates and under-achievers. Of all her rewards and medals and commendations, she realized that the simple pleasure of a private shower was one reward she would miss the most.

The door chimed again.

She hoped that, whoever it was, they would soon give up and leave.

Upon returning to her living chambers immediately after the High Council's sentencing, she had discovered that her sentence had already been carried out. Her living chambers had been swept clean of anything resembling her past rank and position of honor among Purifiers. Her formal greens displaying years of advancements and medals of achievement—including her trial award for her accomplishments in Tartarus—had been taken away, replaced by a simple heather green uniform bereft of note or acclaim. A digital display over the uniform's right breast read:

ARCHANGELS
JANUARY WINTERTON
RANK 100

Winter closed her eyes and stepped directly beneath the cascading water.

Soon, she thought regretfully, relishing every moment the hot water splashed over her face and ran down her shoulders, arms, and back. *Soon, they'll take this away, too.*

The door chimed a third time.

She huffed and turned off the water. She donned her robe and vented the steam from the room.

"Enter!" she called out, more than a little annoyed.

The door hissed open, and Nalara timidly poked her head inside.

"Am I interrupting anything?"

Had it been anyone else, Winter would have said 'yes' and told him or her to come back some other time, but the anxious look on her friend's face made it impossible to turn her away.

Winter sighed out the last of her frustration. "No. Come in. I was just finishing anyway," she lied, grabbing a towel to begin drying her long black hair. "So, what's up?"

Nalara entered the room, and the door slid closed behind her. "I was . . . worried. I thought I'd stop by and see how you were doing."

Winter paused with the towel. "You heard."

Nalara nodded. "Yeah. I asked a Unifier as soon as the hearing was over." Her eyes glanced around the room. "I'm really sorry about the demotion."

"Don't worry about it." Winter went back to soaking up the excess water from her ebony locks. "I made a choice, and that choice cost me. That doesn't mean it wasn't the right choice."

"So . . . no more top twenty then?"

"Nope. And no longer the lieutenant of the Archangels. That'll most likely fall to Scorch." She grabbed a hairbrush from the bathroom and began working out the knots. "And I'm sure I'll be moved back to the dorms soon—which means, no more personal apartment."

Nalara's eyes suddenly lit up with excitement. "Hey!" she exclaimed with glee. "Maybe we could bunk together! That would be so first-tier!"

Winter smiled in spite of herself. She couldn't help but love her friend's near-instantaneous rebound. Nalara always seemed to radiate like the sun through any dark storm.

"What kind of advice do you have for your new bunkmate?" Nalara asked eagerly.

Winter laughed. "Considering what happened to me today, are you sure asking me for advice is the best thing to do?"

Winter returned the hairbrush to the bathroom, where she paused momentarily in front of the mirror. She always loved the bright luster of her dark hair after a shower. Maintaining and intentionally keeping her hair long had been that one indulgence she'd allowed for herself as a Purifier. While Nereza Vossen had been the initial inspiration—a figure she now understood to be anything but *inspiring*—Winter had made it her own.

She lovingly ran her fingers through the soft, moist tips and smiled. This was who she was. Take away all the awards and medals and the private living chambers—but Winter would still be Winter, and that would never change.

"Besides," she called from the bathroom, giving her damp tresses one final caress, "something tells me you'll get by just fine without my help."

"What makes you say that?" Nalara asked from the foyer.

Winter returned to the main room and faced her friend. "You kidding me? With your optimism, it's only a matter of time before you take Olympus by storm."

Nalara beamed. "It's funny you should mention that." She softly bit her lower lip and swiveled back and forth on her heels. "Because I was invited to the Equinox Festival tomorrow evening. It is, after all, the most extravagant event of the season, you know. *Aaaand* . . . you're going to come with me."

"Oh, I am, huh?"

"Yes, you are—even if I have to drag you there myself."

Winter sighed. "Nalara, I'm not really sure that'd be a good idea."

"What? You going or me dragging you?"

"Both," Winter said with a chuckle. "With what happened today, I seriously doubt I'd be welcome."

"Sorry. No excuses."

"More than that," Winter added with emphasis. "I don't *want* to go."

Nalara gave a playful shrug. "Still not good enough."

"What do you mean—?"

"I *need* you to go," Nalara cut in and gave her friend a wink. "I've never been to something like this before, and I am going to need my old friend Janey to be there with me."

"Hm." Winter's voice lowered. "You should know by now: Janey died a long time ago."

Nalara dismissed her statement with a confident shake of her head. "Not possible. I still catch a glimpse of her every now and then."

"That's the only thing that's 'not possible.'"

"Well, doesn't matter. Whether it's Winter or Janey that joins me, I still need you to come with me." Her big brown eyes begged. *"Please?"*

While annoyed with her friend's tried-and-true manipulative tactic, Winter couldn't help but marvel at Nalara's strength of will. In so many ways, Nalara was exactly what she wished she could be: loyal, pure, and indomitably optimistic.

Winter had always been able to share her heart with Nalara, but she paused to be sure she was fully relaxed and open before speaking. "You know, Nalara, I can't apologize enough for being so distant since you graduated."

Nalara seemed bewildered at the unexpected response.

"I remember how alone and helpless I felt after my graduation," Winter expressed openly. "Scorch, my trainer, was . . . he was . . . *preoccupied* with some personal issues at the time, and I never wanted to be that way with you. Until Eagle Eyes eventually became my mentor, I was forced to figure out a lot of things on my own—and I ended up doing the same thing to you. I'm sorry. I wanted to be there for you; I wanted to keep you safe. But I just got blindsided. I got taken off my feet by something so much bigger than you and me—bigger than all of us."

Breathing to steady herself, she finished with: "But . . . I think I've got my bearings now. And I promise, no matter what, I'm here for you."

Nalara grinned, and her whole face brightened. "So, does that mean you'll come?"

Winter smiled back and gave a short nod. "Yeah, Blight me . . . I'll come."

Nalara unexpectedly rushed forward and threw her arms around her in an embrace.

Genuinely shocked, she looked down and softly placed a hand atop her friend's amber hair. "Really that important to you, huh?"

Nalara nodded into Winter's robe and sniffed. "I'm just so happy that you're going to be alright. I was so scared. But not anymore." She gave her friend a tight squeeze. "I want you to know that I'm here for you, too."

Perhaps not the most ideal choice—the Grand Elite surmised as he rode a lift down from the First Tier to the Second—*but the logical one.*

The Master Purifier and captain of the Archangels team, Orrin 'Wraith' Priest, would have been an obvious candidate to observe and report on Winter's movements, but Draven had not become the Grand Elite of Olympus by always doing what appeared to be obvious. In such delicate matters, the Sovereign had taught him that subtlety and tact were often more effective methods than brute-force power.

You don't require a sledgehammer to crush an insect. He smiled at his reflection in the lift's glass doors. *A light, focused swat will do just fine.*

A worthless Purifier would be able to infiltrate and remain undetected where someone of greater significance would be far too conspicuous. Thusly, Winter's latest initiate had been the logical choice.

What was her name again? He couldn't be bothered with such trivialities.

The lift doors opened, and Draven exited into the darkened streets of the Second Tier. He hated descending to this level of the city. As the hour of curfew approached, only a handful of middle-class citizens walked the streets. They bowed and fawned before him as he passed by, but he refused to acknowledge their pitiful obeisance. He received the same adulation from the Elite. If that was his desire, he would have remained on the sparkling crown of Olympus.

No. He had descended to these dismal depths for a purpose.

Entering the Science and Technology Quarter, the squat Archive building near the Biological Research and Development Lab came into view.

Draven had to know. He could have simply assigned Winter to reclamation and have been done with it. That had been the High Council's recommendation, but his authority eclipsed theirs to the same degree the Sovereign's authority eclipsed his own. The verdict had been his decision and his alone.

Winter's testimony to the Council—her words—had been dangerous. It was not enough to simply rid Olympus of her. Draven needed to know the *cause* of such dangerous thoughts—thoughts that had already manifested into action. He needed to discover the root and pluck it up before its infection could spread.

He would do this for the glory of Zeus, and Zeus would surely honor him for it.

Entering the Archive, Draven avoided eye contact with the startled worker behind the desk.

"Bring me all Unifier records for January Winterton," he ordered directly.

Bowing and fumbling, Kara got down from her stool quickly. "Yes, lord Grand Elite. As you command, my lord." Her fingers flew over a touchscreen as she called up all checkpoints, interviews, and briefings for the specified person.

A hologram with digital touch displays was projected before Draven, and he spent several minutes flipping through the various interactions and exchanges. There were no flags on her answers, only a handful of temporary notes, and only one mark made recently on her permanent record.

Kara stood by as the Grand Elite studied the videos and transcripts.

"My lord?" she asked timidly, swallowing down her nervousness.

Draven scoured the records but didn't find what he was looking for. Although, the footage of her post-incident interview for her three-day disappearance on the surface was certainly intriguing.

She appeared so vulnerable.

So . . . damaged . . .

Draven wetted his lips.

"My lord?" Kara repeated a bit louder.

The Grand Elite shot an intense glare at the archivist. "You dare interrupt me?"

She bent towards the floor. "Please, great and powerful Grand Elite. Please, *please* forgive me! But . . . you're looking at the records for January Winterton."

"Yes?" he queried obviously.

"And I just thought you might be interested to know that she was in here. The night of the Ascension, doing research or something."

His eyes narrowed on the ugly, miserable woman. "What research?"

"I can call up the files. She used her security passcode."

"Do it!" he snapped. "I want to see everything she looked at."

CHAPTER THIRTY-SIX

The peace and validation was almost sensual as the earliest light of dawn pierced the clear horizon over the deep blue coastline. Not a single cloud fettered Winter's view of the surface as she finished her morning climb up the outer hull. The danger-fueled adrenaline and endorphin-charged muscle fatigue left her smiling broadly as she sat on the lip of Olympus with her legs dangling over the edge. She let her hair down with a long sigh and ruffled the base of her scalp to free the cohesive strands from her sweaty neck. Liquid ebony cascaded down her back in voluminous luxury.

Life and energy filled her lungs as she breathed in her victory over death the night before. She had stood up to the established system and lived, despite being stripped of everything she had worked to achieve in her professional life. She had successfully spoken to a group of ruling Elite about decency and equality and had not been branded a heretic for it. Her words may have fallen on deaf ears; nevertheless, with the dawning of a new day, she felt assured more than anything that what she knew must be accomplished was, in fact, possible.

The insecurity and pretenses were gone, and the world had not ended as a result.

Winter enjoyed the brisk walk through her beautiful city. The opaline towers and shining windows all seemed to glow under the rippling barrier bathed in morning light.

A small hiccup of uncertainty caught in her throat as she approached the entrance to Purifier Command. There, she intersected with her team, the Archangels; everyone but the captain and Nalara. Winter was nervous as she joined them, but to her surprise, Scorch left the side of his initiate and jostled her shoulder in familiarity.

"You gonna congratulate me on my promotion?" he teased in good humor as they filed into the lift and began the descent.

"Oh, that's low," Winter said with a smile.

"At least now, you've dropped the formalities and just come out as straight up *crazy,*" Sapphire shrugged.

"Ha-ha." Winter secretly enjoyed the hazing. It had been a long time since anyone had felt comfortable enough to poke fun at her to her face. "Jokes on you," she jabbed at Scorch. "Drills are all yours now."

Scorch groaned. "Ugh . . . Blight me. I don't even remember all the lieutenant's duties and procedures. Can we just get through this jump first?"

"It's another drone hunt," Viper joined in.

"Drone hunt?" Winter asked.

"Yep," Havoc said. "I heard them talking in the barracks—another set of drones downed."

Bulletproof mimed an explosion with his hands. *"Pshkww!"* His playful eyes lit up.

The dense smell of sweat hung in the air as the jovial crew exited the lift and walked to the conference room. Winter relished the nostalgic feeling of camaraderie as she and her teammates sat together well before the orientation began.

After several minutes, Winter sat up and scanned the room. "Has anyone seen Nalara?"

The Archangels glanced around and offered their shrugs.

"What, little Kitty Cat gone missing?" Viper teased. "Here, Kitty-Kitty-Kitty! Come here, Kitty!"

"Meow . . ." Sapphire mimicked the sound and pretended to lick her paws clean.

"Ah, there you are, lost little Kitty." Viper gave a scratch behind Sapphire's neck, who proceeded to purr loudly. "Who's a good little Kitty?"

"Meow . . ." was Sapphire's answer.

The team laughed.

Winter turned to Scorch with a questioning look.

Scorch leaned in. "Yeah . . . it's the callsign we've come up with for Nalara. She doesn't know about it yet, but we figured until she's able to earn herself a better one . . . you gotta admit—it sorta fits."

"Very funny." Winter was not amused.

The Master Purifier entered the room. "Purifiers!" Wraith barked over their conversations. "Settle."

The room quieted immediately as the gigantic man took the stand behind the podium. A hologram display behind him illuminated with the projected terrain. Winter immediately recognized the area: a tributary flowing into a wide river out to sea, a small island, and the dome between four bridges.

"You may have heard that we're on a drone hunt today," the authoritative Master Purifier spoke. "Three drones have been downed since yesterday. Teams will coordinate their search patterns. Team captains have already been briefed, and coordinates have been transferred to the pilots. The drones in this area," he indicated to the region southwest of the four bridges, "have been down for the past twenty-four hours, so we're going in blind. The upside is we know we're closing in on a location for a major enemy nest. If we can take the blighters out at the source, this area should be permanently cleared of infection."

Enthusiastic applause filled the conference room.

Winter's heart sank, knowing that this was the immediate region where Joshua and his people lived.

"Our vocation is a glorious one," Wraith said stirringly. "Our Sovereign's strength is ours if we are faithful. We were created to purify the surface, and we will do it with blood and fire!"

Winter felt sick and out of place again as all the Purifiers in the room stood and cheered.

"Purifiers—move out!" Wraith concluded over the wild applause.

All the teams split off to their hubs to gear up.

Viper, Sapphire, Havoc, Bulletproof, Savage, Scorch, and his initiate, Mason Howell, all fanned out within the Archangels' hub and entered their respective codes at their alcoves.

Winter glanced around. "Where *is* Nalara?" she asked earnestly.

Wraith pushed by brusquely, grumbling, "Late as usual."

Winter quickly entered her code at her panel and pulled on her jumpsuit. She sat on the bench and slipped off her climbing shoes, replacing them with the tactical boots that had served her for so many years. As if on autopilot herself, Winter stood up and twisted her long black hair into itself and fastened it tight.

Scorch and Mason laughed and messed around with their gear as they prepared. Winter couldn't help but smile at them as she secured and adjusted her gauntlets.

Nalara finally came trotting in, her face flushed and her breathing labored.

"Sorry, everyone! Sorry! I'm here," she gasped.

"Stop wasting our time and gear up," Wraith snarled from the armory.

"Yes, sir!" Nalara immediately obeyed, not even pausing to acknowledge Winter.

Their alcoves adjacent, Winter couldn't help but notice the faint smell of industrial oil wafting from her friend.

"Where were you?" Winter asked.

"Just slept in . . ." Nalara averted her gaze and began changing into her soft jumpsuit.

The obvious deception was confusing to Winter, and it even hurt a little, especially after the engaging evening of open conversation they had shared the night previous. But she understood that Nalara was her own person, so she put it from her mind.

Nalara shoved her feet into the heavy metallic boots and locked them on before clasping the utility belt around her middle. She cast an anxious glance around at her comrades as she engaged her gauntlet's armor and pulled on her helmet. She was a buzzing whirl of emotion, having botched her special assignment already.

Stupid! Stupid! Stupid! the voice in her head shouted at her.

She knew Winter climbed in the mornings but had no idea what an intricate mess of floor plans one had to navigate to reach the outer hull. She had never felt the fury of Zeus more fully focused on her failure than when she had lost Winter earlier that morning in the lower levels of the city.

I'm sorry! she pleaded in her mind. *I won't mess up again.*

Winter clipped her holster in place and engaged her six-point nano-armor shielding. Her gauntlets began to hum softly. The translucent film slowly seeped up her limbs to meet together at the center of her chest. After securing her helmet and completing the armor's circuit, she lined up with her team to await boarding their shuttle.

She turned her head and looked around at her team. Their faces inside their helmets were tinted red from the overhead light. Winter breathed softly and experienced profound gratitude for this moment of normalcy.

"You okay?" Nalara surprised her by asking.

"First-tier," Winter said before turning forward.

The voice of a man in Flight Control came over the intercom. "Grim Reapers are clear of the barrier. Archangels are go to board."

The doors before Wraith hissed and pulled open to the sides, and the Archangels entered the large bay and proceeded to their shuttlecraft.

"Iron Raiders on deck, prepare to board," Flight Control prompted from the intercom.

Winter boarded their team's shuttle quickly and sat down. She pulled the restraint over her shoulders and locked it between her legs.

The whole team was locked and ready in a matter of seconds.

Winter enjoyed the look of wonder and excitement in the new initiate's eyes.

"Flight Control," the pilot said from the cockpit. "Purifiers on board. Requesting launch permission."

"Shuttlecraft 3FGD-4FRWE," Flight Control's voice flooded from the pilot's console. "Permission granted. You are go for launch."

"Copy that, Control. Initiating flight sequence," the pilot replied in rehearsed uniformity.

The shuttle shifted and launched out into the open sky. Glittering Olympus receded quickly into the blue firmament as the shuttle plunged toward the surface.

Zooming over the canopy, the craft eventually slowed.

"Drop zone 20242," the pilot announced. "Grid fifty-two, sector seven."

The shuttle landed softly, sending dirt, grass, and pink blossoms below flying up into swirling madness.

The glass shields descended. Winter almost stood up on reflex to perform her duty as lieutenant but stopped short when Scorch did. The Archangels exited one by one, receiving their rifles from Captain Priest. They secured the drop zone quickly before meeting back in the center.

The thrusters hummed loudly, and the shuttle slowly pushed up over the trees and flew away.

"We're coordinating our search pattern with the Broadswords," Wraith announced, looking down at his gauntlet display. "Keep your eyes open, I don't want any surprises this jump." His eyes briefly flicked to meet with Winter's, but he averted them instantly. "Everyone, stick to protocol."

"Yes, sir!" the team rejoined.

"Savage, Havoc, Viper—take point."

"Sir!" They trotted away, rifles up.

"Winter and her legacy of failure," Wraith looked directly at Nalara, "are here securing the LZ. Everyone else, with me."

Winter glanced apologetically at Nalara as the team steadily left them behind.

After a long moment of silence, Winter said, "Don't quite understand how my mistakes reflect on you, but I'm sorry."

"It's fine." Nalara tried to not sound crushed. "I'm not going to be on the bottom forever, right?" She lightheartedly pointed to her digital rank display that read *ninety-eight* now that Winter had been stripped of all rank and achievement. "Mason will probably get a killshot before me, though."

"That's not . . ." Winter instinctively started, wanting to tell her friend that killshots were both unimportant and barbaric, but she might as well outright say that their Sovereign was a liar, too. For Nalara, the truth would do more harm than good. "You'll . . . be fine," she concluded unconvincingly.

Winter moved away and began patrolling. It was hard to not feel bitter, even though rank meant nothing to her now. At least, that's what she struggled to remind herself as her eyes inadvertently glanced down to her sorry rank display of *one-hundred*.

The heavy moment passed slowly. She tried to focus on her job. As good as it felt to be back to some sort of normal, she couldn't help but long for the wind on her face and the sweet smell of nature. She recalled the overwhelming taste of the food and the genuine conversations she had shared with Joshua. It all seemed like a pleasant, long-ago dream—one that she couldn't chase from her senses. It was almost like her mind and body ached to be closer to the surface, not separated by the stifling barrier of nano-armor.

She spent the better part of an hour patrolling in slow, ever-widening circles around the drop zone while Nalara blankly wandered around the clearing. Winter was tempted to be annoyed with her, having trained her better than that, but she knew Nalara was a little hurt with her failure-by-association status and decided to leave her be.

With a restless sigh, Winter gave into temptation and holstered her rifle to climb a rock formation that had caught her eye. It honestly looked like it could have been a stone building of some kind centuries ago, but nature had claimed its ruined remains and made it a part of the landscape. She mounted the climb and rose steadily to the peak, eighty feet above the terrain below. As her feet bore her up to stand at the summit, she wanted nothing more than to remove her confining helmet and enjoy the warmth of the sunshine and its gentle cleansing touch.

She turned in a slow circle and smiled to take in the breathtaking sight. Though obscured by the data stream flitting across her helmet display, she could still appreciate the rolling hills of dense forest—a spattering of bright pink blossoms and green budding leaves everywhere from the first unfurling of spring. A few miles away, she could just make out the crest of the familiar bridges she'd used as a compass to find Joshua before.

She activated her gauntlet display and analyzed its readings. Two clusters of pinpoints representing the Archangels and Broadswords teams systematically snaked through the terrain in the direction of the bridges.

Winter knew that their indoctrination concerning the 'blighted' was nothing but a lie. The supposed 'blighted' were not mindless, infected animals aimlessly wandering the landscape in need of purification. They were intelligent human beings. They were highly trained hunters and scouts—like Joshua.

Her eyes fixed on the far horizon, where the slightest peaks of the bridge structures broke above the canopy. She knew Joshua would most likely recognize the danger of the encroaching Purifier teams and seek shelter.

They wouldn't find him.

A twinge of panic gripped her heart. She *hoped* they wouldn't find him, that is.

Winter's breathing quickened as she focused again on her display. Both Purifier teams were now within a mile of the bridges.

It was incomprehensible . . . she couldn't possibly . . .

She looked down to the LZ to find Nalara scanning at the edge the clearing.

Was it wrong to bank on Nalara's incompetence?

Winter bit her lip.

If she was going to warn Joshua, it was either now or never—and she couldn't live with never.

CHAPTER THIRTY-SEVEN

Nalara glanced up at the crest of rocks where Winter still stood. She sighed heavily.

Wraith's cutting words still rang in her mind. She had such a stigma attached to her name. Somehow, she felt like it would always be a part of her.

She just wasn't like Winter. She didn't have it in her to be cold and unattached at a moment's notice. She never had been able to compartmentalize, not since her earliest days of training in the Formulation Quarter.

The stark difference between her and her trainer was overwhelming. It had always been that way, even in the FMQ, and the hellish trials of Tartarus had only served to cement the gap in ability between them.

Winter had *thrived* during the trials.

Nalara had only just barely *survived*.

At her initiation ceremony, she had been so excited to learn that her old friend Janey was going to train her. She had hoped that if she was trained by the best, then she would have had what it would take to be the best—or at least to have a chance—but to see Winter acting so erratically lately made her think that somehow, she had been cheated out of a proper training that might have made things different.

Nalara always tried to wear the mask of optimism, but the truth was . . . she was oftentimes very afraid and plagued by doubts.

Winter seemed to have all the talent and focus in the world, and now, she was frustratingly flippant about throwing away all her accomplishments for who-knows-what reason. She had tried to explain it to her yesterday, but it all sounded like over-thinking nonsense.

And then . . . Winter punched an Elite . . .

An ELITE!

Nalara shook her head. What had all *that* been about? It was unthinkable.

Her fists clenching her rifle, Nalara closed her eyes and tried to vent her frustrations by focusing on her 'special assignment.' The Grand Elite himself had given it to her, and there was no way he would have done that if she didn't have the necessary skills to accomplish her task.

Right?

A smile of confidence broke across her lips. She nodded.

Right.

Nalara Gressen—she daydreamed—*a Purifier worthy of such an important task.*

Reinvigorated by the pleasing thought, she checked the ridge again. Her momentary surge of confidence was shattered, and terror set in. She looked around in a panic.

Winter was gone!

She instinctively opened her com channel, then immediately switched it off again. Captain Priest would only yell at her again, and then he'd undoubtedly tell the Grand Elite of her failure—on her first day!

Her mind raced to find the protocol for this situation, but it simply didn't come.

What do I do?

Nalara took off running toward the towering rock formation. She didn't have the skill to attempt climbing the rock face like Winter had, so she circumvented the base and looked for a passable way up another side. It was long out of the way, but she was determined to do her duty.

No more failure.

Finally reaching the top, Nalara looked around and threw her hands up in exasperation when Winter was nowhere to be found. It had only been an hour since Wraith had taken the team out, and already, she had messed up her prime directive.

She took a moment to catch her breath and collect her thoughts when she realized she hadn't looked for Winter's beacon. A little hope sprung up when she saw it holding steady there on her gauntlet display, but her heart sank when she realized she needed to climb back down.

"You've got to be kidding me . . ." She sighed in frustration before beginning her immediate descent down the trail again. Her ankles felt weak in the heavy boots as she stumbled down the uncertain path. The helmet's view screen analyzed and managed everything before her, making it difficult to discern the uneven terrain.

Fear choked at her throat like a stranglehold and forced her to imagine all the possible scenarios that involved her failure and death. Here she was, in a toxic wilderness with rabid blighters and diseased animals, cut off from communicating with her team and under the distinct possibility of getting lost, left behind, and killed in some horrific way.

She cursed her rotten luck. She'd probably encounter one of those *camels* Scorch had talked about. She could just imagine herself being melted into a puddle of organic goo, only to be slurped down by the dreadful creature.

Thus ends Nalara Gressen—she thought bitterly—*in the belly of a beast.*

Entertaining these dark thoughts, Nalara found herself back at the LZ with still no friend in sight. She checked her gauntlet and started quickly toward Winter's position, sourly mulling over every possible negative outcome of this course of action.

The Grand Elite had told her not to let Winter out of her sight, and she had managed to do exactly the opposite all morning. She knew that Winter got up before the break of dawn to go climbing, but she had become so hopelessly lost trying to tail her through the endless core levels that she almost didn't make it back in time for today's jump. And now, here on the surface, she distractedly had let her wander out of range and sight.

The beacon up ahead was still holding position. Nalara felt sure she could finally start doing right, but she overtook the marker and passed it.

Puzzled, she slowed to a stop and looked around but saw no sign of her friend. She retraced her steps a few paces and cast about at a loss. How was this possible? The gauntlet display indicated she was right on top of Winter, but the rocky, barren area was completely devoid of life. She looked around—feeling ridiculous.

No Winter.

She glanced at her feet and saw the faintest sign of passage in the rocks nearby.

Winter *did* come through here.

What Nalara lacked in aggression, she made up for in survival skills. She had scored slightly higher than average during all simulated tracking exercises in Olympus' controlled environments. It had been one of her favorite skills to practice.

She followed the disturbed ground off to one side where a few large rocks had been displaced. Confused, she pulled one down and gasped in horror when a Purifier helmet rolled out.

Nalara breathlessly snapped her rifle sights up to her eyes and scanned the area. Blood rushing through her ears, she could barely handle the pumping adrenaline that coursed through her body. There was no sign of struggle. The faintest of footprints scuffing the lichen-covered rocks led directly to that place and then away.

This had to be a trick. Or a test. Or a secret mission maybe? Was Winter carrying out some *extra* secret directive? So secret that Nalara was supposed to be her backup but couldn't know what it was?

That must be it.

Nalara swallowed hard. She felt so completely incompetent and overwhelmed. She looked about at a loss and wished with all her heart that there was a clear directive. How could they leave her guessing like this? This wasn't part of her training.

As she tried to slow down her breathing, she figured there were only two options. Either she could go back and secure the LZ as her captain had commanded, or she could follow Winter at all costs as the Grand Elite had commanded. And the Grand Elite did tell her that this assignment was of the 'utmost importance'—superseding all other directives.

The choice was clear. She needed to do her best to catch up with Winter.

With no beacon to follow . . . and no way to communicate . . .

This was her true assignment. This was the test.

Nalara steeled what she could of her courage and began one step at a time, following the trail left by her friend, hoping with all her being that she would not enter a violent encounter during this solitary sojourn into the unknown.

"Don't worry, Winter," she whispered to herself. "I'm coming."

The heavy fall of Purifier boots thumped rapidly through the dense wilderness. Heart pumping wild with both exertion and uncertainty, Winter flew through the landscape.

As she ran, she periodically checked her gauntlet display and altered her path to avoid any encounters with the Archangels and Broadswords. She knew they would be completely occupied by their mission to find the downed drones. It would be a few hours before they'd return to the LZ.

Still, she would have to hurry. Nalara was the main concern. Even acknowledging her initiate's incompetence, Nalara would eventually notice her unwarranted disappearance and would get panicked.

Winter quickened her pace.

Get in, she instructed herself. *Warn Joshua. Get out!*

At first, she was uncertain and conflicted about this foolhardy effort, and her mind generated every scenario of how she could explain her sudden absence. Wraith had warned her she would catch a round between the eyes if she broke protocol on a jump again, and now, after his *educational* beating, she couldn't be sure if it was an exaggeration or not.

But the longer she ran and the more distance she put between herself and the LZ, the easier it was to ignore those problems. Now, as she ran, all she could think of was the safety of Joshua and his people.

That was paramount—even to her own safety.

Winter knew where she was going. She knew she could reach the dome between the four bridges if she followed the river and the giant old road. It was almost too much to hope that Joshua would be waiting there for her again, but she hoped nonetheless.

The warm late-morning sun greeted her as she left the cover of the trees and closed in on the columned domed building where she had first been introduced to the idea of tyranny.

She slowed her pace, knowing that this area was still likely inhabited by surface humans. She had no idea where or how they were living, but she wanted to make sure that her presence caused no further pain or fear.

This area with so many ancient buildings still partially standing was desolate and quiet, like an old silent ghost haunting the lonely forest. Winter kept tight to cover under the looming buildings and picked her foot placement carefully. The buildings, crumbling and unrecognizable and covered by the overgrowth of nature, towered overhead as she passed beneath their shadows. Every opening was dark and empty. Silent testaments of a culture and civilization long since extinct, each hollow building appeared to her as a lifeless corpse.

Winter was suddenly aware that she was being followed. She didn't hear or even see anything, but her internal alarms went off, and she knew to trust her instincts.

She tucked into a direction change under the cover of ancient rubble and doubled back on her position. Her pursuer was clever, predicting her movement and circumventing the course. She knew better than to get pinned down. Even though she fully acknowledged these were surface humans and not ravenous mutants, they would still almost certainly perceive her as a threat and attack given the opportunity.

She needed to find Joshua. He was her only trusted contact on the surface.

Winter moved quickly to put some distance between her and her pursuer in a zig-zag pattern of dead dashes and sharp corners. Monitoring the movement behind her, using only peripherals, she maneuvered toward a more impassable setting where she knew she would have the advantage.

The ancient remains of urban sprawl became her playground. Winter supercharged her speed before jumping across an expanse that bridged a small overpass. She flew through the open air and caught the opposite ledge with her fingertips. Her precision feet skipped upward and she pulled up to stand in an open area filled with rows of gigantic metal containers, each the size of a house, rectangular, and composed of rusted steel. They seemed to fill the whole area in uniform columns and random stacks.

Sprinting forward, with an upward push, Winter caught the lip of a container and pulled herself up to the new level. She dashed across the tops, leaping unit to unit, until she reached the edge where she flipped over the side and tucked into a roll on the gravel below.

Movement behind her telegraphed that she had not gained the distance she'd hoped for. Her efforts to lose her tail seemed fruitless. It was perplexing, considering her genetic engineering, but the home terrain advantage was undeniable.

A crumbling stone wall stood in her way, but it wasn't an obstacle. Winter vaulted up the side and pulled her body over the top with ease. She landed perfectly on both feet and was off running again, full-tilt.

She dodged and flipped through a series of uneven ground layers and turned a blind corner where she skidded to an abrupt stop—face to face with a 'blighter' in full gear.

The tense split-second of panic felt like an eternity.

Heart stopped short, breath caught high in her chest, Winter felt the overpowering instinct to lash out against her opponent, but her vow to prevent the further mindless bloodshed of these people held her in check . . . only just.

Her pursuer suddenly held up its hand, and removed its goggles and cowl.

Joshua's flushed, smiling face greeted her. "You missed the shortcut around the wall." He laughed as he doubled over and leaned on his knees while struggling to catch his breath.

CHAPTER THIRTY-EIGHT

"I can't believe you chased me!" Winter gasped breathlessly. "Blight me! I could have killed you!"

"No doubt," Joshua said, still trying to steady himself. "Wow . . ." He straightened and breathed out. "You. Are. Fast. . . . These are *my* grounds, but you really made me work hard for it."

"I couldn't tell it was you." She meant to sound apologetic, but her voice was edged with adrenaline.

Joshua grinned. "I'm just glad you didn't stab me or shoot me in the face."

"Unbelievable," Winter muttered. "You have a death wish or something?"

He shrugged and held out a small container. "Admit it. You had fun, too." He winked.

Winter cocked her head at the container.

"It's just water," he explained and took a sip to demonstrate its safety.

With some effort, Winter squelched the residual revulsion caused by the thought of consuming 'toxic' surface substances. She embraced her dedication and unclasped the top before enjoying the cold water. It tasted so different from what she was used to.

Fresh. Living.

Joshua couldn't help but smile. The free-running had caused Winter's hair to fall from its bindings, and it rippled down her back in shimmering ebony waves while she drank.

"Thanks." Winter wiped her chin and handed back the canteen.

Joshua indicated to the somewhat faded yet distinct bruises on her face. "Everything . . . okay up there?"

Winter knew what he was getting at. A small stir of fear and shame rippled through her lower chest as she recalled the incident with Wraith. "Things got interesting," she said. "I faced some difficult choices, but I'd like to think I made the right ones. I have, at least, set a precedent for change . . . and I think *I'm* different because of it. More than that, I now know I can't give up. I'm gonna keep going until the purifying is ended."

Joshua smiled warmly. The sincerity in his eyes spoke volumes. "I'm just amazed . . . For you to stand up to your people—to your deity, even. I can't imagine the kind of courage that's gotta take."

"I don't feel courageous," Winter admitted softly.

He waved off her comment. "Feelings are nothing. *Actions* are everything." He paused. "And you should know that your actions have really inspired me."

"Inspired you?" Winter almost laughed. "I'm constantly struggling. I am so far in over my head that sometimes, I don't know which way is up. I have no training for this. I'm trying to find a way to fundamentally change the core beliefs of an entire city with no idea of how to proceed."

"That's why." Joshua pointed at her to emphasize his statement. "The fact that you put so much on yourself and that you have no help but are determined to do it anyway—the fact that you haven't suppressed the unpopular truth to embrace the popular lie—*that* takes courage."

Winter pulled her lips tight together, unsure how to respond. His words of support touched her deeply.

"Look," she said, remembering her reason for being there. "I came to warn you. Two Purifier teams are in the immediate area, and several more are just a few miles away. You need to hide immediately."

Winter could have sworn Joshua began crying inside. His expression didn't change, but somehow, his countenance did. That familiar, penetrating sadness returned to his eyes.

"Thanks for the warning, but you really shouldn't have come here." His voice carried a deathly serious tone. "You need to be more careful yourself."

"What do you mean?" she asked, truly concerned.

Joshua took a few steps back, as if trying to barrier himself against her coming closer. "I wish I could, but I can't stay and talk. I'm really grateful to see you again, Winter, but I only needed to tell you that this has to be the last time."

Winter couldn't deny the sharp, sudden pain that gripped her insides at hearing his words and seeing him withdraw from her like that. "But . . . why?" Her voice trembled slightly. "I—"

"This area's become too close to compromised, too many times." Joshua turned his head away. "More and more drones appear every day."

"You need to tell your people to stop shooting them down," Winter urged. "Olympus has been able to pinpoint the area because—"

"It's not us shooting them." He set a hand on his holster instinctively. "We've never shot at them—nor have we ever gone out of our way to fight with the hunters." He shook his head. "Purifiers." He corrected himself. "Listen, Winter . . . there are things I haven't told you about the surface. There are . . . *horrors* down here—things I doubt even Olympus could dream up."

"Horrors?" Winter repeated.

"You need to leave here—now. Leave, and don't come back." He paused. "I'm truly sorry, but there's just too much at stake. I need to protect my family."

Winter could hear the sorrow in his voice, laced with distinct hints of underlying rage. "Was it me?" She needed to know. "Did I cause this?"

Joshua took a step away as she shifted closer. He didn't answer.

Winter couldn't believe how poignant his silence was. "I just wanted to learn the truth."

"Winter, you know the truth." He almost sounded accusing.

A soft, almost indiscernible shrieking zipped somewhere overhead.

Joshua dodged back and pulled on his cowl and goggles once more. "You have to get out of here—you have to go."

She shook her head in frustration. "I don't want . . ." She struggled with the words for this strange new emotion. "So . . . am I just never going to see you again—ever?"

Joshua shook his covered head. "I'm sorry, but my family comes first."

Winter felt something break inside, and she spoke her true feelings more honestly than she'd ever allowed herself to be. "Joshua, please. Everything I am contradicts everything I've learned. The truth has blindsided me, tortured me, alienated me, and . . . and literally beaten me senseless. The truth has nearly gotten me killed." She almost choked on her emotion. "But through it all, you were the only thing that I could hold on to as evidence of my own sanity. And now, you're leaving, and you'll disappear forever. If you no longer exist—or if you were never real at all—then what *is* real?" Tears rimmed her eyes and blurred her vision. "Joshua, I'm afraid. I'm afraid I'm going to lose myself in this battle of truth and lies. I'm afraid that . . . without you, I'm going to fail."

Joshua paused at the edge of turning to leave.

Winter wished deeply that she could see his soul-stirring eyes just once more.

"Forgive me, Winter. I'm sorry," he whispered under his cowl. "You know the truth. Trust it." His voice broke. "But please . . . don't ever come back."

Joshua broke into a run and disappeared into the ancient urban landscape, leaving Winter alone.

CHAPTER THIRTY-NINE

Nalara couldn't put a name to her feelings; there were too many inside to process. She watched from the edge of the trees as the shuttle came whizzing down to hover over the clearing, snapping tree limbs and tossing clumps of grass with the thrusters as it steadily came to land.

The pilot didn't notice her, consumed with his focus to fulfill his vocation. He didn't even look up before he began the return flight diagnostics. The engine quieted down to a dull hum.

A short time later, markers on Nalara's gauntlet appeared in the immediate vicinity and began closing in. The team was almost there.

Nalara's mind flew. The Grand Elite had commanded her to tell no one of her special assignment—no one, except for Captain Priest. Her countenance lifted in hope. She could tell him the truth. Surely, the Master Purifier would know what to do.

Wraith and the Archangels became visible through the trees and approached the shuttle. Leading the weary team into the clearing, Wraith bore a large drone in one hand. The battered device was covered in earth and oil. A large hole gaped in its hull, and a mess of frayed wires hung out.

Nalara scarcely breathed as she moved forward to meet them.

In the time it took the team to regroup, and before a single word was spoken, Winter came into view at the edge of the clearing as if nothing had happened. She was wearing her helmet, her armor fully engaged.

Nalara averted her eyes and positioned herself with the team between them as a barrier.

"No incident, sir," Winter said with authority as she drew close.

Nalara's mouth fell open and she dared a furtive glance.

Wraith grunted as he walked past directly to the shuttle and entered his code on the outer hatch.

"Check it out." Scorch pointed at the gutted drone. "Blighters took the infrared scanner, the memory—and the engine."

"Smashed the life out of the transponder, too," Viper added.

Winter seemed distracted. "Yeah . . . how about that?"

Nalara barely heard their words. Her frightened eyes were locked on Winter like she was a venomous serpent about to strike.

"Alright, team." Wraith shoved the broken drone into the shuttle's hatch after dousing it with disinfectant. "Let's get home."

"Captain Priest!" Nalara blurted suddenly, drawing everyone's attention.

He turned in brusque curiosity and stared at her with furrowed eyebrows.

"I—" she gasped out, not sure what she was about to say. She couldn't make her report with Winter and the team standing there. "N-no . . . no incident, sir."

The team chuckled.

"*Meow* . . ." Sapphire quietly mocked.

Wraith rolled his eyes and began the boarding process.

Following after their captain, the slow, meticulous routine began with Mason Howell, and the others followed one by one.

Nalara's hands shook. She knew she didn't have all the facts, but she also knew what she had seen. Lying prone on a grassy hill, peering down the scope of her rifle . . . she had seen Winter with a blighter—*talking* to a filthy, diseased, loathsome blighter! And without her helmet, no less!

It was . . . impossible!

At her turn, Nalara stepped up into the scanner, winced as the green lights splayed over her body, and then sighed in relief as she was cleared and sprayed down with disinfectant. The gas vented, and the glass partition raised. She wordlessly checked her rifle, took her seat, and secured her restraint.

Her confusion turned to a low-boiling anger deep inside. No matter how she spun it, everything just felt wrong. Winter wouldn't betray her team like that. Her city . . . her god? It was repulsive. How could she?

Nalara had been working so hard and for so long to just tow the mark, and no matter how she tried, she couldn't seem to do anything right. She had been striving to be a good Purifier—like Winter—since her initiation, and she had come up short every time. She faced constant ridicule or just flat-out being ignored by their team captain. And now to find out that this whole time, Winter was just wasting her natural talent and consorting with the enemy? How could she be sure anything her trainer had taught her was correct now? It was infuriating.

And deeper than the anger, there sat an intense layer of bitter sorrow for her friend and trainer's decision to go against everything they were created to be.

Winter stepped into the scanner.

Nalara held her breath as she remembered the flashing red lights, blaring alarms, and purifying flames that had consumed Trigger. She was certain she was about to witness her friend consumed by those same flames. She didn't want to see Winter die. The thought turned her stomach and made her clutch the restraints in fear.

Green.

Ding

Nalara's eyes widened, and her jaw went slack.

Winter calmly entered the shuttle, handed her rifle off to Wraith, and sat down across from Nalara and buckled in.

The stark feeling of utter incompetence washed over her mind like a wave of black ink. The Grand Elite chose wrong. He should have picked someone who understood complex missions or someone who could think on their feet. It was so unfair. There was no protocol for this. How was she supposed to know what to do?

The inertia of the shuttle takeoff caused their bodies to shift. The whine of the engines built steadily as they lifted off the ground in an arcing line to Olympus.

Nalara kept her eyes fixated on the floor, grateful that Winter made no attempt at conversation for the duration of the return trip.

The shuttle bay was a busy hub of motion while all the teams disembarked and filtered off. Nalara avoided eye contact with Winter as they removed their gear and filed into the conference room for debriefing.

"Teams," the Master Purifier said while they all found their seats. "Excellent work today, all of you. All three drones were located and recovered. A special note of recognition goes out to the Grim Reapers for suppressing a nest of blighters in their search area. Eight confirmed killshots—five by Captain Sharpe."

The room resounded with applause as Lilith raised her hand high.

With her peripheral, Nalara checked Winter. Her head was slightly bowed, and she wasn't clapping.

"Training tomorrow begins one hour later than standard . . ." Wraith groaned and shut his eyes, "in consideration of the Spring Equinox Festival on the Elite tier tonight, to which we are all invited and encouraged to attend." His clenched right hand hit over his heart in salute. "Hail to Sovereign Zeus!"

Everyone instantly rose to their feet, their fists over their hearts. "Hail, Sovereign Zeus!" the Purifiers rejoined in unison.

Nalara's limbs went cold when she again checked Winter with a sideways glance. She couldn't believe her eyes. While Winter was on her feet with everyone else, her right hand was at her side!

"Dismissed." Wraith switched off the hologram projection and exited the room.

Careful to not raise suspicions, Nalara painstakingly filed out of the conference room and to the elevators. Her body desperately wanted to run, but her mind held the reins taut and instructed her to walk calmly with the others. She chose a different lift than Winter's and, packed in tight with a dozen other Purifiers, rode the lift in silence and tried to keep her heartbeat from wildly racing.

The elevator seemed to climb each floor at an agonizingly slow third-tier pace.

3 . . . . . . 2 . . . . . .

Sweat dewed Nalara's forehead, and she fought for every labored breath. *For Sovereign's sake—please hurry!*

1 . . . . . .

At last, the lift doors opened. The Purifiers poured out onto the Second Tier and into the welcoming late afternoon sunlight.

Nalara kept with the pack until she was confident she could break away unnoticed—not that anyone took notice of her at all. Finally, rounding a blind corner, the reins were released. She took off in a dead sprint towards the Hive and the Grand Stairway ascending to the First Tier. Structures and faces flew past in streaks of blurred, unrecognizable motion.

Her mind was zeroed in on the fulfillment of her special assignment. Nothing else mattered. Winter, and possibly Olympus itself, was in serious danger—and only the Grand Elite could help now.

Only the Sovereign's right hand could save Winter.

Four massive Guardians stood as impassable sentinels at the base of the stairway. One took a step forward and lifted his hand as Nalara barreled towards them.

"Halt, Purifier!" the Guardian's deep voice bellowed as the three behind him shifted to fill in his space.

Nalara skidded to a breathless stop before the towering figure.

"The Equinox Festival does not begin for another three hours," the Guardian rumbled. "Return then."

"I'm not here for that." Nalara straightened and spoke as authoritatively as she could. "I need to see the Grand Elite."

The Guardian cocked an eyebrow and smirked sarcastically. "Oh, really?" He seemed amused. "And what makes you think that his greatness, the Grand Elite of Olympus, needs to see *you.*"

"He does!" Nalara's response was as sharp as a knife's edge. The Guardian's mocking smirk disappeared. She moved closer, peering up at the giant man. "It's of the *utmost* importance that you get a message to him. Tell him that the Purifier Nalara Gressen needs to see him—now."

CHAPTER FORTY

With a gratifying sigh, Wraith entered the private office of the Master Purifier. The automated doors slid closed behind him, and he enjoyed the noise-canceling pane. The quiet room was simple, practical, and spacious and held many exclusive comforts: a padded chair at the desk, a private shower, and a small kitchen that was restocked daily.

He took a quick sweep of the room before retrieving a blood-red apple from the kitchen. He sat at the desk, eased into the chair's comfortable backing, and entered his security code to unlock the desk's holographic display.

"Good afternoon, Master Purifier Orrin Priest." The computer's placid female voice welcomed him.

A deep sense of satisfaction set in, and a smile twitched in the corner of his lips.

Master Purifier.

Finally, after all the years of sweat and blood and living in the long shadow of his predecessor, the honored title was *his*. He was *Master Purifier*. Nothing and no one could take that from him.

"Would you care to review the teams' movement patterns for today's jump?" the computer asked politely.

"No," Wraith replied curtly as he took a loud bite out of the apple. "Show me the blast-cam footage for the Grim Reapers, starting with its captain."

"Accessing . . ."

Lilith Sharpe's image and rank data appeared before him along with multiple individual windows.

"Twelve rifle rounds were recorded," the computer explained, "totaling five confirmed killshots—rounds two, five, six, nine, and eleven. Which would you care to view?"

"All killshots, and slow to one percent."

Five individual windows zoomed close while the other seven faded into the background. The videos began playback at one percent speed.

Wraith grinned as he watched each slowed video in turn, enjoying the anticipated release of adrenaline as each well-aimed rifle round honed in on a blighter and exploded through their disfigured, mutated bodies. He chuckled as round nine burst directly through the head of one of the wretched creatures.

"Ooo . . . headshot." Wraith crunched into the apple; juice sprayed across his lips and trickled down his stubbled chin. He wiped it away with the back of his hand as he munched in delight. "Nice one, Razor."

The computer's voice returned once each video had been viewed. "Would you care to view additional footage from the Grim Reapers' team?"

Wraith finished the apple with another crisp bite and tossed the core aside. Someone else would clean it up.

"Nah." He wiped the last of the juice from his lips. "Bring up the movement patterns for the Archangels—Winter's pattern and the pattern for that . . . pathetic excuse of a Purifier."

"Please specify second pattern."

Wraith huffed. "I'll have to teach you that one." He still couldn't fathom the Grand Elite's reasoning for selecting literally the worst Purifier for such an important surveillance mission. But then, it wasn't his place to question the motives of a god's closest and most trusted aide. The Grand Elite would have his reasons.

"Nalara Gressen for the second pattern," he clarified.

"Patterns confirmed," the female voice replied, and an aerial view of the surface's terrain blipped on.

Wraith yawned as he studied. He accelerated the timeline somewhat and blankly watched the two patterns guarding the LZ. Gressen's movements were haphazard and aimless. Wraith rolled his eyes and cursed that such an incompetent, third-tier pod child was assigned to his team.

But not for long.

Once her assignment was completed, he'd order her transferred to another team—to let someone else deal with the useless amateur. He'd then put in a transfer for one of the more proficient Purifiers to join his team.

He smiled broadly as he mused. *It's good to be Master Purifier.*

Soon enough, the Archangels would overtake the Grim Reapers as the first-ranked team.

And in time, he would take his rightful place among the glorified Ascended in Elysium as the first-ranked Purifier.

He flashed a toothy grin. With Winter's recent humiliating demotion, the rank of *first* was guaranteed to remain his.

Wraith turned his attention to Winter's marker. Her movements were more expected: professional and systematic, circling the drop zone in an ever-widening pattern. She ascended to the summit of a nearby mound, and then . . .

Wraith leaned in as something strange caught his eye. After descending, Winter's marker crossed a field, entered the forest, and became stationary.

He scanned several minutes through the timeline.

Stationary.

"Hm." He scanned further.

Still stationary.

Nine minutes later, Gressen's marker suddenly dashed across the LZ, ascended the same mound from around the back, then quickly descended, and eventually met up with Winter's marker. Both held position for only a moment before Gressen darted quickly into the wilderness—alone.

"What the . . .?" Wraith cocked his head and played it again.

A ding at the intercom signaled an incoming call.

Wraith growled and paused the playback before accepting it.

"What is it!?" he barked.

"Uh . . ." the caller stammered. "Master Purifier, sir, you are summoned to the personal residence of his lordship, the Grand Elite. He's expecting you now."

"Now?" Wraith queried.

"Yes, sir, right now. Sovereign's guidance ever upon you, sir." The caller discontinued transmitting.

Wraith breathed out and took one last quick look at the odd movement patterns. "Right now," he repeated the order quietly and switched off the display.

The Master Purifier stood, straightened out the wrinkles in his uniform, and exited his office in professional timeliness.

CHAPTER FORTY-ONE

The golden sunlight of the early evening cut low through the barrier and bathed the Elite tier in bright hues of yellow and orange. The glittering streets were all a bustle of servers and decorators passing by, laden with food and wine and every sort of colorful finery.

Nalara knew every Elite was preparing for 'the most extravagant event of the season,' as Elite Alexander had put it.

As she made her way from the Administerial Hall towards the sloping steps to the Second Tier, her spirits were somewhat lifted by the breathtaking sights. There was a huge pavilion set up for the Equinox Festival behind the giant fountain at the center of the main plaza. Draped silk of every color, twinkling candles on every table, and flowers absolutely everywhere filled the interior.

The horrors of what she had witnessed on the surface pleasantly faded as the beautiful blue eyes and striking features of Alexander Sterling Belmont entered her mind.

Nalara breathed in the wonderful fragrance of the festival's flowers. She smiled as she imagined Alexander smiling back, taking her hand in his, and laying another gentle kiss on her prickled skin.

She unconsciously cooed at the heavenly memory.

Things weren't as awful as they seemed. After all, an *Elite* had personally invited her to the festival as his guest.

Whatever she felt about Winter at the moment, or the unspeakable thing she'd seen on the surface, Nalara clung to the hope that tonight was going to be magical. All she wanted in the whole world was to just forget the hard and tiresome worries of the day and soak in the sublime comfort and fine company.

But the memory of Winter consorting with the repulsive blighter relentlessly clawed its way back to the forefront of her mind—replacing Alexander's beautiful face with the stuff of nightmares.

She sighed wearily and began the long descent from Olympus' lavish heights.

Everything was supposed to be better once she became a full-fledged Purifier, but it had only gotten harder and more complicated. Nalara knew she wasn't prepared for her vocation. She wasn't prepared for anything up here. This world only seemed to be a never-ending tangle of confusion and second-guessing.

She almost found herself wishing to be back in her tiny bunk in the crowded Formulation Quarter. Her upbringing seemed simple and straightforward by comparison to what she was now experiencing. She missed the simplicity of waking, studying, training, and sleeping. She missed someone constantly telling her exactly what to do, when to do it, and how to get it done. In the FMQ, there had been no conflicted interests and no opportunity for mistakes—at least, no mistakes that seemed to jeopardize the very fate of Olympus. There had been one continual stream of information and clear-cut orders, rather than this confusing world of seeing and having to discern for herself.

Nalara could only hope that unwinding at the festival tonight would make everything better.

Her steady descent was stopped short when she halted at the sight of her commanding officer.

The Master Purifier stalked up the stairs in haste, his footfalls resounding like sharp drumbeats. He glanced at her only briefly in passing and didn't slow his pace at all.

Nalara watched the burly, intimidating man's ascent and didn't think to move again until he was all the way up the steps and far from her. She exhaled at length and quickened her steps.

Reaching the security checkpoint at the base, a Guardian halted her with a silent gesture. He looked stern and immovable as any other. Nalara wondered to herself how they told each other apart.

The eerie, bald census worker by the Guardian's side scanned the mark on Nalara's hand and spoke flatly, "Identify."

"Nalara Gressen," she answered clearly.

The Unifier studied the feedback on his display. "How are you feeling today?"

"Well enough, I guess."

The light turned red. "Signs of deception detected," the Unifier stated without emotion.

The Guardian shifted.

Nalara rubbed an eye. "I'm just really, *really* tired right now."

Green.

"You are experiencing difficulty in your vocation?"

"It is very hard," Nalara admitted.

"If you experience difficulty in fulfilling your vocation, you should reapply yourself in an effort to improve."

Nalara's shoulders slumped. Again, from a whole new source, she was being called inadequate. The feeling of helplessness and worthlessness clouded her insides like thick ink.

"I have put a temporary watch note on your record." The Unifier dismissed her without making eye contact. "Proceed in your service to our Sovereign."

"I am thankful for my ability to serve," Nalara added as if she were trying to convince the uninterested census worker. She moved on toward the Purifier Quarter.

Her room on the ground floor was shared with three other Purifiers of similar rank. A bunkbed sat in either corner of the room, with a trunk and small closet for each of them on the far wall. They shared a bathroom across the hall with the room next door, which is why Nalara often chose to shower in the team hub.

Two of her roommates were absent; Anissa Draper was sleeping in her bunk. The windowless room held no furnishings whatsoever, other than the beds and the trunks.

Nalara walked carefully to the tiny closet where all of her worldly possessions resided. Her trunk held nothing but sleeping clothes, hygiene essentials, and undergarments. Her dress boots sat by the trunk, and her dress greens hung as the only occupant on the small rail.

It was a sad feeling, being limited so harshly in options. If she had been formulated as an Elite, she could own as many outfits as she wished. She could wear whatever she wanted for any occasion. She would never even have to wear the same thing twice if that was her desire.

There were always those stories, floating around the lower ranks, of Purifiers who found favor with the Elite crowd and were excluded from dangerous missions, or even received special advancements or comforts.

Alexander's smiling face again flashed in her mind.

She sighed, praying fervently that maybe that would be her one day.

Then . . . she told herself. *Then things will be different. Then things will be better.*

Nalara changed quickly into her ceremonial uniform, hanging her athletic clothing in the closet as haphazardly as her uniform had been. She made a slight effort to brush off the shoulders and front but lost interest quickly. The plain cloth adorned by nothing but her name and rank was a sorry sight. She always figured that eventually, she would earn some kind of recognition or honors. At least, that's what she'd been telling herself from the earliest days of the FMQ.

She reached into her trunk and retrieved her hairbrush. Her chocolate hair fell in creamy curls down to her shoulders.

The tiny mirror on the wall made her think that her features would be better displayed when framed by her shiny hair, but protocol dictated that she tie it up above her shoulders when in uniform.

The grim reality of the moment struck her—that she suddenly wished more than anything that she had been assigned to a different vocation. Truly, anything on the middle-tier but a Purifier would have been preferable. As a Purifier, she was given the opportunity to achieve Elitehood through Ascension—something that no other vocation was offered. But there was no way she would ever be *that* good. Having the opportunity but no ability to achieve it was the cruelest thing of all.

A knock at the door halted her train of thought.

Nalara put down the hairbrush and opened the door. Her heart stopped in her chest to see Winter standing before her. She instinctively held her breath and took a defensive step back into the room.

"Hey," Winter said. "You all recovered after our *grueling* assignment today?" Her teasing was sarcastic, but the humor was lost on Nalara, who could only see the deception.

"I don't want to talk about it," Nalara deflected.

"Want to get something to eat at the cafeteria?" Winter offered. In her arms, she bore a bundle wrapped in delicate tissue paper. It crinkled when she moved.

Nalara shook her head. "I'm getting ready for the festival, and I don't want to use up my allotments when I don't need to."

Winter paused and pursed her lips. She seemed unconvinced.

"Sorry, but I really need to finish getting ready," Nalara moved to close the door.

"In that case, you'll be needing this." Winter pushed in with a knowing smile.

Nalara opened her mouth in protest but said nothing as Winter entered her room. She held her breath again and edged towards the closet. Fear gripped her chest as only one word screamed in her mind:

Blighted!

Winter closed the door before pulling aside the paper and unfurling a rippling cascade of cream-colored silk; she held up a breathtaking formal gown.

Nalara's jaw dropped in spite of herself as all her fears melted into the dress' milky magnificence. "This? For me?" She gasped in disbelief. "It's so first-tier . . ."

"First-tier is right," Winter said with a satisfied smile at her friend's reaction. "It was a gift from an adoring Elite. He gave it to me after my trials. I've now had it for four years, and I've literally *never* worn it. And now, even if I wanted to, it wouldn't fit me. But you . . ." She lifted the dress out at the shoulders and eyed the measurement to Nalara's smaller frame. "Probably just about right for you."

Nalara impulsively reached out and touched the fabric as if confirming it was real. "Whoa . . . it's so soft." She ran her fingers down the length of the sparkling gown. "I've never worn anything so nice."

Winter handed the gown to her and watched in contentment as Nalara beamed at her gift.

"Well, go on," Winter encouraged. "Try it on!"

Nalara suddenly felt the sick pulling of resentment deep in her soul. Her smile faded as the image of Winter conversing with the cursed blighter resurfaced. At the horrid thought, Winter's gift no longer seemed beautiful and alluring, but loathsome and possibly even diseased.

"Why give this to me?" she asked directly, holding the gown out away from her body by her fingertips.

Winter shrugged. "Like I said, it doesn't fit me anymore. And I know you really like these parties, so I thought you should have it."

Nalara wasn't convinced and made it show.

Winter took the hint and paused before explaining herself. "Last night, when you came to see me, I told you that I really haven't been here for you since your graduation. The truth is, I've failed you as your trainer, and in many ways, I suppose I've failed you as a friend, too. And I'm sorry about that." She cleared her throat. "I've been so wrapped up with . . . things lately. I just wanted to show you that I *truly* cherish you as a friend."

Nalara tried to not be swept away by Winter's expression of good will. She seemed so sincere, but how could she trust that sincerity? How could she trust anything Winter said or did—now that she knew what *things* she'd been wrapped up in?

Things like treason.

Maybe Winter's words were just more lies—nothing but an endless torrent of lies and betrayal.

"You . . ." Nalara fought back the tears that wanted to come; her simmering anger helped to keep them in check. "You promised me that, no matter what, you'd be there for me."

"The promise stands," Winter replied directly.

"And—" Nalara pressed further, offering her friend one last chance to come clean— "you promised me you would tell me what was going on with you the *moment* you figured it out."

Winter nodded. "That stands, too."

They shared a moment of awkward silence together. What had been an indivisible childhood friendship was now being divided by an ever-widening chasm of lies.

Where have you gone, Janey? Nalara thought, her heart aching to know.

She sniffed and half-heartedly folded up the dress. Pressing the gown into the depths of her open trunk, Nalara closed the lid, then reached for a bottle of sanitizing lotion and spritzed her hands and forearms before returning to her festival preparations.

Winter cocked her head in confusion. "You're not going to wear it to the party?"

"Maybe next time," Nalara said casually and began to pin up her hair. "Thanks for the gift, but I really don't want to be late."

"Some things are worth waiting for, don't you think?" Winter gave her a wink, attempting to inject some levity into the unexpectedly dark moment. "Like maybe you showing up in that dress."

"No, thanks," Nalara's response was curt and cutting. "Next time."

Anissa stirred in her bunk and leaned up on her elbows. "You mind?" she groaned. "Trying to get some rest here."

"Sorry, Dagger," Winter apologized.

The weary Purifier collapsed back into the mattress and covered her face with the pillow.

Nalara finished fixing her hair neatly under the crisp beret. She sighed at her tiny reflection, seeing her slightly wrinkled ceremonial uniform bereft of accolade and merit.

She relaxed her body, closed her eyes, and tried to focus on picturing the heavenly face and lustrous blue eyes of Elite Alexander Sterling Belmont. She yearned to see that face again, to hear his voice, and maybe even feel his lips touch her tingling skin.

Soon . . . she dreamed longingly.

Even without talent or merit, Nalara had still been personally invited to the Equinox Festival as the 'guest' of an Elite. She had also found enough favor in the eyes of the Grand Elite himself to receive a special assignment, and after successfully fulfilling that assignment, he had even congratulated her.

"Well done, Purifier," Draven had told her earlier with an appreciative smile. "You have glorified our Sovereign with your excellent service."

Remembering his words infused her with a boost of confidence and pride. Nalara couldn't help but grin. Maybe she would receive her accolades yet. Maybe her time to shine was yet to come, and she would do it without Winter's help.

Nalara turned from the mirror and faced Winter, seeing her for the first time as more of a stranger than a friend.

Janey truly was dead.

In that moment, Nalara accepted the sad reality that her friend was gone. The cold and unfamiliar Purifier known as 'Winter' was now in the capable hands of the Grand Elite of Olympus. Only his wisdom could save her. Only he could bring her friend back.

Winter smiled and whispered, "Come on, I'll walk you there."

Nalara lifted her hand as she brushed past and exited the room. "I know the way."

CHAPTER FORTY-TWO

The color-shifting barrier domed the celestial illuminated Elite tier, drowning out all but the brightest stars in the deep, dark sky. Candlelight and stringed music radiated throughout the luxurious plaza. The marble fountain at its center was not spouting; the surface of the water was covered in tiny floating candles amid a blanket of pink and white flower petals. Laughter and conversation filled the air as the giant pavilion behind the fountain housed most of the Elite citizens in their finest apparel. Jewels and glasses clinked in chorus, fire-breathers delighted, face-painted dancers in multicolored attire entertained, and specially formulated servers wearing white and black rushed about, catering to everyone's deepest satisfaction.

"Blight me! Look at all the food," Nalara said as she crested the top of the Grand Stairway and entered the glistening, bustling plaza.

Winter trailed close behind. She found Nalara's behavior since returning from the day's jump odd, but she had already surmised that Nalara was simply seeking to find her independence in post-FMQ society and decided to leave it alone. Still, even though she didn't care to admit it, she felt hurt to not see her friend wearing her gift.

She remembered timid little Nalara from the Formulation Quarter with fondness. Cords of pride and sorrow were simultaneously plucked to see her now maturing into an adult woman—striking out on her own to find her place and fulfill her role. She only hoped that she'd be able to bring about enough change on Olympus so that Nalara would have the freedom to choose that role for herself. She hoped that her actions could spare Nalara's hands from becoming blood-soaked—unlike her own.

And she would now have to do it without Joshua's help.

Winter, breathing in her recommitment to her cause, came to stand next to Nalara. "This is your first celebration of the Spring Equinox." She gestured to the grand array of exquisite delicacies and entertainment before them. "There's really nothing like it. The only thing that comes close is the Fall Festival six months from now."

Nalara appeared lost in the world of the Elite, as if her mind helplessly raced to translate what her eyes saw into a language she could comprehend. She eventually pointed enthusiastically. "Wow! The fountain—look at the flowers!" Her head swiveled from side to side to take in the whole scene.

Winter nearly laughed. This would be her fifth celebration of the Spring Equinox. The pomp and glamour had already become dull to her senses in years previous—even more so since learning of the ever-present, strangling lie of Olympus' Sovereign and his blessed 'Elite'—but seeing the festivities with renewed eyes through Nalara's childlike perspective somehow brought back those past sensations of delight and wonder.

This was Nalara's very first time enjoying the comforts of the Elite. Seeing her face illuminate with inexpressible glee, Winter savored the moment. She was secretly overjoyed that whatever troubles seemed to be afflicting her friend's mind were waylaid, at least for the moment.

"Just have fun tonight." Winter took Nalara by the arm and gently led her into the plaza, steering her towards the open buffet. "And," she added with a tone of sincerity, "be careful. You're too unguarded."

"Uh-huh," Nalara agreed distractedly.

Upon reaching the buffet tables laden with tantalizing confections, Winter took a small bite of a sweet tart while Nalara shoved a whole cream-filled pastry into her mouth.

"I don't . . . know what . . . this is . . ." Nalara attempted to talk as her cheeks bulged comically. She munched for a moment longer, then swallowed and licked some cream from her lips. "But I know that I like it."

Winter chuckled as she opened her mouth to take another bite, but someone shoved her from behind and caused her to drop her refreshment.

"You are not welcome here," said a familiar, snide voice.

And there he is, Winter thought with an annoyed huff. She turned slowly to face the young, red-faced Elite dressed in white with gold trim.

Nearby partygoers ceased their conversation to watch the spectacle. Some of them were no doubt hoping for a diversion, while others were obviously disgusted at the sight of her.

Winter spoke very clearly in a soft, yet warning tone. "Bad things happen when you touch me, Remington Adolphus Blackburn."

"It's high time, filth, for you to understand: I do whatever I please to whomever I please," he declared, no doubt regurgitating the words he'd been fed his entire life. "I am a favored child of a god. You can't touch me."

Winter leaned in and smiled sarcastically. "I think we *both* know how wrong you are there. Maybe you should calm down."

"And maybe you should leave!" he raised his voice, obviously tainted with drink.

Many heads were now turned as the belligerent scene played out.

Winter turned to face a worry-stricken Nalara. "That'd probably be best."

"Yeah, okay . . ." Nalara relented with a nod.

"Be careful." Winter gave Nalara a quick hug. "And have fun."

"I said leave, you foul, putrid garbage!" Remington blurted.

Winter clenched her fists, her muscles tensing beneath her uniform. Her every instinct roared at her to stand her ground, but she knew that doing so would accomplish nothing but her own demise. She was determined to fight the injustices perpetuated by the Elite and their 'god,' but she begrudgingly accepted that this was neither the time nor the place.

There could be no victory here.

With every eye focused on her and with retreat as her only option, Winter straightened and made her exit as deliberate and dignified as she possibly could.

"That's right, go!" Drink in hand, Remington followed her outside the pavilion. "You worthless, third-tier genetic trash!"

Winter did her best to ignore the raucous Elite, but his presence was unrelenting.

"Defective waste of a Purifier!" He spat at her. "You should never have come here. Miserable, wretched, maggot-loving *wench!*"

Reaching the top of the Grand Stairway, Winter suddenly spun around and eyed her assailant with a dangerous, deathly glare.

Remington stumbled to a halt as a mixed look of panic and sheer terror overtook him.

A breathless hush fell over the plaza as everyone watched and waited.

Staring down at the pathetic, shaky figure before her, Winter strangely felt the urge to laugh. Knowing the truth made all the outward splendor and gaudy magnificence of the Elite seem like a bad joke. Olympus' image of *perfection* was nothing but a well-groomed coward sporting a fancy suit and a big mouth.

The Elite.

All show. No substance.

Their strength stemmed only from the perception of strength bestowed upon them by the Sovereign—then all-too-willingly granted by the people. Their power was merely the illusion of power. But by exposing the Sovereign's lie through the bright, penetrating light of truth, the Elite appeared as little more than weak, vulnerable insects scurrying for the safety of the shadows.

Winter breathed out and relaxed her posture, then calmly turned and began the long descent.

This time, Remington didn't follow.

"Th-that's . . . that's r-right." His voice wavered. He brought his glass to his lips with trembling hands and poured more liquor down his throat. "As I said, you'd better go! And never, *ever* return!"

Descending into the comforting darkness of the Second Tier, Winter whispered back, "Don't worry. I won't."

Under the pavilion, Nalara stood rooted in place by the buffet table. She watched Winter disappear from sight, then sighed with relief when she heard the music and carefree conversations start up again.

"Well, that was certainly uncomfortable," a soothing voice spoke to her from behind.

Nalara felt her face flush as she turned and met the beautiful eyes of Alexander Sterling Belmont.

"I'm positively elated to see you again." Alexander flashed his heart-stopping smile. "How is my guest enjoying the festival?"

Nalara offered him a short, sincere bow. "Oh, I'm having a really great time. Honest." She took another pastry from the table. "And these are just to die for!" Remembering proper manners this time as she stood in the presence of an Elite, she carefully nibbled a bite from the pastry's corner instead of shoving the whole dessert in her mouth. "What's it called?"

"An éclair—filled with vanilla custard and iced with triple-chocolate fondant." His voice was as smooth as the pastry's cream.

Nalara unintentionally moaned as she took another delectable bite. *"Mmmm.* An éclair. It sounds just as delicious as it tastes."

Wearing that same brilliant smile, Alexander took a step closer. Nalara felt her heart skip a beat.

"I'm pleased you are enjoying yourself, Nalara. I truly am thrilled you came."

"Well . . . almost all the Purifiers are here." Nalara glanced around at the familiar faces mixed into the crowd of Elite.

"And yet, you are the only one I was hoping to see," he assured her with that butter-smooth voice.

Nalara shifted self-consciously as her face went from warm to hot. She suddenly wished she was wearing the dress. "Th-thank you, Elite Alexander Sterling Bel—"

"Please." He held up his hand. "For you, 'Alexander' will do wonderfully."

Nalara's nerves caused a soft giggle to escape. "Okay. Alexander."

The music changed and he held out his arm. "Come with me."

Stuffing the last of the pastry into her mouth, Nalara nodded and complied eagerly.

He laughed as she took his arm.

"What?" she asked with her mouth half-full as she was led out into the plaza.

"It's just rather . . . amazing to see someone enjoy food the way you do." He shrugged as they exited the pavilion. "Living here on the First Tier makes one, I don't know—somewhat *numb* to it, I suppose. As delicious as éclairs are, I wouldn't describe them as 'to die for'."

Nalara swallowed. "Am I embarrassing you?" Her question was laced with mortification. She fully understood how out of place she was.

"No." Alexander shook his head, not ruffling a single blonde hair. "Not even a little. I find your fascination . . . well . . . fascinating. Captivating, actually."

The way he looked at her in that moment made Nalara feel like she had done everything in her life perfectly right, and suddenly, it was all worth it.

Out in the open plaza, Alexander led her to the fountain side and gestured for her to sit with him. Nearby, a worker sifted tiny bits of rubbish from the rippling, candle-filled pool.

Once Nalara sat down, Alexander snapped his fingers with authority at the worker.

Nalara smiled in blank curiosity as the worker immediately shifted to a device near the fountain.

"Close your eyes," Alexander instructed.

Nalara's heart thumped wildly as she obeyed. Sitting in darkness, her other senses were heightened as the aching anticipation grew. She heard Alexander snap his fingers again, then came the distant, soft sound of controls being maneuvered.

"What's happening?" Nalara questioned with a grin.

"Patience," was his soothing reply. "You'll see."

A moment later, through the fleshy veil of her eyelids, she sensed that the immediate area had brightened with soft, flickering lights—slowly dancing all around her.

"Now . . ." Alexander whispered in her ear. "Open your eyes."

Nalara did so and let out a breathless gasp. The hundreds of floating candles from the fountain's pool now floated in midair—hovering, twirling, lifting, and sinking as if caught in an imaginary breeze.

The Elite and the Purifier sat together, bathed in an ocean of golden, swirling firelight.

Alexander leaned in. "You like it?"

Nalara placed a hand over her mouth. "Sovereign's blessings. I had no idea. It's . . ." She fought to find the words, the rims of her eyes glistening with tears. "It's more beautiful than anything I could have ever imagined."

"It certainly is." Alexander smiled, his blue eyes focused intensely on Nalara. "It's not meant to be displayed until after the toasts and various other formalities, but I decided you deserved a private showing."

Nalara couldn't answer. Her big brown eyes danced in the gentle glow of the floating candles. All she could do was smile ear to ear.

Alexander edged closer and licked his lips.

Nalara closed her eyes again and held her breath . . . waiting . . . wanting . . . *needing* . . .

"*Stupid, wasteful, third-tier trash!*" Remington stumbled around the corner. His face was red and his movement lethargic.

Letting out an exasperated sigh, Alexander muttered angrily under his breath, "By Zeus' right eye!" He snapped his fingers again at the worker, who quickly operated the device by the fountain. The candles moved in sync at his commands, returning to hover over the pool, then gently lowering until they kissed the surface of the water and came to rest amid the flower petals.

"Broken, defective . . ." Remington ranted. "I hate . . . *hate* that vile harpy! I hate all Purifiers!" He noticed Nalara sitting there in her uniform. His cruel eyes narrowed on his target. "You! You're a Purifier!" He stumbled closer and pointed an accusing finger. "I command you—leave this place immediately!"

"I must apologize, Nalara," Alexander excused himself and moved to intercept his inebriated friend.

The intoxicated young man pointed again at Nalara. "Don't you dare lookit me like that. I know you *heard* me. Leave! Now!" He sneered hatefully as Nalara sat motionless on the fountain's edge.

"I believe that's enough excitement for you, Rem." Alexander took him by the shoulders and marched him away in another direction. He mouthed *'I'll be right back'* to Nalara and pushed his friend along.

Nalara watched the two Elites walk off, giving her a chance to calm the beating of her heart.

"You can't do thisss to me," Remington slurred as he slumped his weight heavily into Alexander. "I'm a godsssson chosen child. Special. I'm . . . I'm power and glory."

"Let's call it a night, shall we?" Alexander encouraged as they walked together.

"It's not my fault everyone hates me." He broke into a fit of sobbing and moaning. "Everyone hates me!"

"Nobody hates you, Rem."

"Yesss . . . yes, they do, too. But, you—you understand, don't you, Xander? You know it's all *her* fault. She's done this to me—making me look a fool." Remington spat on the street and cried again. "I hate her so, *soooo* much."

"Yes, yes. Me, too." Alexander kept him walking. "Now, let's get you home."

"You know what, Xander? You wanna know what?" Remington threw his friend's guiding hand off his arm. "Immunna . . . make this right. She's gonna pay for what she's done. She can't do this to me. I'm . . . Remington Adolphus . . . Adolphusss."

"Come along, Rem," Alexander encouraged. "I'm going to take you home."

"No! Get off me!" Remington thrashed. "Get away from me!"

"Going home is the right thing to do right now."

"No! I said she's gonna pay—so she's gonna pay!" Remington's already red face turned crimson.

Alexander sighed sharply with impatience and glanced back at the fountain. He paused for only a brief moment before his eyes lit up and a smile twitched the corner of his mouth.

"You know what, Rem?" Alexander cooled the tone of his voice as he draped his arm around his friend's shoulder and began leading him in the opposite direction, back toward the stairs descending to the Second Tier. "I think that's a wonderful idea."

Remington, trying to not stumble over his own feet, looked bewildered. "You . . . you do?"

"Absolutely!" Alexander returned with conviction. "But not 'pay' as in she should suffer. No. What she needs to do is *pay* you an apology."

"An apology?" He made no attempt to hide the disgust in his voice.

"Yes, she needs to apologize to you for making you look like a fool. She owes you that apology, and only you can get it from her. Only you can make her respect you."

Remington blinked. "Only . . . only me?"

"Only you, Rem." They reached the top of the Grand Stairway, where Alexander gave his friend a confident pat on the back as he pointed down into the deep darkness of the Second Tier. "You go right on down there, and you tell her to apologize to you. She'll then apologize, and you'll have regained your respect."

Remington sniffed and attempted to straighten his posture. His head wobbled as he nodded half-heartedly. "My respect?"

"Yes, your respect. Once she apologizes, you will have won."

A wide, toothy grin spread across Remington's face. "Yes . . . yesss, you know what? You're right! She needs to apologize."

"She absolutely needs to apologize, and you're the man who's going to get her to do it."

"She can't do this to me!"

"No, she cannot, and you're going to make it right."

Remington swayed and pointed down the stairs. "Immunna go down there!"

"You are going to go right down there!"

"And make her *pay!*"

"And you're going to make her pay you that apology. Yes, you're going to get that apology; that's exactly what you're going to do."

Remington chortled in his throat and took a few staggering steps down. He stopped and half-turned to his friend on the landing, suddenly appearing unsure. "You . . . you're coming with me, right?"

"Oh, I wouldn't dream of it, Rem!" Alexander seemed appalled. "Absolutely not, I could never do that to my friend—for I would only rob you of the sweetness of your victory."

Remington gave a puzzled look.

"Winter stole your honor and your dignity," Alexander explained in earnest. "She took that from *you*—so *you* and *you alone* need to get it back from her. And when you do, your victory will be complete. You will have won, and you will have done it all yourself." He drew Remington's attention again down the stairs. "You go down there, and you demand that she apologize. You demand from her the respect you deserve—and you'll get it!"

Remington smiled. "Yeah . . . The respect I deserve." He straightened his suit and nodded resolutely. "I'm gonna get what I deserve."

"You are going to get *exactly* what you deserve," Alexander reassured confidently. "Now, you know where she lives, right?"

Remington blew out derisively with his lips, ejecting flecks of spittle into the night air. "Do I know where she lives?" He howled with laughter. "What do I look like—some kinda fool or something?"

He slowly made a winding path down the steps to the Second Tier and trudged toward the Purifier Quarter, muttering the words 'respect' and 'she's gonna pay' as he went. It was dark and quiet, and the streets were all but empty. When he leaned up against a random building to calm his swimming head, a pretty face caught his eye.

"Finally . . . found you . . . and you're gonna pay." He sighed wearily as he slumped against the wall.

"Hello there, handsome," she spoke enticingly.

CHAPTER FORTY-THREE

Winter was exhausted.

The trip back to her quarters was delayed as the empty streets beckoned her to come play. She pushed herself to go faster, leap farther, and reach higher than she had before. The fulfillment within as she pushed herself beyond past limits released the much-needed endorphins.

The exertion helped to burn off the pulsing anger that she was struggling to keep down. Being accosted by that Elite child again had stirred something dangerous within her. She was also plagued by the uncertainty of what was bothering Nalara and how she might help. And on top of all that, she felt hollowed out inside at the thought of being the reason Joshua and his people might be forced to evacuate from their home. Her heart ached every time she thought of it.

There was nothing to do; there seemed no way to fix any of it. She just needed to adapt and carry on without his steadying presence.

Somehow, she would do it. She had to—or the senseless murdering would continue.

Winter reached her door and entered the code into the panel. A yellow warning signal flashed on the pad and a computerized voice spoke:

"Remove all personal items from this residence within the next twenty-four hours and report to the Purifier Main Office for room reassignment."

Well, there it was . . . the inevitable manifestation of her new reality.

Winter sighed in acceptance as the doors hissed open to the side.

Her empty chambers stretched out before her in pristine impersonality. It didn't really feel like her home at the moment. It just felt like a shell. At one point, it had been filled with a sense of comfort and achievement, but now, it was empty of anything but practicality. It was just . . . there.

Winter changed into her sleeping clothes and performed some light exercises before crawling into bed. Her head spun with possibilities, momentarily preventing her from settling into any sort of sleep.

The comforting thing was that she had orientation now. She'd fallen to as low as she could go, and now, she at least knew where she was: rock bottom. Here, she could begin the upward climb toward her new goal.

Imaginary scenarios played through her mind—scenes of citizens treated equally and fairly and of open trade with the surface humans as they worked in unity to build a good and prosperous society together. With all the surface resources and all the Olympian technology, they could be unified in creating the paradise everyone had dreamed of since formulation.

Winter's eyes closed slowly, and a smile flicked in the corner of her mouth as she slowly drifted into sleep.

If she took the challenges of her goal one day at a time, she knew it was possible.

Eventually, the Sovereign and his lies would be exposed. Even if it took her the rest of her life, she knew she would fight to bring the truth to Olympus with the same relentless tenacity she had fought to be the greatest Purifier of her generation.

She swore that she'd see the day when her people were set free.

"I have sworn upon the altar of God . . ." she whispered with a deep yawn. "Eternal hostility against every form of tyranny . . ." Another yawn. " . . . Over the mind of man."

Sleep took her gently, transitioning seamlessly from her positive thoughts to empty and peaceful unconsciousness. She was not troubled by dreams or restlessness. She felt calm and comfortable. She finally had her footing to begin achieving what she'd tortured herself about for weeks now.

Winter's eyes opened.

She was unsure how many hours of sleep she'd been able to capture, but her rest was poignantly disturbed by something unknown. The stillness was paramount. Nothing seemed amiss; there wasn't even movement out in the hallway.

Consciousness slowly came to her as she blinked. Gradually becoming aware of her room, Winter felt like she was in a vacuum—no sound or movement. Everything was completely and utterly quiet.

Her practicality told her she was being ridiculous, but her instincts begged her to take action.

Winter shifted silently out of bed, gracefully transitioning flat against the wall without making a sound just as the front door hissed open and heavy feet—many of them—infiltrated her apartment.

Sliding silently to the doorway of the bedroom, Winter waited.

Whoever they were, she could tell they moved in formation—which meant they were most likely armed. They fanned out and progressed directly to the bedroom.

Suppressing her breath and adrenaline until the first one was past the threshold, Winter paused so she could see what she was up against.

It was dark, but she could tell they wielded unfamiliar weapons, metal rods with electric prongs at one end. She could just make out their faces.

Purifiers!

The first one went directly to the bed and checked the covers.

"Negative!" Warlord from the Hellhounds hissed. "She's not here."

A second figure entered the room.

Move forward!

Winter materialized from the shadows and planted her foot directly to the second's face.

A cry of pain, a splatter of blood, and Winter instantly switched to high precision mode. She wrapped her arm around the face she'd just struck—recognizing him as Specter from the Dragon Slayers—and threw him into Warlord near the bed. Not pausing, she launched at them, stepped on Specter's back to kick Warlord hard in the face. She landed on the bed as a third attacker rushed into the room. Titan from the Black Ghosts charged her, arcing the unfamiliar weapon at her face; sparks flew from the prongs as he lunged. She grabbed the bed sheet and whipped it around his arm. The flickering, buzzing weapon hung useless in the air as she twisted around, leading the arm behind her until it reached the end of its range—then snapped!

With a scream of pain, Titan crumbled into a heap, cradling his arm.

Winter charged the doorway and met another Purifier: Judge from the Iron Raiders. He thrust another weapon forward. Blinding sparks flew past her face as she dodged to the side. She wrapped an arm around his face and twist-stepped, changing places with him before pulling with all her bodyweight to bring his face into the doorframe.

Blood dribbled from his impacted face and he bellowed in pained fury.

Massive arms wrapped around Winter's shoulders from behind and crushed inward. Taken by surprise at their strength, it took a beat to regain her breath as the person lifted her clear off the ground.

Winter relaxed her arms and exhaled. Shifting her shoulders to hitch slightly within his grip, she whipped her hand at his groin and found her footing as he collapsed forward, gasping. The Guardian that had grabbed her didn't have time to regain his composure before she struck him with her elbow hard across the jaw.

Two more Guardians lumbered forward, hands first.

Winter dashed forward and whipped around, sliding to the floor as she swept the feet out from under one of them while evading the grasp of the other.

She had a straight shot to the door and ran to it, not wasting any time as the intruders all scrambled to regroup.

She hit the button on the door panel and glanced over her shoulder in mounting panic.

The doors hissed to the side and the Master Purifier's scowling face met her gaze.

Winter, stunned in confusion by years of conditioning, was unable to press her escape now faced with her commanding officer. The reality of his presence became suddenly clear as Wraith kicked her hard in the middle and sent her careening back into the living chambers. She rolled and bounced to a stop, gasping desperately to collect herself after the stunning blow.

Wraith stepped inside, his enormous frame filling the doorway.

"Reckoning time, Winterton," he growled.

Winter shook her head and found her feet again, snapping back to a fighting posture. She advanced fast, running and jumping into a flying punch at his face. It connected. Wraith grunted, but was undaunted. He returned with a massive blow.

Lights exploded in Winter's head, and she tasted blood.

She recoiled and latched onto his face with both hands and jumped to knee him in the head twice before he shoved her away. She used his push to propel her momentum into a wide spinning back kick to his head.

Wraith wavered only slightly. "Not this time," he snarled, grabbing her by the arms and violently tossing her against the wall.

With adrenaline helping to mask the pain, she hit the ground and rolled to her feet to again face her aggressor.

Thumping sounds from behind telegraphed the approach of the Guardians, and Winter felt a sharp stab at her waist. When she put her hand there to investigate, she pulled out a tiny dart and her vision blurred.

The Guardians grabbed at her, but she was still too fast.

Desperate to get out to the hall, she threw herself at Wraith again, dodging the giant hands that swiped at her.

Her flurry of attacks and circle-stepping gave her a window of opportunity, but she failed to see Specter and Warlord close in from the bedroom.

"For Sovereign's sake, use the bolt staves!" Wraith shouted as his hand-to-hand with Winter continued.

The strange weapons made contact with her bare flesh and sent jolts of electricity through her whole body. Winter lost control of her limbs as they shocked straight. Wraith took hold and threw her against the kitchen counter. Warlord seized her throat and held her down.

Lungs burning and body shaking from the shock of the bolt staves, she winced and choked against the stranglehold. She jabbed Warlord in the throat hard and caused his grip to fail.

"What is this?" Winter demanded once his hand was off her neck.

"Judgment." Wraith wiped some blood from his lip as Specter produced electromagnetic bracers.

He approached and reached for Winter's wrists, but she snapped into motion, shifting Specter's weight off-center and grabbing the mag braces in one motion. She fought through the mounting vertigo and struck Warlord in the face with the braces as he grabbed for her again; simultaneously, she buckled Specter's knee with a sharp downward kick.

He screamed.

Wraith seized a giant handful of her hair and punched her hard in the torso.

Winter grunted in pain as she felt a rib displace. She channeled the pain into rage and wrapped her arm around his. She pulled upward sharply in an attempt to dislocate his arm, but his massive size was insurmountable.

"Enough!" Wraith brought her face down hard into the countertop, cracking it.

Specter, crying out in pain, called for backup.

The injured but unrelenting Purifiers closed in around her.

Winter saw her own blood pool on the counter beneath her. She kicked hard behind her and checked Wraith in the armpit, weakening his grip. She shifted as his grip eased and twisted out of his grasp, coming to stand again.

She roared and lunged forward, channeling all her pain and strength into a powerful elbow strike to his head.

Wraith stumbled back in a daze as the blow connected and blood dribbled from his chin.

The backup rushed in with their bolt staves and the Guardians with their arms wide.

Winter paused.

It was only a moment.

The dark room went blurry once more and her knees felt weak.

Should she stop fighting . . .?

The sound of her own breath echoed in her ears as the world around her slowed. If she stopped fighting, what would happen to her? If she continued fighting, what would happen to her comrades? She knew what she was capable of; she knew what a student of the old art taught by Eagle Eyes could do. The moral quandary of her predicament thumped in her mind like a hollow drumbeat.

Winter set her jaw.

A flurry of motion—jaws cracked, knees buckled, and blood spattered the floor as she tore into them like a demon unchained. She could feel the effects of the dart dulling her senses, but she refused to give in and submit. The room filled with desperation and screams of pain. Back and forth, she flew from one opponent to the next in cold efficiency, wreaking gruesome devastation upon all with whom she connected.

The realization of her folly came suddenly.

Her focus was off.

She should have carved a way to the door and made escape her priority—not this meaningless destruction. She should have seen the whole picture.

Open gaze . . . See everything . . .

She'd failed.

Locked in combat, completely consumed with the attack, she didn't see one of them slip her guard with a bolt staff and fill her limbs with jolting electricity.

A Guardian charged and barreled her over, crushing her to the ground. The Purifiers piled in and jolted her again and again with their weapons.

Winter's body locked up. Her limbs were completely unresponsive amid the constant barrage of electric shock; she could not even draw breath with the massive Guardian atop her.

Her vision faded in and out as she screamed with her last breath at the brutal, relentless onslaught.

Wraith approached and kicked her in the face. Fireworks exploded in her head, and her vision went black as blood trickled into her eyes. She struggled, but the application of more bolt staves ensured she was unable to move. Judge ground his knee into her ear and pulled her arms behind her back while Specter snapped on the mag braces.

The level of pain in her head was unbearable. She trembled from the exhaustion of aftershock and adrenaline. Small wisps of steam rose from the contact points of the searing electricity. Her face throbbed and stung sharply. Her lungs felt heavy and her breathing labored as the effects of the tranquilizer finally took full hold.

"That's it, stand her up!" Wraith barked.

Winter was almost limp as the two Guardians pulled her to her feet. She stood on weak legs and painfully swallowed a mouthful of blood.

"Surprised?" Wraith taunted, though purposefully remaining outside her range.

Winter blinked hard, trying to clear her eyes. The room was spinning.

The battered Purifiers gathered around, staring at her—Warlord, Specter, Judge, Titan—scowling with bloodied faces.

"Blight me," Titan groaned, holding his dislocated arm. "What in Zeus' name was that?"

Winter slumped as her legs gave out. She was at a complete loss. All these top achievers had trained with her, had served with her. Wraith's hatred was commonplace at this point, but why would the rest of these Purifiers attack her like this?

"I . . . don't understand," Winter gasped out. "Why . . .?"

"January Winterton," the Master Purifier sneered. "By order of the Grand Elite of Olympus, you are under arrest." He snapped at the Guardians. "Bring her." He exited the residence.

The Purifiers followed closely, each staring down Winter as they limped by, their eyes full of hatred and scorn. Judge roughly pulled a black bag over her head, then struck her in the face with a single, final vindictive jab.

Winter gasped for air and fought for any sense inside the stuffy cowl.

How could this be happening?

Truth and liberty felt a lot like defeat now . . . and they tasted like blood.

CHAPTER FORTY-FOUR

Indiscernible buzzing and churning filled Winter's senses. She could tell it was the dead of night. Nothing but thick blackness filled her vision when she was able to hold open her eyes. Her rushing escorts' footfalls were the only sound on the street. In her half-conscious, tranquilized delirium, she couldn't move a muscle to hinder their passage.

The miserable throbbing in her face made everything else distant and intangible. The musty smell inside the cowl over her face was the only tangible thing she could sense, other than the waves of pain—so intense that they made her wince and clench her teeth against them.

Her escorts didn't utter a word. Their focus was on the speed of their passage. They had obviously coordinated and planned this carefully.

Through the swirling dizziness of the tranquilizer, Winter forced her mind to focus. She knew the Second Tier so well that, after a moment to gain her bearings, she was able to map out in her mind exactly where they were going. She knew the steps leading into the Hive; she knew the doorway to the understage.

At the moment they were to pass over the threshold, Winter summoned all her strength and faculties in an attempt to wrench from their grip. She shifted her shoulders and braced her feet against the door frame.

The Guardians halted short and nearly lost their grip. Winter twisted and shoved against the door frame with all her might, but in her tranquilized, brutalized state it was not nearly enough.

Someone behind her grabbed a handful of hair through the cowl while another pulsed her full of lightning with a bolt staff.

Winter screamed through clenched teeth.

The Guardians dropped her as the shockwaves jolted their hands.

She fell hard on the tile, but even in her weakened state, she refused to give in. She immediately scrambled to find her footing, but with her wrists secured behind her back and her face obscured by the cowl, it was impossible to do before being shocked by their bolt staves again and again.

Her body went rigid with the excruciating electricity. She relaxed as the merciless onslaught ceased when Wraith's voice commanded, "Enough! Just get her in there."

Winter shook and panted as hands gripped her all over and hauled her limp body through the doorway.

Her breath came only in stuttered gasps, and her limbs twitched with aftershock. She lost consciousness for a brief moment . . . or maybe several minutes. When she regained awareness, she was on her knees, pinned up against a wall by her shoulders while they paired the mag braces to the surface behind her. Once paired, the braces were immovable. Their hands released her suddenly, and Winter's full weight collapsed forward as her taxed frame refused to support her. She gasped softly as footsteps shuffled around her.

She was a maelstrom inside—so full of wrath and vengeance, yet tempered by confusion and betrayal, and completely washed over by surging waves of agony and burning.

"Tell me . . . what's going on," she mustered the strength to demand.

"Shut up, betrayer!" one of the Purifiers yelled as she was kicked in the gut hard enough to drive the air from her lungs.

Winter gaped and struggled to breathe. The foreign and terrifying feeling of helplessness crept into her heart and planted seeds of worthlessness deep inside. She fought to remain in control of her senses, but the fear seemed to slowly and mercilessly strangle her like a cold noose.

"Excellent work, Master Purifier," spoke a refined, slithery voice from the doorway.

Winter knew *that* voice. She felt the noose tighten.

"Olympus truly smiles upon you this day."

"Thank you, my lord," Wraith answered, striking his fist over his heart. "Fulfilling the Sovereign's will is my only desire."

"Of course, of course," came the offhanded reply.

Within the thick blackness of the musty cowl, Winter fought to calm her breathing and collect her wits.

His footsteps approached, each noisy *tap* evincing the luxurious design of his shoes. "How damaged is she?"

Someone pulled off the bag, leaving a tangled mess of blood-matted hair in Winter's face.

She glared at her captors and clenched her jaw.

Three Guardians, four Purifiers, the Master Purifier, and Grand Elite Draven Constantine Rothgard all stood looking at her like she was some rabid, caged animal. There was a table to one side, laden with ropes, gags, and various metallic instruments too appalling to discern.

Draven's lips splayed with a maniacal smile. "Nearly there, but we'll have to bloody her up a bit more before tomorrow." He paused. "Leave us."

"But, my lord—" Wraith objected.

"Leave!" the Grand Elite roared, then added as they began to move for the door, "I require privacy."

Winter snarled in defiance and lunged violently against the restraints, causing Draven and everyone else in the room to flinch.

Draven backed off one step, then pointed to one of the Guardians. "You. Stay. Everyone else, leave!"

The single Guardian soundlessly obeyed the command, assuming a sentinel position by the door once the room cleared.

Winter's head drooped heavily as she fought the nauseating aftereffects of the tranquilizer. Through the swirling madness and the glaring white lights, she thought she recognized the statue-like sentry.

The Grand Elite licked his lips and cautiously stepped closer.

"This interaction is beneath me," he said, breaking the silence while gently sweeping the hair from her face. He appeared to be enjoying the scene in an unnatural way.

"We're . . . just animals to you." Winter tossed her head to escape his touch. She clenched her fists and strained against the electromagnetic restraints behind her.

"Hm. Certainly some more than others," Draven admitted frankly, standing over her. "But I have such *fun* with my pets." He gritted his teeth and retrieved a small knife from the table nearby. "Not many citizens of the lower tiers know this, but the Sovereign takes what he needs from the ranks of the young Elite. Coming to *know* the Sovereign is an honor reserved for only the most beautiful and delicate of his Elite sons. These boys are often given one of his creations as a show of favor with our god. I'm sure you've seen them."

His countenance shifted slightly in sick pleasure. "You remind me of my first pet—a dog the Sovereign gave me so many years ago—needy, troublesome, incessant, and entirely useless."

Winter faded backward as Draven crouched near her and inched the blade slowly toward her face.

"Was I supposed to love that pathetic creature? Care for it?" He almost laughed. "It gave me nothing. Offered me nothing." The blade touched the skin of her jaw. "The only pleasure it provided me is when I made it scream. . . . Mmmm, oh, yes. Now *that* was fun."

"Get away from me!" Winter shouted.

He smirked. "He gives you Purifiers so much power. He makes you so strong, so . . . resilient. Durable." He seized a handful of Winter's hair and wrenched her head to the side. "It feels good, doesn't it? Having all that power stripped from you?" The knife pressed into the soft tissue.

Winter struggled in vain.

"It feels good to lose your power—when you . . . give it . . . all to me." Draven looked entranced as he pressed the blade into her flesh, drawing a shallow cut.

Winter screamed through clenched teeth as a small trickle of blood trailed down her neck.

"I haven't given you *anything!*"

"Oh, but you will. One way or another, you will." Draven pulled back on her hair and held her face, though she fought against him. "I offered it to you before, but your simple little mind could not see. I offered you a place at my side, January. You could have enjoyed a life of unthinkable luxury and unbridled pleasure." He pulled her face very close. "All you had to do was beg me, and it would have been yours. I would have made all this go away."

He held her eyes with his for a terrifying moment. In his dark eyes, Winter could see the truth of Olympus' Grand Elite. When he had made his offer to her after the hearing, she had believed that his primary desire was only a base lust for her—seeing only some new flesh to satisfy his every physical need and whim.

But she had been wrong. She now understood.

With him, it wasn't about lust. It was about power—domineering, absolute power.

She had lied to him that day, feigning humility in order to survive, but in so doing, she had also denied him his ultimate desire.

He had wanted a new *pet.*

She had been a fool to think he'd let that go.

"And here you are, once again," Draven explained, "with your fate in my hands." His jaw trembled and his lip twitched with contempt. "And now

. . . you *are* going to beg me. I *will* have my fun with you."

Winter clenched her jaw and returned his gaze with fierce defiance. "NEVER!" she roared furiously. "I know that there are some fates worse than death! I'd rather be thrown over the edge of Olympus than to have anything to do with you."

Draven's expression melted into hot rage. With her hair still locked in his grip, he whipped her head back against the wall with a furious roar.

Once, twice . . . three times.

"Whore! Stupid, stupid whore!"

With each brutal impact, Winter saw the room go momentarily dark. Her muscles went limp. She slumped her full weight against the restraints, feeling a trickle of warm blood running down the back of her neck.

"Being thrown over the edge is far too good for you. I have something else in mind." Draven released her hair and stood up. "I've taken everything from you—your title, your rank, your prestige. I've turned the Purifiers against you. Even your own initiate has betrayed you . . ." He couldn't help but grin at Winter's puzzled expression at the statement. " . . .and you still slap my hand away? I offer you everything, and you refuse *me! The Grand Elite!*" He kicked her hard in the ribs.

Having sustained an injury there already, Winter couldn't hold back a cry of pain.

Draven grinned murderously and kicked her again, causing another scream.

"But you've chosen *this* instead!" He shouted with another kick. "Why!? Why do you resist me!?"

"Because it's all a lie!" Winter answered through the searing pain. She looked up at her bloodthirsty warden, disgust rampant in her eyes. "I've seen the truth! This war we wage is against humanity itself. There are no blighted humans on the surface!"

Draven smiled, as if taken a little by surprise.

Winter recognized in the blink of a moment as his expression betrayed yet another truth, the same truth she had caught a glimpse of when he had presented her with the drummed-up 'Survivor's Award': The Grand Elite was already fully aware.

In that moment, she wondered if the other Elites knew as well, or was it just him and the Sovereign?

Draven scoffed. "You pathetic, delusional waste! These are the lies you'd tell?"

"You know I'm not lying!" she returned defiantly. "And the greatest lie of all is that Olympus is ruled by a god—when really he's just a *mortal* man!"

Winter recognized the sudden change in Draven's expression—one of genuine confusion.

"You . . ." she began quietly, "you *do* know he's not a god, right?"

Draven seemed appalled. "You scorn and forswear our very creator?" He landed another kick, harder than any before, directly into her gut. "The Sovereign gives us life; he gives us everything! The very air we breathe is his. Your existence, even your ability to spit in his face, is all thanks to his benevolence in creating you. Zeus is a god! He is *our* god!"

Winter coughed, retching up blood. "I don't care . . . if I die . . . for speaking the truth. I know he's not. I know he's nothing but a liar . . . and I hate that I've murdered so many people in his name." Her eyes dewed with tears as she drowned beneath surging waves of physical and emotional agony. "I've seen the surface world with my own eyes. I've breathed the air—"

"You wretched liar! You imagined all this!" Draven cut her off. "Your delusions are nothing more than the ravings of a diseased lunatic."

"I have walked the surface unshielded, multiple times," Winter nearly pleaded, speaking more for her own reassurance than anything else. "I've eaten the food. I've drunk the water. And here I am—unblighted! I'm not diseased—because *there is no Blight!*"

The Guardian, Drake Rowan, looked to the Grand Elite for his reaction.

"So now you're a god, are you?" Draven laughed. "Everyone should bow down to worship the great and invincible January Winterton. Is that it? You think you're better than our Sovereign? You think you can usurp him? That people will just believe you? Follow you?"

"No! I never—"

"No one is going to believe you," Draven growled. "You're nothing!" He was becoming so impassioned that his hands shook. "No one's going to even *hear* you!" He seized a gag from the instrument table and swiftly fell to his knees.

Winter struggled against his grip as he wound the gag around her mouth and pulled it so tight that even her pressed lips couldn't keep it from forcing in-between her teeth. She cried out in pain as he roughly tied the fabric behind her head.

"Shh, shh, shhhhh . . ." he soothed gently as he stroked her blood-soaked face with a finger. "Don't cry just yet, not when there's so much left to cry for."

Winter looked into his eyes and saw a black hole. *Nothing.* The complete absence of empathy . . . remorse . . . compassion . . .

A tangible, strangling fear gripped her heart once again as she realized what someone becomes when their life is devoid of truth and their soul devoid of feeling.

Draven Constantine Rothgard was . . . pure evil.

Gagged, restrained, and helpless, Winter trembled as she actively held back her tears and bottled her rage while Draven stood again.

He crossed the room to the door and nodded to Drake, who opened it for him. The five Purifiers and two other Guardians filed back in slowly, glaring at Winter like a pack of hungry dogs.

"I'm finished here," Draven breathed in resigned disgust. "This is a very sad day for Olympus." He pointed at Winter. "This monster has just confessed to the murder of Elite Remington Adolphus Blackburn."

Winter's eyes popped wide in shock and utter confusion.

WHAT . . .!?

The Purifiers shook their heads somberly.

"It just doesn't make any sense," Titan muttered.

"Sickening," Judge growled.

"You said it," Specter agreed.

"How could one of *us* fall so low?" Warlord lamented.

"What are your orders, lord Grand Elite?" Wraith asked dutifully.

"Keep her secured. Do *not* remove the gag," Draven warned. "But do whatever you want to her." He sneered. "I just need her alive for tomorrow—but no one needs to recognize her."

Wraith's nostrils flared.

Draven moved to the exit, then turned at the threshold as if he'd forgotten something. He retrieved a spherical holo-camera from within his robes. "Oh, and be sure to record this. You'll deliver it to me when the work is done."

"By your will, great one," Wraith said with a bow, taking the holo-cam from the Grand Elite as he left the room.

The door closed, and the lock engaged.

Wraith and the others stepped toward Winter slowly.

Stranglehold.

The Master Purifier activated the holo-cam. It left his hand and hovered silently in the air, scanning and recording every inch of the room.

"Just so you know, Winterton," he revealed calmly, retrieving a bolt staff from the table laden with instruments of torture, "I'm gonna enjoy this. Very much."

Winter swallowed hard and tried to keep from shaking, but terror gripped her frame as tightly as the gag in her mouth.

CHAPTER FORTY-FIVE

Eyes closed, savoring the tantalizing sensation of his dominance, Draven stood in the Sovereign Tower's lift as it ascended on and on toward the pinnacle.

Having slept better than most nights, his mind played over every possible advantage his actions had created for him. He imagined Zeus' pleasure and favor, and what it would mean for his future. He had already arranged everything that morning, including the assembly announcements throughout all Olympus. All would gather in the Hive—First, Second, and Third Tier citizens—and in just a short while, he would solidify his position forever in the chronicles of time.

In one hand, he twirled the small sphere that had recorded the night's bloody entertainment. He was eager to view its holographic contents, but it would have to wait until he retired to his private estate.

No matter. In the Hive, a greater pleasure awaited him.

Soon, he thought, relishing in the thrill of expectation of what was to come. *Very soon.*

He tucked the holo-cam into his robes as the doors opened to the celestial penthouse. Violent coughing greeted Draven's ears as he stepped inside. Following the sound to the conference room without a word, the Grand Elite found the Sovereign with the vault door just sealing shut behind him.

Though disappointed at once again missing his opportunity to see the wonders inside that door, Draven smiled anyway.

Zeus stepped away from the vault when Draven appeared. "You did not announce yourself, my child." He tried not to sound surprised.

"Forgive me, holy majesty." Draven dipped his head. "My eagerness to be in your divine presence caused me to forget."

"Indeed." The Sovereign crossed the room, his silk-slippered feet gliding noiselessly on the marble. "Yesterday, my Purifiers discovered yet another nest. My power has just finished coursing through Olympus—incinerating all traces of the vermin."

Draven was fascinated. "You truly are the one who brings purification to all." He fawned. "Every day, I yearn to witness your purging glory."

Lord Zeus looked amused. "As it should be, young one." He set a glass syringe on the table and eased into the comfort of his massive throne. "What news do you bring?"

"Dissension and heresy, Sovereign lord," Draven spoke with flare and let the words hang dramatically. "I discovered last night that the Purifier, January Winterton, knows about the surface world. In her own words: *There is no Blight.*"

The Sovereign's wrinkled brow furrowed in vexed meditation. "And how exactly did she come to know this?"

"From what I've determined, she's been consorting with surface dwellers since the night of Derrick Zinda's Ascension. With how many . . .? That I am uncertain," Draven admitted, then was quick to add, "but you'll be pleased, lord Zeus, to know that my efforts have contained the matter." He took a step closer to the throne and bowed low. "We await only your glorious presence to purge this traitor from our midst."

The Sovereign shook his head. "I'm surprised at you, Draven. Are you not my eyes and ears among the people?" He spoke rhetorically. "It should never have gone this far."

Draven's ego was stabbed through the heart. This is not what he had in mind. He desired only praise. Correction was hateful to him.

He bowed his frame lower in hopes of drawing out a measure of mercy—and with it, commendation.

The Sovereign was silent for a moment. "Did she say anything else?"

Draven straightened, dreading to answer. "Yes . . . eternal one." He swallowed nervously, feeling Winter's lying words settle like sickening bile in the pit of his stomach. "She had the impertinence . . . the disgusting arrogance to breathe out threats against your supreme holiness, saying that you were not a god, but merely a mortal man."

Zeus' sun-like, radiant countenance darkened. His eyes filled with burning rage.

Draven shivered as he thought the room grew cold. "But," he added, "she is a traitor and speaks the lies of a traitor. After today, none will dare speak such heresies again. January Winter—"

"DO NOT!" Zeus' voice cracked like thunder, *"speak* her name in my presence. Ever! She is to be labeled 'The Heretic,' and nothing more. Is that understood?"

Draven grinned broadly at his god's judgment. "Yes, lord Zeus. Yes.

She is The Heretic, now and forever. She is a cursed parasite, the fallen one—and we all long to see you condemn and burn her out of existence."

Silence hung heavy in the throne room for a long while. The Sovereign's countenance brightened somewhat, and Draven sensed the warmth in the room finally return.

"You have always been my favorite," the Sovereign spoke at length, hiding a shaking hand beneath the folds of his golden robe. He tried to not sound winded. "My trust in you has not been misplaced. And so, I give to you the fulfillment of the task."

Draven's lips parted. He couldn't believe the momentous responsibility he'd just been granted. This changed everything.

"My holiness . . . I—"

"But mark me, Draven," the Sovereign cut him off in a stern warning. "You are to *eradicate* this Heretic fully and thoroughly. Not one speck of her heresy is to remain among my children." Leaning forward in his throne, the god of Olympus lowered his voice to apply the full gravity of his words. "It dies today. Is that clear?"

Draven couldn't hide his toothy grin. "Crystal, your eminence," he answered fervently. "I will happily carry out your command."

The Sovereign eased back and closed his eyes. "I trust you will."

Draven took the dismissal and bowed eagerly. "I will not fail you, glorious lord Zeus," he promised before taking his leave.

On the ride down, the Grand Elite trembled slightly with the exhilaration of this unexpected success. This was a greater achievement than he had dared to dream. The Sovereign granting him complete authority in a matter of such monumental significance—he could scarcely contain the powerful surge of adrenaline coursing through him.

It had been a long time since he'd felt such delectable pleasure.

He—Draven Constantine Rothgard, the Seventh ordained Grand Elite of eternal Olympus—had been granted the unilateral power to crush 'The Heretic' and reestablish order among the populace.

With such trust placed in him, it was only a matter of time before the Sovereign would take him deeper into his graces.

Perhaps, he mused enthusiastically, *unrestricted access to the Sovereign's vault is within my grasp.*

Draven laughed out loud.

At the base level of the Tower, he considered using the Sovereign's signature private entrance to the Hive—briefly. To do so would be a little blasphemous, he knew, but truly not farfetched in his mind.

All in good time.

Walking instead with the normal Elite, Draven put on his most charming and engaging smile as they migrated toward the upper Hive entrance, indifferently greeting all whom he passed. Each Elite parted way at his presence and honored the greatest among them with a bow of respect—as they should.

The ornately carved walls and gold filigrees of the Elite tier entry transitioned to the commonplace practicality of the lower citizens' living.

Draven was deeply satisfied to see the Hive already partially filled, with citizens steadily pouring in from every tier.

There at the base, separated by the class partition, he was met by the desperate gaze of that vaguely annoying little Purifier he'd used.

"My lord Grand Elite!" she called pleadingly over the echoing din of selling spectators. "Lord Grand Elite—*please!* I beg just a moment of your presence!"

Draven grinned like a feline playing with an injured rodent and diverted his course in curiosity to come stand across the divider from her.

"What is it, Purifier?"

Nalara bowed herself in half before him. "Thank you, great one, for speaking with me." She looked up with big doll-like eyes, wild and tearful. "My lord . . . is it true? Did Winter really kill that Elite?"

"The evidence is undeniable," he said in mock concern. "As you'll soon see for yourself."

She shook her head, and a tear rolled down her cheek. "I can't believe she could do this."

Draven suppressed a laugh deep inside at the sight of her horror-stricken expression. "Her hatred for Olympus and the Sovereign's blessed Elite eventually consumed her." He leaned in close and put on a grave mask. "You know it's true. After all, you were witness to her striking honored citizen Remington Adolphus Blackburn, were you not?"

Nalara's mouth fell open with no words. She nodded slowly.

"Then it shouldn't be any wonder," he concluded. "Her madness drove her to commit this terrible crime against Olympus, against the Elite, and against the Sovereign himself."

Draven turned away and approached the stage, finding it impossible to hide the cruel sneer on his lips.

Ever since she had heard the charges for which Winter was arrested, Nalara had felt like she was hanging from a cliff, desperately grasping at vain possibilities for saving her friend. Now that the Grand Elite had confirmed to her the unfathomable depths of Winter's treachery, all hope was gone.

She stared dumbfounded. Gripped by hopelessness and despair, she slumped against the dividing wall and burst into desperate tears. All she could feel was the emptiness inside, like falling into nothingness without end.

Alexander Sterling Belmont suddenly appeared on the Elite-side of the divider.

"Nalara?" he said softly. "Are you alright?"

Nalara's big teary eyes looked up at him. She sobbed silently.

Alexander's expression changed to reflect genuine concern. He looked as if he'd been cut to the core. "She wasn't just your trainer, then?" he surmised.

"No," Nalara sniffed, desperately fighting to get a handle on her emotions but failing to do so. "Winter was . . . my best friend. I don't know what's going to happen to her, and there's nothing I can do to help." She gritted her teeth as an ocean of rage and self-loathing overtook her. "I feel like such an idiot! I could have helped her! Before . . . before she went and . . ." She hung her head and wept uncontrollably.

Alexander reached over the partition and grasped her hand. "I don't know what's going to happen either. But I'll stand right here with you—as long as you need me."

Nalara looked up into his eyes and saw nothing but sincerity. It didn't stem the tides of her grief, but this one lifeline at least offered a faint glimmer of light in the cold darkness she had been plunged into.

"Blessed Elite of Sovereign Zeus! And all citizens of Olympus!" the Grand Elite's projected voice flooded the immense stadium over the loudspeakers. He stood in the center of a large stage composed of raised hexagonal tiles, twenty feet above floor level. His broad smile widened as applause met his greeting, and he turned a slow circle with arms outstretched, savoring every single second, basking in his glory. "You are here today to witness a defining yet horridly grim event in the history of our chosen people."

The audience settled in hungering fascination.

"Long have the years proceeded in peace and comfort for our fair city. In fact, I'd wager that not one of you can name an incident that disrupted our blissful way of life—not until this recent upset, when a crime of unprecedented scale and monolithic horror has taken place."

Draven paused as hushed mutterings of awe filled the Hive.

"I understand your shock," he went on, pacing across the stage. "Trust me, I share in it, as I for one cannot *comprehend* the actions of a deranged and defective piece of indiscriminate waste that has entered our beloved home—not as a menace . . . not as a villain . . . but as a hero." Draven nodded. "A *hero!*" he repeated with emphasis. "I, too, was deceived by her presence. I, too, was beguiled by her looks, her talents, and her seemingly boundless potential. The truth is, we were *all* beguiled!"

The restlessness of the crowds intensified.

"Good people of Olympus! This is to serve as a warning to us all. We must always be on guard for defectiveness and corrosion all around us—no matter the deceptively pure form in which it may manifest its hideous self."

Draven lowered his head for a brief moment, only to conceal the smirk that flitted across his lips.

"We have been given a beautiful home. We have been blessed to live above the poison and terror of the world below. Our Sovereign gives us life. He gives us peace and safety. Our Sovereign is merciful and great. And in return for our lives and happiness, he asks only for our gratitude and service." He lowered himself gently to his knees. "Let us join together now to show our gratitude for his magnanimous light!"

Chime, Chime

The intercom signaled.

Every soul in attendance followed the Grand Elite's example and dropped to their knees in unison, then raised their voices as they'd been programmed to do since formulation.

Hail to his supreme holiness.
Hail to our Sovereign ruler.
Hail to our living god.
Your name is a light to our path.
Your wisdom guides us through darkness and death.
Your power governs the whole earth.
It is to you and you alone, o gracious lord, that I swear my life, my loyalty,
and my unconditional obedience.
I swear to live for you.
I swear to die for you.
Live forever, o glorious king—for in you, we are granted life.

The intercom chimed again, and everyone returned to their seats.

"Our thanks will forever pale to his blessings," Draven reminded them as he rose to his feet. "Our thanks must be in the form of guarding these blessings. Our thanks must be to protect our home—even if that means protecting it from threats from within." He paused and hung his head dramatically. "If I could spare you this sight, I would. But all of you must witness for yourselves the ghastly effects of corruption. All of you here today are to hold these images in your hearts. I charge you in the name of our Sovereign, do not let this memory fade. For in this way, we will *together* safeguard our home from future corruption."

A buzz of approval swept through the galvanized crowd.

This is too good, the Grand Elite celebrated as his ego devoured the audience's validation.

"Blessed, favored Elite! And all lower citizens of Olympus! Hear me! Last night, we witnessed a crime of the most heinous nature, and it was our fault for not ousting this monster at the first sign of her wicked dissension. One of our Sovereign's favored children, one of our beloved own . . . was brutally murdered last night. The defective creature who perpetrated this act held no remorse, no repentance as she confessed to the vicious killing . . . Prepare yourselves."

Draven entered a command on his handheld panel, and the Hive's giant holographic projections displayed a grisly image for all to see.

The audience cringed and gasped, even screamed in horror. Several vomited on themselves and on their neighbors. Many more passed out completely.

"Many of you knew our beloved Remington Adolphus Blackburn," Draven said over the commotion. He fell silent and let the image soak in.

The projected image displayed a mortifying scene: Remington sprawled out on an apartment floor, his face and body carved almost beyond recognition, laying in a massive pool of his own blood. A close-up of his face showed deep bruising beneath the open gashes. His blank eyes stared lifelessly in unsettling stillness. Deep, gory stab wounds covered his torso. Blood spatter covered the furniture and walls surrounding the noxious image, and a blood-covered blade lay idly near the corpse.

The Elite shook their heads in disgust and muttered to one another. The middle-tier citizens erupted in tumultuous conversation. The lower-tier workers booed and hissed loudly.

"Unspeakable! Unthinkable! *Unimaginable!*" Draven's voice boomed loudly across the Hive. "And where, I ask you, was Elite Remington's body discovered?" His voice dipped low to utter the cursed name of The Heretic. "None other than in the living chambers belonging to the Purifier—January Winterton!"

Draven bathed in rapt indulgence at the crowd's revulsion.

"It's . . . it's just not possible," Nalara whimpered as the nightmarish images played in a loop.

"This is all my fault," Alexander almost whispered. "I should have sent him home!"

Nalara looked to the Elite now grasping her hand tighter than ever. "What do you mean?"

Alexander lowered his head in shame. "At the Equinox Festival last night, I first had the thought to send him home. But he was insistent! He said he needed to make Winter pay." He looked at Nalara, this time with tears rimming his eyes. "I acted stupidly. I convinced him that she owed him an apology, and I sent him down to the Second Tier to seek it." His lips trembled. "I . . . I mean . . . he was so drunk, I was certain he'd never make it to the Purifier Quarter. I believed he'd pass out long before he even got close to reaching Winter's apartment. By the morning, he'd awake in the streets to have forgotten the whole ordeal—and that was supposed to have been the end of it!"

He dared another glance upward at the revolving holographic projection of his mutilated late-friend.

"And even if he did make it," he justified with a quivering voice, "I swear by Zeus' name, I could never have imagined *this* would be the result!"

Nalara reached out her other hand and cupped it gently over their already interlocked embrace.

They stared into each other's grief-stricken, reddened eyes.

"None of us could," Nalara replied sorrowfully.

"I am sorry to expose you to such brutal and disturbing images—but it is necessary." Draven shook his head. "The unthinkable act was perpetrated by the same one who had caused violence and chaos in our streets already. Her erratic acts of brutality had already cost this innocent Elite his dignity. And now, her unchecked behavior has cost him his very life!" He waited one sickening moment longer before entering another command on the panel, and Remington's bloody image flickered in the air and disappeared.

"January Winterton," he explained, "was arrested last night after resisting with violent and destructive—flippant—dismissal of order. She assaulted her own comrades and later confessed to the killing. I think you'll agree that this wretched creature has no place among our civilized and peaceful city."

A roar of agreement filled the Hive.

Draven felt the timing was perfect and punched the appropriate command on his panel. A section of floor lifted near the center of the stage. Slowly, January Winterton herself was raised from the understage into full view of one hundred thousand fevered spectators.

The electromagnetic bracers still held her immovably against the pillar, kneeling.

She was practically unrecognizable.

The audience howled deafeningly at the sight of her. The mob mentality had whipped them into a madness. Even former fans and Archangel comrades called out for her death.

"Murderer! *Murderer!*" Viper hissed.

"You're a disgrace to all Purifiers, Winter!" Havoc shouted.

"Sovereign curse you forever!" Savage screamed.

"Traitor to our god!" Sapphire yelled.

"I hope you rot in Tartarus for this!" Bulletproof condemned.

"Y-yeah!" initiate Mason Howell joined in. "Rot . . . you evil scum!"

Scorch buried his face in his hands and sobbed bitterly. "How? . . . Why would you do this, Winter?"

"Best. Day. *Ever,*" Wraith, the Master Purifier, whispered with a grin.

Beaten within an inch of her life, Winter's face was bloodied and swollen, contorted and broken. Her arms and legs bore dozens of superficial tears and dark bruises. Her hair was filled with caked blood, and her face was bound by a brutally tight gag.

She didn't even look human.

"Look, citizens of Olympus!" Draven's voice resounded. He smiled deeply, the thrill of power surging wildly in his heart. "Look upon the face of treason and heresy!"

CHAPTER FORTY-SIX

P*ain* . . .
Every moment that passed was a victory over death. Every beat of her heart and every breath she forced into her lungs was one more moment Winter refused to succumb to the mind-numbing pain that consumed her being. Fire burned deep inside her chest, inescapable and maddening. The room in which she was left alone for hours unthinkable was dark as pitch. She couldn't even see the floor beneath her face as she hung forward against the vice of the mag braces that held her fast.

It had been forever since she felt any sensation at all in her legs. It was probably a blessing for the beating they'd sustained. The endless torture, the mindless brutality . . . seemed to never end—until suddenly, it did, and her sweaty and satisfied attackers left her utterly alone with the pain.

The pain . . .

Ebbing and flowing black tides continuously crashing down. An ocean of unrelenting agony.

Winter had always assumed that there was a certain threshold of torment that the mind couldn't cross. She thought that once the body reached a certain register, it would all be the same after that . . . but she had discovered she was wrong. The chilling curve of agony continuously rose and rose with every passing hour—even after the torture had ceased. No sweet unconsciousness took her away from it; no threshold was reached where she could grit down and bear it. Pain she could have never comprehended consumed her body and throbbed through every inch of her frame.

Salty tears stung her abused face as they trickled down her cheeks—at least they had for the first few hours. Now, there were no tears left, and her body simply shook with agony.

The endless hours of solitude played with her mind; the consuming blackness gnawed at her sanity. She imagined darkly that had she been formulated as anything other than a Purifier, death would have arrived long ago to claim its prize.

Winter cursed her fate silently.

She valued her life, and something deep inside—whether it was courage or dogged determination or simply raw stubbornness—kept her clinging to the weakening thread of it, but there was an ever-growing part of her that wished to let go. At this point, death wouldn't be a punishment, but a release.

When the muffled sound of movement first began, Winter nearly jumped out of her skin. Her heightened senses magnified every footfall as the Hive overhead filled steadily with what sounded like a brimming full house. She recognized the stage above being rearranged—the subtle grinding of hexagonal tiles. She latched onto the sounds with her heart and mind, refusing to focus on anything but the distant thumping of feet and the soft murmur of voices as thousands of them conversed somewhere overhead—anything to distract her from the surging waves of pain.

At length, the loudspeaker blared with such volume that the walls around her vibrated. Winter started and cried out at the explosion of sound, but she couldn't make out the words being spoken. It was so unnatural and unsettling—the feeling that clouded her mind as she tried to listen. She could almost believe that she had fallen asleep and was experiencing a nightmare. There were people just outside the reach of her perception; there was darkness so thick that there was no difference when her eyes were opened or closed, and for several disconcerting minutes, she could not quite determine if she was actually awake or asleep.

The answer became blatant when suddenly, the tiles on the ceiling shifted, flooding her vision with blinding light. Squinting against the sharp assault on her senses, she struggled to lift the weight of her head as the tiles beneath and behind her began to steadily rise.

Along with the searing flood of light came an overwhelming rush of audible madness. The packed stadium echoed with disparaging howls of hatred.

Winter remained as still as possible, realizing suddenly that she was the one on display here in the center of the Hive. The Grand Elite of Olympus stood several paces off to one side, gesturing to her and shaking his head. Powerless to make it end, she stifled her shaking hands and forced herself to bear it with whatever dignity she had left.

Because her vision was blurred and obscured by swollen eyes and blood-matted hair, she was unable to identify any individuals in the distant crowd.

"Look upon the face of treason and heresy!" Draven exuded self-satisfaction; his voice washed over the Hive speakers and quieted the crowd somewhat. "This . . . this *thing* dismisses the order and wisdom of our dear Sovereign. As you've all witnessed with your own eyes, she viciously assassinated one of our own beloved—and we know her to be murderer!" He waved an outstretched arm over the crowds, pointing with a finger. "Aside from the fact that Elite Remington's body was found in her own living chambers, how many of you saw her assault him in the gardens only a few days ago?"

A small outburst issued from both the Elite and the working-class seats.

"And how many of you witnessed the embarrassing display last night at the Equinox Festival?"

A giant chorus of agreement from Elites and Purifiers flooded the air.

Winter bit down on the gag and tried to swallow, only to find her throat too parched to successfully complete the task. She couldn't remember the taste of anything other than blood.

"But, apparently," the Grand Elite continued, "for this loathsome, contemptible creature, physical aggressions and public humiliations would not be enough." He spun around and pointed at Winter accusingly. "Nothing would satisfy her insatiable bloodlust until he lay DEAD AT HER FEET!"

As the crowds roared in unbridled hatred, Draven strode victoriously past his victim. Tapping a single command on his control screen to switch off his microphone, he spoke just loud enough for Winter to hear: "I promised I would have my *fun* with you—one way or another. And now, here we are . . . having fun."

Winter had already come to the realization that the Grand Elite was pure evil—but it was impossible for her to fathom the true depths of his malevolence.

All she knew was this is what he had planned. This was the game he would play with his pet.

Draven switched his microphone back on to again address his audience. "All of you here today are blessed and enlightened by our Sovereign. He gives us good, comfortable, meaningful lives. How does it feel to have one so blessed spit in the face of our great god?"

The Hive reverberated with their thunderous howling.

"How does it feel to live your vocations to the best of your ability, only to see this pariah throw aside the gifts she was given—to squander and abuse her blessings to such an unthinkable degree?"

His audience renewed their cries of disapproval.

Draven lifted his arms to the shrieking masses. "I ask you, dear and honorable citizens of Olympus, those who worship our beloved Zeus without guile or treachery in your hearts—what is to be done with such a sickening pestilence? What fate would be just for this vile Heretic!?"

"DEATH! DEATH! DEATH!" the bloodthirsty crowds took up the chant as five giant Guardians joined the Grand Elite onstage.

"No," Nalara whispered, gripping Alexander's hand even tighter. "No, no, no . . . This can't be happening—it just *can't* be happening!" Just when she had felt there were no more tears to cry, another dam broke wide open within her heart and released its reservoir in a torrent of uncontrollable sobbing.

Alexander reached over the partition and gently guided her head to rest against his shoulder.

Nalara complied without any resistance, where she cried . . . and cried.

From his seat among the Purifiers, Scorch looked around at his companions shouting the death chant and felt sick.

"It's just not fair," he mourned softly as a single tear rolled down his cheek. "Why'd you have to go and do it, Winter? Why?"

First, he thought bitterly, *I lose Samantha. And now, I'm gonna lose you.*

"It's just not fair," he repeated in a whisper as the crowds chanted on and on.

Lev 'Boom' Sellers, captain of the War Wolves, shook his head dejectedly.

Nothing about this seemed right—*real* even. On his left hand and on his right, his teammates shouted the call of *"DEATH! DEATH! DEATH!"* with the rest of Olympus.

Only one month ago, it had been Winter of the Archangels who had saved them from a certain and unspeakable fate at the hands of a vicious horde of blighters.

And now . . . they were living proof of their namesake: War Wolves.

Like a pack of wild dogs, with a ravenous hunger for blood in their eyes, they howled for the death of the 'Angel' they owed their very lives to.

Unreal.

Depressed and heartbroken, Boom wordlessly stared on in disbelief as the mindless droning of the mob drowned out all memory of when Winter had been the best of them.

As Olympus chanted on, Draven paused to enter the appropriate commands on his panel. He made no effort to hide his grinning face as a platform rose steadily from the understage, laden with the tools of his malfeasance.

Winter's skin began to crawl, and an otherworldly chill ran down her spine as she viewed the strange items. Arranged in perfectly straight lines atop the platform sat an old rusted knife, some dull shears, and an odd-looking short metal rod with a round disc at one end. She also recognized the bolt staff on the table with the other items.

On its own platform, separated from the rest of the objects, also lay the glistening Ascension blade—the mark and most celebrated aspiration of the Purifier class.

"This monster refuses the Sovereign's way and order," Draven spoke authoritatively, bringing his audience's death chant to an end. "She laughs in the face of your dedication! She does not wish to be counted among the blessed. She has made the choice to be a cursed child of Hades instead of an honored child of Zeus. Therefore . . . it is our divinely commissioned responsibility to separate this abomination from us!"

A roar of satisfaction filled the Hive.

Winter gasped involuntarily when the Guardians grabbed her by the shoulders and unpaired the mag braces from the pillar.

"We must . . . *alter* her from the blessed," Draven sneered with a maniacal smile, "that we might discern this filth and not be led astray." He turned from the cheering crowd. "Bring her," he commanded the Guardians and approached the table.

Winter's numb legs suddenly shocked and radiated with burning, throbbing pain as the Guardians lifted her up. Her lifeless feet dragged beneath her limb body. She couldn't run; she could barely struggle with their grip as they hauled her toward the harrowing instruments.

"The Sovereign gives freely to his faithful," Draven reminded the multitude. "And when his gifts are spurned, they can be taken away." He picked up the shears and gestured to the Guardians.

The massive hands forced Winter to double over, pushing her head down so that her long raven tresses fell before her face.

"Deny the gifts and calling of our dear Sovereign, and you deny your identity as one of his children," the Grand Elite spoke over the boisterous crowd. "Deny being one of his children, and you become nothing more than a craven animal!" He gripped a handful of Winter's thick hair and roughly sheared it off with a grinding, clanging *thwack.*

Thwack, thwack . . .

The cruel scissors chewed through her tresses, and Winter lost all sense of the moment. She couldn't breathe.

Was this really happening?

As Draven worked through handful after handful, Winter watched in horror as long strands of her beautiful black hair fell to the stage floor. She couldn't believe it, even as she flinched in pain when the shears nicked her scalp over and over.

She screamed desperately into the gag, but no one heard her. No one would make it stop.

Thwack, thwack . . .

More painful than the cutting into her scalp with the careless shearing was the feeling of something inside her die as the blood-matted ebony locks fell one after the other in ragged clumps.

Almost as if every effort and every accomplishment of her life was represented by the once-beautiful strands, she watched them fall. All her medals in the FMQ . . . all her commendations as a Purifier . . . every drop of sweat . . . every drop of blood . . . it fell to the floor in black piles of failure and regret.

As he had told her, Draven had taken *everything* from her.

Even this.

Even herself.

Winter had thought that there were some things that would never change—some things that could never be taken away. She had been wrong.

The crowd grew wild with carnal gratification. To see her suffer whipped them into laughter and cheering of the most scornful, base nature.

Draven was neither careful nor thorough in his task and left her head a tufted, sliced up mess.

Winter felt warm blood trickle down her scalp.

Draven dropped the instrument on the table. "Stand her up," he commanded the Guardians.

They roughly seized her chin and hauled her up for the cheering multitude to see.

For one brief, desperate moment, Winter looked up to the Ascended statues ringing the uppermost level of the Hive. She saw the glistening white statues of Nereza 'Nightmare' Vossen and Derrick 'Eagle Eyes' Zinda. In her heart, she couldn't help but cry out to them.

Help me! she wailed silently.

But her former hero Nereza and former mentor Derrick remained silent and motionless.

Please! PLEASE help me!

No answer.

Winter's heart broke. They would not answer her cries. Even they had forsaken her.

"There can be no quarter for the unfaithful!" Draven triumphed to the ecstatic crowd. "Shorn like an animal for the slaughter, this wretched thing will know no mercy for the indignity she has inflicted upon our way of life! Just as she showed no mercy for the Elite son of Zeus whom she murdered in cold blood."

Draven replaced the shears on the table and took up the bolt staff. As the audience erupted into another series of derisive ridicule toward Winter, Draven switched the controls so that his voice was no longer projected over the stadium. "You recognize these . . ." He smiled at Winter. "Such outdated and crude instruments—more conducive to pain than efficiency—the *perfect* instrument to punish my disobedient pet."

Winter bit down into the gag, baring her teeth and bloodied gums. Able to finally move her feet, she stretched and rolled her ankles as the Guardians dragged her to the table and held her face-down against the surface. Her eyes were parallel to the strange iron shaft with the disc at one end.

The crowds hummed in surprise as Draven activated the bolt staff and sparks flew from the arcing electric connection.

Winter flinched as he brought the torturous instrument within inches of her face and held it against the iron disc surface. Wincing against the growing heat, she struggled to be free of the hands holding her face to the table while the disc steadily grew red hot.

Draven's smile drew up watching Winter's desperation mount as the heated metal began to glow.

All five Guardians gathered around when Draven nodded to them. Winter saw the face of Drake Rowan, the one Guardian she knew, among them. He joined in dutifully as they worked together to hold her against the table.

They disengaged the mag braces and Winter felt circulation reach her fingers. At the moment of her release, she found a tiny spark of willpower to fight back. She lashed and struggled violently, but in her weakened state, even her best efforts were pitiable.

One Guardian on either side gripped a shoulder each and held her in place down on her knees. One pulled her left hand out to the side. Two of them seized her right hand and forced it flat against the platform's surface.

With her palm down, Winter could see the mark of the Purifiers on the back of her hand—the Ascension blade wreathed in tongues of red flame. How much pride she once had in its appearance, how very settled she had once been in the identity it gave her, and how it had once filled her with such gratitude to salute her fist over her heart to her 'god'. The image that had once prescribed her entire purpose in life was now the only thing left of her Purifier being.

Draven activated a holo-cam and held up the searing-hot brand. Holographic projectors displayed the unknown symbol for all Olympus to see.

Draven's voice reengaged over the loudspeakers. He pointed to the symbol on the glowing red disc at the end of the rod. "Good citizens of Olympus . . . *biohazard,* they once called this."

He held his audience in rapt attention.

"In the world that existed before," he explained, "this symbol was used as a warning, to protect the populace from being exposed to harmful and corrosive and deadly substances. Anything marked as a 'biohazard' was recognized as something to be avoided at all costs. To come in contact with a 'biohazard' was to risk a horrible, agonizing death."

Draven lowered the brand close to Winter's right hand.

Her eyes widened in alarm.

He wouldn't.

The sudden, horrifying thought crossed her mind—and then another came just as sudden and just as horrifying.

Yes . . . he would.

"If we are to successfully purge this demon from our midst," Draven spoke with tangible disgust, "we must first purge her from among the ranks of our dear Sovereign's honorary Purifiers. By order of Sovereign Zeus himself, January Winterton is no longer to be remembered as a Purifier of Olympus. She is only to be remembered as 'The Heretic', as she *is* this dangerous biohazard that we fear. And in order to remove the sacred symbol of the Purifier class from her, we shall purge her cursed flesh with iron—and with fire!"

The Grand Elite swiftly brought the brand down roughly into the back of Winter's hand, searing her flesh and destroying the Purifier's mark.

Shrieking in agony, though muffled by the gag, Winter thrashed wildly for relief, but it was to no avail as the Guardians held her fast. Her tissue sizzled and popped as tiny flames licked upward.

The merciless audience clapped and hollered in approval.

Draven gave one extra, vindictive push to the brand before pulling it from her.

Winter's vision went black for a moment, and then her frame relaxed, shuddering with pain as she gasped for air. New tears streaked down the old blood on her face. She fought to hold her focus and refused to relinquish consciousness.

Draven returned the brand, smoking with burnt flesh, to the platform and turned to the Guardians. "Hold her up. Let the people look upon The Heretic."

They hauled her upright. The holo-cam captured the grisly scene for the Hive's projectors to display a close-up of her hand's disfigured, charred skin.

All Olympus resounded with gratification.

"How did that feel?" one of the Guardians coldly chuckled into her ear.

Winter channeled her mind to focus on bringing life back to her legs, blocking out the sickening smell of her own burnt flesh. She began working and writhing her lips and jaw in an attempt to loosen the gag.

Draven addressed the fanatical mob. "Here you see where once a Purifier bore the sacred mark of her class, now bears a symbol of scorn and desecration and plague." He pointed to Winter's mutilated hand and the raw, bright red branding of the 'biohazard' covering her Purifier mark.

Draven turned away to goad the surging mass, and the Guardians dropped her in disinterest. Winter's limp, shaking form hit the arena floor hard.

They didn't even recognize her as a person anymore.

She was just a *thing*—a piece of discarded waste.

Winter flexed her legs, encouraging the blood to return. She was going to die today; she knew and accepted that fact. There was no way to avoid it or flee from it; she could only embrace it.

But before she died, if only her voice could somehow be heard—maybe . . . *maybe* someone would hear the truth. If it was her fate to die, she surged with a sudden, overwhelming determination to make certain the truth did not die with her.

Draven continued his droning on and on to his adoring audience. He spoke of honors and glory in the life to come. He pandered to the hype-crazed multitude, catering to their base hatred and lust for entertainment.

He paused, and Winter knew the moment had come. It was now or never. Drawing upon every last ounce of strength she had left, she pushed up from the arena floor, gripped the cruel gag in her mouth and torqued her head to fully escape it.

Ignoring the aching of her cracked ribs, Winter drew a deep breath and shouted for every single soul to hear:

"MY EYES ARE OPEN!"

Draven stopped short, and all Olympus fell silent as 'The Heretic's' strong voice echoed throughout the Hive.

"I see the truth!" she spoke quickly but projected forcefully. "You're all prisoners to the Sovereign's lies! Zeus is *not* a god!"

"Shut her up!" Draven shouted over the loudspeakers. "NOW!"

"He's just a man with amassed power because of your blindness!"

The nearest Guardian raced over and kicked her in the stomach.

Winter coughed violently, but even through the agonizing pain, an indomitable resolve won out. She was dead anyway; this was her one and only moment. The opportunity to free the minds of her people would never come again.

"Everything you know is a lie! There is no Blight on the surface!"

Two Guardians laid hands on her and pulled her up while another struck her hard in the face.

With a surge of adrenaline masking the pain, Winter struggled against their grip, fully supported by her own legs now. She shifted her shoulders and experimented with their strength.

"I know the truth!" she shouted desperately. *"My eyes are open! Open yours!"*

A fourth Guardian, with arms the size of tree-trunks, drove the wind from her lungs with a single, stunning fist to the pit of her stomach.

Winter gaped, and her middle seized in fruitless desperation to draw breath. The gag was again shoved into her mouth and quickly retied.

She fought a desperate, losing battle to breathe, but the air refused to come. The lights and noise of the Hive suddenly retreated into a distant pinpoint of light and sound as all faded into darkness . . .

. . . and peace.

At long last, in one agonizing instant, air rushed into her lungs, and she was jolted back into a world flooded by hatred and torment. She ached all over. Every short, labored breath racked her body in excruciating pain.

In that moment, she wished to go back into that quiet darkness.

Soon . . .

Draven paused for only a moment before turning back to his stunned audience. "You see!?" he exclaimed. "This only proves it! This proves that she is, in fact, *The Heretic*—a scourge upon our blissful society!"

Several voices rang out, gradually followed by more and more.

"These are the lies this despicable creature would tell!" Draven incited them again once he had their attention. "You've now heard it with your own ears! She even speaks blasphemies against most holy Zeus himself!"

With that, Olympus was again in an uproar, reviving the chant of:

"DEATH! DEATH! DEATH!"

Winter's heart sank, not because she knew she was about to die. She was filled with a deep hurt for her people. There really was no hope for them. Her one final attempt to reach them with the truth had failed. The lies imprisoning their minds were simply too strong, the chains too reinforced for even the sharpest of truths to cut through.

As the Guardians dragged her back to the pillar, Winter mourned for her people. How easily the Grand Elite was able to win them over. Her words had been drowned by his. She now knew that all Olympians would remain the Sovereign's slaves forever.

She would soon be dead, and despite her best efforts, the truth would die with her.

Winter's eyes met briefly with Drake's as he assisted in securing her to the pillar. A curious melancholy emoted from them.

She didn't really take notice as the giant Guardian paired the mag braces to the pillar, but suddenly took interest when he failed to secure them around her wrists.

Her hands floating behind her back, Drake Rowan—First Lieutenant of the Elite Guard Order—pushed her against the pillar, one large hand on her chest. Their gaze collided for only an instant, where Winter saw something in his eyes she never could have expected: He knew exactly what he'd just done.

Winter stood dumbfounded and motionless as Drake stepped back nonchalantly to stand with the other four Guardians.

Her mouth fell open.

Was . . . was this real . . . ?

Winter tested her fingers and slowly rolled her wrists, finding them unbound.

Her mind raced as her eyes darted through the Hive's ascending terrain.

This sudden, startling development changed everything.

She swallowed and tried to quiet her heart.

Draven glared menacingly at her as he momentarily turned from the crowd to take up Ascension, brandishing it high above his head for all to see.

The immaculate blade shone brilliantly under the hot lights—its curved steel and razor edge framed magnificently by the golden, gemstone-studded guard and blood-red hilt.

"This . . ." Draven spoke dramatically. "This is the honor to which every worthy Purifier aspires. A blessed life given in honorable service to our Sovereign is one that merits the ultimate reward. All Purifiers who perish in their vocation spend eternity among Elysium's honored dead. But only a few—the rarest and most gifted among them—earn a place in the next life, not as a Purifier, but as a transfigured, *ascended* Elite. And this sacred blade, held by lord Zeus himself, is the doorway that transports those greatest achievers to that next life of Elitehood."

He reverently replaced Ascension back on its stand.

"That future *could* have been hers," Draven went on with a shake of his head, feigning sorrow, "had she remained faithful. But that honor has been blithely rejected by this unholy filth!" He seized the old rusty knife from the platform and approached Winter. "Filth is what she has chosen—so filth shall be her end."

The audience screamed and howled. Their frenzy and bloodlust filled the stadium with ringing evidence of their blindness to the Grand Elite's lies.

"I searched long and hard through the archives of Olympus for a fitting end to trash like January Winterton." Draven looked upon Winter with rampant disgust and loathing, gripping the decrepit blade with brimming anticipation. "I found none. And so, left to resolve one myself, I could only think to end this animal's life *by* trash—by this discarded and defiled and unworthy blade."

The Grand Elite's dark eyes were filled with a rageful hunger. "She's been beaten. She's been shorn. She's been branded. And now, the time has come!" He lifted up the ugly knife in view of one hundred thousand screaming fans.

"THIS IS THE DEATH SHE DESERVES!"

CHAPTER FORTY-SEVEN

"Thus ends the fallen Purifier, January Winterton—The Heretic!" Draven taunted mercilessly as he handed the third-tier kitchen knife with a long, serrated edge to a Guardian standing nearby. He switched off his microphone and ordered the obedient giant: "Be sure to remove the gag first. I want to hear her scream."

"With pleasure, great one." The Guardian bowed before his master.

Winter stood against the pillar, her hands still held behind her back, watching as the world slowed around her. The approaching Guardian bore murder in his eyes. The braying crowd spewed hatred from their lips. Draven's wicked glare of sick satisfaction leered over her . . . and the Ascension blade rested on the platform twenty feet away.

Winter's heart raced, her breathing quickened—but her mind narrowed into a laser-like point.

Over the din, she heard the voice of Eagle Eyes echo in her mind: *"Open gaze, Winter . . . See everything . . ."*

She was ready to seal her belief with her own blood, but that would have to be after she could fight no more. And that time was not yet.

The Guardian, gripping the knife, seized her neck and slammed her against the pillar. He grabbed the gag and ripped it from her bloodied mouth.

Winter gritted her teeth through the pain and stared him down fearlessly.

The Grand Elite's microphone was switched back on.

"SAW HER HEAD OFF!" Draven howled, and the crowd joined with him.

"DEATH! DEATH! DEATH!"

Winter felt the Guardian move to rip the repulsive blade through her throat.

Closing her eyes, centering her mind, Winter exhaled, breathing out all the tension in her body.

". . . *And* . . ." Derrick's disembodied voice drowned out all others. ". . . *Move forward.*"

Exploding into motion, she shifted her shoulders, secured the Guardian's blade-wielding wrist, and simultaneously drove her fist into his larynx with the full momentum of her bodyweight.

His grip disappeared and Winter shifted the other way, manipulating his arm forward and bringing up the knife to rip through his own neck. Blood spurted from the jagged tear. The Guardian stumbled back, leaving the knife behind in Winter's hand as he clutched his throat, trying desperately to stem the flow of blood between his fingers.

Winter's deathly-cold eyes fell on the Grand Elite of Olympus.

Draven Constantine Rothgard's smug grin disappeared.

In a split second of a snapped, blurred motion, Winter hurled the blade at him.

Draven had just enough time for his perfect, Elite face to contort in true, chilling terror as the knife spiraled through the air. He made his best effort to fall away from the menacing projectile, but its sawtoothed edge caught his face and laid it deeply open from the crest of his ear to the tip of his jawline.

The Grand Elite collapsed backward to the stage floor, cupping his blood-gushing face. His screams of pain shook the Hive over the loudspeakers.

Olympus erupted into utter panic and chaos.

Drake Rowan—calmly, quietly—turned and walked off stage.

The three other Guardians closed in, arms outstretched, eyes filled with hate.

With a feral snarl, Winter charged and collided with the nearest offender who had struck her moments before, and drove him back off his heels. She launched off of him and utilized her momentum to crash down in a driving kick to the next attacker's knee, cracking it into a ghastly sideways angle. Tucking into a roll toward the instrument platform, she evaded the slow sweeping grab of another. The first weapon she could get her hands on were the large shears, which she used with her momentum to flip around in sweeping arcs. Slinging flecks of blood in continuous, deadly spinning motions, Winter held the remaining Guardians at bay as they advanced from all sides.

Draven continued screaming as the crowds in the stands shrieked in horror and stampeded every which way.

Winter accidentally dropped the shears as two massive arms closed in around her from behind. The snide Guardian who'd made the brusque comment after her branding crushed in and lifted her from her feet. He suplexed her body into the platform, then picked her up again, seizing the back of her head. Winter was close enough; she kicked down on the long iron brand lying nearby and leveraged its end off the edge. It flipped toward her, and she caught it in hand.

Its end still slightly aglow, Winter whipped it down against the Guardian's shin, loosening his grip. She spun in the second she felt give and latched one arm around his neck. Winter shoved the brand deep into the Guardian's face with a searing sizzle. He fell back with a howl, and she slacked her grip to the end of the shaft to swing it in a wide arc upward. The iron brand connected hard with the Guardian's jaw, and he fell backward to the floor in a heap.

"How did *that* feel!?" Winter growled and moved to exit the stage.

Suddenly, she realized the floor was filling with Purifiers from every team. They blocked her escape from the main doors as armed Guardians fresh from the security checkpoints outside came rushing in. Winter hit the floor as they fired indiscriminately toward her, but hitting many in the crowd behind her.

The screaming and chaos mounted around her as Winter settled into cold practicality. She could not fight them all—not in her condition.

Ascension . . .

The thought came quickly, and she acted on it without hesitation.

Winter darted to the side and snatched up the glimmering blade, flipping over the platform for cover. As she came to stand once more, the firing Guardians came rushing in to surround her methodically.

Winter moved forward.

Her lethal dance of efficient and calculated movement cut through her attackers like grass. Blood sprayed. Limbs were cleanly severed. A few heads hit the stage with a hollow *thud* and rolled.

She wielded Ascension as if it were an extension of her own body.

So easy . . . so smooth . . . so deadly.

Winter did what she needed to do to open a clear path, leaving dismembered Guardians gasping and bleeding all over the stage floor in the wake of her dance of death. Fighting through the pain of her incarceration, sheer willpower alone pumped her aching legs toward the swiftly emptying Elite stands.

Vaulting the partition separating Elite from commoner, Winter dashed up the long stairs toward the statues of the Ascended, with several former Purifier comrades close on her heels.

The silent statues of Nereza and Derrick stared on in eternal indifference as she bolted past and came to a skidding stop at the high ledge. Winter seized Ascension between her teeth with determination and utilized a skill almost no other Purifier shared. Acting purely on instinct, she began scaling down the outside of the massive Hive wall.

A three-hundred-foot sheer drop.

Winter didn't pause to notice the Purifiers above slide to a stop and fall immediately prone above her, reaching frantically to catch hold of her before she descended out of reach.

"Go around!" someone overhead commanded. "She's climbing down! Go around!"

Winter's laser focus latched onto the wall like her strong fingertips and worked her abused, fatigued limbs in coordination. *Escape* the only thing on her mind, she didn't pause for a moment to think of what her next move would be.

Screaming and pandemonium echoed in torrents from both inside and outside the Hive. With the Hive exits blocked by fleeing, terrified Olympians of every tier and class, she knew she would have at least a minute or two before any Purifiers would be able to escape that mess.

Over the Hive's loudspeakers, Winter could still hear the Grand Elite moaning in pain.

She bit harder into the blade, regretting only that she had missed Draven's heart—if he even had one.

When her feet eventually touched down on the street, she crouched to absorb the impact. She took the blade in hand once more as she came to stand in the rising heat of late-morning.

A flood of frantic pedestrians washed out from the Hive's main exit. Some were wounded; all were in shock. Several stumbled amidst the panicked masses and were unsympathetically crushed beneath the turbulent, surging sea of flailing bodies stampeding for safety.

Winter's mind raced over every possible scenario.

Olympus was no longer her home. Branding her both literally and societally as 'The Heretic,' the Grand Elite had made sure of that. If she was to survive, she knew there was only one course of action.

The surface . . .

Growling in raw determination, she willed her body to get moving. Her legs buckled and wobbled for the first few steps, but she pushed through until they found their rhythm. The empty streets she knew so well flew past as she ran for her life. Her years of free-running aided her. With this advantage, she was able to put a good deal of distance between her and any pursuing Purifiers.

Reaching the lift in the Purifier Quarter, her hands shook with adrenaline as she entered the command and rode it down to the command deck. She knew the way so well that it was strange to fly through without procedure. The lack of a plan was a side note to her driving need to escape—to be free.

Tearing into the flight deck, Winter knew she had merely moments before her pursuers caught up. She raced to the first shuttle parked in the bay, her heart thumping with courage and her lungs anticipating that first sweet breath of freedom.

She was so close. Just a little further . . .

Her heart sank to find the cockpit hatch locked with a keypad. Winter had never seen a pilot enter a shuttle in her life; they were always just *there* by the time the Purifiers arrived.

Breathlessly, she entered a jumble of guesses into the touchscreen, receiving denial every time.

A distant sound from the Purifier hub emphasized the utter lack of time she had available.

Her eyes darted around for solutions. They fell on the Ascension blade in her hands.

With a steadying breath, Winter pulled back, winding her core, and thrust the blade forward into the hatch seam. Sharp sparks flew from the impact. Determination like fire in her eyes, she hauled to the side, leveraging the hatch open a crack. With Purifier amplified strength, and with every ounce of will she had left, she pried her fingers into the seam and pulled.

Slowly, and with great, agonizing effort, the door budged open just as heavy footfalls entered the bay.

Winter squeezed inside and glanced over the myriad of touchscreens, buttons and controls.

"The shuttle! She's in the shuttle!" an exasperated voice rang out.

"Seal off the bay!" another shouted.

Winter sat in the pilot seat and shut her eyes. She set Ascension against the control panel, then took a moment to settle her focus. Channeling her hyperawareness and perfect recall, she pored through her memory files of the hundreds of times she'd seen the pilot's hands move over the controls.

She copied his motions, mimicking without thinking and without opening her eyes.

"Fire at will!" an enraged command was given.

Electric rifle blasts rang out and exploded against the hull.

Winter flinched but refused to give up her focus. Her fingers flew, her mind scanning through each memory. With nothing more than faith and perhaps dumb luck guiding her hands, she could do nothing but hope that something would happen.

Please . . . Please! she begged.

One more memory.

One more command.

One last hope.

As deafening blasts of gunfire resounded, and several dozen more Purifiers and Guardians poured into the bay, she breathed in and entered the final command.

The craft vibrated beneath her with a familiar hum as the engines roared to life.

Winter opened her eyes and breathed out, honestly amazed that it had worked at all.

More shots rang out. Sparks of flame and shards of metal flew in every direction.

Scorch ran up to the side of the shuttle, rifle sights up.

Time slowed as she took in his earnest and bewildered face.

"Winter, stop!" he pleadingly ordered.

Her heart ached for him, a friend doomed to forever remain the Sovereign's prisoner. But not in a prison built of walls, consisting of gates and bars and locks—not a prison for his body. Rather, a prison built of lies—to encage his mind and heart and soul.

The most insidious prison of all—an invisible prison he would never think to try and escape.

In that single, breathless moment, she desperately wished things were different—that at the very least, he would choose to come with her. But she knew there was absolutely *nothing* more she could do for him or for any Olympian. They had made their choice, and now, she would have to make hers.

And she had already made it.

Scorch fingered his rifle's trigger and called out again. "Please, just stop!"

. . . No!

Winter punched the throttle. Thrusters rocketing, the shuttle lurched forward through the bay's open doors as his single, reflexive rifle blast impacted near the hatch in an explosion of glass.

Dozens more followed in distant echoes.

Shoved back by the inertia, Winter gripped the sides of the pilot seat and struggled to pull the harness over her head. Gravity and motion pushed her stomach up into her throat, and her whole body floated, weightless as the shuttle launched beyond the reach of the city's barrier and dipped sharply toward the surface world.

The frigid blast of wind from the open hatch obscured all thought and coherence. Winter's vision blurred, and her ears rang. Red lights flashed, and alarms blared.

Warning! Warning! Starboard engine severely damaged!

Through the bullet-riddled cockpit window, the sun shone brightly in an endless ocean of brilliant blue sky.

Winter fought and pulled and was just able to secure her harness as the shuttle plummeted into the patchy clouds.

For a moment, within the tranquil beauty of the glowing clouds, Winter's heavy and swollen eyes threatened to close. Her abused and broken body relaxed in the seat, and the weary functions of her mind receded into passive observance. She felt, in that moment, like everything had been a terrible dream, and now, she was simply free-falling in the endless billow of soft reverie before waking.

Falling had often been a part of her nighttime dreams. But she couldn't fall forever . . . that's what she'd always told herself.

"Not forever . . ." she muttered in half-delirium. "I can't . . . I *can't* fall forever."

Sink rate! Altitude 10,000 feet. Pull up! Pull up!

The computerized statement forced her eyes open as the earth rushed up to consume her view. Winter gasped and tore madly at the throttle.

The horizon spun as the craft dove in a wild spiral.

Sink rate! Sink rate! Altitude 8,000 feet. . . . 7,000 feet.

Her body pressed into the side of her harness as if by an unseen hand, Winter strained and reached to take the controls, easing them carefully in the opposite direction.

The sickening spin slowed, then stopped.

Altitude 4,000 feet. . . . 3,000 feet. Terrain! Terrain! Pull up!

Hoping to save her life, Winter gently pulled back.

Terrain! Altitude 1,000 feet. Brace for impact!

She took a deep breath . . . and waited.

The nose of the shuttle tipped upward mere seconds before shuttering against the hard branches of the canopy. The craft shook violently. Trees snapped, metal tore, and shards of broken glass flew.

Winter gripped her restraints and shut her eyes tight. Her head bashed back and forth in the harness. Her jaw clenched. Her every muscle tensed.

The shattering of wood and screeching of metal against earth grew to a deafening climax.

Bouncing and deflecting, rolling and sliding, the wrecked shuttle ripped wildly through the forest and finally ground to a stop in a tidal wave of earth, billowing smoke and fumes inside a trench of its own making.

The cockpit was almost entirely crushed, half-immersed in raw soil and gravel. Pools of engine fluid and fuel spilled out into the trench, crowned and surrounded by a mass of splintered trees.

Winter slowly breathed out . . . and fell into darkness.

"We've lost the signal, sir," a flight control technician reported, shaking her head.

"Just pin down the area," the Master Purifier growled.

"Copy that, sir. Dispatching drones now."

Wraith nodded in grave determination. "Assemble all Purifiers. We're going after her."

CHAPTER FORTY-EIGHT

The sharp, earthy smell of deep soil filled Winter's senses as she gradually came to. Her eyes opened—or nearly opened—one partially and the other bruised and swollen shut.

She attempted to move but quickly realized that her arms and legs were completely immobile. Breathing came in short, painstaking rasps as the pressure on her chest was nearly unbearable. The glass panel before the cockpit was completely shattered, giving way to the influx of earth and gravel that buried the front of the shuttle and her up to her eyes.

Winter spat and blew the dirt away from her mouth and struggled to get her face above ground, fighting to keep her heart rate under control. Her head spun from the crash, and she coughed and writhed to escape her prison.

But every attempt proved fruitless. She was still locked into the pilot's harness, and the soil had cemented her in. As she desperately clawed with her buried fingers to dislodge the dirt surrounding her hands, thus providing her with some mobility, the topsoil quickly collapsed in to fill the void and seal her in again.

After multiple failed attempts, her breathing quickened, and her heart thumped wildly as the familiar terror of utter powerlessness overcame her. She tried to fight off the panic and the mounting claustrophobia, tried to remain in control of her faculties. But with each passing, paralyzing second, the crushing fear buried her in an ever-deepening pit.

All instruction and training from Eagle Eyes about maintaining mental focus and control instantly vanished as she saw herself back in that room— locked in place by the immobilizing electromagnetic bracers, while Wraith and the others pummeled her with their fists, kicked with their legs, and shocked her over and over with the cruel bolt staves.

Winter let out an involuntary wail as tears streamed from her swollen eyes.

Overhead in the afternoon sky, the whining sound of an engine rushed by.

She couldn't turn her head to see if it was a drone or a shuttle, but it didn't matter. Whatever it was, it signaled the reality that her time was short. If she failed to escape this new, earthen prison, death squads from Olympus were sure to find her.

And then, it would be over.

Her fight for survival—her struggle for the truth—would end.

Enraged, blazing anger rushed in to replace the fear and panic. Winter screamed and strained with all her might. Her chest burned with hot, sharp pain. She kicked as best she could and torqued her body, triggering a blinding pain that spasmed through her lungs and strangled her breath. She tasted fresh blood mingled with the dirt.

In the distance, she heard the soft rustling of tree limbs, and then came the unmistakable sound of heavy footfalls racing through the forest.

Purifiers! her mind shouted.

Refusing to give up and ignoring the pain, Winter clenched her teeth and pushed and writhed. She struggled desperately and, with one final roar of determination, was finally able to free one arm. Immediately, she began digging about to free her second arm.

But something was terribly wrong.

Her head suddenly stabbed with knifing agony. Her ears rang. Her vision blurred and the cockpit began to spin nauseatingly. She lost all focus. The world began to recede back into darkness.

"No . . ." Winter whispered as her head drooped heavily and came to rest in the dirt. "Not . . . not now."

It was no use. In her weakened, battered state, the tremendous exertion required to free herself had only succeeded at securing her demise.

She had fought. She had run. She had escaped Olympus and even made it to the surface alive.

But now, the end had come; her struggle was over. With nowhere left to run or hide, only the fires of *purification* awaited her.

As pitch darkness swallowed her mind, the fast approaching footfalls echoed on and on. They came to a stop above the cockpit, and a voice called out before all consciousness was lost.

"Winter! I'm here!"

"Aaaaargh!" the Grand Elite roared at the medical attendant dabbing his mutilated face. "You imbecilic, reclamation sludge!"

"Please forgive me, masterful one!" she implored, bowing low. "Please, please! I'm so sorry! I'm almost finished."

He shot her a menacing, hateful glare, then huffed and folded his arms. "Then finish already, goat!"

After another bow, she quickly and carefully patched a bandage over the wound.

Draven Constantine Rothgard sat in the center of the Hive in the midst of pooled blood and carved Guardian corpses. Spattered and smeared footsteps bore macabre manifestation of the struggle that had occurred not long ago. The bodies of crushed Olympians—hundreds of them—littered the stadium seating and main entrance. Aside from the cursed little medic at his side, their only company was the reclamation workers hauling the broken, mangled bodies away, one by one, and the cleaners mopping up buckets of blood.

The death-filled silence of his surroundings fueled Draven's rage. He shook with adrenaline and frothing lust for revenge. In one hand, he gripped the rusted serrated blade that The Heretic had used to wound him so. Clutching it tightly, it was now a tangible symbol of the roiling maelstrom of his hatred for her.

January Winterton, he swore in his seething wrath, *I will rip you to pieces!*

The medic suddenly gasped. Quivering, she immediately stopped her work and made hasty and fervent obeisance on the bloody tiles.

The Grand Elite, confused, turned to see the Sovereign himself approaching their position. A young Elite boy followed closely at his heels, holding up his silken gold robes to keep them from being stained by commoner's blood.

Draven quickly stood and faced his maker, fighting to contain his mounting vexation. He quietly slipped the third-tier knife into his robes, reluctantly dropping it into a deep pocket.

Sovereign Zeus was painfully silent. He took in the ghastly scene and shook his head ever so slowly.

"In all my years, never before . . ." the god of Olympus spoke at length, "have I witnessed such calamitous, deplorable incompetence."

Draven's mouth went dry. "Lord Zeus, nothing you see here was my doing." He licked his lips nervously. "This was not my fault."

Zeus' eyes were hard as stone as they stared down his Grand Elite.

Draven's eyes fell to the floor, unable to hold the harsh gaze of his god.

"When you're my Grand Elite of my city, Draven," the Sovereign's voice was edged with malice, "it will *always* be your fault. Thus is your burden and your responsibility." He again cast his eyes about to survey the carnage. "It's about time you understood that."

Draven's anger approached its boiling point. He knew he was justified. His finger tapped aggressively against his thigh. "Begging your forgiveness, Sovereign Zeus, but my plan—"

"Was nothing but childish!" the Sovereign cut him off sharply. "Your plan was utter foolishness and a complete disaster—can't you see that?" Zeus winced as if pained by Draven's idiocy, then paused to consider his next words. "When you left my chambers this morning, what was my final word to you?"

Draven swallowed hard. "You told me—"

"I *warned* you," Zeus corrected sternly.

"Yes, great lord . . . you *warned* me, saying that I was to eradicate The Heretic completely."

"So that," the Sovereign continued, "not *one speck* of her heresy was to remain among my children." His robed arm waved over the bodies of the dead. "And *THIS!*" his voice thundered, causing all in the Hive to bow lower before their god. "*This* is what you give me!"

He turned in a wide circle, the Elite boy trailing behind him just able to keep his robes from skirting the bloody ground. "Initial estimates are that over six hundred are dead—ninety-eight percent of them crushed as they fled the Hive in mass panic. Thousands more are injured! Many of them so injured that they're now useless to me and must be processed through reclamation." His hate-filled eyes again fell on his Grand Elite. "My reclamation facilities were not designed to handle that kind of load, DRAVEN!"

The Grand Elite's name echoed and reverberated throughout the Hive. Draven began to tremble—from a strange mixture of rage and fear and humiliation. It was a new and terrible, sickening sensation to him.

"You were to take this dissension up by the roots and burn it," Zeus spoke again. "You were to extinguish every last trace of The Heretic as swiftly and as completely as was in your power. But instead, you orchestrate this charade—this paltry show of power that you believe is actually yours."

He shook his head sorrowfully. "You even allowed her to escape with my glorious Ascension blade. That sword was one of a kind—*not* easy to create." His voice grew in volume. "The very symbol of my honored Purifiers now in the hands of The Heretic! It's blasphemy!"

The Sovereign stepped closer to Draven and lowered his voice to a harsh whisper. "And on top of all that, what's this I hear about her *speaking* during this momentous disaster of yours?"

Draven flinched as the words of his god sliced him deeper than the gash across his face. "I . . ." he started, his voice shaking. "It was only for a brief moment, my lord. She said nothing of note—certainly nothing anyone would remember. I had her silenced immediately."

"Silenced immediately? Oh, really?" The Sovereign took a long look around. "Not 'immediately' enough, as is painfully obvious! Not only did you allow her to speak—you allowed her to write her words in BLOOD!"

"But I didn't allow it, my lord!" Draven pleaded earnestly. "Something happened . . . I don't know what exactly . . . but—"

"Your fault, Draven!" Zeus reminded and added with emphasis: "*Your* fault."

After a long pause, the Sovereign touched Draven's face and turned it up to see the bandaged area. "You have received the rewards for your actions, I see . . . You are truly hideous now."

Draven took a breath. "The effects of Winter's betrayal will be erased with regeneration therapy. In time, there won't even be a scar."

Lord Zeus recoiled. "That's what *you* believe!"

Draven couldn't fathom his meaning.

The Sovereign's expression melted into disgust. "You think *this* . . ." Taking the top corner of the bandage, he angrily ripped it from Draven's face.

Draven bottled the howls of pain inside and doubled over, cupping his freshly bleeding face.

" . . . is the effect of the Purifier's betrayal?" the Sovereign continued. "And you think *this* . . ." He gestured to the bloody massacre surrounding them, " . . . is the full effect of that betrayal?"

"I . . . I don't understand, my lord," Draven said through clenched teeth.

"No, you don't," Zeus derided. "You don't understand a shred of what

I have been trying to teach you for so many years. You keep saying you are ready . . . my favorite boy . . . but you continue to show me that you are far from it. You don't understand that the people and the things are not the danger—the betrayal is not the danger." He tapped a finger dramatically on his own temple. "The *idea*, Draven. The *idea* is the danger. Ideas are a disease—worse than any plague in all the world's history—responsible for more deaths than any war that has ever been waged. Give a mortal a sword, and he will slay what he needs to thrive. But give a mortal an idea, and he will slay until all he views has either been destroyed or consumed by that same idea."

His gray eyes looked up at the lifeless bodies scattered throughout the Hive's seating. *"On résiste à l'invasion des armées; on ne résiste pas à l'invasion des idées* . . . Do you know what that means, Draven?"

"No, my lord," he admitted.

The Sovereign spoke in a dangerous quiet, *"We withstand the invasion of armies; we cannot withstand the invasion of ideas."* He turned back to face Draven. "Devotion means nothing to the weak and malleable mortal. They cannot be given the option of new ideas because their minds have no capacity for constancy. What I have created here in the clouds is a haven from ideas—a place where mortals can live within the safety of *my* constancy. Your mortal weakness aside . . . you believed the enemy was a person—a person who could be broken and humiliated. A person who could be destroyed for the entertainment of your adoring masses. You sad child . . . you never heard what I was trying to teach you. Our enemy was not the Purifier but the sickness she bore."

"But . . . the Blight . . .?" Draven ventured to understand.

"The *idea*, you fool!" the Sovereign roared suddenly. "This carnage is not the effect of betrayal, nor is your disfigured face! The effect is the unseen decay within the minds of Olympus—now, not so unseen. Now, out and in the open."

Draven prostrated himself before his god. "Great lord Zeus, I will kill The Heretic. I promise you, I will kill her and bring an end to her heresy."

The Sovereign nodded. "I hope so, Draven, for your sake. Because until you do, you will bear that hideous mark of your failure like a badge."

Draven's face turned pale as the blood continued to ooze. "My . . . my lord . . .?"

"Allow me to be perfectly clear. Until The Heretic is dead, and Ascension has been returned to me, and I am fully satisfied that *the idea* has been purged from Olympus—" the Sovereign pointed at the bleeding wound "—you will receive no regeneration therapy. You will carry that scar until I say otherwise."

The Grand Elite's stomach lurched as if he'd been slugged in the gut. His breath caught in this throat and he tried to sputter out a protest, but the Sovereign was already walking away.

Draven became suddenly hopeful when Zeus stopped as if he'd forgotten something, but the hope quickly disappeared when the Sovereign turned to address the trembling, groveling medic on the stage floor.

"You there, child. What's your name?"

The medic cautiously, fearfully raised her head. "A-Abigail Sp-Sparrows, great Sovereign Zeus."

"Abigail Sparrows," Zeus spoke in gentle tones, "I have two commands for you, my child, and you will obey me."

"Of course, my Sovereign. Anything."

"What you have heard today is not for your ears, nor for the ears of any other Second or Third Tier citizen." His voice grew stern. "I order you to take charge here, directing and overseeing the clean-up of the Hive and the reclamation of the dead. Afterwards, you and all Third Tier workers currently assigned here will likewise be reclaimed." His voice again gushed with benevolence. "This is a great day for you, my child. I give you my word: you will have your place in Elysium."

Abigail's face blushed wildly. Her mouth dropped in awe, and she bowed her head again to the floor. "Thank you, lord Zeus! Thank you! I will do as you have said."

"Go now, and see that you do."

With another bow, the medic jumped to her feet and hurriedly left the stage to carry out her god's command.

The Sovereign turned again to his speechless Grand Elite. Zeus' eyes burned with consuming power. "You see, poor, poor Draven. Where there's even the *possibility* of the idea being planted in the minds of my people, you uproot it and cast it out immediately. May that grotesque mark on your face help you to remember that."

"Great and mighty Zeus," Draven entreated earnestly, "I pledge to do as you have said. I swear it."

The Sovereign's hard eyes glared in disgust. "To return into my good graces, you have a very, very big mountain ahead of you. Start climbing, boy."

Before Draven could respond, Zeus had turned and was leaving the arena, the small Elite boy shuffling quickly behind with golden robes in his arms.

Draven stood alone in the center of the bloody carnage, his mind soaking up the scene of death like a sponge.

"I *will* kill her," he promised himself. "I will see my glory restored. No matter what."

He swept out toward the main entrance, face still seeping blood down his neck and staining his Elite robes. His humiliation was paramount when all who encountered him in the street cringed or gasped as they bowed. Their obeisance meant nothing to him now. Everywhere he went, he felt eyes on him—staring at him.

Seething with rage by the time he rode the lift down to the command deck, Draven found the Master Purifier hunched over a digital display of surface topography.

Wraith didn't look surprised to see him; he barely looked up from his work.

"Update, now!" Draven demanded, startling the technicians with his volume.

Wraith complied immediately with an annoyed huff. "Winterton's hijacked shuttle impacted on the surface. The signal disappeared, but the drones located the crash site. My Purifiers are closing in on the shuttle as we speak."

"Tell them to find the body," Draven ordered.

Wraith glared at the table in silence.

A moment later, a voice issued from the console. "Master Purifier, sir. We've located the stolen shuttle."

"Confirmed, Hellhounds," Wraith spoke into the com. "Now, find me a body."

"It's a real mess down here, sir," the voice came back. "I don't think anyone could survive this."

"Just find me a body," Wraith repeated in a slow, menacing tone.

Silence followed for a long moment.

Draven paced like mad, scratching at his neck like one possessed.

"Lord Grand Elite," Wraith asked, attempting to hide his frustration at Draven's continued distracting presence, "shouldn't you get that looked at?" He indicated to the Grand Elite's dribbling face wound. "We have control of the situation here."

"Silence!" Draven snapped. "Mind your own business, and hurry up the search!"

Wraith locked his jaw and flared his nostrils. "Team, status."

"Sir, we've searched the cockpit," the voice crackled over the intercom. "It's been crushed, and it's filled with dirt, but there are clear signs of digging around the pilot's seat. She's gone, sir. She must have dug herself out."

Draven suddenly lost grip on his desperation and rage. He lashed out and struck one of the technicians across the face, sending him careening off his seat in abject shock.

Wraith gritted his teeth and clenched his fists on the table as the bloodied technician apologized profusely and climbed back into his seat, replacing his headgear.

The other technicians kept their faces focused directly on their work, not daring to even glance in the Grand Elite's direction.

"Get down there and find her!" Draven roared, stalking up to Wraith with hostility.

"My shuttle's already prepped," Wraith said in cold control.

"You find her and you kill her!" he shouted in Wraith's face, flecks of blood spraying the Master Purifier.

Wraith stepped back without reaction. "Yes, lord Grand Elite. It will be done."

As Wraith went through the process of preparing for a jump to the surface, he promised himself that Winter's luck had now permanently run out. He steeled his mind in its course and approached the shuttle where the Archangels were geared up and standing by.

"None of you wants this stain on our reputation." He locked eyes with each of them in turn. "This isn't about numbers or ranks. Today, our mission is to reclaim our honor," he said through clenched teeth. "We are Purifiers of Sovereign Zeus, and this defamation to his great name must be corrected. This unbearable disgrace must be righted. The Heretic, January Winterton, must be purified."

CHAPTER FORTY-NINE

"*Winter . . . Winter . . .*"

A voice echoed through the void, the words so distant and unfamiliar. *It* knew instinctively that they shouldn't be, but no matter how *it* tried to listen, to focus on the words being spoken, their source and meaning were imperceptible. The words would come and hang in the stale air for a moment, and *it* would fight to decipher them, but they all too quickly would pass away into the invisible ether from which they came.

"*Winter . . . Just hang on . . .*"

It suddenly perceived a body—a woman . . . *maybe* a woman—floating weightless amid an eternity of dark wisps of cloud. *It* was strangely aware that the woman was *its* own self, but somehow . . . not. Or maybe *it* . . . no . . . no, that wasn't right. Maybe *she* wasn't herself. That must have been it. Her body appeared different.

Changed.

Tormented.

Damaged.

Able to act only as a remote observer, she watched in odd fascination as her detached and motionless body floated in the cloudy sea. Wherever she was—if that beaten *thing* even was her—at least she appeared to be at peace. She didn't seem to be in any pain.

No more pain.

Yes.

That was nice.

"*Oh, no you don't . . . Don't you give up on me . . .*"

Featureless, black shadows darted at the borders of her consciousness. They swirled with the clouds, gathered their strength, then advanced in force. They reached out with clawed limbs to take hold of her suspended body. She could feel their presence, cold and forbidding. It was impossible to understand exactly how, but she could sense that the shadows wanted more than just her body. She could hear it in their desperate howling and feel it in their feral hunger.

The body was just a shell. They wanted more than that. They wanted *her*—all of her.

They wanted to take her somewhere.

But . . . where?

Was it a place she wanted to go?

She sensed not. Whatever the shadows were and whatever they wanted, she perceived they meant her ill. They bore 'destruction' on their breath and 'hate' in their touch.

Their kiss was 'death.'

"Winter . . . Don't go . . ."

That voice again. It came more insistently this time.

She tried to focus on it—to repeat those words.

Winter . . . Winter.

That was her, right? That was who she was—and whatever the voice was, it was calling out to her. The voice seemed very different from the shadows. She sensed it was trying to help her—maybe even trying to save her.

But where did it go?

She channeled her focus and strained to hear it again. She needed to hear that voice again.

"Winter . . . I've got you . . . Just stay with me . . ."

It came so much clearer this time. She felt like she could understand it—trust it. Believing that it would act like a compass to point the way, she reached out with her mind and took hold of it.

The black shadows suddenly recoiled and shrieked in agony. They screamed, lashed out, and tried to reach for her again, but they were being pulled away by an unseen force—further and further, and then gone.

Winter planted her feet on solid ground. Looking around, she knew where she was.

Olympus. The Hive.

The vast stadium was empty and silent, dark—like nightfall, but very different. Everywhere, from the mid to upper seating areas, was enshrouded in dense fog. Standing alone on the hexagonal-patterned arena floor, she could see nothing beyond it.

Then, a solitary figure appeared out of the darkness.

Winter turned, and her mouth dropped to see Derrick 'Eagle Eyes' Zinda striding towards her. He wore his usual charismatic smile.

This can't be real, she thought. *You're dead.*

Behind him, standing at the edge of the fog, a lone woman with long blonde hair stood, watching. She seemed so familiar.

Eagle Eyes came forward to stand before her, as big as life.

"Hey, kid." He gave her a playful wink. "You're awake."

Winter blinked, confused. "I'm . . . I'm what?"

"Thank heaven, you're awake."

With one eye half-open, Winter looked up at a gray ceiling with shadows dancing by dim firelight. Her other eye was covered with something.

Drawing in a breath was painful as she blinked rapidly to clear her fuzzy vision. It was dark, and there was a hollow, cold feeling in the air. A strange taste filled her mouth—something other than blood.

"How are you feeling?"

Winter turned her head, triggering intense vertigo. She blinked again and tried to focus on the concerned face nearby. She opened her mouth to speak, but her voice came in barely more than a weak whisper.

"J . . . Josh . . . ua . . .?"

He was standing over in a doorway of sorts, returning her gaze with those eyes that spoke volumes of sadness.

Winter lightly shook her head and looked again, checking to see if he was actually there, unsure whether she was still dreaming.

"W-what . . .?" Winter croaked, discovering the fiery pain burning through her all over again.

Nope, she thought as stabs of agony filled her chest. *I'm not dreaming.*

She winced and tried again. "What are you . . . doing here?"

"Just what I can," he said. "You really gave me a scare a few times there. It's good to have you back."

With a grunt, Winter lifted her head.

"Don't—" Joshua began, but she was already up on her elbows "—move." He smiled in defeat.

Winter checked her surroundings. They were in a long rectangular room of what seemed to be the ancient remains of a building. The floor and ceiling were concrete, cracked and broken with age. Rubble and overgrowth filled the ruin. A tiny fire smoldered nearby, radiating heat and warming a small container suspended above it.

The Ascension blade lay propped up against the wall across from her, its gold and steel and gemstones reflecting the soft red glow of the coals. She subconsciously leaned away from it.

There was one partially collapsed entrance where Joshua stood, looking outside every minute or so.

"What is all—" Winter began, but the whine of an engine flew somewhere overhead.

Joshua looked up at the pre-dawn, starlit sky. "They're getting closer."

"How long . . . have I been here?" Winter asked, gingerly touching the bandage draped over her shut eye. That's when she noticed the crude wrappings around her arms and the back of her right hand. She was also covered by Joshua's canvas coat. His tactical pack had been the pillow her head had rested on.

After one last check outside, Joshua approached with sincere concern set in his expressive eyes. He knelt beside her. "Two days here. One day at another location. I had to move you as the drones and search parties were getting too close."

"Three . . . days?" she restated in disbelief. She swallowed down that strange taste in her mouth. "How . . .? How did you find me?"

"Well—" Joshua rolled his eyes as a childlike smile spread across his lips "—you *did* make quite the entrance."

The traumatic events that led her to this point suddenly assaulted Winter's mind with their sharp flood of brutal and soul-raking memories. The sick and broken feeling stabbed her tangibly, deep inside her gut, and she realized that she had stopped breathing.

Joshua noticed. "Winter? You okay?"

She could put little focus on his words. In her mind, she was tied up in a room . . . dark . . . helpless . . . she felt trapped in a black vortex, devoid of control. All the agony of her body was overshadowed by the intense feeling of dread and worthlessness.

"Winter, focus. Look at me." Intense worry laced his voice.

Winter didn't respond—didn't seem to hear him—but jumped violently and sat up fully when he touched her forehead.

"Sorry," he apologized and felt her rising temperature. "How much pain are you in right now?"

"I . . . I . . ." Winter trailed off, her head swimming. One big gasp of air reestablished her bearings. "I don't—"

"Here, drink this," Joshua offered and poured the warm contents of the container over the fire into a small tin mug. "It'll help keep the pain down a little."

Unable to respond, Winter didn't fight it when Joshua guided her hands to hold the mug and bring it to her lips. It was bitter, earthy, and acidic, but Winter couldn't deny the comfort of warm liquid pouring down her weary throat. At least now, she had an answer for what that strange taste was.

After finishing, Winter again studied her surroundings.

"It's not great," Joshua commented, "but it's secure—at least for now."

"You . . . live here?" Winter asked, deeply concerned.

"No." Joshua laughed. "My compound is roughly ten miles north of here. This is just a safe spot to rest for now. There are many like it. They're used for emergency overnights if anyone gets cut off from the compound."

"You shouldn't have brought me here," Winter warned, terror reflecting in her one blue eye. "They're not going to stop looking."

"What do they want?" Joshua couldn't help but ask.

"They want to kill me," Winter stated unemotionally. "They want to kill me because I told the truth."

"And they banished you?"

Winter swallowed silently; she shook her head. "I got away," she almost whispered. Glancing down at her sorry, battered self, she suddenly felt like she didn't 'get away' at all.

"We should move then," Joshua suggested. "There's another safe spot I know of about a mile south of here. It's several floors deeper. We'll be safer there."

"No, not *we.*" She trained her one eye on him. "If they find you with me, they'll kill you, too."

Joshua paused to think about how to respond. He shrugged. "And how would that be different from any other day?" He smiled. "Besides, they haven't met me yet. The last Purifier I talked to didn't kill me."

"Lucky for you." Winter tried to laugh, but instead only managed a weak cough. "She happens to like you alive."

"I like me alive, too." He chuckled. "And if both of us are going to stay that way, we'll need to get moving soon." He surveyed his medical work. "But first things first, we need to take care of you." He reached for the bandage covering her eye, then stopped short. "May I?" he asked permission this time.

Winter nodded, internally fighting off the involuntary dread that overcame her at someone's touch—even the touch of a friend.

Joshua gently took the bandage and slowly peeled it away. "Hm. Seems to be healing up nicely. That's a bit of good news, at least," he said lightheartedly. "I told you before that I've played the role of a field medic a time or two. Admittedly, I never thought you'd give me the opportunity to put those skills to the test. Had I known that, I would have insisted on more training."

Winter smiled at his humor and carefully tested her injured eye. She was worried at first when all the room appeared as only a darkened blur, but after several blinks, her vision began to clear up, and everything came into focus.

"So, how is it?"

"It still hurts a little, but I can see fine," Winter replied with a few more blinks.

She attempted to swallow down the last of her nervousness and make the conscious decision to open up to Joshua—possibly the only person in all the world who wanted to help her.

So strange, she mused, mulling over the overwhelmingly improbable odds of this friendship.

Several weeks ago, she was the ideal Olympian Purifier, designed specifically for and charged by 'a god' with the task of exterminating any and all surface dwellers—a task she had excelled at as few others could. She hadn't been just a Purifier. She had been an exceptionally proficient Purifier. And now, here she was—a beaten outcast, a hated pariah: 'The

Heretic'—sitting in an ancient ruin with one of those surface dwellers, and he was the one taking care of her while her own people wanted her dead.

Oh, the irony, she thought bitterly.

All her life, she'd been indoctrinated to believe that those on the surface were horribly diseased, mutated monsters, deserving only of purification.

All a lie.

The true monsters had now revealed themselves. She had been created by them, lived among them, served them, honored them, loved them, and aspired to be them—*real* monsters.

So, so strange, she thought again with a labored sigh.

"Thank you, Joshua," she finally said with sincerity. "Thank you for getting me here."

He shrugged. "It was no problem. You're not that heavy."

Winter half-smiled. "That's not what I meant. Thank you for saving me . . . and for taking care of me."

"Yeah, I knew what you meant." He smiled in return. "You're very welcome. But I'm not done yet. They really did a number on you. It'll still be some time before you're back to one-hundred percent—even with all that . . . 'genetic superiority' of yours." He winked.

She didn't smile. Everything hurt. Everything reminded her of the lie that was her existence.

Joshua must have noticed her discomfort. His smile disappeared. "Well," he said and cleared his throat, "before we leave, I'll need to change your wrappings. And to do that, I'll need to gather some more herbs to make a poultice—speeds up the healing. I'll be back soon." He stood up to leave.

"Your compound is really ten miles from here?" Winter spoke suddenly, causing Joshua to pause and kneel back down.

He nodded. "Give or take half a mile. Why?"

"That just seems like a long way away." Her blue eyes locked with his hazel. "I thought . . . I thought I was never going to see you again. What are you even doing out here?"

Joshua didn't miss a beat. "Looking after a friend, obviously."

And there it was: that deep reservoir of sadness dammed up behind those bright eyes. He tried to hide it with his tender smile, but Winter recognized it immediately. It frightened her.

She leaned in. "Did . . . something happen?"

He smiled again, the sadness never leaving. "Let's just worry about you for now, okay? I'll change your wrappings and we'll—"

"Joshua, please," Winter cut him off, unable to keep the fear and insistence out of her voice. "What happened?"

"It doesn't matter. We just—"

"Tell me!" she yelled in frustration and flinched at the sharp ache in her ribs. *"Please,"* she begged softly. "Just tell me."

Joshua was silent for a long while. He glanced away, but Winter saw his eyes dewed with tears in the dying glow of the fire.

He sniffed and breathed out. "You . . . uh . . . you remember Joel, Alyssa, and Zack?"

Winter nodded slowly, seeing the terror-stricken, lifeless faces of Joel and Alyssa in her mind all over again. It had been some time since their faces had haunted her mind—not since she'd learned that Zack had survived her assault.

No . . .

Her eyes widened at the thought.

No, no, no . . .

Winter took a deep breath and waited for Joshua to continue.

"Zack . . . uh . . . ." he began, and a single tear dropped from his eye. "Zack's dead."

Winter's heart shattered. The third and final member of Joshua's team—the only one she hadn't killed—was dead.

Time seemed to slow; the air grew cold, and Winter forgot to breathe out.

I . . . she realized in horror. *I killed him, too. I killed them all.*

"It just doesn't make any sense," Joshua went on explaining, but his words were distant as the full gravity of Winter's actions that terrible day crushed her heart to dust. "He seemed to be getting better. Our physicians were hopeful he'd make a full recovery. Then, about a week ago, he suddenly fell ill. Infection set in, and even though we tried everything we could, he just kept slipping further and further away. And then, four days ago . . . he was . . . gone."

His lip quivered as he drew a breath. "It's true I don't normally venture out this far from home—except for seasonal hunting trips—but, this time . . . I just needed to get away. I needed some time alone." His hand trembled as he wiped at his nose. "I left in such a hurry, I even forgot my rifle. Such a stupid thing to do." He let out an empty chuckle. "But, on the bright side . . . if I hadn't left, I wouldn't have found you."

Winter understood the depth of his words, even if he didn't mean them in that way. At the cost of his friend's life, he was now there to save his friend's murderer.

The dead faces of Joel and Alyssa again flashed in her mind. This time, they were joined by the cowled, shadowed face of Zack—a face she had never actually seen, but that didn't matter. He was dead, and she was to blame.

She suddenly wished she'd never survived the shuttle crash. That way, at least justice would have been done, and she wouldn't have to face Joshua, their last surviving team member . . . all thanks to her.

It wasn't fair that Zack was dead and she was alive. Nothing about it was fair.

"Why, Joshua . . .?" Winter finally began, trying desperately to put words to her turbulent emotions. Hot tears stung her eyes, and she trembled to be in his presence. "Why are you helping me?"

He seemed strangely confused by her question, so she pressed on.

"I've brought nothing but misery and death to you and your people. I've killed your entire team and probably many more of your people before that." Her voice grew in volume and desperation. "I've done nothing to deserve your help. I don't deserve it. I deserve to die!" The tears began to flow freely down her cheeks. She let them. "Tell me—why!? Why are you helping me?"

Shaking, Winter looked into Joshua's eyes. She couldn't name the emotion behind them. It wasn't sadness. It wasn't pain. It wasn't hatred. It was something she'd never seen before.

What was it?

Joshua eventually drew up a warm smile and answered in a whisper: "Because I choose to."

Winter broke down sobbing. "No, no. You shouldn't. You *should* hate me. Please—tell me you hate me!" she cried out. "Please, tell me I should die! I know I should!"

Joshua shook his head. "No, Winter. I don't hate you."

"But I *want* you to hate me!" she wailed in agony. "I *need* you to hate me! Please, just tell me you hate me and that I'm a monster!"

Joshua said nothing.

"Tell me!" she bawled uncontrollably.

Joshua looked away, his eyes staring into the cooling coals. With the dying of the fire, the room had fallen into shadow, but the faint bluish glow of pre-dawn was beginning to trickle in through the building's vine-covered entrance.

When he finally turned back, his face was stern, and for a moment, Winter was sure she'd get her wish.

"No," he said unequivocally, denying her. "I will not lie to you, Winter. I can't tell you I hate you—because I'd be lying if I did." His focus on her was so intense, she was suddenly reminded of Eagle Eyes. "Listen to me: I do not hate you, and I do not wish you were dead. Your death would accomplish nothing. It wouldn't bring my friends back. If you were dead, that would only mean I will have lost another friend—and how could I possibly wish for that?"

"But . . ." Winter protested, her eyes still filled with tears. "But I killed them. I killed them all. I don't deserve your friendship."

"Maybe not," he shrugged unapologetically. "Still, I wouldn't trade it for the world."

Winter's jaw went slack. She couldn't understand it. It made no sense. She'd given him every possible reason to hate her and to want her dead, but he somehow refused.

Her head drooped in surrender.

It was simply impossible. Joshua *was* impossible.

They sat in silence for a long time, with only the melodic birdsong in the trees outside to serenade them.

"Listen," Joshua said at last, rising to his feet, "I'm gonna gather those herbs. It won't take long. You good staying here till I get back? I'll redress your wounds, and we'll move out. Okay?"

Winter nodded in defeat.

It was a lie. She'd already made up her mind. She wouldn't risk Joshua's life to help save her own.

"Okay," he whispered, reaching down to snatch up his tactical pack. "Try to get some more rest. I'll be back before sunrise." He took hold of his canvas coat. "Sorry, but I'll be needing this. It helps to camouflage me from the drones."

"Please, take it," Winter whispered.

He pulled it off her legs, revealing more of his bandages and wrappings around her thighs and calves. Winter winced involuntarily at the sight of them, remembering the punches and kicks and repeated electric shocks of the bolt staves.

Slipping on his coat, Joshua walked to the entrance, then turned and matched her gaze. He stood there wordlessly for a moment, concern in his eyes.

"You go. I'll be fine," Winter assured him.

Joshua nodded, then pulled on the cowl and exited the structure.

Winter waited several minutes in silence before pulling her knees up to her chest, experiencing the various symphonies of pain throughout her body as she did. Her body was torn and broken but still functional. With her advanced genetic makeup, and with Joshua's help, her body was already well into healing most of her less serious injuries.

She looked down at her hand that had once been the symbol of her pride and identity. The back of her hand that had been the hallmark of her lifetime of service was now bandaged in a bloody gauze wrap.

Terror gripped her heart as she dared not explore her scalp where her cherished tresses once had been.

Everything was gone.

She had no intention of waiting for Joshua's return. His inexplicable nature would not allow her to survive the surface world alone, but that's exactly what she planned to do. Until they saw her corpse, the Olympians would never rest in their hunt for her. The longer she was alive, the longer the truth would be undeniable, but she could not live with herself if her survival meant putting Joshua or his people at risk.

She couldn't live in the fantasy that it was possible to simply run away from the Purifiers. They would find her eventually, no matter where she hid. They would hunt her relentlessly.

After all, it's what she would do in their place.

Once she was sure Joshua wouldn't double back, Winter slowly and carefully pulled herself to stand. Her head felt heavy and off-center.

She took a moment, then kicked dirt on the last remaining embers of the fire. Her bare feet were scraped and speckled with dried blood. She had nothing on but the nightgown she'd been wearing at the time of her arrest, now ripped and stained with dirt and blood.

Once the fire was out, her eyes rested on Ascension leaning against the crumbling wall.

Practicality drove her hand to grip its finely crafted hilt before setting out on her quest for survival, but as the light glinted off the master craft blade, she caught sight of her reflection in its mirror surface. Though obscured by copious amounts of dried blood, she saw herself in the blade's reflection, and the image was truly harrowing.

She saw a mangled creature, bruised and torn beyond recognition. She saw the patchy scalp where once grew her beautiful hair in which she took so much pride. Her once sharp, icy eyes were now lackluster pools of emptiness.

In her mind, she couldn't help but remember the beauty of Olympus. There, she felt the comfort of order—immaculate, wholesome order. The sparkling barrier, the pristine streets, the golden halo of the First Tier, her perfect living chambers . . .

Winter didn't notice her heart begin to race as she looked at her broken reflection and the blood that obscured it. She didn't notice her breathing stop as she gingerly, disbelievingly touched her scalp as if to confirm the nightmare was real.

She gazed at the bloody surface and recalled using the blade to carve through the ranks of Guardians—hacking, slicing, whirling madness and rampant death. The efficiency and perfected execution was exactly what she'd trained for, but she recalled the falling limbs, the spraying blood, and the screaming enemies as they fell one by one . . . so many . . . the work of her own cold detachment and gritted survival-driven focus.

Derrick's intense eyes suddenly looked at her through the blood. His face became clear in her mind. He gazed at her with approval and confidence, and Winter watched again in horror as this same blade—in the hands of the god of Olympus—severed his head clean from his shoulders. His eyes became cold and lifeless, and a river of blood washed over her perception.

Winter gasped, drawing breath for the first time in minutes. Gravity intensified around her. She shook all over and collapsed backward, dropping the blade of death and oppression as if it were searing hot. As the blade clattered to the ground, Derrick's head toppled to the stage floor and rolled to a dead stop. Winter fell back against the wall, gasping and shaking, her heart palpitating wildly.

Fear and disgust stirred in her chest, and she couldn't bring herself to touch the blade again. For the first time, she saw it for what it truly was. It was a representation of the Sovereign's tyranny of the mind. Forged in the flames of his lies, it represented the vanity and utter uselessness of the Purifier class. The source and pinnacle of all Purifier ambition, its razor edge was the instrument of death to every Purifier *fortunate* and *talented* enough to reach that lofty goal called "Ascension."

In short, it represented her life, wasted in bloodshed, pursuing an imaginary paradise . . . purifying an imaginary threat. And she had, without thought or remorse, wielded it to the gruesome demise of too many Olympians.

After a long moment of collecting herself, her breathing and heart rate returned to normal, and her hands were shaking a little less. She breathed out slowly and stood once more.

The mission had not changed, but, terrified at her own ability to wreak death and pain, Winter resolved that her survival would never be dependent upon bloodshed again. The blade called "Ascension" was the Sovereign's tool of control, not hers. She wouldn't have anything to do with it.

Turning away from the hateful thing, Winter limped to the exit and left it behind.

Outside, the sun was threatening to rise within the hour. It was about to get much easier for the Purifiers to find her. Another drone shrieked somewhere nearby, and she forced down her trepidation. Joshua had said his compound was to the north. She turned her back to it and determined in her heart to lead any search parties as far away as possible.

She had a chance to finally do some good—at great personal cost. She knew she was going to die, but at least she would die ensuring Joshua and his people were safe.

If she could survive just long enough to show any pursuing Olympians that the surface wasn't toxic, maybe those who found her would see the truth.

She would fight to keep the truth alive for as long as possible.

She *was* the truth now.

CHAPTER FIFTY

Breathing rhythmically with her own footfalls, Winter fortified her mind against the damage her body bore as she moved quickly through the dense forest. She gritted her teeth as each step stung her bare feet with loose gravel, broken twigs, and dry pine needles. The cold soil turned her toes red and amplified the sting of every sharp edge.

The search patterns of the drones had been closing in on her movement in smaller and smaller circles, and she was sure they had her pinned down by now. The fact that she hadn't seen any shuttles only meant to her that they had predicted her direction and landed ahead of her already.

The crisp, chill morning broke, and the slate-colored sky bled golden hues into the horizon. Winter had no destination in mind but knew that she needed more than anything to keep moving. At her best, no one in the Purifier ranks could keep pace with her. In her current state, however, she had no idea how fast they might catch up.

With that thought in mind, she continued to push herself harder and harder to keep going.

Another drone whined and zipped overhead; it undoubtedly saw her.

Something about the terrain made Winter's senses uncomfortable. If she were the hunter here, she would have picked a spot like the one up ahead for an ambush. She didn't pause or second-guess her instincts and changed direction sharply to veer to the side.

An electric blast tore through the air and exploded into the ground where she had just stood moments before. She tucked into a roll and took cover behind a large tree. With the sudden movement, her body rang with alarms and howled with pain. She winced and bore down against it, knowing that the flowing adrenaline would soon help to mask it and help her power through.

How could she bring herself to fight them? It was painful to think of them hunting her after all they had experienced together as teammates and comrades, but she could not allow herself to fall to them. They had to see the truth, but they also needed to live to tell it.

She had to move. Tactics dictated that they close in and flank her, but running away would be no good; everyone she knew was more effective at long range.

Move forward.

Winter set her jaw and spun into the tree, peeking around the cover. Two helmeted, full-armored Purifiers charged toward her, rifles up and ready. She didn't pause. She dashed forward, darting this way and that as fire rained down on her until she closed the distance. She stepped off the line past the rifle barrel and latched onto his trigger hand. Locking her elbow down, she swung the rifle to the side with her bodyweight. The next shot exploded into the ground near the other Purifier's feet. As the near-death experience caused him to fall backward in surprise, Winter reversed her motion and drove the rifle into its owner's helmet hard enough to crack the screen. He fell, stunned.

Winter didn't wait to see if the other would recover; she dug down into a dead run in the direction of the most unfriendly terrain. She lacked the protective armor they had, but the advantage in mobility was undeniable. Anyone who pursued her from here was quickly left behind. The handful of rifle blasts that followed didn't come near her as she wound back and forth between the trees.

A drone zipped overhead.

Winter's ankle buckled and she stumbled, scraping her legs on the bare earth. Her pause gave one of the Purifiers a chance to close the distance.

"Winter, don't move!" Savage warned, sights up to her eyes as she skidded to a stop at her elbow.

With no hesitation, Winter wrapped her arm around the rifle and stood up, jerking and dislocating the shoulder.

Savage screamed and collapsed.

Winter wanted to help her, felt deep remorse for hurting her, but she hurled the rifle into the foliage and moved on.

She consciously cut her mind off from seeing or recognizing any faces; it was too painful. It would only distract her, and she couldn't entertain the risk of being soft right now. She ran and hid; she sprinted and took cover.

The forest was thick with Purifiers. If she could avoid them, she did, but more than a few met with her non-lethal physical devastation. Cold and calculating, Winter swept over the landscape, trying to put as much distance between herself and Joshua as possible.

Survive.

She was cut short by another Archangel bursting through the trees before her. He struck her with his rifle, and Winter's head swam as she doubled over. She latched onto the inside of his knee with one hand and pushed hard at the crook of his hip with the other.

Havoc crashed backward into the ground, his arms splayed wide.

Winter shot to her feet and threw the rifle away, but Havoc was quick to stand and drew his sidearm. As he raised the sights, she shifted off the line. Two shots tore past her torso, missing her by inches. Winter buckled his elbow, turned, then wrenched it downward with a sickening *crunch.*

Havoc roared in agony and dropped the firearm, but his force of will won out as he drew his knife and slashed wildly at Winter.

Adrenaline coursing through her survival-driven heart, she evaded the blade arcs and stepped in closer. With a soft deflection, she countered the strike and pulled on the inner elbow to drive the knife into Havoc's face.

His helmet protected him, but the shock at nearly being stabbed in the face was so great that he fell back. Winter took the knife with a simple disarm and turned to tear into the woods at the moment of opportunity.

"Coward! *Heretic!*" she heard him scream as she entered the trees.

Half a mile into the forest, Winter moved into a rocky area. She was careful not to get closed in by the layout as she flew in a mad dash for life itself. It had been several minutes since she'd seen a Purifier. As she stumbled through the unpredictable landscape, she flinched as an electric shot blasted through the air. It came so close to her face, she could have sworn she felt the bullet graze her cheek.

Winter switched into evasive movement and crouched against the nearest large rock she could find.

Crunching ground telegraphed the approach of more on foot, though the shot came from the outcropping up above.

She gripped the knife tighter and prepared to dart toward the sound of footsteps, intending to use the approaching Purifier as a body shield against the sniper.

Coiled and ready to strike, Winter lunged out from behind her cover only to meet head-on with the Master Purifier himself: Orrin 'Wraith' Priest, captain of the Archangels.

Through his helmet, she caught the unmistakable flash of his toothy grin.

The shock of seeing him set her back a moment—a moment too long as his trigger finger was faster than her recovery.

Move forward! MOVE FORWARD!

Her instincts seemed to scream, but her shock and fear delayed her movement long enough that when she moved to shift off line, the rifle fired off a searing electric round that tore through the side of her lower abdomen.

Winter's mind jolted blind with pain, so much that it seemed to numb her other senses.

Wraith clocked her in the face with the butt of his rifle. As she fell to the ground, he pinned her down with the stock against her throat.

"Hello, Winterton," Wraith spat hatefully. "Fancy meeting you here."

Winter kicked and struggled as his weight crushed down on her, feeling that familiar sensation of helplessness when the pressure began to cut her off from consciousness.

She fought to move at all beneath the strength of his massive body. His hatred and malice was not obscured by the helmet's shield. Winter saw the rage-fueled madness there, burning within his eyes.

Desperate to loosen the pressure on her throat, she pumped the blade at his center but was deflected repeatedly off his shoulder and elbow.

The attempt, though fruitless, reminded Winter of her first close encounter with surface humans. She remembered her focus had been completely derailed by her armor losing its seal.

She reversed the grip on the knife and plunged it into his armored thigh. The armor held up to the impacts, rippling wildly in order to compensate against the fierce blows.

One, two solid impacts, and Winter's vision began to go black.

But at the wild warning signals flashing across his helmet's visor, Wraith's grip relaxed slightly—his eyes wide with disbelief.

Winter seized the moment to shift her shoulders and buck him off.

The instant he was off her, another shot exploded dangerously near Winter from up above. The sniper up on the rocks was going to make it impossible to fight Wraith on even terms.

She took hold of Wraith's rifle, torqued it out of his hands, and threw it away in panic.

"You little—" he began.

"Save it!" Winter snapped as she struck him hard in the face shield.

Wraith went straight for his sidearm, but Winter already expected that. She kicked it back into the holster as he attempted to draw it out. He returned with a backhand to her face, sending her reeling, and immediately drew his sidearm with practiced accuracy. Winter used her momentum to spin around into a butterfly kick, driving his weapon out wide.

Wraith stepped back to line up the shot and fired. The only reason Winter survived the bullet that whizzed past her was her drilled-in response from Derrick's training to move forward. The shot exploded into the earth; she answered by channeling all her strength and momentum into a deft strike to his ribs.

Wraith's side buckled, though there was no damage due to the nano-armor. He pistol-whipped her across the face and threw her to the ground.

She screamed, powering through the pain with unbottled rage.

"Your luck is up, Winterton," he snarled and lined up the sights.

Joshua tramped into the ruin after being forced to take an alternative route for the unusual amount of Olympian patrols cutting him off on his return trip from gathering the medicinal herbs. He was not surprised to find the room empty. He removed his cowl and nodded in affirmation as his prediction proved true.

Winter was gone.

"Women." He shook his head.

Sighing in frustration, he turned to leave when he noticed the otherworldly blade he had found in the shuttle wreckage with Winter.

Why would she leave it behind?

He stooped and retrieved it from the ancient concrete floor.

The craftsmanship was like nothing he'd ever seen in his life. He could tell just by looking at the blade that it was sharper and more durable than any Shenandoah steel. He felt its weight in his hand; it was surprisingly light and strangely well balanced considering its wide, curved blade.

Its mirrored surface was caked with dried blood . . .

He couldn't imagine what Winter must have gone through to escape.

The screaming of engines tore overhead. They had been multiplying in frequency for the last thirty minutes. He hoped with all his heart that it didn't mean they'd found her.

His spirit sank when the faint echo of rifle blasts drifted through the morning air.

Joshua pulled on his hood again and gripped the strange weapon before ducking deeper into the crumbling structure. The ancient stairwell had collapsed in several places, but he knew the safe steps by heart. Breaching the roof, he came to a skidding stop at the lip and looked down into the valley terrain. It only took a moment for him to locate the source of the skirmish. He could see a shuttle landing in a clearing to the south and, further up the dell, the unmistakable bright blue muzzle flashes of Purifier rifles. They were spread out somewhat, but it was obvious they were converging toward a single point.

Winter was outnumbered and outgunned, and in no condition to fight them.

Back down the stairs, he sprinted, skipping steps and jumping levels when possible. He reached the entrance and didn't pause as he dug deep and pushed as hard as he could toward the sounds of battle.

His feet hitting the ground in rapid rhythm, his arms pumping wildly, gripping the blade in his hands, Joshua spoke softly through his puffing breath:

"God of my fathers, please grant me the speed to reach her in time!"

CHAPTER FIFTY-ONE

"**Y**our luck is up, Winterton."

Wraith's cold voice growled as he raised the pistol to her face. "I told you before, this is how it would end. One round, right between those pretty blue eyes . . ." He paused, seeming to be savoring the moment. "Although not so pretty anymore, are you?"

Winter's vision blurred; she clutched her bullet wound and felt the hot blood spilling over her fingers. "Wraith, please! You can see that I'm not affected," she said with conviction. "Why can't you accept that the Blight is a lie? The Sovereign lies to you!"

"You just don't know when to quit, do you?" Wraith shook his head. "And not affected? Ha! Are you serious!? Have you bothered to take a look in the mirror? You're a *freak*, Winter!"

"The Blight didn't do this to me. Draven did," Winter snarled between clenched teeth. "YOU DID!"

"And it," Wraith said, cocking back the hammer on his sidearm, "was my pleasure."

Wraith's insufferable, willful ignorance lit a flame inside Winter's chest, and she settled into her cold, feral instinct-driven mentality. She closed her hand around some loose gravel.

"Lights out, Heretic," Wraith said and squeezed the trigger.

Winter snapped to the side, throwing the handful of gravel at his face. The damage was nonexistent, but she knew the view screen would target and analyze every single particulate. As the chaos exploded across Wraith's view screen, the wildly flashing lights obscured his vision, causing the shot to miss by inches.

Winter circle-stepped to the side before Wraith could react, but the sniper was faster. Another shot buried into the ground near her bare feet.

"The Master Purifier has engaged the target," Ryan 'Hatchet' Hart of the Broadswords spoke into his com as he followed the fight through his scope.

"If you have the shot, take it!" the Grand Elite's aggravated voice ordered.

"Copy that, lord Grand Elite."

Ryan focused on the skirmish below, keeping The Heretic in his sights as she exchanged blows with Wraith. He took a shot every time he saw an opening, but they were moving too fast.

"Carve her up, Wraith," he muttered. "Ooh!" he exclaimed at a brutal hit.

He fired again, missing by a hair's breadth. The round exploded into the rocks near her feet.

"Blight me!" he swore, then readjusted his grip and position on the sights. "You're mine, Heretic . . ."

He squeezed the trigger slowly, with Winter's torso square in his sights.

Winter swung around behind Wraith in a snap of motion, latched onto his neck, and wrenched, sinking all of her bodyweight to the ground.

Wraith grunted in pain as a series of small pops issued from his tortured spine.

She would not relent. Hanging on with all her might, she wrapped one arm around the front and pushed down hard with the other from behind.

He gripped her arm and attempted to pry it off, but every struggling movement let her sink in her hold a little deeper. He switched tactics and grabbed her leg from behind.

She didn't see it coming fast enough. Both feet came up off the ground, and Wraith buried her beneath him as he fell backward, hard. With at least one broken rib already, she felt a crunch inside her chest and gagged on a mouthful of blood as they landed.

His rage mounted, and he spun around swiftly. His response came in the form of a full-fisted, brutal strike to her face. The unbridled impact was severe—worse than anything he'd dealt to her on Olympus.

Winter's splayed form, impacted on the rocks, relaxed a little.

"Give it up, Winterton," the Master Purifier said, training his pistol at her head. "Accept your fate."

Winter didn't blink as she looked him square in the eyes.

A resounding shot made her flinch, but it wasn't for her. A bullet from above blasted against Wraith's armor and drove him back half a step.

Joshua heard Winter scream. He heard the violent, rapid sound of blows. As he moved to charge into the rocky clearing, he stopped short. Another sound caught his ear, and he paused to scan the area more carefully.

Whispering a prayer of thanks, Joshua caught sight of movement up on an overhang. Moving as swiftly as possible, he focused on stealth as he changed course to intercept the higher ground.

He came upon a Purifier, lying flat on the rock with his rifle trained down below.

The Purifier fired a thunderous electric blast. "Blight me!" he said, then lined up another shot. "You're mine, Heretic . . ."

He was so focused on the grudge match below, he didn't notice Joshua creeping up until it was too late.

Adrenaline coursing, Joshua hefted a large rock and scored a stunning strike on the turning Purifier's helmet with all his strength.

He crumpled, helpless.

Taking up the fallen Purifier's rifle, Joshua trained it on the scene below. He looked down the scope and witnessed the violence in breathless agitation. At his first opportunity, he fired off a round, striking Winter's attacker. The enormous man staggered somewhat, but the armor seemed unaffected by the bullet.

"WIN-TER!" Joshua called out at the top of his lungs.

Winter, lying beaten on a rock, glanced weakly up at him.

With all his might, Joshua hurled the master craft blade towards her. Whirling through the chilled morning air, the sword briefly caught the light of the rising sun, then clattered down on the rocks ten meters from her.

Joshua cupped his hands around his mouth and breathed deep. *"GO ALL OUT!"*

Winter quickly moved to retrieve the blade.

Joshua fell prone and propped himself on his elbows to give her supporting fire, for whatever it was worth.

A crackling noise came from inside the unconscious Purifier's helmet. Joshua overheard.

"Do you have the shot!?" a voice cried desperately over the line. "Answer me! Do you have the shot!?"

"GO ALL OUT!"

The moment of distraction was all she needed. Winter snapped to her feet and ran to retrieve Ascension—promises to never wield it again all forgotten amid her frantic fight for survival.

She snatched up the weapon and spun around as Wraith raised his pistol to end her. On instinct, she positioned the wide blade in front of her as he fired. The bullet ricocheted off the steel with a loud clang. Wasting no time, she rolled forward to close the gap between them.

Another shot fired.

Miss.

Coming to her feet, Winter brought Ascension around in a wide, deathly arc. Its razor edge sheared off Wraith's thumb right through his metal gauntlet. Sparks and blood flew from the impact and he shouted in surprise as pain and horror filled his expression. The firearm fell from his lifeless grip.

His response was immediate and fierce. He kicked Winter hard in the middle, sending her reeling to keep her balance. He held his mutilated hand close and drew his knife with the other. He pounced almost faster than Winter could defend. She caught his blade with hers and strained to keep his mass from driving her into the rocks.

Wraith's knife just inches from her face, Winter clenched her teeth with breathless exertion.

"Just DIE already!" he roared.

"You first!" she shouted back. She shifted her shoulders and split the pressure, sending his weight at a diagonal. He toppled forward and was forced to catch himself from falling rather than bury his blade in her face.

Both of them shot to their feet, blades in hand.

Another gunshot from Joshua glanced off Wraith's helmet. Winter lunged forward. The jarring impact aside, he caught her weapon with his and brought his bloodied fist down hard on her shoulder. She kicked her knee up into his side twice as forcefully as she could. He returned with a strike to her ribs. She twisted, crashing her elbow into his face shield, but he responded by grabbing her head and wrenching it to the side. He lifted his knife to sever her head, but she plunged Ascension up through the bicep of his arm grabbing her.

Wraith jolted in shock, staring blankly at the Ascension blade sticking out of his arm. He dropped his knife and let go of Winter.

Taking advantage of his pause, she latched onto his face and flew into a jumping knee-strike, pulling his head down to meet her blow.

Stumbling backward as a spray of blood coated the inside of his face shield, Wraith struggled to keep his footing.

Winter witnessed with her own eyes that the Ascension blade passed right through the nano-shielding technology but still couldn't believe it. For an instant, she felt like she had won the upper hand, but her vision blurred and her limbs became heavy. She blinked and tried to steady herself, only to find that she was still oozing blood from her gunshot wound. The adrenaline and panic had driven the injury from her mind, but now that she saw it, it burned suddenly and fiercely as though it was making up for lost time.

Wraith stood his ground and slowly drew out Ascension from his arm without making a sound. "You're not worthy of this sacred blade," he said scornfully. "Not to wield it, nor to be killed by it." He tossed it away. "It's sickening to even think that your cursed fingers have touched it—staining it. You've stained my path to be an Ascended Elite!"

Winter swallowed down the pain and tasted thick blood. "Wraith, you're wrong. I've told you the truth. The Sovereign is a liar." Her fatigued, tortured frame could barely support her now.

"You're not a god, Winter!" Wraith seethed. "You don't get to decide what's true or not!" He tucked into a head-down rush that drove Winter back off her feet.

He landed on top of her, crushing her body into the ground. She kept her head and struck at his helmet, right in the center. He pummeled her, fist over fist in crippling carnage. Winter fought to keep her consciousness. When he paused, she struck again. This time the screen cracked deeply and his nano-armor flickered and disappeared.

Winter recognized the explosion of terror in his eyes, and took his moment of sudden horror to devastate his larynx. He coughed and choked, but his single-minded, murderous intent was not to be dissuaded. Enraged at being exposed to the *blighted* surface world, Wraith unleashed a barrage of pounding like never before.

"I'm going to kill you, Winterton!" he screamed. "You're dead! *You're dead!*"

Winter's body couldn't take much more. She knew that Wraith was beyond reach. He would never see nor hear the truth, and he wouldn't stop until she was a bloodied stain on the rocks.

The brutality and overwhelming agony was unbearable. Her vision passed in and out of blackness as she desperately tried to shield her face and ribs from his unrelenting barrage. Her mind could not possibly ignore the pain, so instead she shifted from avoiding it to embracing it. She screamed in rage and let him get a hard strike in so she could shoot a hand up behind his neck and pull him close.

He struggled, but Winter was able to latch on to her own wrist with her other hand and steadily tighten her grip, slowly crushing her shoulder into his throat for all she was worth.

Wraith's face turned purple and his helmet rolled off as he clawed at her arms to pry them off. Winter consciously tightened . . . and tightened her grip by tiny increments every time he struggled. He coughed and tried to gasp, but her constricting force was too great. She strained every muscle in her body, fighting to hold out until the end. She felt his body begin to give way, when suddenly he bound up again and drove his fist into her wound with the last of his gathered strength.

Winter roared and clenched her teeth, embracing the pain and using it as fuel. She gripped tighter. He punched again, but she would not let go.

Wraith dug his one good thumb into her bullet wound and suddenly lights exploded in her head. The tidal wave of burning pain overwhelmed all senses. She told her grip not to fail, but as white lights flashed across her vision, and a shrill ringing filled her ears, it was impossible to hold on.

Wraith lifted her clear off the ravine floor and smashed her back down. Winter gasped as her arms fell limply to the side.

Her head spun and swam. She rolled to her side and attempted to scramble away, but her efforts were menial. She watched in helpless horror as Wraith lifted a large boulder over his head. His eyes were fiery with pain and unbridled rage. He meant to crush her skull in once and for all. She sucked in a sharp, bracing breath and shielded her face.

A shot rang out, striking Wraith in the shoulder. He grunted in pain and dropped the boulder behind him.

Winter gathered her strength and stumbled away, pushing through the blinding pain.

Wraith took hold of her ankle and dragged her backward. "Where do you think you're going!?" he snarled.

Winter twisted and kicked his face with her other foot, knocking him down.

The moment of shock gave her enough time to scramble away. Her mind held only one thought:

Ascension . . . got to reach . . .

Wraith got to his feet and came in swinging. He struck her hard and sent her flying backward to land on the rocks.

As she winced in pain, she wearily lifted her eyes.

Ascension was just barely beyond her grasp.

"You sick . . . sad . . . worthless . . ." he slurred in a daze, panting hoarsely over her fallen form. "You should have killed yourself years ago. You're so worthless, Winter. You always have been."

As the Master Purifier bent over her with hands outstretched to strangle her dead, Winter rolled weakly to the side and shot a hand out to grip the blade. She twisted around with everything she had left, Ascension swinging wide. The blade made contact at his knee and sliced through, severing his leg cleanly off.

Wraith collapsed, howling out in excruciating pain.

Winter crawled away and agonizingly pulled herself to her feet, just out of reach as Wraith clutched his blood-gushing leg.

"Worthless or not . . ." she retorted through the throbbing, full-body pain. Her chest heaved, and her every muscle ached. Her face was terribly pale, and she could barely hold herself upright with the massive loss of blood and the all-over trauma to her frame. "I'm the only one . . . standing."

Confident the terrible struggle was finally over, she let Ascension slip from her bloody grip and clash noisily to the ground.

Wraith sucked in air through his teeth, clenched his eyes shut, and fell backward to land on his side. His severed leg continued to spurt blood over the rocks.

A new emotion unexpectedly flooded Winter's senses. Seeing her old captain moaning in agony and bleeding out, she was overcome with intense pity for the man.

After all they had gone through together, and even after all the suffering he had personally put her through, it still pained her deeply to see him like this: the giant among the Purifiers brought down. The Master Purifier defeated.

Yet another Olympian soon to be dead—again, by her own hand.

And for what?

Winter, trembling all over from the battle's aftermath, shook her head remorsefully.

For nothing. Nothing at all.

She fought back the tears that threatened to surface. "I never wanted this, Orrin," she stated truthfully. "I never, ever wanted this."

Wraith opened his eyes and glared at her with malice. "To Hades with what you want," he spat at her. "You're a curse, Winterton. *You* are the Blight of all Olympus." He toppled heavily to his back and stared up into the sky.

After a moment of silence, Wraith suddenly began to laugh. Starting as a quiet chuckle, his laughter grew in volume and intensity until it approached a sinister cackle.

Winter blinked, unsure what brought this on.

"And . . ." Wraith spoke through fits of howling laughter. "And you're gonna die, Winterton! You're gonna DIE!"

Suddenly, Joshua was at Winter's side, breathing hard. He gripped her firmly by the elbow.

"Winter!" he shouted to get her attention. "We need to go—NOW! Look!"

His finger pointed skyward, drawing her gaze.

Winter's breath caught in her throat as she saw the city of Olympus hovering almost directly overhead, with an unmistakable red light gathering and pulsating at its base.

The Eye of Zeus.

"RUN!" Joshua screamed, tugging at her arm.

She immediately turned and limped after him.

"Yes, run! *Run,* Heretic!" Wraith shouted after her. "Run all you like—

but you've got nowhere to hide!" His mocking laughter rang out through the forest. "Zeus will find you, Winterton! He'll find you and BURN YOU!"

"Do you have the shot!?" the Grand Elite screamed into the console. "Answer me! Do you have the shot!?"

"I'm sorry, lord Grand Elite. No response." The control technician shook his head.

"Obviously!" Draven threw his hands up in exasperation. "He said that the Master Purifier had engaged The Heretic."

"Yes, great one, that was the last communication."

"Authorize the Eye of Zeus," Draven quickly ordered, "half-mile radius."

Shocked, everyone in the control room looked at the projected terrain. More than a dozen Purifier beacons were within that range.

"Don't just sit there, worthless maggots!" Draven screamed. "Target Wraith and FIRE!"

No one dared refuse or even question his order.

A tech opened the channel. "Engineering, prepare the Eye of Zeus for wide-beam discharge. Radius—" she swallowed "—half-mile."

There was a pause on the other end of the com.

"Please confirm, Control. Did you say '*half-mile*' radius?" the engineer finally asked incredulously.

"Confirmed, Engineering," the tech replied coolly. "Half-mile radius."

"Alright, we copy. Now, a radius of that size will require a longer charge time. Stand by." The line again went silent. A moment later, the engineer returned. "You got it. Estimated time to wide-beam discharge: Two minutes, forty-five seconds."

"Copy that, Engineering—two minutes, forty-five seconds. Beginning countdown."

The techs all focused on their respective procedures for the execution, their eyes fixed forward with total compliance.

"Lord Grand Elite . . .?" one of them timidly ventured, raising a shaky hand.

Draven eyed him like he was a slug.

"M-my lord . . . s-should we issue a recall for the Purifiers in the area? Procedure states—"

"Skip procedure!" Draven snapped. "You want to risk The Heretic escaping?"

"But, my lord, there are so many—"

Draven seized the technician by the hair and drove his face into the tabletop with all his strength. Blood exploded out the man's crushed nose and his vacant eyes rolled into the back of his head.

"Does anyone else have a problem obeying my orders!?" Draven screamed, veins pulsing in his temples. The remaining techs quickly returned to their duties as the unconscious body of their coworker slipped off his chair, smearing blood across the table as he fell in a heap.

The apt motivation caused their fingers to fly even faster than before.

"One minute, twenty seconds to Eye of Zeus discharge," a tech volunteered the information without looking up.

Draven tapped his foot impatiently, his finger drawing long, anxious strokes along the stitched and bandaged wound across his face. He'd neither eaten nor slept in three days, having sworn to not rest until The Heretic had been eradicated and her corruption purified.

That time was finally here.

His victory was at hand.

With strained, blood-shot eyes, the Grand Elite counted down the seconds.

"Thirty seconds to Eye of Zeus discharge, my lord."

"Have Engineering contact the Sovereign—" Draven licked his lips "—and fire when ready."

Her blood-soaked feet clapping against the cold earth in uneven, desperate succession, Winter's foot snagged on an upraised tree root as she attempted to run. She collapsed forward and hit the dirt hard. Her broken ribs burned within and stole her breath. The lack of oxygen robbed her vision.

She had nothing left. She'd given her everything.

All perception of time and place, understanding of purpose and resolve, was immediately lost as her utterly spent body gave up and resigned itself to the end.

Just . . .

Nothing . . .

Left . . .

In a moment, she felt the sensation of weightlessness as she was raised from the hard ground and borne in strong arms.

Through the waves of darkening delirium, she saw Joshua's sweat-streaked, strained face framed by the passing blur of green foliage and flashes of sunlight.

Overhead, the ruby-red light continued to pulse and brighten. A low, barely perceptible *thrum* vibrated the otherwise still air.

Relaxing into his arms, she felt suddenly at peace with her head propped against his muscular shoulder.

If this was the end . . .

She smiled weakly.

. . . not a bad way to go.

Faster! Run faster!

Joshua drew deep to push his body harder and pump his legs faster than ever before. He flew through the forest, leaping downed logs and sailing through groves of budding oak and sycamore—a limp and bleeding Winter bouncing in his arms.

A strange, menacing electricity filled the air, causing the hair on his neck and arms to stand straight. Not a breath of wildlife was in sight. Not a single animal darted at his passing nor bird flitted through the trees.

They'd already fled. They knew what was coming.

Faster! his mind screamed. *FASTER!*

Up ahead, through one last stand of trees, the overgrown entrance of his destination came into view. The ancient stone ruin, swallowed almost entirely by the encroaching landscape, was their only hope.

Please! Just a little more!

A distinct pressure change preceded a faint ringing so high it was almost impossible to hear.

Then . . . a *quiet*—a terrible, all-consuming, deathlike quiet.

Joshua took a breath, drinking deep from a wellspring of untapped speed and strength, and madly dove for the entryway.

Then . . . a *noise*—one he prayed to never hear again.

White clouds parted, deafening thunder exploded, crimson light ripped the azure sky wide open, and the forest burst into flames.

Joshua shielded Winter's taxed body with his own as he felt blistering heat on his back and legs. Through the ruin's entry they dove, hitting the collapsed, slanted floor inside, and tumbling down . . . down . . . down into the depths.

Fire burst through somewhere overhead. All oxygen was sucked out. Everything shook violently. The thunderclaps grew to an ear-shattering crescendo. The heat intensified to a hair-singeing, skin-scorching climax.

Joshua and Winter tumbled head over heels, deeper and deeper into the ruin.

And finally . . . into darkness.

CHAPTER FIFTY-TWO

Draven Constantine Rothgard sighed long and grinned openly, feeling the vibration of the energy blast through the floor of the command center. The Sovereign's glorious power was truly something to behold. A mile-wide red blotch representing the diameter of the blast projected on the terrain hologram display. He watched in sated silence as all the Purifier beacons within the area flickered, then disappeared.

The steady vibration through the city slowed and then came to a dead stop.

"Eye of Zeus . . . s-successfully discharged, lord Grand Elite," a tech said shakily. "The target zone has been eliminated."

Draven flicked away the beads of sweat dewing his eyebrows. "And the Master Purifier's signal?"

"His beacon is gone, great one . . ." the tech paused, "along with . . . fourteen other Purifiers."

Draven didn't hesitate for an instant. "Send in any surrounding Purifiers to confirm that The Heretic is dead."

"Yes, lord Grand Elite," she whispered before opening the surface broad channel.

Two Guardians entered the control room. One took up a sentry position by the door while the other approached Draven and took a knee before him.

"Any word?" Draven asked flatly, untouched by the brute's veneration.

"Yes, mighty one." The massive man bowed lower. "The Hive's security footage has been reviewed, and the one responsible has been detained."

"Good." Draven's eyes narrowed hatefully as he drew a finger slowly across the bandage on his face. "Make him . . . *uncomfortable* until I arrive."

Winter jerked awake with a start. She gasped and lurched upward as sharp, shooting pain exploded through her midsection.

Joshua's hands went up apologetically. "I'm sorry, but I had to cinch it tight—to keep pressure on it."

Her breathing came in raspy gasps for oxygen. The air—what little of it there was—was both stale and acrid. With a hand clutching her side, Winter's bloodshot eyes darted through the room, wildly scanning every darkened corner and crevice for signs of danger. The room's only light was a single candle burning nearby. Wherever they were—some kind of ancient concrete bunker from what she could tell by her brief inspection—they at least appeared to be alone.

After she was confident that they were in no immediate danger, Winter glanced down to inspect herself. New bandages covered sections of her arms and legs, and what appeared to be torn strips from Joshua's coat were wrapped around her midsection and tied off at her abdomen.

She looked into Joshua's sad candlelit eyes.

His unexpected smile dulled the sadness. "I know I'm not the best medic there is," he admitted frankly, "but with you constantly giving me opportunities to practice, I'm sure I'll be an expert in no time." His smile faded as his humor had no effect on Winter. He shifted and pointed to her side. "I did what I could to stitch you up, but you lost a lot of blood. Try to move slowly. I don't want the wound to reopen."

Winter attempted to swallow against the arid desert in her throat, finding that breathing was still difficult. The scent of smoke hung heavy in the still air. Her eyes scanned the dark room again, this time more thoroughly.

"W-wh . . ." The words failed to form. She swallowed again and licked her dry lips. "Wh-where . . . are we?"

"Safe," was Joshua's soft reply. "About a mile south of the last safe spot. You know, we got here just in time."

His eyes lifted upward.

Winter followed his line of sight to a tiny opening at the apex of several collapsed concrete floors. A single shaft of gray daylight shone through the entrance. Through the opening, she could see towers of smoke rising into a darkened sky.

Fuzzy, delirious images of the Eye of Zeus firing down upon them burned through her mind. She shook her head. She couldn't believe that even *he* would have gone that far just to see her dead.

But, then again . . .

She checked her right hand. The horrific burn of the biohazard brand beneath Joshua's wrappings still throbbed painfully. With the same hand, she nervously reached up to touch her scalp, almost daring to hope to find her precious, familiar ebony tresses there. Her heart sank as her fingers only ran through savagely sheared hair amid clumps of dried blood.

Her hand dropped heavily into her lap. She knew all too well that the Sovereign and the Grand Elite of Olympus were capable of *anything*.

She turned back to Joshua. "You seem to be saving me a lot lately," she whispered hoarsely.

"Please try not to make a habit of needing me to," he replied, giving her a playful wink.

She couldn't help but smile at his uncanny ability to bring life where there was only death. "No promises, but I'll try."

She moved to stand, half expecting Joshua to try and stop her. Surprisingly, he reached out to gently take her by the arm and help her to her feet.

Their eyes met in the candlelit darkness of what could have very nearly been their tomb.

"Thank you, Joshua," Winter said gratefully. "Thank you for saving me. . . . again."

He shrugged and gave her a little squeeze. "Anytime."

That's when Winter noticed Joshua's arm. It was difficult to tell in the enveloping darkness, but she could still see the intense redness and inflammation along his forearms and biceps.

Her eyes filled with concern as she looked on. "Are you okay?"

"Yeah. I'll be fine," he answered unreassuringly, checking his arms up and down. "One heck of a sunburn, though. That Sovereign of yours sure packs a punch."

Her expression turned a shade of disgust. "He's no 'Sovereign' of mine," she replied bitterly, turning around to look up to the entrance. "Zeus is no god. He's a monster."

The angry, rage-filled faces of thousands of Olympians, each hatefully chanting *"DEATH! DEATH! DEATH!"* flashed through her mind.

She winced at the horrid memory and whispered to herself, "They *all* are."

Joshua took Winter by the wrist and guided her arm to drape across his broad shoulders. "Come on," he said, lending her his support. "Let's get you out of here."

Winter's mouth opened slightly as she stared into the hazel depths of his sad eyes.

Who was this person? the thought suddenly came to her.

Joshua was unlike anyone she had ever met before. She had done nothing but take and take from him, and in return, he only continued to give and give. More than that, it even seemed like he *wanted* to give and give.

Out of everyone she'd ever met before, Joshua was the most mysterious. Complicated. Baffling. His actions made no sense to her.

She had given him every single reason imaginable to hate her and want her dead. She had even killed his team—his friends. And yet, staring into his eyes, she saw no hatred.

Her realization from before again came to mind. All her life, she had been taught that those on the surface were blighted, mutated creatures—savage monsters deserving only of purification by death and fire.

But the truth was so perfectly opposite what she had been taught to believe.

After all the masks were taken off and everyone's true face had been revealed, it was the surface world that contained the most 'human' of anyone, while the real monsters were the very people she had lived among and served with . . . and murdered for.

And she had been one of them—a *real* monster.

In that moment, Winter realized that she didn't know nor understand who Joshua truly was, but there was a sudden hope that maybe, one day, she would.

"How about it?" Joshua asked with a warm smile. "Time to go?"

Winter slowly nodded and allowed him to take the lead, grateful for the support he offered to her battered, weakened body.

Together, one carefully placed step at a time, they climbed the collapsed floors of the ancient building towards its lofty entrance. With each painstaking step, the smell of smoke thickened until it burned their lungs and stung their eyes, and whenever Winter's bare, bloodied feet slipped on the slanted ascent, Joshua was there standing firm, his feet planted securely and his shoulders offering her stability until she found her footing again.

At long last, they emerged from the ruin's basement levels to gaze upon a foreign, gray world. As a Purifier, Winter had witnessed the power of the Eye of Zeus several times before—but nothing like this. For a thousand meters in every direction, the target area was a devastated, smoking cinder. The few trees left standing were blackened, lifeless husks. Massive columns of thick smoke billowed high along the distant border of the blast zone, where the fires continued to burn hot. A blood-red sun descended towards the western horizon, its light barely able to cut through the thick, choking haze.

"This is . . ." Winter started.

" . . . Unbelievable," Joshua finished.

Stifling a cough, Joshua began leading Winter away from the ruin and through the charred wilderness. The barren, rocky earth was mildly hot beneath her feet, but Joshua chose their path carefully, steering her away from the regions still smoldering with glowing coals.

Winter groaned with every staggered step, wincing as her ribs shifted with each labored breath.

"Why did you come back?" she heard herself unexpectedly ask the question, unsure of where it came from or if she even wanted to know the answer.

Joshua looked at her as they walked together but said nothing.

"I left you behind on purpose, you know," she continued without any emotion.

"Oh, I know," he finally replied. "And I had my suspicions that you'd run if I left you alone."

Winter clenched her teeth against the sharp pain shooting through her side. "So . . . why'd you come back then?"

"You're the strongest person I've ever met, Winter," Joshua said while smiling reassuringly. "But with all you've set yourself up to do, I think you could stand to have a friend or two to help. Don't you?"

When she eventually spoke, her voice was as cold as death. "All my friends have tried to kill me." Her head lowered in shame. "I just didn't want to get you involved in any of this."

"Too late for that," he said plainly. "I *am* involved—and that's not going to change by you running away."

"I only ran because I wanted to keep you and your people safe."

He nodded. "I know, I know. But why don't you let me worry about that?" Turning his eyes back to the blackened path ahead of them, he stopped suddenly and peered forward. " . . . Wait . . . What's that?"

Winter looked but failed to see anything of interest. Everything was obscured through the smoke and ash and devastation. "What's what?"

Joshua guided her a few more steps over some large rocks, then pointed at the ground nearby. "There." He checked with her first. "You good to stand?"

Winter braced herself to stand on her own without the support. "No problem," she lied.

Gingerly, Joshua guided her arm off his shoulders and checked on her again before moving away. He walked several paces, stooped down, reached into a bed of cooling ashes, and pulled up the Ascension blade.

Winter's stomach churned to see the cursed sword again, appearing in pristine condition even through the intense blast of the Eye of Zeus.

"Wow," Joshua said in surprise, giving a drawn-out whistle between pursed lips. "This thing actually survived." He looked to Winter inquisitively. "Other than the obvious . . . what is this thing anyway?"

"It's called 'Ascension,'" she answered, making no attempt to hide the revulsion in her voice.

She closed her eyes as a bloody, sickening spray of images flooded her mind. The same blade the Sovereign used to murder her fellow Purifiers— all for the sake of the lie—she again saw herself wield to cut down all who stood in her path, including Wraith.

She scanned the immediate area, wondering if anything of her former captain remained, but she saw nothing but ashes and dust.

"And I want nothing to do with it," she finally said, turning her back to Ascension.

A welcome gust of cool wind blew through the rocky vale, driving away enough of the smoke to temporarily open up the sky above. Winter's eyes lifted heavenward. Through the haze, she saw the city of Olympus hovering high over them—a shining crown in the evening clouds.

Her eyes focused in cold hatred on her old home and the now dormant Eye of Zeus at its base.

She snarled and spoke defiantly against the city's false god, "You missed."

Twenty meters away, the rocky earth crunched loudly, immediately drawing their attention.

Winter's heart stopped as she found herself staring down the barrel of a Purifier's rifle.

On the high ground, a lone Purifier took aim. "But I won't."

CHAPTER FIFTY-THREE

Winter fought to remain standing, weakened as she was. Even with all her senses wildly oscillating between a trained focus and a near unconscious state, she undeniably recognized the Purifier's voice.

Her oldest, dearest friend had her finger on the trigger.

"Nalara," Winter called out, her hands raised defensively. "Please. You don't have to do this."

Nalara tensed.

Joshua stood motionless, holding his breath.

Winter waited at the end of death's barrel.

"I . . ." Nalara's hands shook, her finger squeezing the trigger dangerously close. "I . . . I don't know what to do! Blight me, I don't know what to do!"

Her hands still up, Winter took one step closer.

Nalara reflexively stepped back and screamed, "Stay back, Heretic! I swear to Zeus, I'll END YOU right now!"

Winter stopped. By force of will alone, she focused her mind to partition off her body's agony and summon the strength to speak with a strong voice. "Nalara, please calm down. I am not your enemy."

"Yeah, right," Nalara said sarcastically. "You've become The Heretic, Winter. You're the enemy of all Olympus. Y-you . . . you murdered Remington—an Elite son of Zeus!"

Winter's teeth clenched in rage at hearing her friend ignorantly spew the Grand Elite's lies. "I did not!" she snapped, suddenly not caring whether or not Nalara pulled the trigger. "I didn't kill him. I didn't even see him again that night after he forced me to leave the festival."

"And, what? I'm just supposed to believe *you?* You've been acting weird for weeks, Winter. You attacked him. I *know* you did that! I was there, remember? I saw you do it!"

Winter huffed angrily. "Yes, *that* was me. But I didn't kill him."

"The Grand Elite says you did. He was found dead in your living chambers!"

"He's lying to you, Nalara! I promise you, he's lying. I swear, I did not kill Remington."

"Then who did!?" Nalara shouted in panicked, terrified anger.

"I DON'T KNOW!" Winter shouted back as loud as she could. "Okay!? I don't know who did! All I know is that it wasn't me."

Winter drew in a deep, steadying breath to allow the rage to pass. She still couldn't believe she was staring down Nalara's rifle. When she spoke again, she fought to keep her tone in check. "Nalara, please. Please put the gun down."

Despite Nalara's trembling, the rifle stayed trained on her.

Winter bit her lip, weighing the situation.

Twenty meters.

She knew that, under normal circumstances, she'd easily be able to close that distance to disarm the weapon and coldcock the threat. But in her current impaired state—even with a shaky shooter with abysmal aim—Winter accepted that her one and only hope was to reach Nalara with her words.

Words had failed her every single time before, but with her arsenal of options now completely depleted, words were all she had left. She would either reach Nalara with her words, or she would die.

With a frustrated sigh, Winter's hands dropped to her sides. "Well, Nalara," she said with a shrug, "if you really believe I'm 'The Heretic,' and if you really believe I killed Remington . . . you might as well get it over with."

Joshua stiffened in horror. "Winter . . ." he whispered harshly.

She ignored him, never taking her eyes off her friend behind the rifle's sights. "Go on, Nalara. I'm not going anywhere. You'll never get a clearer shot. Do it." After a brief pause, she decided to push her luck one step further and raised her voice to a shout. "Do it! If you're going to end me—then DO IT already!"

Nalara nearly stumbled over her own feet. The rifle's barrel swayed madly with her shaking. "Blight me, Winter!" she cried, tears streaming down her face. "Blight me! What do I do!?"

One small victory, Winter thought. *Now, move forward.*

"Maybe you could try thinking for yourself for a change," she suggested.

"I *am* trying to!" Nalara bawled. "Do I purify you now? I can't remember my training. I can't remember anything—it's all so crazy!" She began hyperventilating. "This isn't how it was supposed to be!"

"First, slow down," Winter cautioned. "Try to breathe normally."

"Winter, you've gotta help me out!" Nalara begged. "You're blighted, right? I thought I was insane, but I saw you before without your helmet talking to a blighter. And now, here you are with another one!" She made no effort to even look in Joshua's direction. "You need to be purified, right!?"

"Nalara, deep breaths. There's a lot you don't understand."

"I was trained just like you!" Nalara snapped, her tears turning to anger. "I'm tired of being told I'm not enough! I *know* I'm nothing like the great, amazing January Winterton with all her talent and brains and beauty! But we had the same training. Why am I not like you!?"

"Nalara," Winter sighed, "you don't have to be like me."

"Yes, I do!" Nalara jostled the rifle at her. "I always looked up to you. I always trusted you. I was so excited when I found out I was being assigned to the Archangels—that you were going to train me." Her crying turned to uncontrollable wailing. "I was supposed to be able to trust you! I don't get it! I don't get why I'm not good at anything."

"Nalara, I—"

"What am I missing? Huh? What am I missing!? TELL ME!" Nalara screamed through her tears. "You didn't prepare me for this! You didn't train me to stand by and be okay with not understanding! Why didn't you train me for this!?"

"I wasn't trained for this either!" Winter cried back in equal distress. "I wasn't prepared for anything—not *anything*—you get me? You always act like I'm just *ready* for whatever comes, but the truth is I've been just as scared as you are now. I still am scared! I don't have anything that makes me more special than anyone else! I wasn't more prepared for the FMQ, or the trials, or to be an active Purifier than you were. No one is!"

Winter could barely keep her swollen eyes open—for what it was worth, since her vision was blurry anyway. Her frame was so weak that it took all her energy just to remain standing.

Fighting to keep conscious, she pushed herself to continue and hoped to speak the right words. "Maybe the only thing that makes me different is I never wait for a challenge that fits my ability, but I always force myself to *grow* to meet every challenge. If you want to be more like me, then stop waiting for orders from me or anyone else, and start thinking for yourself!"

"So, you did go off-orders." Nalara shook her head. "You really are crazy, just like everyone's saying."

Winter clenched her fists, ignoring the burning pain of the biohazard brand. "I am *not* crazy, Nalara. I stopped following our orders because I found something that the rest of you wouldn't believe."

"What—that the Blight is all a lie?" was Nalara's sardonic reply. "Yeah, I heard you back at the Hive. I also saw what you *did*. You attacked the Grand Elite, and you murdered those Guardians!"

Winter felt the smoldering ember inside her explode into a raging inferno. "LOOK AROUND YOU!" she roared at the top of her lungs, and pointed emphatically at Joshua. "Open your eyes, and just LOOK! See him! See that he's not blighted. He's human—just like you and just like me! There is no Blight!"

Nalara didn't look. "How am I supposed to believe what I see when it goes against everything I've been told? How am I supposed to believe my eyes when it goes against everything I am? How am I supposed to do that, Winter!?" Her voice seethed with anger and pain. "Maybe . . . maybe my eyes are playing tricks on me. Maybe the Blight is more than something physical. Maybe it's deeper than that. Maybe he's infected your *mind* with his Blight—and that's the reason you've been acting so crazy!"

Winter threw up her arms in frustration. "Yeah . . . and maybe the sky is green and grass is blue! Maybe up is down and down is up! How about that?"

Nalara shook her head in a rage. "STOP TRYING TO CONFUSE ME!"

"I'm not, Nalara," Winter replied calmly, clinging to one last desperate hope that the truth could penetrate through the veil of lies and reach her friend's heart. "All I'm saying is that sometimes, the truth really is what you see. Sometimes, it really is right in front of you, in plain sight all along." She pointed again at Joshua. "You throw all these 'maybes' out there. While you're at it, maybe you could consider the possibility that what you're now seeing and now hearing is the real truth—that there is no Blight, and we've all been living a complete and total lie since our formulation."

Joshua suddenly took a step forward. "Nalara, it's true. I'm just—"

Nalara instantly snapped the rifle to train it on him. "DON'T MAKE A MOVE, BLIGHTER!" she ordered vehemently.

His hands went up, and he slowly backed off.

"Please, Nalara," Winter begged. "Trust me. He is a friend."

Nalara aimed the rifle back at her and started sobbing again. "I thought . . . I thought you were my friend, Winter."

Something broke inside her, and Winter wanted to cry. "Oh, Nalara . . . I am. If you can't believe anything else, I just hope you can believe that. I hope you can trust that *I am your friend.* Now and always." The tone of her voice grew more desperate. "I just may be the only true friend you have!" Winter gestured to her own sorry, miserable condition, and her eyes began flowing with tears. "Just look at what they DID TO ME! Look what they did to *your friend!*" she wailed in agony. "Don't think for one second that they wouldn't do the exact same thing to you—or to anyone else who tries to expose their lies!"

Winter dared to make a few cautious steps forward.

Sixteen meters.

Nalara didn't move. The rifle didn't lower.

"My one and only desire was to bring the truth of the surface world to Olympus," Winter continued with increased confidence. "But I was stupid. I was naïve. I was too open with my new beliefs, and I ended up exposing myself too soon. If I could do it all differently, I would. I would try to influence Olympus one at a time—person by person—instead of trying to influence the whole." She lightly shook her head, a foolish mistake as it brought on waves of dizziness and throbbing pain. After a moment, she recovered and pushed forward. "I can now clearly see that as soon as I got the attention of the Elites . . . it was all over for me. Once I got Draven's attention—all hope was gone."

Nalara's rifle wavered. "But . . ." she paused and breathed. "But the Elites care for us. They are . . . the chosen children of Zeus."

Winter sighed. "No better than you or I, Nalara. Or . . . for that matter, maybe no worse either." She looked thoughtfully down at her trembling, calloused, bloodied hands. "I've got blood on my hands, just as they have blood on theirs." She smiled warmly at her friend. "But that's what makes me so hopeful for you. You haven't killed anyone yet."

"Don't rub it in," Nalara quickly replied with bitterness.

Winter smiled and suppressed a weak chuckle. "Sweetie . . . it was meant as a compliment. What I'm saying is that you're not *like* me—you're *better* than me. Your hands are still clean!" She took another few steps closer.

Twelve meters.

Nalara's tear-streaked face was now clearly in view through her helmet's face shield.

Her rifle was still pointed at Winter's heart.

"Please, Nalara," she pleaded. "I'm begging you, please don't start now. Don't start with your friend."

"Stop right there," Nalara ordered, her voice stern but calm.

Winter obeyed.

"I just . . . I need time to think." Nalara paused for several moments. "No . . . no, no . . . wait . . ." she finally said, her frustration returning. "If there's no Blight, like you say—then what about Trigger?"

Winter silently cursed, remembering Trigger's horror-stricken face in the shuttle's chamber just moments before the flames of 'purification' consumed him. She knew then that Trigger's death—on Nalara's first day as an active Purifier—would remain with her for a long time.

"I saw him infected with the Blight, Winter!" Nalara insisted with urgency. "You saw it, too! You saw him purified! If there's no Blight, then explain *that.*"

Unpleasantly, Winter gave a shrug in response. "I'm sorry, but I don't know. I don't have an answer for you, other than to say I have personally walked through the surface world completely unprotected for days on end—and I've been able to pass through security checkpoint after security checkpoint with no problem whatsoever."

"Okay," Nalara pressed, "then maybe the Blight is real as we've been taught, and maybe you're just immune to it. How about that?"

Winter remembered when she had considered that possibility once before, but she'd long since discarded the thought as she came to see all the evidence against the Blight's existence far outweighed any evidence in support of it. She recalled the holographic images she saw at Olympus' Archive—images of horrific monstrosities of nightmarish origins. In all the time she'd spent on the surface, she'd never once seen anything so grotesque. On the contrary, what she had seen was a surface world filled with beauty and purity and goodness.

"No, Nalara," she finally said plainly. "That's just not true. Because of what I've seen and what I've heard for myself, I know the truth: the Blight does not exist. The surface isn't toxic, and the people here are all human." She gestured back to Joshua. "And there's your evidence, right there—standing right there!"

Nalara's mouth fell open in fear as her eyes darted back and forth between Winter and Joshua. "You actually want me to believe that there's no poison on the surface?" she asked disbelievingly. "The Sovereign says the Blight is real. We have a barrier around Olympus. We live our lives centered inside it," she said, trying to verbally justify her beliefs. "That's why Olympus was created in the first place. That's why we Purifiers exist!"

"Trust what you see," Winter encouraged. "You don't have to believe everything you're taught."

"What you say is treason," Nalara countered. "That's why you're The Heretic—because you speak these heresies!"

"I know," Winter returned with such impassioned zeal that her arms began to shake. "But it's only treason and heresy against lies, and I have paid for it with blood—MY OWN BLOOD!" Winter didn't stop in her fervent testimony. "The Sovereign is not a god. He's mortal just like you and me. All the shields and barriers are there *not* to keep us safe, but only to keep us *enslaved* to a false god! And it makes me absolutely sick inside when I think of all the hundreds of people I've murdered—all for the sake of a lie, and all in the name of *Antiochus Ignatius Theodosius Zeus!*"

Nalara's eyes went wide with terror at the mention of her god's full name. She began shaking again. "You . . . you blaspheme his name when you speak it."

Winter breathed in and let out a long sigh. "I promise you, Nalara, he's just a man—and *not* a good one. I now know what a good man is like," she said, pausing to think of Joshua, "and the Sovereign is *nothing* like one. He is not worthy of your worship or your adoration. He's only worthy of your contempt."

"No! That's not true!" Nalara yelled back, then proceeded to parrot a line from their upbringing: "The Sovereign preserves and protects us. In him, we are granted life."

"Just listen to yourself!" Winter pleaded. "You're not defending truth! You're just regurgitating the lies you've been told!"

Winter stepped closer, further closing the distance between them.

Seven meters.

"Nalara, you are a slave to that evil man," she insisted. "You are a prisoner trapped inside a prison of his creation, and he's got his invisible chains wrapped tightly around you. And the saddest part is, right now, you are just a pale shadow of what you *could be* if those chains were broken."

"I don't know what you're talking about," Nalara admitted, "but I don't believe you. Zeus can't just be a man. That's impossible! Olympus has existed for almost two-hundred-fifty years—and Zeus has been the Sovereign for all that time. So, tell me," she goaded, "if he's just a man, how could he live for so long?"

Winter was already well beyond her breaking point. The partition she'd thrown up in her mind to hold back the waves of physical agony had crumbled, and she now fought a desperate, losing battle just to remain conscious.

"Tell me!" Nalara shouted.

"I don't know!" Winter blurted angrily, her vision going black for a split second. "I don't have all the answers! To be honest, I only have very few."

Nalara eyed her narrowly. "You know, that's not exactly comforting, Winter."

"I know. But at least it's the truth," she boldly returned. "I have questions, Nalara, just like you. I'm sorry that I don't have all the answers. I'm sorry that I don't understand everything. There was so much more I wanted to find out. But I . . . I just ran out of time before I could."

Winter finally closed the distance between them, but she intentionally didn't step off line of Nalara's rifle barrel. Instead, she calmly reached up, took hold of it, and planted its end firmly between her breasts.

Nalara's eyes widened in shock and dewed with tears.

"Point-blank, my friend . . ." Winter whispered. "If you honestly believe that I'm your enemy . . . and if you cannot believe what I've told you . . . then please . . . just get this over with." Requiring considerable effort, she hefted her deadening arms out wide. "Just kill me now."

Nalara's brown eyes blinked out a stream of tears. "I hoped you had died in the crash," she spoke through gritted teeth. "I hoped you were already dead! That way, I wouldn't have to hunt you down. And now . . . now you're forcing me to choose between what our Sovereign says is true and what *you* say is true. You're forcing me to choose between him and you!"

"Nalara . . . I'm not *forcing* you to do anything," Winter returned quietly. "You're the one with the gun. The choice . . . the power is all yours."

Pockets of fire burned nearby. Thick plumes of smoke ascended and filled the valley.

Time slowed.

Two lifelong friends held their breath . . . and waited.

Suddenly, Nalara's com crackled and a voice came through her helmet. Winter heard every word.

"Archangels, this is Olympus Control," the voice said. "Final report. Any sign of The Heretic?"

Nalara sniffed and blinked away her tears. With one hand steadying her rifle on Winter's heart, she slowly reached up and activated her com.

"Control," she spoke confidently, resolutely.

Winter's heart stopped.

"Nalara Gressen reporting in. I've found—"

All day long, the several dozen Purifier beacons displayed across the projected terrain had circled systematically around the border of the blast zone, and—once the extreme temperatures within the zone had dropped to acceptable levels—they had proceeded with their search within the mile-wide blast area.

All teams had already made their final reports and were now returning to Olympus.

All teams, except one: the Archangels.

Draven bit a knuckle of his fist to hold in the anger and impatience that boiled within. He stepped around the dried pool of blood of the unconscious technician on the floor and paced.

"L-lord Grand Elite," a tech volunteered shakily, raising her hand.

"What!?" Draven exploded.

All the technicians flinched, but kept their eyes on their work.

"The Archangels have finished their final sweep, my lord," the tech answered.

"About time!" he shouted. "Contact them."

"Yes, my lord." The tech signaled the last Purifier team on the surface. "Archangels, this is Olympus Control. Final report. Any sign of The Heretic?"

The com crackled, then the voices of the Archangels came through one by one.

"Havoc, reporting in. Nothing on my end."

"Viper here. That's a negative."

"Bulletproof. No sign."

"This is Sapphire. Nothing to report."

"Uh, this is Mason Howell. I haven't found anything."

"Yeah . . . Scorch here." There was a pause. "She's gone."

"Control. Nalara Gressen reporting in. I've found no sign of The Heretic. Nothing could have survived that."

The Grand Elite clenched his fists and grinned broadly in silent triumph.

"Copy that, Archangels," the technician responded. "Return to the LZ for immediate recall to Olympus."

Draven hummed in self-satisfaction as he made a swift exit from the hateful control center where he'd spend the last three and a half days. Taking the lift up to the Second Tier, he stepped out into the smoke-reddened evening sun and turned towards the Guardian Quarter.

A dull, ruddy glow bathed the entire city. He almost laughed. It was the beautiful color of victory—his victory!

And now, his final victory over The Heretic was nigh.

With this one last loose end tied up, he would finally be rid of her forever.

"I've found no sign of The Heretic. Nothing could have survived that."

Nalara deactivated her com, took a step back, and lowered her rifle to the ground.

Winter breathed out, her heart finally able to beat normally again. "Thank you, Nalara," she expressed sincerely. "Thank you."

Nalara smiled. "The Heretic is dead," she stated unequivocally. "You're safe. No one will come looking for you anymore."

Having witnessed the conflict come to an end, Joshua strode up to stand next to Winter, sliding one arm under hers for support and bearing her up.

Winter welcomed the support and immediately weighed into him, almost collapsing.

Nalara looked inquisitively at them, her eyes locked firmly on 'the blighter' standing in her presence.

"So," she said suspiciously, "this is your surface human, huh?"

Winter nodded. "Nalara Gressen—meet Joshua."

Joshua hesitated for only a second before extending his free hand in greeting.

Nalara glanced at his hand and tried to not look repulsed. "Look, uh . . ." she swallowed sickeningly. "Just because I'm now convinced you're human, that doesn't mean I want to touch you."

The hand dropped. "Fair enough," Joshua replied with a smirk. He angled his mouth close to Winter's ear and whispered: "By the way, that makes *two* Purifiers I've talked to that haven't killed me."

Winter tried not to chuckle, as it caused burning stabs of pain throughout her torso.

She turned her attention to Nalara. "What are you going to do?"

Nalara shrugged without emotion. "Go back home."

Winter's dry lips parted and her chin quivered. "You won't consider staying here with me?" she asked hopefully, but she already knew what the answer would be.

"You know I can't," Nalara replied softly. "I've already reported in. If I don't go back, it'll only raise suspicions, and they'll come looking. For your sake, I need to go back home." She looked again at Joshua. "Besides . . . I'm not ready for that yet, and to be honest, I don't know if I ever will be."

Winter sighed, but nodded in understanding.

Nalara half-turned. "Goodbye . . . Janey."

Winter's heart shattered inside her as her friend moved away. "Wait, Nalara!" she called out in sudden desperation.

Nalara stopped and looked over her shoulder.

"There's . . . there's a building," Winter began explaining, trying to hold back her tears. "It's in the ancient city to the north of here, about ten miles away. It's a domed building located between four bridges." Tears began flowing freely from her eyes; it was a futile effort to try and stop them. "If you ever get the chance, and if . . . if you ever want to see me again . . . I'll be around there. Okay?"

Nalara's eyes also filled with tears. She nodded and simply said, "Okay."

Before parting ways, they exchanged a long, meaningful glance. In that singular, brief moment, all the years of friendship and hardship and suffering and triumph they had shared together came to one solid fact that they both felt simultaneously without words. They both knew without speaking that each would ultimately sacrifice everything, and hazard anything, for the safety of the other.

Nalara turned south and disappeared into a thick plume of smoke.

Winter was beyond exhausted. She hung limply on Joshua's arm, doing everything in her power to not pass out.

"Let's get moving," Joshua said and steered her in the opposite direction.

As she stumbled along with him, she took notice of the Ascension blade tied off at his hip, its mirror-like surface bouncing lightly against his leg as they walked.

She had the fleeting thought to protest him bringing the cursed sword along, but she neither had the heart nor the energy.

"Whatever," she whispered silently and instead focused all her energy on placing one foot in front of the other.

Move forward, she thought. *Always, always move forward.*

CHAPTER FIFTY-FOUR

Draven Constantine Rothgard leaned against the wall of the 'white room,' a special studio exclusive to Guardians where the massive brutes could condition one another to endure all manner of abuse.

Ten feet away, hanging suspended by his wrists from the ceiling, was the perpetrator of this whole catastrophe—the Guardian who had failed to secure The Heretic to the pillar. Puddles and splatters of blood ornamented the floor beneath him as two of his comrades pummeled him with their large fists.

With crossed arms, the Grand Elite of Olympus viewed and enjoyed the delicious brutality, smiling with each solid impact. Not a single word was spoken; not a sound filled the room but the heavy impacts of their fists and the small grunts of pain and exertion.

The suspended Guardian winced and coughed and groaned, completely inert as the beating continued.

"Enough!" Draven finally shouted and stepped forward.

The two Guardians lowered their muscular arms and panted, sweat streaming down their faces, their training clothing drenched.

Draven approached the hanging Guardian, but kept well outside his range. Even though the animal was shackled and beaten like Winterton had been, he wouldn't take any chances. He wasn't about to make the same mistake twice.

"Do you know who I am, beast?" he asked with disgust rife in his voice.

The bruised and bloody man looked down at him with swollen eyes. "Lord Grand Elite . . ." he answered quietly, blood dribbling from his mouth through broken teeth, "Draven . . . Constantine Rothgard."

"Yes." Draven licked his lips in simmering fury. "Do you see my face?"

The monstrous brute gave a single nod.

"And do you know what happened to it?"

"She . . . cut it," the weary Guardian responded.

"SHE CUT *ME!*" Draven roared, his raged-filled voice reverberating throughout the room. "The Heretic cut ME! And the only reason she was able to was because of your disgusting defectiveness!"

Draven gave the signal, and one of the Guardians nearby struck the prisoner's face again. A tooth clattered to the floor, along with a spray of blood.

"Your absolute failure in the Hive not only resulted in *this!*" he jutted a thumb at the bandage across his face, "but also in The Heretic escaping in the first place! Wretched filth such as you have no place in Olympus, Guardian! The only thing you deserve—"

"Drake," the man interrupted.

Draven balked in disbelief. "What? What did you say to me?"

"My name . . . is Drake. Drake Rowan."

"A Guardian dares to correct *me?*" Draven spoke in bewilderment. "Without first being directly addressed, what flaw makes you think you can even speak to an exalted Elite, let alone to *me?* What defect has driven you to defy the very power of Olympus?"

Drake sighed and looked the Grand Elite in the eye. "I don't . . ." He swallowed a mouthful of his blood. "I don't want to be a Guardian anymore."

Draven blinked.

The two Guardians looked disbelievingly at one another.

"I don't want to be a Guardian anymore," Drake repeated. "And I didn't want to see her die."

Draven took one step closer and lowered his voice. "And just what exactly was she to you?"

Drake considered the question carefully, then answered, "She's my friend."

The Grand Elite shook his head, then laughed loudly. "Was!" he corrected. "She *was* your friend! She's dead now, you stupid monstrosity! She's dead, and you will be joining her." He turned to the two Guardians standing at attention. "Beat this . . . this *thing* until it stops breathing—then beat it some more. When you're finished, it is to be tossed over the edge of Olympus."

"Yes, my lord!" they answered in unison and immediately went to work.

Draven turned away as the brutality resumed and left the room.

As he made his way towards the First Tier, he reflected on the Sovereign's words. Though the Sovereign obviously had, there was no way Draven could have foreseen the havoc and destruction that The Heretic's nonconformity had wrought. Lord Zeus had warned him, of course, but it was the unfathomable depths of her depravity that was really to blame.

The fault was *not* his own.

Draven scratched madly at the bandage until it bled through, eager to claim his regeneration therapy. Soon, this physical imperfection would be erased from existence, just like Winterton—just like every last trace of her heresy.

Ascending the Grand Stairway to his lofty, glistening Elite home above the lowly squalor, a sudden and terrifying thought entered his mind, stopping him mid-stride.

The Heretic had successfully manipulated a single Guardian with her treasonous ideas, and the fallout had been disastrous.

But that was no matter. That despicable, flawed thing would soon be dead and discarded forever. His treacherous blood would never be reclaimed and passed on to future Olympian generations.

But what if Winter had successfully manipulated others?

Draven made a slow turn on the stairs and looked out across the city and its many inferior inhabitants.

What if the idea—*her idea*—had already taken root? If so, what would the fallout be then?

The Grand Elite tried to push the terrifying thought away—but relentlessly, it persisted, gnawing mercilessly at his mind.

What if this wasn't the end?

What if this was only the beginning?

AUTHOR'S ACKNOWLEDGMENTS

HELENA FAUST

Helena is a true friend and inspiration in my life. I first began work on *The Winter Saga* in December 2014, but it wasn't until I began working with Helena in the summer of 2016 that the dream became a reality. Without her help, *The Winter Saga* would have remained an unattainable dream. She's a writer, a fighter, and a lover of all things science-fiction and fantasy. My dear friend, Helena, with all my heart, "Thank you."

www.SteveArgyle.com

STEVE ARGYLE

I first discovered the beautifully creative work of Steve in the mid-2000's on DeviantArt. As a young man with a passion for the arts, I immediately fell in love with his incredible work, and I remember my excitement whenever his next masterpiece would be posted. It's been an honor to have worked with one of my all-time favorite artists on *The Winter Saga*.

www.Aiven.net

YVAN FEUSI

I just recently discovered the amazing work of Yvan. After searching for literally months for that one artist with the talent necessary to illustrate the city of Olympus, I came across Yvan's art on Pinterest. As soon as I saw his work, I said, "He's the one." It's been a pleasure working with him and I'm grateful to call him my friend.

ABOUT THE AUTHOR

Christian Rivers

Ever since the age of fourteen, it's been Christian's deepest desire and greatest dream to be a sci-fi and fantasy novelist. On December 8, 2014, while working in his home studio, a fictional character named January 'Winter' Winterton walked into his life . . . and *The Winter Saga* was born.

Winter's Fall is his first published work.

Christian's greatest treasures in all the world are his two beautiful daughters.

JANUARY WINTERTON
WILL RETURN IN

THE WINTER SAGA

WINTER'S
RISE

BOOK TWO